DEAD OF NIGHT

DEAD OF NIGHT

CHARLAINE HARRIS

AMANDA STEVENS

 HARLEQUIN® MIRA®

Recycling programs for this product may not exist in your area.

ISBN-13: 978-0-7783-1476-9

DEAD OF NIGHT

Copyright © 2013 by Harlequin Books S.A.

The publisher acknowledges the copyright holders of the individual works as follows:

DANCERS IN THE DARK
Copyright © 2004 by Charlaine Harris

THE DEVIL'S FOOTPRINTS
Copyright © 2008 by Amanda Stevens

For questions and comments about the quality of this book, please contact us at CustomerService@Harlequin.com.

Printed in U.S.A.

CONTENTS

DANCERS
IN THE
DARK

CHARLAINE
HARRIS

My thanks to dancers past and present: Coco Ihle, Larry Roquemore, Jo Dierdorff, Shelley Freydont and the very helpful Molly McBride. Special thanks go to Doris Ann Norris, reference librarian to the stars, who can look up the inner dimensions of a sarcophagus faster than I can whistle "Dixie."

1

Rue paused to gather herself before she pushed open the door marked both Blue Moon Entertainment and Black Moon Productions. She'd made sure she'd be right on time for her appointment. Desperation clamped down on her like a vise: she had to get this job, even if the conditions were distasteful. Not only would the money make continuing her university courses possible, the job hours dovetailed with her classes. *Okay, head up, chest out, shoulders square, big smile, pretty hands,* Rue told herself, as her mother had told her a thousand times.

There were two men—two vampires, she corrected herself—one dark, one red-haired, and a woman, a regular human woman, waiting for her. In the corner, at a barre, a girl with short blond hair was stretching. The girl might be eighteen, three years younger than Rue.

The older woman was hard-faced, expensively dressed, perhaps forty. Her pantsuit had cost more than three of Rue's outfits, at least the ones that she wore to classes every day. She thought of those outfits as costumes: old jeans and loose shirts bought at the thrift store, sneakers or hiking boots and big glasses with a very weak prescription. She was concealed in such an ensemble at this moment, and Rue realized from the woman's face that her appearance was an unpleasant surprise.

"You must be Rue?" the older woman asked.

Rue nodded, extended her hand. "Rue May. Pleased to meet you." Two lies in a row. It was getting to be second nature—or even (and this was what scared her most) first nature.

"I'm Sylvia Dayton. I own Blue Moon Entertainment and Black Moon Productions." She shook Rue's hand in a firm, brisk way.

"Thank you for agreeing to see me dance." Rue crammed her apprehension into a corner of her mind and smiled confidently. She'd endured the judgments of strangers countless times. "Where do I change?" She let her gaze skip right over the vampires—her potential partners, she guessed. At least they were both taller than her own five foot eight. In the hasty bit of research she'd done, she'd read that vampires didn't like to shake hands, so she didn't offer. Surely she was being rude in not even acknowledging their presence? But Sylvia hadn't introduced them.

"In there." There were some louver-doored enclosures on one side of the room, much like changing rooms in a department store. Rue entered a cubicle. It was easy to slide out of the oversize clothes and the battered lace-up boots, a real pleasure to pull on black tights, a deep plum leotard and fluttering wrap skirt to give the illusion of a dress while she danced. She sat on a stool to put on T-strap heels, called character shoes, then stood to smile experimentally at her reflection in the mirror. *Head up, chest out, shoulders square, big smile, pretty hands,* she repeated silently. Rue took the clip out of her hair and brushed it until it fell in a heavy curtain past her shoulder blades. Her hair was one of her best features. It was a deep, rich brown with an undertone of auburn. The color almost matched that of her deep-set, dramatic eyes.

Rue only needed her glasses to clarify writing on the black-board, so she popped them into their case and slipped it into her backpack. She leaned close to the mirror to inspect her makeup. After years of staring into her mirror with the con-fidence of a beautiful girl, she now examined her face with the uncertainty of a battered woman. There were pictures in a file at her lawyer's office, pictures of her face bruised and puffy. Her nose—well, it looked fine now.

The plastic surgeon had done a great job.

So had the dentist.

Her smile faltered, dimmed. She straightened her back again. She couldn't afford to think about that now. It was showtime. She folded back the door and stepped out.

There was a moment of silence as the four in the room took in Rue's transformation. The darker vampire looked gratified; the red-haired one's expression didn't change. That pleased Rue.

"You were fooling us," Sylvia said. She had a deep, raspy voice. "You were in disguise." *I'd better remember that Sylvia Dayton is perceptive,* Rue told herself. "Well, let's try you on the dance floor, since you definitely pass in the looks depart-ment. By the way, it's Blue Moon you want to try out for, right? Not Black Moon? You could do very well in a short time with Black Moon, with your face and body."

It was Blue Moon's ad she'd answered. "Dancer wanted, must work with vamps, have experience, social skills," the ad had read. "Salary plus tips."

"What's the difference?" Rue asked.

"Black Moon, well, you have to be willing to have sex in public."

Rue couldn't remember the last time she'd been shocked, but she was shocked now. "No!" she said, trying not to sound as horrified as she felt. "And if this tryout has anything to do with removing my clothes…"

"No, Blue Moon Entertainment is strictly for dancing," Sylvia said. She was calm about it. "As the ad said, you team with a vampire. That's what the people want these days. Whatever kind of dancing the party calls for—waltzing, hip-hop. The tango is very popular. People just want a dance team to form the centerpiece for their evening, get the party started. They like the vamp to bite the girl at the end of the exhibition dance."

She'd known that; it had been in the ad, too. All the material she'd read had told her it didn't hurt badly, and the loss of a sip of blood wouldn't affect her. She'd been hurt worse.

"After you dance as a team, often you're required to stay for an hour, dancing with the guests," Sylvia was saying. "Then you go home. They pay me a fee. I pay you. Sometimes you get tips. If you agree to anything on the side and I hear about it, you're fired." It took Rue a minute to understand what Sylvia meant, and her mouth compressed. Sylvia continued, "Pretty much the same arrangement applies for Black Moon, but the entertainment is different, and the pay is higher. We're thinking of adding vampire jugglers and a vampire magician— he'll need a 'Beautiful Assistant.'"

It steadied Rue somehow when she realized that Sylvia was simply being matter-of-fact. Sex performer, magician's assistant or dancer, Sylvia didn't care.

"Blue Moon," Rue said firmly.

"Blue Moon it is," Sylvia said.

The blonde girl drifted over to stand by Sylvia. She had small hazel eyes and a full mouth that was meant to smile. She wasn't smiling now.

While Sylvia searched through a stack of CD cases, the blonde stepped up to Rue's side. She whispered, "Don't look directly in their eyes. They can snag you that way, if they want to, turn your will to their wishes. Don't worry unless their fangs run all the way out. They're excited then."

Startled, Rue used her lowest voice to say, "Thanks!" But now she was even more nervous, and she had to wonder if perhaps that hadn't been the girl's intention.

Having picked a CD, Sylvia tapped the arm of one of the vampires. "Thompson, you first."

The dark-haired taller vampire, who was wearing biking shorts and a ragged, sleeveless T-shirt, came to stand in front of Rue. He was very handsome, very exotic, with golden skin and smooth short hair. Rue guessed he was of Eurasian heritage; there was a hint of a slant to his dark eyes. He smiled down at her. But there was something in his look she didn't trust, and she always paid attention to that feeling...at least, now she did. After a quick scan of his face, she kept her eyes focused on his collarbone.

Rue had never touched a vampire. Where she came from, a smallish town in Tennessee, you never saw anything so exotic. If you wanted to see a vampire (just like if you wanted to go to the zoo), you had to visit the city. The idea of touching a dead person made Rue queasy. She would have been happy to turn on her heel and walk right out of the room, but that option wasn't open. Her savings had run out. Her rent was due. Her phone bill was imminent. She had no insurance.

She heard her mother's voice in her head, reminding her, "Put some steel in that spine, honey." Good advice. Too bad her mother hadn't followed it herself.

Sylvia popped the disk in the CD player, and Rue put one hand on Thompson's shoulder, extended the other in his grasp. His hands were cool and dry. This partner would never have sweaty palms. She tried to suppress her shiver. *You don't have to like a guy to dance with him,* she advised herself. The music was an almost generic dance tune. They began with a simple two-step, then a box step. The music accelerated into swing, progressed to jitterbug.

Rue found she could almost forget her partner was a vampire. Thompson could really dance. And he was so strong! He could lift her with ease, swing her, toss her over his head, roll her across his back. She felt light as a feather. But she hadn't mistaken the gleam in his eyes. Even while they were dancing, his hands traveled over more of her body than they should. She'd had enough experience with men—more than enough experience—to predict the way their partnership would go, if it began like this.

The music came to an end. He watched her chest move up and down from the exercise. He wasn't even winded. Of course, she reminded herself, Thompson didn't need to breathe. The vampire bowed to Rue, his eyes dancing over her body. "A pleasure," he said. To her surprise, his voice purely American.

She nodded back.

"Excellent," Sylvia said. "You two look good together. Thompson, Julie, you can go now, if you want." The blonde and Thompson didn't seem to want. They both sat down on the floor, backs to one of the huge mirrors that lined the room. "Now dance with Sean O'Rourke, our Irish aristocrat," Sylvia told her. "He needs a new partner, too." Rue must have looked anxious, because the older woman laughed and said, "Sean's partner got engaged and left the city. Thompson's finished med school and started her residency. Sean?"

The second vampire stepped forward, and Rue realized he hadn't moved the whole time she'd been dancing with

Thompson. Now he gave Sylvia a frigid nod and examined Rue as closely as she was examining him.

Dust could have settled on Sean, he stood so still. He was shorter than Thompson, but still perhaps two inches taller than Rue, and his long straight hair, tied back at the nape of his neck, was bright red. Of course, Sean was white, white as paper; Thompson's racial heritage, his naturally golden skin, had made him look a little more alive.

The Irish vampire's mouth was like a capital *M*. The graven downturns made him look a little spoiled, a little petulant, but it was just the way his mouth was made. She wondered what he would look like if he ever smiled. Sean's eyes were blue and clear, and he had a dusting of freckles across his sharp nose. A vampire with freckles—that made Rue want to laugh. She ducked her head to hide her smile as he took his stance in front of her.

"I am amusing?" he asked, so softly she was sure the other three couldn't hear.

"Not at all," she said, but she couldn't suppress her smile.

"Have you ever talked to a vampire?"

"No. Oh, wait, yes, I have. A beauty contest I was in, I think maybe Miss Rockland Valley? He was one of the judges."

Of all the ways Sean the vampire could have responded, he said, "Did you win?"

She raised her eyes and looked directly into his. He could not have looked more bored and indifferent. It was strangely reassuring. "I did," she said.

She remembered the vampire judge's sardonic smile when she'd told him her "platform" was governmental tolerance toward supernatural creatures. And yet she'd never met a supernatural creature until that moment! What a naive twit she'd been. But her mother had thought such a topic very current and sure to attract the judges' attention. National and state governments had been struggling to regulate human–vampire relationships since vampires had announced their existence among humans five years before.

The Japanese development of a synthetic blood that could satisfy the nutritional needs of the undead had made such a revelation possible, and in the past five years, vampires had worked their way into the mainstream of society in a few countries. But Rue, despite her platform, had steered clear of contact with the undead. Her life was troublesome enough without adding an element as volatile as the undead to the mix.

"I just don't know much about vampires," she said apologetically.

Sean's crystalline blue eyes looked at her quite impersonally. "Then you will learn," he said calmly. He had a slight Irish accent; "learn" came out suspiciously like "lairrn."

She focused safely on his pointed chin. She felt more at ease—even if he was some kind of royalty, according to Sylvia. He seemed totally indifferent to her looks. That, in itself, was enough to relax her muscles.

"Will you dance?" he asked formally.

"Yes, thank you," she said automatically. Sylvia started the CD player again. She'd picked a different disk this time.

They waltzed first, moving so smoothly that Rue felt she was gliding across the floor without her feet touching the wood. "Swing next," he murmured, and her feet did truly leave the floor, her black skirt fluttering out in an arc, and then she was down again and dancing.

Rue enjoyed herself more than she had in years.

When it was over, when she saw that his eyes were still cool and impersonal, it was easy to turn to Sylvia and say, "If you decide you want me to work for you, I'd like to dance with Sean."

The flash of petulance on Thompson's face startled Rue.

Sylvia looked a bit surprised, but not displeased. "Great," she said. "It's not always easy…" Then she stopped, realizing any way she finished the sentence might be tactless.

Julie was beaming. "Then I'll dance with Thompson," she said. "I need a partner, too."

At least I made Julie happy, Rue thought. Rue's own partner-to-be didn't comment. Sean looked neither happy nor sad. He took her hand, bowed over it and let it go. She thought she had felt cold lips touch her fingers, and she shivered.

"Here's the drill," Sylvia said briskly. "Here's a contract for you to sign. Take it home with you and read it. It's really simple." She handed Rue a one-page document. "You can have your lawyer check it over, if you want."

Rue couldn't afford that, but she nodded, hoping her face didn't reflect her thoughts.

"We have personnel meetings once a month, Blue Moon and Black Moon together," Sylvia said briskly. "You have to come to those. If you don't show up for an engagement, and you're not in the hospital with a broken leg, you're fired. If you fight with Sean, it better not show in public."

"What are the meetings for?" Rue asked.

"We need to know one another by sight," Sylvia said. "And we need to share problems we have with clients. You can avoid a lot of situations if you know who's going to be trouble."

It was news to Rue that there could be "trouble." She crossed her arms over her chest, suddenly feeling cold in the plum leotard. Then she looked down at the contract and saw what she would be paid per appearance. She knew that she'd sign; she'd have the contract in Sylvia's hands the next day, so she could start work as soon as possible.

But after she'd gotten back to her cheap apartment, which lay in a decidedly unsafe part of Rhodes, Rue did study the contract. Nothing in the simple language was a surprise; everything was as Sylvia had told her. There were a few more rules, covering items like giving notice and maintaining any costumes she borrowed from the company stock, but the contract was basic. It was renewable, if both parties wanted, after a year.

The next morning, Rue bundled up in the brisk midwest spring morning and set out early to the campus so she would have time to detour. There was a mail slot in the door of the old building that housed Blue Moon/Black Moon. Rue poked the folded paper through the slit, feeling profound relief. That night Sylvia called Rue to schedule her first practice session with Sean O'Rourke.

2

Wearing cutoff sweatpants and a sleeveless T-shirt, Sean waited in the studio. The new woman wasn't late yet. She would be on time. She needed the job. He'd followed her home the night she'd auditioned. He'd been cautious all the years he'd been a vampire, and that had kept him alive for more than 275 years. One of his safety measures was making sure to know the people he dealt with, so Sean was determined to learn more about this Rue.

He didn't know what to think of her. She was poor, obviously. But she'd had years of dance lessons; she'd had good makeup, a good haircut, the good English of privilege. Could she be an undercover operative of some kind? If she were, wouldn't she have taken the opportunity to work for Black Moon, the only remotely interesting thing about Sylvia's enterprises? Perhaps she was a rich girl on a perverse adventure.

His first fifty years as a vampire, Sean O'Rourke had done

his best to conceal himself in the world of humans. He'd stayed away from others of his kind; when he was with them, the temptation to explore his true nature had grown too strong. Sean had been abandoned by the man who'd made him what he was. He'd had no chance to learn the basic rules of his condition; in his ignorance, he'd killed unfortunates in the slums of Dublin. Gradually, Sean had learned that killing his victims wasn't necessary. A mouthful of blood could sustain him, if he had it every night. He'd learned to use his vampiric influence to blot out his victims' memories, and he'd learned to blot out his own emotions almost as successfully.

After fifty years, stronger and colder, he'd begun to risk the company of other vampires. He'd fallen in love a time or two, and it had always ended badly, whether the woman he loved was another vampire or a human.

His new partner, this Rue, was beautiful, one of the most beautiful women he'd seen in centuries. Sean could admire that beauty without being swayed by it. He knew something was wrong with the girl, something hidden inside her. He hadn't watched people, observed people, all these years without learning to tell when a human was concealing something. Maybe she was an agent for one of the fanatical organizations that had formed to force vampires back into the darkness of the shadows. Maybe she suffered from a drug addiction, or some physical condition she was hoping to hide for as long as possible.

Sean shrugged to himself. He'd speculated far too much about Rue's possibilities. Whatever her secret was, in time he would learn it. He wasn't looking forward to the revelation. He wanted to dance with her for a long time; she was light and supple in his arms, and she smelled good, and the swing of her thick mahogany hair made something in his chest ache.

Though he tried to deny it to himself, Sean looked forward to tasting her more than he'd looked forward to anything in decades.

The practice room was a larger studio behind the room in which she'd met Sylvia and the others. "Sean/Rue" was scrawled on the sign-up sheet for the six-thirty to eight o'clock time slot. Julie and Thompson would be practicing after them, Rue noticed.

She was nervous about being alone with the vampire. He was waiting for her, just as still and silent as he'd been two nights before. As a precaution, she'd worn a cross around her neck, tucked under the old gray leotard. The black shorts she'd pulled on over the leotard were made out of a shiny synthetic, and she'd brought ballet shoes, tap shoes and the T-strap character shoes she wore for ballroom dancing. She nodded to Sean by way of greeting, and she dumped the shoes out on the floor. "I didn't know what you'd want," she explained, all too aware that her voice was uneven.

"Why are the initials different?" he asked. Even his voice sounded dusty, as though it hadn't been used in years. To her dismay, Rue discovered that she found the slight Irish accent charming.

"What do you mean? Oh, on the shoe bag?" She sounded like an idiot, she thought, and bit her lip. She'd had the shoe bag for so many years, she simply didn't notice anymore that it was monogrammed.

"What is your real name?"

She risked a glance upward. The brilliant blue eyes were just blue eyes; they were fixed on her at the moment, but he wasn't trying to rope her in, or whatever it was they did. "It's a secret," she said, like a child. She smacked herself on the forehead.

"What is your true name?" He still sounded calm, but it was clear he was going to insist. Actually, Rue didn't blame him. She met his eyes. She was his partner. He should know.

"I go by Rue L. May. My name is Layla LaRue LeMay. My parents liked the song? You know it?" she asked doubtfully.

"Which version? The original one by Cream, or the slower Eric Clapton solo?"

She smiled, though it was an uncertain smile. "Original," she said. "In their wilder years, they thought it was cool to name their daughter after a song." It was hard to believe now that her parents had ever had years of not being afraid what people would think, that once they'd been whimsical. She looked down. "Please don't tell anyone my name."

"I won't." She believed him. "Where do your parents live now?" he asked.

"They're dead," she said, and he knew she was lying.

And though he would need to sample her blood to be sure, Sean also suspected that his new partner was living in fear.

After they warmed up, that first practice session went fairly well. As long as they both concentrated on the dancing, the conversation was easy. When they touched on anything more personal, it wasn't.

Sean explained that they were almost never called on to tap dance. "People who hire us want something flashy, or something romantic," he said. "They want a couple who can tango, or a couple who can do big lifts, for the charity balls. If it's something like an engagement party or anniversary, they want a sexy, slow dance, always ending with the bite."

Rue admired how impersonally he said it, as if they were both professionals in this together, like actors rehearsing a scene. In fact, that was exactly appropriate, she decided.

"I've never done this," she said. "The biting thing. Ah, do

you always bite the neck?" As if she didn't care, as if she was quite matter-of-fact about the finale. She was proud of how calm she sounded.

"That's what the audience likes. They can see it best, and it's traditional. In real life, of course—if I can use the phrase 'real life'—we can bite anywhere. The neck and the groin have the big arteries, so they're preferred. It isn't fatal. I'll only take a drop or two. We don't need much as we get older."

Rue could feel her face flood with color. This matched what she'd learned from the university's computers, though she'd felt obliged to have Sean confirm what she'd read. She needed to know all this, but she was embarrassed, just the same. It was like discussing sexual positions, rather than the more comparable eating customs: missionary vs. doggy-style, rather than forks vs. chopsticks.

"Let's try a tango," Sean said. Rue put on her character shoes. "Can you wear a higher heel?" her partner asked impersonally.

"Yes, I can dance in something higher, but that would put me too close to your height, don't you think?"

"I'm not proud," he said simply. "It's all in how it looks."

Aristocrat or not, he was a practical man. To Rue's pleasure, Sean continued to be a great partner. He was very professional. He was patient, and since she was rusty, she appreciated his forbearance. As the session continued, Rue grew more confident. Her body began to recover its skills, and she began to enjoy herself immensely.

She hadn't had fun in forever.

They ended up with a "cool-down" dance, a dreamy forties romantic song performed by a big band. As the music came to a close, Sean said, "Now I'll dip you." Then he lowered her, until her back was almost parallel with the floor. And he held the position. A human couldn't have sustained it for long, but his arm under her shoulders was like iron. All she had to do was keep her graceful alignment with his body. "Then, I bite," he said, and mimed a nip at her neck. He felt her shiver and willed her to relax. But she didn't, and after a moment, he assisted her in standing up again.

"We could have a booking this weekend, if you feel you're up to it," he said. "We'd have to practice every night, and you'd have to have your costumes ready."

She was relieved to have a safe topic to latch on to. Julie and Thompson were standing by the door, waiting for their turn in the practice room. They were listening with interest.

"Sylvia said there was a wardrobe of costumes?"

"I'll show you," Sean said. He sounded as calm and indifferent as he had at the beginning of the session.

After she'd glanced in the room off Sylvia's office, where costumes were hanging in rows on rolling racks, she went to the ladies' room. As she was washing her hands, Julie came in. The young blonde looked especially happy, with flushed cheeks and a big smile.

"I gotta tell you," Julie said. "I'm really glad you picked Sean. I always thought Thompson was pretty hot, and Sean is as cold as they come."

"How long have you been dancing for Sylvia?" Rue asked. She wanted to steer clear of discussing her partner.

"Oh, a year. I have a day job, too, clerking at an insurance agency, but you know how hard it is to get along. I settled in Rhodes because I thought a city in the middle of the country would be cheaper than either coast, but it's hard for a girl to make it on her own."

Rue was able to agree with that wholeheartedly.

"Hard to understand why the vampires do this," she said.

"They gotta live, too. I mean, most of them, they want a nice place to live, clean clothes and so on."

"I guess I always thought all vampires were rich."

"Not to hear them tell it. Besides, Thompson's only been a vamp for twenty years."

"Wow," Rue said. She had no idea what difference that would make, but Julie clearly thought she was revealing a significant fact.

"He's pretty low down on the totem pole," Julie explained. "What's unusual is finding a vamp as old as Sean performing. Most of the vamps that old think it's beneath their dignity to work for a human." She looked a wee bit contemptuous of Sean.

Rue said, "You all have a good practice, Julie. I'll see you soon."

"Sure," Julie said. "Have a good week."

Rue hadn't meant to be abrupt. But she had some sympathy for Sean. Just like her, he was making a living doing what he did best, and he didn't have false pride about it. She could draw a lesson from that herself.

That sympathy vanished the next night, when Rue discovered that Sean was following her home. After getting off the bus, she caught the barest glimpse of him as she walked the last block to her apartment. She ran up the steps as quickly as she could, and tried to act normally as she unlocked the common door and climbed up to her tiny apartment. Slamming the door behind her, her heart hammering, she wondered what she'd let herself in for. With the greatest caution, she left the lights off and crept over to the window. She would see him outside, looking up. She knew it. She knew all about it.

He wasn't there. She fed her cat in the dark, able to see the cans and the dish by the light of the city coming in the windows. She looked again.

Sean wasn't there.

Rue sat down in the one chair she had, to think that over.

Her heart quit hammering; her breathing slowed down. Could she have been mistaken? If she'd been a less-experienced woman she might have persuaded herself that was the case, but Rue had long since made up her mind not to second-guess her instincts. She'd seen Sean. Maybe he wanted to know more about his partner. But he hadn't watched her once she was inside.

Maybe he'd followed her to make sure she was safe, not to spy on her.

It was hard for Rue to pay attention in her History of the British Isles class the next morning. She was still fretting. Should she confront him? Should she stay silent? She'd let her hair go all straggly for class, as she usually did, and she tucked it behind her ear while she bent over her notebook. She was so jangled by her indecision that she let her mind ramble. Her professor caught her by surprise when he asked her what she thought of the policy of the British during the Irish potato famine, and she had a hard time gathering up an answer to give him. To make the day even more unpleasant, while Rue was working on a term paper in the college library, she realized that the brunette across the table was staring at her. Rue recognized that look.

"You're that girl, aren't you?" the girl whispered, after gathering her nerve together.

"What girl?" Rue asked, with a stony face.

"The girl who was a beauty queen? The one who—"

"Do I look like a beauty queen?" Rue asked, her voice sharp and cutting. "Do I look like any kind of queen?"

"Ah, sorry," stammered the girl, her round face flushing red with embarrassment.

"Then shut up," Rue snarled. Rudeness was the most effective defense, she'd found. She'd had to force herself, at first, but as time went on, rudeness had become all too easy. She outstayed the flustered student, too; the girl gathered up her books and pencils and fled the library. Rue had discovered that if she herself left first, it constituted an admission.

After dark, Rue set out to dance rehearsal with anger riding her shoulders.

She debated all the way to Blue Moon. Should she confront her new partner? She needed the job so badly; she liked dancing so much. And though it embarrassed her to admit it to herself, it was a real treat to sometimes look as good as she could, instead of obscuring herself.

Rue reached an internal compromise. If Sean behaved himself during this practice as well as he had during the first, if he didn't start asking personal questions, she would let it go. She could dance this Friday and make some money, if she could just get through the week.

She couldn't prevent the anger rolling around her like a cloud when he came in, but he greeted her quite calmly, and she crammed her rage down to a bearable level.

The dancing went even better that night. She was on edge, and somehow that sharpened her performance. Sean corrected a couple of arm positions, and she carefully complied with his suggestions. She made a few of her own.

If he followed her home, she didn't catch a glimpse of him. She began to relax about the situation.

The next night, he bit her.

"You don't want the first time to be in front of a crowd," he said. "You might scream. You might faint." He seemed quite matter-of-fact about it. "Let's do that thing we were working on, that duet to 'Bolero.'"

"Which is maybe the most hackneyed 'sexy dance' music in the world," she said, willing to pick a fight to cover her anxiety.

"But for a reason," Sean insisted. "Reason" came out "ray-son." His Irish accent became more pronounced when he was upset, and Rue enjoyed hearing it. Maybe she would irritate him more often.

The duet they'd been working on was definitely a modern ballet. They started out with Sean approaching Rue, gradually winning her, their hands and the alignment of their bodies showing how much they longed to touch. Finally they entwined in a wonderful complicated meshing of arms and legs, and then Sean lowered her to finish up in the position they'd practiced the night before, leaning Rue back over his arm.

"We'll go very low this time," he said. "My right knee will touch the ground, and your legs should be extended parallel to my left leg. Put your left arm around my neck. Extend your right."

"Can you sustain that? I don't want to end up in a heap on the floor."

"If I brace my right hand on the floor, I can hold us both up." He sounded completely confident.

"You're the vampire," she said, shrugging.

"What's my offense?" He sounded stung.

"I didn't realize you were going to be the boss of us," she said, pleased to have jolted him out of his calm remove. "Aristocrat," Sylvia had called him. Rue knew all about people who thought their money provided them with immunity. She also knew she wasn't being reasonable, but she just couldn't seem to stop being angry.

"You'd like to be the one in charge?" he asked coldly.

"No," she said hastily. "It's just that I—"

"Then what?"

"Nothing! Nothing! Let's do the damn finale!" Every nerve in her body twanged with anxiety.

She got into position with a precision that almost snapped. Her right leg extended slightly in front of her, touching his left leg, which he swept slightly behind him. He took both her hands and clasped them to his chest. His eyes burned into hers. For the first time, his face showed something besides indifference.

It wasn't smart of me to have a fight with him right before he bites me, Rue told herself. But the music began. With a feeling of inevitability, Rue moved through the dance with the vampire. Once she moved too far to the right, and once she lost track of her place in the routine, but she recovered quickly both times. And then she was leaning back gracefully, her left arm around Sean's neck, her right arm reaching back, back, her hand in an appealing line. Sean was leaning over her, and she saw his fangs, and she jumped. She couldn't help it.

Then he bit her.

All her problems were over, her every muscle relaxed, and she was whole again. Her body was smooth and even, and everything inside her was perfect and intact.

The next thing Rue knew, she was weeping, sitting on the floor with her legs crossed. Sean was sitting by her side, leaning over with his arm around her shoulders.

"It won't be like this again," he said quietly, when he was sure she would understand him.

"Why did that happen? Is it that way for everyone?" She rubbed her face with the handkerchief Sean had handed her. Where he'd kept it, she couldn't imagine.

"No. The first time, you can see what makes you happiest."

Can, she noted. She was sure it could also hurt like hell. Sean had been generous.

"It will feel pleasant next time," Sean said. He didn't add, "As long as I want it to," but she could read between the lines. "But it won't be so overwhelming."

She was glad he'd had enough kindness to introduce her to this in private. Of course, she told herself, he hadn't wanted her to collapse on the dance floor, either. She would look stupid then, and so would he. "Can you tell what I'm feeling?" she asked, and she deliberately turned to look him in the eyes.

He met her dark eyes squarely. "Yes, in a muffled way," he said. "I can tell if you are happy, if you are sad—when I bite."

He didn't tell her that now he would always be able to tell how she felt. He didn't tell her that she had tasted sweeter than his memory of honey, sweeter than any human he'd ever bitten.

3

They danced together for two months before Sean discovered something else about Rue. He wanted to call her "Layla," her real name, but she told him he would forget and call her that in front of someone who…and then she'd shut down her train of thought and asked him to call her Rue like everyone else.

He followed her home every night. Sean wasn't sure if she'd seen him that second night, but he made sure she never saw him again. He was careful. His intention, he told himself, was simply to make sure she arrived at her apartment safely, but he inevitably analyzed what he saw and drew conclusions.

In all those nights, Sean saw her speak to someone only once. Late one Wednesday night, a young man was sitting on the steps of her building. Sean could tell when Rue spotted him. She slowed down perceptibly. By then Sean had bitten her five times, and he could read her so closely that he registered a tiny flinch that would have gone unnoticed by anyone else.

Sean slid through the shadows silently. He maneuvered close enough to be able to help Rue if she needed it.

"Hello, Brandon." Rue didn't sound pleased.

"Hey, Rue. I just thought I might…if you weren't busy… Would you like to go out for a cup of coffee?" He stood up, and now the streetlight showed Sean that the young man was a little older than the common run of students, maybe in his late twenties. He was very thin, but attractive in a solemn way.

Rue stood for a second, her head bowed, as if she were thinking what to do next. The parts of her that Sean had begun to know were brittle and fragile, forged by fear. But now he felt her kindness. She didn't want to hurt this man. But she didn't want to be in his company, either, and Sean was dismayed by how happy this made him.

"Brandon, you're so nice to think of taking me out for coffee," she said gently. "But I thought I made myself real clear last week. I'm not dating right now. I'm just not in that mode."

"A cup of coffee isn't a date."

Her back straightened. Sean considered stepping out of the shadows to stand by her side.

"Brandon, I'm not interested in spending time with you." Her voice was clear and merciless.

The man stared at her in shock. "That's so harsh," he said. He sounded as though he was on the verge of crying. Sean's lip curled.

"I've turned down your invitations three times, Brandon. I've run out of courtesy."

The man pushed past her and walked down the street in such a hurry that he almost knocked over a trash can. Rue swung around to watch him go, her stance belligerent. She might look ruthless to the human eye, but Sean could tell she was full of shame at being so stern with a man as guileless as a persistent puppy. When she went up the steps, Sean drifted down the street, wondering all the while about a beautiful woman who didn't date, a woman who camouflaged what she was under layers of unattractive clothing, a woman who was deliberately rude when her first inclination was to be kind.

Rue May—Layla LaRue LeMay—was hiding. But from what? Or who? He'd been dancing with her for two months now, and he didn't know anything about her.

"We got a call from Connie Jaslow," Sylvia said two weeks later. "She wants to hire three couples to dance at a party she's putting on. Since it's warm, she's determined to have a tropical theme."

Rue and Sean, Julie and Thompson, and the third pair of dancers, Megan and Karl, were sitting in the padded folding chairs that Sylvia usually pushed against the walls. For this meeting, they'd pulled the chairs in front of Sylvia's desk.

"She'd like the gals to wear sort of Dorothy Lamour–style outfits, and the guys to wear loincloths and ankle bracelets. She wants some kind of 'native-looking' dance."

"Oh, for God's sake!" said Karl, disgust emphasizing his German accent.

"Connie Jaslow is one of our big repeat customers," Sylvia said. Her eyes went from one to the other of them. "I agree the idea is silly, but Connie pays good money."

"Let's see the costumes," Julie said. Rue had decided Julie was a good-hearted girl, and almost as practical as Sylvia.

"This was what she suggested," Sylvia said. She held up a drawing. The women's costume showed belly button; it was a short flowered skirt, wrapped to look vaguely saronglike, with a matching bra. The long black wig was decorated with artificial flowers.

Rue tried to imagine what she would look like in it, and

she thought she'd look pretty good. But then she reevaluated the low-rider skirt. "It would be that low?" she asked.

"Yes," Sylvia said. "Showing your navel is in right now, and Connie wanted a sort of update to the island look."

"Can't do it," Rue said.

"Something wrong with your button?" teased Thompson.

"My stomach," Rue said, and hoped she could leave it at that.

"I can't believe that. You're as lean as you can be," Sylvia said sharply. She wasn't used to being thwarted.

Rue had a healthy respect for her employer. She knew Sylvia would demand proof. Better to get it over with. Dancers learned to be practical about their bodies. Rue stood abruptly enough to startle Sean, who was leaning against the wall by her chair. Rue pulled up her T-shirt, unzipped her jeans and found she'd worn bikini panties, so she hardly had to push them down. "This would show," Rue said, keeping her voice as level as she could.

The room was silent as the dancers gazed at the thick, jagged scar that ran just to the left of Rue's navel. It descended below the line of the white bikinis.

"Good God, woman!" Karl said. "Was someone trying to gut you?"

"Give me a hysterectomy." Rue pulled her clothes back together.

"We couldn't cover that with makeup," Sylvia said. "Or could we?"

The other two couples and Sylvia discussed Rue's scarred stomach quite matter-of-factly, as a problem to solve.

The debate continued while Rue sat silently, her arms crossed over her chest to hold her agitation in. She became aware that she wasn't hearing a word from Sean. Slowly, she turned to look up at her partner's face. His blue eyes were full of light. He was very angry, livid with rage.

The dispassionate attitudes of the others had made her feel a bit more relaxed, but seeing his rage, Rue began to feel the familiar shame. She wanted to hide from him. And she couldn't understand that, either. Why Sean, whom she knew better than any of the other dancers?

"Rue," Sylvia said, "are you listening?"

"No, sorry, what?"

"Megan and Julie think they can cover it up," Sylvia said. "You're willing to take the job if we can get your belly camouflaged?"

"Sure," she told Sylvia, hardly knowing what she was saying.

"All right, then, two Fridays from now. You all start working on a long dance number right away, faux Polynesian. You'll go on after the jugglers. Julie and Thompson are booked for a party this Saturday night, and Karl and Megan, you're doing a dinner dance at the Cottons' estate on Sunday. Sean, you and Rue are scheduled to open a 'big band' evening at the burn unit benefit."

Rue tried to feel pleased, because she loved dancing to big band music, and she had a wonderful forties dress to wear, but she was still too upset about revealing her scar. What had gotten into her? She'd tried her best to conceal it for years, and all of a sudden, in front of a roomful of relative strangers, she'd pulled down her jeans and shown it to them.

And they'd reacted quite calmly. They hadn't screamed, or thrown up, or asked her what she'd done to deserve that. They hadn't even asked who'd done it to her. To Rue's astonishment, she realized that she was more comfortable with this group of dancers than she was with the other college students. Yet most of those students came from backgrounds that were much more similar to hers than, say, Julie's. Julie had graduated from high school pregnant, had the baby and given it up to the parents of the father. Now she was working non-stop, hoping to gather enough money to buy a small house. If she could do that, she'd told Rue, the older couple would let her have the baby over for the weekends. Megan, a small, intense brunette, was dancing to earn money to get through vet school. She'd seen Rue's stomach and immediately begun thinking how to fix it. No horror, no questions.

The only one who'd reacted with deep emotion had been Sean. Why was he so angry? Her partner felt contempt for her, she decided. Scarred and marred, damaged. If Rue hadn't felt some measure of blame, she could have blown off Sean's reaction, but part of her had always felt guilty that she hadn't recognized trouble, hadn't recognized danger, when it had knocked on her door and asked her out for a date.

That night, when they both left the studio, Sean simply began walking by her side.

"What are you doing?" Rue asked, after giving him a couple of blocks to explain himself. She stopped in her tracks.

"I am going in the same direction you are," he said, his voice calm.

"And how long are you gonna be walking in that direction?"

"Probably as far as your steps will take you."

"Why?"

There it was again, in his eyes, the rage. She shrank back.

"Because I choose to," he said, like a true aristocrat.

"Let me tell you something, buddy," she began, poking him in the chest with her forefinger. "You'll walk me home if I ask you to, or if I let you, not just because you 'choose' to. What will you do if I *choose* not to let you?"

"What will you do," he asked, "if I choose to walk with you, anyway?"

"I could call the police," she said. Being rude wasn't going to work on Sean, apparently.

"Ah, and could the police stop me?"

"Not human cops, maybe, but there are vamps on the force."

"And then you wouldn't have a partner, would you?"

That was a stumper. No, she wouldn't. And since vampires who wanted to dance for a living were scarce, she wouldn't be able to find another partner for a good long while. And that meant she wouldn't be working. And if she wasn't working…

"So you're blackmailing me," she said.

"Call it what you choose," he said. "I am walking you home." His sharp nose rose in the air as he nodded in the right direction.

Frustrated and defeated, Rue shouldered her bag again. He caught the bus with her, and got off with her, and arrived at her building with her, without them exchanging a word the whole way. When Rue went up the steps to the door, he waited until she'd unlocked it and gone inside. He could see her start up the inner stairs, and he retreated to the shadows until he saw a light come on in the second-floor front apartment.

After that, he openly walked her home every night, in silence. On the fourth night, he asked her how her classes were going. She told him about the test she'd had that day in geology. The next night, when he told her to have sweet dreams, he smiled. The *M* of his mouth turned up at the corners, and his smile made him look like a boy.

On the sixth night, a woman hailed Sean just as he and Rue got off the bus. As the woman crossed the street, Rue recognized Hallie, a Black Moon employee. Rue had met all the Black Moon people, but she did her best to steer clear of them all, both vampire and human. Rue could accept the other Blue Moon dancers as comrades. But the Black Moon performers made her shrink inside herself.

"Hey, what are you two up to?" Hallie said. She was in her late twenties, with curly brown hair and a sweet oval face. It was impossible not to respond to her good cheer; even Sean gave her one of his rare smiles.

"We just left practice," Sean said when Rue stayed silent.

"I just visited my mother," Hallie said. "She seems to be a little better."

Rue knew she had to speak, or she would seem like the most insufferable snob. *Maybe I am a snob,* she thought unhappily. "Is your mom in the hospital?"

"No, she's in Van Diver Home, two blocks down."

Rue had walked past there a couple of times, and thought what a grim place it was, especially for an old folks' home. "I'm sorry," she said.

"She's in the Alzheimer's wing." Hallie's hand was already waving off Rue's expression of sympathy. "If I didn't work for Sylvia, I don't know how I could pay the bills."

"You have another day job, too?"

"Oh, yes. Every day, and nights I don't work for Sylvia, I'm a cocktail waitress. In fact, I'm due back at work. I ran down to see Mom on my break. Good to see both of you."

And off Hallie hurried, her high heels clicking on the pavement. She turned into a bar on the next block, Bissonet's.

Rue and Sean resumed the short walk to Rue's building.

"She's no saint, but it's not as simple as you thought," Sean said when they'd reached her building.

"No, I see that." On an impulse, she gave him a quick hug, then quickly mounted the steps without looking back.

Two weeks later, Blue Moon's three male vampires and

three human women were dressing in a remote and barren room in the Jaslow mansion. Connie Jaslow had no consideration for dancers' modesty, since she'd provided one room for both sexes. To an extent, Mrs. Jaslow was correct. Dancers know bodies; bodies were their business, their tools. At least there was an adjacent bathroom, and the women took turns going in to put on their costumes and straighten the black wigs, but the men managed without leaving.

Rick and Phil, the two vampires who ordinarily worked together at "specialty" parties for Black Moon, had polished a juggling act. They would go on first. They were laughing together (Phil only laughed when he was with Rick) as they stood clad only in floral loincloths. "At least we don't have to wear the wigs," the taller Rick said, grinning as he looked over the dancers.

"We look like a bunch of idiots," Julie said bluntly. She tossed her head, and the shoulder-length black wig fell back into place flawlessly.

"At least we're getting paid to look like idiots," Karl said. The driver of the van that had brought them all out to the Jaslow estate, Denny James, came in to tell Karl that the sound system was all set up and ready to go. Denny, a huge burly ex-boxer, worked for Sylvia part-time. Megan and Julie had told Rue that Denny had a closer relationship with Sylvia than employer/employee, much to Rue's astonishment. The ex-boxer hardly seemed the type to appeal to the sophisticated Sylvia, but maybe that was the attraction.

Anxious about the coming performance, Rue began to stretch. She was already wearing the jungle-print skirt, which draped around to look like a sarong, and matching bikini panties. The bra top matched, too, a wild jungle print over green. The shoulder-length wig swung here and there as she warmed up, and the pink artificial flower wobbled. Rue's stomach was a uniform color, thanks to Julie and Megan.

Karl had brought the CD with their music and given it to the event planner who'd designed the whole party, a weirdly serene little woman named Jeri. On the way into the estate, Rue had noticed that the driveway had been lined with flaming torches on tall poles. The waiters and waitresses were also in costume. Jeri knew how to carry through a theme.

Rue went over the whole routine mentally. Sean came to stand right beside her. On his way out the door with Phil, Rick gave her a kiss on the cheek for luck, and Rue managed to give him a happy smile.

"Nervous?" Sean asked. It came out, "Nairvous?"

"Yes." She didn't mind telling him. *Head up, shoulders square, chest forward, big smile, pretty hands.* "There. I'm okay now."

"Why do you do that? That little…rearrangement?"

"That's what my mother told me to do every time I went on stage, from the time I was five to the time I was twenty."

"You were on stage a lot?"

"Beauty pageants," Rue said slowly, feeling as though she were relating the details of someone else's life. "Talent contests. You name it, I was in it. It cost my parents thousands of dollars a year. I'd win something fairly often, enough to make the effort worth it, at least for my father." She began to sink down in a split. "Press down on my shoulders." His long, thin fingers gripped her and pressed. He always seemed to know how much pressure to apply, though she knew Sean was far stronger than any human.

"Did you have brothers or sisters?" he asked, his voice quiet.

"I have a brother," she said, her eyes closed as she felt her thighs stretch to their limit. She hadn't talked about her family in over a year.

"Is your brother a handsome man?"

"No," Rue said sadly. "No, he isn't. He's a sweet guy, but he's not strong."

"So you didn't win every pageant you entered?" Sean teased, changing the subject.

She opened her eyes and smiled while rising to her feet very carefully. "I won a few," she said, remembering the glass-fronted case her mother had bought to hold all the trophies and crowns.

"But not all?" Sean widened his eyes to show amazement.

"I came in second sometimes," she conceded, mocking herself, and shot him a sideways look. "And sometimes I was Miss Congeniality."

"You mean the other contestants thought you were the sweetest woman among them?"

"Fooled them, huh?"

Sean smiled at her. "You have your moments." The sweetness of that downturned mouth, when it crooked up in a smile, was incredible.

"You knock my socks off, Sean," she said honestly. She was unable to stop herself from smiling back. He looked very strange in his costume: the flowered loincloth, ankle bracelets made of shells and the short black wig. Thompson was the only one who looked remotely natural in the getup, and he was gloating about it.

"What does that mean?"

She shook her head, still smiling, and was a little relieved when Denny knocked on the door to indicate that Jeri, the party planner, had signaled that it was time for their appearance. Karl lined the dancers up and looked them over, making a last-minute adjustment here and there. "Stomach looks good," he said briefly, and Rue glanced down.

"Julie and Megan did a good job," she admitted. She knew the scar was there, but if she hadn't been looking for it, she would have thought her own stomach was smooth and un-marred.

After Karl's last minute adjustment of the bright costumes and the black wigs, the six barefoot dancers padded down the carpeted hall to the patio door, and out across the marble terrace into the torch-lit backyard of the Jaslow estate. Rick and Phil loped past them on their way inside, burdened with the things they'd used in their act. "Went great," Rick said. "That backyard's huge."

"It's probably called the garden, not the backyard," Thompson muttered.

Karl said, "Sean, is this the sort of place you grew up in?"

Sean snorted, and Rue couldn't tell if he was deriding his former affluence, or indicating what he'd had had been much better.

Since Rue was shorter than Julie, she was in the middle when the three women stepped out across the marble terrace and onto the grass to begin their routine. Smiling, they posed for the opening bars of the drum music. Julie looked like a different person with the black wig on. Rue had a second to wonder if Julie's own mother would recognize her before the drums began. The routine began with a lot of hulalike hip twitching, the three women gradually rotating in circles. The intense pelvic motion actually felt good. The hand movements were simple, and they'd practiced and practiced doing them in unison. Rue caught a glimpse of Megan turning too fast and hoped the torchlight was obscuring Megan's haste. In her sideways glance, Rue caught a glimpse of a face she'd hoped she'd never see again.

All the years of training she'd had in composure paid off. She kept her smile pasted on her face, she kept up with the dance, and she blanked her mind out. The only thought she permitted herself was a reminder—she'd thought even Julie's family wouldn't recognize her, in the costume and the wig. Neither would her own.

Maybe Carver Hutton IV wouldn't, either.

4

The music was mostly drums, and the beat was fast and demanding. While Megan, Julie and Rue held their positions, the men leaped out, and the crowd gave the expected "Oooooh" at how high the vampires could jump. Sean, Karl and Thompson began their wild dance around the women. It was a good opportunity for her to catch her breath. Without moving her head from its position, she looked over at the spot where she'd seen him standing. Now there was no one there who reminded her of Carver. Maybe it had just been an illusion. Relief swept through her like sweet, cool water through a thirsty throat.

When Sean came to lift her above his head, she gave him a brilliant smile. As he circled, stomping his feet to the beat, she held her pose perfectly, and when he let her fall into his waiting arms, she arched her neck back willingly for the bite. She was ready to feel better, to have that lingering fear erased.

He seemed to sense her eagerness. Before his fangs sank in,

she felt his tongue trace a line on her skin, and her arm involuntarily tightened around his neck. As the overwhelming peace flooded her anxious heart, Rue wondered if she was becoming addicted to Sean. "Hi, I'm Rue, and I'm a vampire junkie." She didn't want to become one of those pitiful fang-bangers, people who would do almost anything to be bitten.

The audience gave them a round of applause as the women stood up, the men sweeping their arms outward to mark the end of the performance. The crowd goggled curiously at the two dots on the women's necks. Rue stepped forward with Julie and Megan to take her bow, and as she went down she thought she saw Carver Hutton again, out of the corner of her eye. When she straightened, he wasn't there. Was she delusional? She pasted her smile back onto her face.

The six of them ran into the house, waving to the guests as they trotted along, like a happy Polynesian dance troupe that just happened to (almost) all have Caucasian features. They were expected back out on the terrace in party clothes in fifteen minutes. Meanwhile, Denny James would be dismantling their sound system and loading it into the van, because an orchestra was set up to play live music.

When they were scrambling out of the costumes, Rue made her request. "Julie, Megan…do you think you could leave your wigs on?"

The other dancers stopped in the middle of changing and looked at her. Julie had pulled on some thigh-high hose and was buckling the straps of her heels, and Megan had pulled on a sheath dress and gotten her "native" skirt half off underneath it. The male dancers had simply turned their backs and pulled everything off, and now all three were in the process of donning the silk shirts and dress pants they'd agreed on ahead of time. Rick and Phil were helping Denny gather up the costumes and all the other paraphernalia to store in the van.

But they were all startled by Rue's request. There was a moment of silence.

Julie and Megan consulted with each other in an exchanged glance. "Sure, why not?" Julie said. "Won't look strange. We're all wearing the same outfit. Same wig, why not?"

"But we won't be wearing ours," Karl said, not exactly as if he were objecting, but just pointing out a problem.

"Yeah," Megan said, "but we look cute in ours, and you guys look like dorks in yours."

Karl and Thompson laughed at the justice of that, but Sean was staring at Rue as if he could see her thoughts if he looked hard enough. Phil, who never seemed to talk, was looking at Rue, with worry creasing his face. For the first time, Rue understood that Phil knew who she was. Like the girl in the library, he'd matched her face to the newspaper photos.

The black wig actually looked better with the shining burgundy sheath than Rue's own mahogany hair would have. She would never have picked this color for herself. Megan was wearing a deep green, and Julie, bronze. The men were wearing shirts that matched their partner's dress. Burgundy was not Sean's color, either. They looked at each other and shrugged simultaneously.

Out on the terrace, minutes later, the three couples began dancing to music provided by the live band. After watching for a few minutes, other people began to join them on the smooth marble of the terrace, and the professional couples split up to dance with the guests. This was the part of the job that Rue found most stressful. It was also the most difficult for her partner, she'd noticed. Sean didn't enjoy small talk with companions he hadn't chosen, and he seemed stiff. Thompson was a great favorite with the female guests, always, and Karl was much admired for his sturdy blond good looks and his courtesy, but Sean seemed to both repel and attract a certain class of women, women who were subtly or not so subtly dissatisfied with their lives. They wanted an exotic experience with a mysterious man, and no one did mysterious better than Sean.

John Jaslow, the host, smiled at Rue, and she took his hand and led him to the dance floor. He was a pleasant, balding man, who didn't seem to want anything but a dance.

Men were much easier to please, Rue thought cynically. Most men were happy if you smiled, appeared to enjoy dancing with them, flirted very mildly. Every now and then, she danced with one who was under the impression she was for sale. But she'd met hundreds of men like that while she was going through the pageant circuit, and she was experienced in handling them, though her distaste never ebbed. With a smile and a soothing phrase, she was usually able to divert them and send them away pacified.

Rue and John Jaslow were dancing next to Megan and her partner, who'd introduced himself as Charles Brody. Brody was a big man in his fifties. From the moment he'd taken Megan's hand, he'd been insinuating loudly that he would be delighted if she went to a hotel with him after the party.

"After all, you work for Sylvia Dayton, right?" Brody asked. His hand was stroking Megan's ribs, not resting on them. Rue looked up at her partner anxiously. John Jaslow looked concerned, but he wasn't ready to intervene.

"I work for Blue Moon, not Black Moon," Megan said, quietly but emphatically.

"And you're saying you just go home after one of these affairs, put on your jammies and go to bed by yourself?"

"Mr. Brody, that's exactly what I'm saying," Megan said.

He was quiet for a moment, and Rue and Mr. Jaslow gave each other relieved smiles.

"Then I'll find another woman to dance with, one who'll give a little," Brody said. Abruptly, he let go of Megan, but before he turned to stalk off the terrace, he gave the small dancer a hard shove.

The push was so unexpected, so vicious, that Megan didn't have time to catch herself. She was staggering backward and couldn't catch her balance. Moving faster than she'd thought she was able to move, Rue got behind Megan in time to keep her from hitting the ground.

In a second, Megan was back on her feet, and Mr. Jaslow and Sean were there.

The gasp that had arisen from the few people who'd watched the little episode with Brody gave way to a smattering of applause as Megan and bald Mr. Jaslow glided across the terrace in a graceful swoop.

"Smile," Rue said. Sean had gotten everything right but that. As he two-stepped away with her, his lips were stiff with fury.

"If this were a hundred years ago, I'd kill him," Sean said.

He smiled then, and it wasn't a nice smile. She saw his fangs.

She should have been horrified.

She should have been scandalized.

She should have been mortified.

"You're so sweet," she murmured, as she had to a thousand people during her life. This time, she meant it. Though Sean had defused the situation, she had no doubt he would rather have punched Brody, and she liked both reactions.

In five more minutes, their hour was up, and the six dancers eased themselves out of the throng of party guests. Wearily, they folded and bagged the costumes for cleaning and pulled on their street clothes. They were just too tired to be modest. Rue saw a pretty butterfly tattoo on Megan's bottom, and learned that Thompson had an appendectomy scar. But there was nothing salacious about knowing one another like this; they were comrades. Something about this evening had bonded them as no other event ever had.

It had been years since Rue had had friends.

Denny was waiting at the side entrance. The van doors were open, and when Rue scrambled into the back seat, Sean climbed in after her. There was a moment when all the others stared at Sean in surprise, since he always sat in front with Denny, then Megan climbed in after Sean. The middle row was filled with Karl, Julie and Thompson; Rick and Phil clambered in the front with Denny.

It was so pleasant to be sitting down in circumstances that didn't require polite chatter. Rue closed her eyes as the van sped down the long driveway. As they drove back to the city, it seemed a good idea to keep her eyes closed. Now, if she could just prop her head against something…

She woke up when the van came to a stop and the dome light came on. She straightened and yawned. She turned her head to examine her pillow, and found that she'd been sleeping with her head on Sean's shoulder. Megan was smiling at her. "You were out like a light," she said cheerfully.

"Hope I didn't snore," Rue said, trying hard to be nonchalant about the fact that she'd physically intruded on her partner.

"You didn't, but Karl did," Thompson said, easing his way out of the van and stretching once he was on the sidewalk.

"I only breathe loudly," Karl said, and Julie laughed.

"You gotta be the only vampire in the world who takes naps and snores," she said, but to take any sting out of her words, she gave him a hug.

Rue's eyes met Sean's. His were quite unreadable. Though she'd had such a good time with him before they had danced at the Jaslows', he was wearing his usual shuttered look.

"I'm sorry if you were uncomfortable the whole way back," she said. "I didn't realize I was so tired."

"It was fine," he said, and got out, holding out a hand to help her emerge. He unlocked the studio door; Karl and Thompson began unloading the sound system and the dancers set the costumes on a bench outside Sylvia's office. Denny drove off in the empty van.

The small group split up, Megan and Julie getting in the cab they'd called, Karl and Thompson deciding to go to Bissonet's, the bar where Hallie worked. "Why don't you come, Sean?" Karl asked. "You could use some type O."

"No, thanks," Sean said.

"Showing your usual wordy, flowery turn of phrase." Karl was smiling.

"I'll see Rue home," Sean said.

"Always the gentleman," Thompson said, not too fondly. "Sean, sometimes you act like you've got a poker up your ass."

Sean shrugged. He was clearly indifferent to Thompson's opinion.

Thompson's fangs ran halfway out.

Rue and Karl exchanged glances. In that moment, Rue could tell that Karl was worried about a quarrel between the other two vampires, and she took Sean's arm. "I'm ready," she said, and actually gave him a little tug as she started walking north. Sean's good manners required that he set off with her. They took the first two blocks at a good pace, and then turned to stand at the bus stop.

"What frightened you?" he said so suddenly that she started.

She knew instantly what he was talking about: the seconds at the party when she'd thought she'd seen an all-too-familiar face. But she couldn't believe he'd noticed her fear. She hadn't missed a beat or a step. "How'd you know?" she whispered.

"I know you," he said with a quiet intensity that centered her attention on him. "I can feel what you feel."

She looked up at him. They were under a streetlight, and she could see him with a stark clarity. Rue struggled inside herself with what she could safely tell him. He was waiting for her to speak, to share her burden with him. Still, she hesitated. She was out of the habit of confiding; but she had to be honest about how safe she felt when she was with Sean, and she could not ignore how much she'd begun to look forward to spending time with him. The relief from fear, from worry, from her sense of being damaged, was like warm sun shining on her face.

He could feel her growing trust; she could see it in his rare smile. The corners of his thin mouth turned up; his eyes warmed.

"Tell me," he said, in a voice less imperative and more coaxing.

What decided her against speaking out was fear for his safety. Sean was strong, and she was beginning to realize he was ruthless where she was concerned, but he was also vulnerable during the daylight hours. Rue followed another impulse; she put her arms around him. She spoke into his chest. "I can't," she said, and she could hear the sadness in her own voice.

His body stiffened under her hands. He was too proud to beg her, she knew, and the rest of the way to Rue's apartment, he was silent.

5

She thought he would stalk off, offended, when they reached her place, but, to her surprise, he stuck with her. He held her bag while she unlocked the front door, and he mounted the stairs behind her. While she sure couldn't remember asking him up, Rue didn't tell him to leave, either. She found herself hoping he enjoyed the view all the way up both flights. She tried to remember if she'd made her bed and put away her nightgown that morning.

"Please, come in," Rue said. She knew the new etiquette as well as anyone. Vampires had to be invited into your personal dwelling the first time they visited.

Her cat came running to meet Rue, complaining that her dinner was overdue. The little black-and-white face turned up to Sean in surprise. Then the cat stropped his legs. Rue cast a surreptitious eye over the place. Yes, the bed was neat. She retrieved her green nightgown from the footboard and rolled it into a little bundle, depositing it in a drawer in an unobtrusive way.

"This is Martha," Rue said brightly. "You like cats, I hope?"

"My mother had seven cats, and she named them all, to my father's disgust. She told him they ate the rats in the barn, and so they did, but she'd slip them some milk or some scraps when we had them to spare." He bent to pick up Martha, and the cat sniffed him. The smell of vampire didn't seem to distress the animal. Sean scratched her head, and she began to purr.

The barn? Scraps to spare? That didn't sound too aristocratic. But Rue had no right, she thought unhappily, to question her partner.

"Would you like a drink?" she asked.

Sean was surprised. "Rue, you know I drink…"

"Here," she said, and handed him a bottle of synthetic blood.

She had prepared for his visit, counting on it happening sometime. She had spent some of the little money she had to make him feel welcome.

"Thank you," he said briefly.

"It's room temperature, is that all right? I can heat it in a jiffy."

"It's fine, thanks." He took the bottle from her and opened it, took a sip.

"Where are my manners? Please take off your jacket and sit down." She gestured at the only comfortable chair in the room, an orange velour armchair obviously rescued from a dump. When Sean had taken it (to refuse the chair would have offended her), she sat on a battered folding chair that had come from the same source.

Rue was trying to pick a conversational topic when Sean said, "You have some of the lipstick left on your lower lip."

They'd put on a lot of makeup for the dance, and she

thought she'd removed it all before they'd left the Jaslow estate. Rue thought of how silly she must look with a big crimson smudge on her mouth. "Excuse me for a second," she said, and stepped into the tiny bathroom. While she was gone, Sean, moving like lightning, picked up her address book, which he'd spotted lying by the telephone.

He justified this bit of prying quite easily. She wouldn't tell him anything, and he had to know more about her. He wasn't behaving like any aristocrat, that was for sure, but he easily suppressed his guilt over his base behavior.

Flipping through the pages, Sean copied as many numbers as he could on a small piece of notebook paper from Rue's pile of school materials. Several were in one town, Pineville, which had a Tennessee area code. He'd had a vampire friend in Memphis a few years before, and he recognized the number. He'd just replaced the address book when he heard the bathroom door open.

"You're taking the history of my country," Sean said, reading the spines of the textbooks piled on the tiny table that served as Rue's desk.

"It's the history of all the British Isles," she said, trying not to grin. "But yes, I am. It's an interesting course."

"What year have you reached in your course of study?"

"We're talking about Michael Collins."

"I knew him."

"What?" Her mouth fell open, and she knew she must look like an idiot. For the first time, she realized the weight of the years on Sean's shoulders, the knowledge of history and people that filled his head. "You knew him?"

Sean nodded. "A fiery man, but not to my taste."

"Could—would—you talk to my class about your recollections?"

Sean looked dismayed. "Oh, Rue, it was so long ago. And I'm not much of a crowd pleaser."

"That's not true," she said, adding silently, *You please me.* "Think about it? My professor would be thrilled. She's a nut about everything Irish."

"Oh, and where's she from?"

"Oklahoma."

"A far way from Ireland."

"You want another drink?"

"No." He looked down at the bottle, seemed surprised he'd drained it. "I must be going, so you can get a little sleep. Do you have classes tomorrow?"

"No, it's Saturday. I get to sleep in."

"Me, too."

Sean had actually made a little joke, and Rue laughed.

"So do you sleep in a regular bed?" she asked. "Or a coffin, or what?"

"In my own apartment I have a regular bed, since the room's light-tight. I have a couple of places in the city where I can stay, if my apartment's too far away when it gets close to dawn. Like hostels for vampires. There are coffins to sleep in at those places. More convenient."

Rue and Sean stood. She took the empty bottle from him and leaned backward to put it by her sink. Suddenly the silence became significant, and her pulse speeded up.

"Now I'll kiss you good-night," Sean said deliberately. In one step he was directly in front of her, his hand behind her head, his spread fingers holding her in exactly the right position. Then his mouth was on Rue's, and after a moment, during which Rue held very still, his tongue touched the seam of her lips. She parted them.

There was the oddity of Sean's mouth being cool; and the oddity of kissing Sean, period. She was finally sure that

Sean's interest in her was that of a man for a woman. For a cool man, he gave a passionate kiss.

"Sean," she whispered, pulling back a little.

"What?" His voice was equally as quiet.

"We shouldn't…"

"Layla."

His use of her real name intoxicated her, and when he kissed her again, she felt only excitement. She felt more comfortable with the vampire than she'd felt with any man. But the jolt she felt, low down, when his tongue touched hers, was not what she'd call comfortable. She slid her arms around his neck and abandoned herself to the kiss. When Rue felt his body pressing against her, she knew he found their contact equally exciting.

His mouth traveled down her neck. He licked the spot where he usually bit her. Her body flexed against his, involuntarily.

"Layla," he said, against her ear, "who did you see that frightened you so much?"

It was like a bucket of cold water tossed in her face. Everything in her shut down. She shoved him away from her violently. "You did this to satisfy your curiosity? You thought if you softened me up, I'd answer all your questions?"

"Oh, of course," he said, and his voice was cold with anger. "This is my interrogation technique."

She lowered her face into her hands just to gain a second of privacy.

She was half inclined to take him literally. He was acting as if she was the unreasonable one, as if all the details of her short life should belong to him.

There was a knock on the door.

Their eyes met, hers wide with surprise, his questioning. She shook her head. She wasn't expecting anyone.

Rue went to the door slowly and looked through the peephole. Sean was right behind her, moving as silently as only vampires could move, when she unlocked the door and swung it open.

Thompson stood there, and Hallie. Between the two, awkwardly, they supported Hallie's partner, David. David was bleeding profusely from his left thigh. His khakis were soaked with blood. The vampire's large dark eyes were open, but fluttering.

Thompson's gaze was fixed on Rue; when he realized that Sean was standing behind her, he was visibly startled.

"Oh, come in, bring him in!" Rue exclaimed, shocked. "What happened?" She spared a second to be glad none of her neighbors seemed to be up. She shut the door before any of them roused.

Hallie was sobbing. Her tears had smeared her heavy eye makeup. "It was because of me," she sobbed. "Thompson and Karl came in the bar. David was already there, he'd been having words with this jerk…." While she was trying to tell Rue, she was helping David over to Rue's bed. Thompson was not being quite as much assistance as he should have been.

Sean whipped a towel from the rack in the bathroom and spread it on Rue's bed before the two eased the wounded David down. Hallie knelt and swung David's legs up, and David moaned.

"It was the Fellowship," Thompson said as Hallie unbuckled David's belt and began to pull his sodden slacks down.

The Fellowship of the Sun was to vampires as the Klan was to African-Americans. The Fellowship purported to be a civic organization, but it functioned more like a church, a church that taught its adherents the religion of violence.

"The other night I turned down this guy in the bar," Hallie said. "He just gave me the creeps. Then he found out I worked for Black Moon, and that I performed with David, you know, for the show, and he was waiting for me tonight...."

"Take it easy," Rue said soothingly. "You're gonna hyperventilate, Hallie. Listen, you go wash your face, and you get a bottle of TrueBlood for David, because he needs some blood. He's gonna heal."

Snuffling, Hallie ducked into the bathroom.

"He decided to get Hallie tonight, and David intervened?" Sean asked Thompson quietly. Rue listened with one ear while she stanched the bleeding by applying pressure with a clean kitchen towel. It rapidly reddened. She was not as calm as she'd sounded. In fact, her hands were shaking.

"David likes her, and she's his partner," Thompson said, as if David's intervention required an excuse. "Karl had left earlier, and David and I came out just in time to catch the show. The bastard had his arm wrapped around Hallie's neck. But he dropped her and went for David real fast with a knife."

"Out on the street, or in the bar?"

"Behind the bar, in the alley."

"Where's the body?"

Rue stiffened. Her hands slipped for a moment, and the bleeding began again. She pressed harder.

"I took him over the rooftops and deposited him in an alley three blocks away. David didn't bite him. He just hit him—once."

Rue knew no one was thinking of calling the police. And she was all too aware that justice wasn't likely to be attainable.

"He'll heal faster if he has real blood, right?" she said over her shoulder. She hesitated. "Shall I give him some?" She tried to keep her voice even. She had hardly exchanged ten words with David, who was very brawny and very tall. He had long, rippling black hair and a gold hoop in one ear. She knew, through Megan and Julie, that David was often booked to strip at bridal showers, as well as performing with Hallie in private clubs. In her other life, Rue would have walked a block to avoid David. Now she was pulling up the sleeve of her sweater to bare her wrist.

"No," said Sean very definitely. He pulled the sleeve right back down, and she stared at him, her mouth compressed with irritation. She might have felt a smidgen of relief, but Sean had no right to dictate to her.

Hallie had emerged from the bathroom, looking much fresher. "Let Sean give blood, Rue," she said, reading Rue's face correctly. "It won't make him weak, like it would you. If Sean won't, I will."

David, who'd been following the conversation at least a little, said, "No, Hallie. I have bitten you already three times this week." David had a heavy accent, perhaps Israeli.

Without further ado, Sean knelt by the bed and held his wrist in front of David. David took Sean's arm in both his hands and bit. A slight flexing of Sean's lips was the only sign that he'd felt the fangs. They all watched as David's mouth moved against Sean's wrist.

"Sean, what a dark horse you are, me boyo, visiting the lady here after hours." Thompson's attempt at an Irish accent was regrettable. His eyes lit on the empty TrueBlood bottle by the sink. "And her all ready for your arrival."

"Oh, shut up, Thompson." Rue was too tired to think of being polite. "As soon as Sean finishes his, ah, donation, all of you can leave, except David. He can rest here for a while until he feels well enough to go."

After a few minutes, David put Sean's arm away from him, and Sean rolled his own sleeve over his wrist. Moving rather carefully, Sean picked up his jacket, carefully draped it over his arm.

"Good night, darlin'," he said, giving her a quick kiss on

the cheek. "Kick David out after a couple of hours. He'll be well enough by then."

"I'll stay," Hallie said. "He got hurt on account of me, after all."

Sean looked relieved. Thompson looked disgruntled. "I'll be shoving off, then," he said. Hallie thanked him very nicely for helping her with David, and he was unexpectedly gracious about waving her gratitude away.

"We'll practice Sunday night," Sean said to Rue, his hand on the doorknob. "Can you be there at eight?" He'd been making plans for Saturday night while David had been taking blood from his wrist.

"I forgot to tell you," Thompson said. "Sylvia left a message on my cell. We have a company meeting Sunday night, at seven." It would just be dark at seven, so the vampires could attend.

"I'll see you there, Rue," Sean said. "And we can practice, after."

"All right," Rue said, after a marked pause.

Thompson said, "Good night, Rue, Hallie. Feel better, David."

"Good night, all," she said, and shut the door on both of them. She had one more bottle of synthetic blood, which she gave to David. She sat down in the chair while Hallie perched on the bed with David as he drank it. She tried valiantly to stay awake, but when she opened her eyes, she found two hours had passed, and her bed was empty. The bloody towels had been put to soak in the bathtub in cold water, and the empty bottles were in the trash.

Rue was relieved. "You and me, Martha," she said to the cat, who'd come out of hiding now that the strangers were gone. Rue's bed looked better than anything in the world, narrow and lumpy as it was. In short order, she'd cleaned her face and teeth and pulled on her pajamas. Martha leaped onto the bed and claimed her territory, and Rue negotiated with her so she'd have room for her own legs.

Rue was really tired, but she was also shaken. After all, there was a human dead on the street. She waited to feel a wave of guilt that never hit shore. Rue knew that if Hallie had been by herself, it would be Hallie lying bleeding on the street.

Been there, done that, Rue told herself coldly. *And all I got were the lousy scars to prove it.*

As for the shock she'd gotten at the Jaslows', a glimpse of the face she feared above all others, she was now inclined to think she'd imagined it. He would have made sure she noticed him, if he'd known she was there. He would have come after her again.

He'd sworn he would.

But it was funny that tonight, of all nights, she'd thought she'd seen him. At first, she'd imagined him everywhere, no matter how many times she'd called the police station to make sure he was still in the hospital. Maybe, once again, it was time to give Will Kryder a call again.

She imagined Sean lying in a coffin and smiled, just a curve of the lips before she drifted off to sleep.

Actually, Sean was on the road.

Sean had a feeling he was doing something wrong, going behind Rue's—Layla's—back like this, but he was determined to do it, anyway. If he'd asked Thompson to help, he had no doubt the younger vampire could have tracked down any information Sean needed on the damned computer. But Sean had never gotten used to the machines; it might take him twenty more years to accept them.

Like cars. Cars had been tough, too. Sean hadn't learned to drive until the sixties. He had loved phonographs from their inception, though, because they'd provided music for dancing, and he had bought a CD player as soon as he could. Words were hard for Sean, so dancing had always been his means of expression, from the time he'd become free to dance.

So here he was, off to collect information the old-fashioned way. He would get to Pineville tonight, find a place to hole up until he woke the next night, and then get his investigation under way.

Sean knew Rue had a fear that ran so deep she couldn't speak of it. And once he'd decided Rue was his business, it had become his job to discover what she feared. He had done some changing through the centuries, but the way he'd grown up had ingrained in him the conviction that if a man claimed a woman as his family—or his mate—he had to protect her.

And how could he protect her if he didn't understand the threat?

While Rue rose late to have a leisurely breakfast, clean her apartment and wash her clothes, Sean, who had consulted his housing directory, was sleeping in the vampire room of the only motel large enough to boast one, right off the interstate at the exit before Pineville. He had a feeling it was the first time the clerk had rented the room to an actual vampire. He'd heard that human couples sometimes took the room for some kinky playacting. He found that distasteful. The room—windowless, with two aligned doors, both with heavy locks, and a black velour curtain in between—had two coffins sitting side by side on the floor. There was a small refrigerator in the corner, with several bottles of synthetic blood inside. There was a minimalist bathroom. At least the coffins were new, and the padding inside was soft. Sean had paid an exorbitant amount for this Spartan accommodation, and he sighed as he undressed and climbed into the larger of the two coffins. Before he lay down, he looked over at the inner door to make

sure all its locks were employed. He pulled the lid down, seconds before he could feel the sun come up.

Then he died.

6

When Sean felt life flowing back into his body that night, he was very hungry. He woke with his fangs out, ready to sink into some soft neck. But it was rare that Sean indulged himself in fresh human blood; these days, the sips he took from Rue were all he wanted. He pulled the synthetic blood from the refrigerator, and since he didn't like it cold, he ran hot water in the bathroom and set the bottle in the sink while he showered. He hated to wash the scent of Rue from his skin, but he wanted to seem as normal as possible to the people he talked to tonight. The more humanlike a vampire could look and act, the more likely humans were to be open to conversation. Sean had noticed that interactions were easier for Thompson, who still had clear memories of what it was like to breathe and eat.

He'd written down the numbers and names from Rue's book, just in case his memory played tricks with him. One of the numbers was self-explanatory—"Mom and Dad," she'd written by it. "Les," she'd written by another, and that was surely one he would have to explore; a single man might be a rival. The most interesting numbers were by the notation "Sergeant Kryder." She'd labeled one number "police station" and the second number "home."

Pineville looked like almost any small town. It seemed to be dominated by one big business—Hutton Furniture Manufacturing, a huge plant that ran around the clock, Sean noted. The sign in front of the library read Camille Hutton Library, and the largest church complex boasted a whole building labeled Carver Hutton II Family Life Center.

The tire company was owned by a Hutton, and one of the car dealerships, too.

There was no sign crediting the Huttons with owning the police force, but Sean suspected that might be close to the truth. He found the station easily; it was right off the town square, a low redbrick building. The sidewalk from the parking area to the front door was lined with azaleas just about to bloom. Sean opened the swinging glass door to see a young policeman with his feet up on the counter that divided the public and private parts of the front room. A young woman in civilian clothes—short and tight civilian clothes—was using a copier placed against the wall to the left, and the two were chatting as Sean came in.

"Yes, sir?" said the officer, swinging his feet to the floor.

The young woman glanced at Sean, then did a double take. "Vampire," she said in a choked voice.

The man glanced from her to Sean in a puzzled way. Then he seemed to take in Sean's white face for the first time, and he visibly braced his shoulders.

"What can I do to help you, sir?" he asked.

"I want to speak with Sergeant Kryder," Sean said, smiling with closed lips.

"Oh, he retired," called the girl before the young man could answer. The man's name tag read "Farrington." He wasn't pleased at the girl's horning in on his conversation with the vampire.

"Where might I find him?" Sean asked.

Officer Farrington shot a quelling glance at the girl and pulled a pencil out of his drawer to draw Sean a map. "You take a left at the next stop sign," he told Sean. "Then go right two blocks, and it's the white house on the corner with the dark green shutters."

"Might be gone," said the girl sulkily.

"Barbara, you know they ain't left yet."

"Packing up, I heard."

"Ain't left yet." Farrington turned to Sean. "The Kryders are moving to their place in Florida."

"I guess it was time for him to retire," Sean said gently, willing to learn what he could.

"He took it early," the girl said. "He got all upset about the Layla LeMay thing."

"Barbara, shut up," Officer Farrington said, his voice very sharp and very clear.

Sean tried hard to look indifferent. He said, "Thank you very much," and left with the instructions, wondering if they'd call ahead to the ex-sergeant, warn him of Sean's impending visit.

Sergeant Kryder had indeed gotten a call from the police station. His front light was on when Sean parked in front of his modest house. Sean didn't have a plan for interrogating the retired policeman. He would play it by ear. If Rue had written the man's phone number in her book, then the man had befriended her.

Sean knocked at the door very gently, and a slim, clean-shaven man of medium height with thinning fair hair and a guarded smile opened the door. "Can I help you?" the man asked.

"Sergeant Kryder?"

"Yes, I'm Will Kryder."

"I would like to speak with you about a mutual friend."

"I have a mutual friend with a vampire?" Kryder seemed to catch himself. "Excuse me, I didn't mean to offend. Please come in." The older man didn't seem sure about the wisdom of inviting Sean in, but he stood aside, and Sean stepped into the small living room. Cartons were stacked everywhere, and the house looked bare. The furniture was still there, but the walls were blank, and none of the normal odds and ends were on the tables.

A dark-haired woman was standing in the doorway to the kitchen, a dish towel in her hand. Two cats rubbed her ankles, and a little Pekingese leaped from the couch, barking ferociously. He stopped when he got close to Sean. He backed up, whining. The woman actually looked embarrassed.

"Don't worry," Sean said. "You can never tell with dogs. Cats generally like us." He knelt and held out a hand, and the cats both sniffed it without fear. The Pekingese retreated into the kitchen.

Sean stood, and the woman extended her hand. She had an air of health and intelligence about her that was very appealing. She looked Sean in the eyes, apparently not knowing that he could do all kinds of things with such a direct look. "I'm Judith," she said. "I apologize for the appearance of the house, but we're leaving in two days. When Will retired, we decided to move down to our Florida house. It's been in Will's family for years."

Will had been watching Sean intently. "Please have a seat," he said.

Sean sank into the armchair, and Will Kryder sat on the couch. Judith said, "I'll just go dry the dishes," and vanished into the kitchen, but Sean was aware that she could hear them if she chose.

"Our mutual friend?" Will prompted.

"Layla."

Will's face hardened. "Who are you? Who sent you here?"

"I came here because I want to find out what happened to her."

"Why?"

"Because she's scared of something. Because I can't make it go away unless I know what it is."

"Seems to me if she wanted you to know, she would tell you herself."

"She is too frightened."

"Are you here to ask me where she is?"

Sean was surprised. "No. I know where she is. I see her every night."

"I don't believe you. I think you're some kind of private detective. We knew someone would be coming sooner or later, someone like you. That's why we're leaving town. If you think you can get rid of us easy, let me tell you, you can't." Will's pleasant face was set in firm lines. He suddenly had a gun in his lap, and it was pointed at Sean.

"It's easy to see you haven't met a vampire before," Sean said.

"Why is that?"

Before Will could pull the trigger, Sean had the gun. He bent the barrel and tossed it behind him.

"Judith!" Will yelled. "Run!" He dove for Sean, apparently intending to grapple with Sean until Judith could get clear.

Sean held the man still by clamping Kryder's hands to his sides. He said, "Calm yourself, Mr. Kryder." Judith was in the room now, a butcher knife in her hands. She danced back and forth, reluctant to stab Sean but determined to help her husband.

Sean liked the Kryders.

"Please be calm, both of you," he said, and the quiet of his voice, the stillness of his posture, seemed to strike both of the Kryders at the same time. Will stopped struggling and looked at Sean's white face intently. Judith lowered the knife, and Sean could tell she was relieved to be able to.

"She calls herself Rue May now," he told them. "She's going to the university, and she has a cat named Martha."

Judith's eyes widened. "He does know her," she said.

"He could have found that out from surveillance." Will was not so sure.

"How did you meet her?" Judith asked.

"I dance with her. We dance for money."

The couple exchanged a glance.

"What does she do before she goes on stage?" Judith asked suddenly.

"Head up, chest out, shoulders square, big smile, pretty hands." Sean smiled his rare smile.

Will Kryder nodded at Judith. "I reckon you can let go of me now," he told Sean. "How is she?"

"She's lonely. And she saw something the other night that scared her."

"What do you know about her?"

"I know she was a beauty queen. I know she danced in a lot of contests. I know she never seems to hear from her family. I know she has a brother. I know she's hiding under another name."

"Have you seen her stomach?"

"The scars, yes."

"You know how she got that way?" Kryder didn't seem to be concerned with how Sean had come to see the scars.

Sean shook his head.

"Judith, you tell him."

Judith sat on the couch beside her husband. Her hands clasped tightly in her lap, she appeared to be organizing her thoughts.

"I taught her when she was in tenth grade," Judith said. "She'd won a lot of titles even then. Layla is just…beautiful. And her mother pushed and pushed. Her mother is an ex-beauty queen, and she married Tex LeMay after she'd had two years of college, I think. Tex was a handsome man, still is, but he's not tough, not at all. He let LeeAnne push him around at home, and at work he let his boss stomp on what was left of his…manhood."

Sean didn't have to feign his interest. "His boss?"

"Carver Hutton III." Will's face was rigid with dislike as he spoke the name.

"The family that owns this town."

"Yes," Judith said. "The family that owns this town. That's who Tex works for. The other LeMay kid, Les, was always a dim bulb compared to Layla. Les is a good boy, and I think he's kept in touch with Layla—did you say she calls herself Rue these days? Les is off at college now, and he doesn't come home much."

"Carver IV came back from his last year of college one Christmas, two years ago," Will said. "Layla'd been elected Christmas Parade Queen, and she was riding in the big sleigh—'course, it's really a horse-drawn wagon, we don't get snow every year—and she was wearing white, and a sparkly crown. She looked like she was born to do that."

"She's a sweet girl, too," Judith said unexpectedly. "I'm not saying she's an angel or a saint, but Layla's a kind young woman. And she's got a backbone like her mother. No, I take that back. Her mother's got a strong will, but her backbone doesn't even belong to her. It belongs to the Social God."

Will laughed, a small, choked laugh, as if the familiar reference sparked a familiar response. "That's the god that rules some small towns," he said to Sean. "The one that says you have to do everything exactly correct, follow all the rules, and you'll go to heaven. Social heaven."

"Where you get invited to all the right places and hang around with all the right people," Judith elaborated.

Sean was beginning to have a buzzing feeling in his head. He recognized it as intense anger.

"What happened?" he asked. He was pretty sure he knew.

"Carver asked Layla out. She was only seventeen. She was flattered, excited. He treated her real well the first two times, she told me. The third time, he raped her."

"She came over here," Judith said. "Her mom wouldn't listen, and her dad said she must be mistaken. He asked her didn't she wear a lot of perfume and makeup, or a sexy dress." Judith shook her head. "She'd—it was her first time. She was a mess. Will called the chief of police at the time. He wasn't a monster," Judith said softly. "But he wasn't willing to lose his job over arresting Carver."

"She shut herself in the house and wouldn't come out for two weeks," Will said. "Her mother called us, told us to quit telling lies about the Huttons. She said Layla had just misunderstood the situation. Her exact words."

"Then," said Judith heavily, "Layla found out she was pregnant."

The buzzing in Sean's head grew louder, more insistent. He had never felt like this before, in his hundreds of years.

"She called Carver and told him. I guess she thought something so serious would bring him to his senses. Maybe she imagined that his parents had brought on all his violence. Maybe she thought he would do right by her somehow. She was just seventeen. I don't know what she thought. Maybe she wanted him to take her to a doctor, I don't know. She didn't want to tell her parents."

"He decided to take care of it himself," Sean said.

"Yeah," Will said. "He lost his mind. Usually, he can act like a real person when other people are around." Will Kryder sounded as detached as if he were discussing the habits of an exotic animal, but his hands were clasped in front of him so tightly that they were white. "Carver couldn't maintain the facade that night. He pulled up in front of the LeMays' house, and Layla came out, without saying anything to Tex or LeeAnne about where she was going. But Les was watching out the window, and he saw...he saw..."

"After he socked her in the face a few times, he broke his soda bottle and used that," Judith said simply. There was a long moment of silence. "Les got him off in time to save Layla's life, by hitting Carver with his baseball bat...he was on the high school team, then."

"Go on," Sean managed to say. They'd been lost in these tragic memories, but when they heard his voice, they looked up, to be absolutely terrified by Sean's face. "I'm not angry with you," Sean said, very quietly. "Go on."

"The scene at the hospital was—you can imagine," Will said, his voice weary. "She lost the baby, of course, and there was considerable damage. Permanent damage. She was in the hospital for a while."

"No one could ignore *that*," Judith said bitterly. "But the Huttons got a good lawyer, of course, and he made a case for insanity. Here in Pineville, of course, a Hutton won't get convicted of jaywalking. He was declared temporarily insane, and the judge sentenced him to time in a mental institution and ordered his family to pay all Layla's medical expenses. He did grant Layla a restraining order against Carver ever contacting her again, or even coming within a hundred feet of her. I guess that's worth the paper it's printed on. When the mental doctors decided Carver was 'stabilized,' he could be released, and he had to go through so many courses of outpatient anger management and other therapy. That took four years." She shook her head. "Of course, that doesn't mean jack."

"He mutilates Layla, he causes the death of his own child in her womb, and after a token sentence, he walks free." Sean shook his head, his expression remote. "Since I've lived in America, I've admired its justice system. So much better than when I was a boy in Ireland, when children could be hung for stealing bread when they were hungry. But this isn't any better."

The Kryders both looked embarrassed, as if they were personally responsible for the injustice. "That's another reason we're moving," Will said. "Sooner or later, when we least expect it, Carver III will make us pay for backing Layla up. She stayed with us some, when she was convalescing. She didn't want to see her parents. Les used to come over, visit her. Not LeeAnne. Not Tex."

Sean didn't express incredulity, and he didn't comment on Layla's family's behavior. He'd seen worse in his long life, but he hadn't seen worse done to someone he cared about as much as he cared about Layla LaRue LeMay.

"Does she call you?" Sean asked.

"Yes, she does, from time to time. She'll call here, or she'll call the station to talk to Will, to find out if Carver's out yet."

"And is he?"

"Yes. After four years, he's off all supervision now. He's footloose and fancy-free."

"And is he living here?"

"No. He left town right away."

"She saw him," Sean said out loud.

"Oh, no. Where?"

"At a party, where we were dancing."

"Did he approach her?"

"No."

"Did he see her?" Judith had hit the nail on the head.

Sean said slowly, "I don't know." Then he said, "But I have to get back. Now."

Will said, "I hope you're planning on being good to her. If I hear different, I'll come back and track you down with a stake in my hand. She's had enough trouble."

Sean stood and bowed, in a very old-fashioned way. "We'll see you in Florida," he said.

He left Pineville, pushing the rental car to its limit, so he could make the last plane that would get him into the city in time to find a daytime resting place. There was a safe apartment very close to the airport, maintained by the vampire hierarchy. He called ahead to reserve a coffin, and got on the plane after making sure there was an emergency space in the tail where he could wait if sunlight caught them. But all went well, and he was in a room with three other occupied coffins by the time the sun came up.

7

The personnel of Blue Moon Entertainment and Black Moon Productions were draped around the big practice room in various positions of weariness. It was a scant hour after darkness had fallen, and some of the vampires looked sluggish. Every one of them clutched a bottle of synthetic blood. Most of the humans had coffee mugs.

Rue had come in full disguise. The more she'd thought about the glimpse she'd had of the man who'd looked so much like Carver Hutton IV, the more spooked she'd gotten. Between that fear and her upsetting spat with Sean, and the remembered tingle she'd felt when they kissed, she hadn't been worth anything during the weekend so far. She'd performed her regular weekend chores, but in a slapdash fashion. She hadn't been able to study at all.

When Sean came in, wearing sweatpants and a Grateful Dead T-shirt, her pulse speeded up in a significant way. He folded to the floor by her, his back against the glass of the mirror as hers was, and scooted closer until their shoulders and hips touched.

Sean was silent, and she was too self-conscious to look up at his eyes. She'd half expected to hear from him the night before, and when the phone hadn't rung and there'd been no knock at her door, she'd felt quite disconcerted. Men had seldom walked away from her, no matter how rocky their relationship had grown. *I am* not *going to ask him where he's been,* she swore to herself.

Sylvia was talking on the phone and smoking, which all the human dancers detested. She was doing it to prove she was the boss. Rue made a face and tried to arrange herself so her back was comfortable. The wall wasn't friendly to her spine, which had been jolted when she caught Megan after Charles Brody had shoved her. Megan was moving a little stiffly. Hallie looked subdued and David seemed healed, as far as Rue could tell. She hoped this week would be a better one for the entertainment troupe as a whole.

Rue sighed and tried to shift her weight slightly to her right hip. To her astonishment, in the next moment she felt herself being lifted. Sean had spread his legs, and he put her down between them, so her back rested against his stomach and chest. He scooted his butt out from the wall to give her a little incline. She was instantly more comfortable.

Rue figured if she didn't make any big deal out of it, no one else would either, so she didn't say a word or betray the surprise she felt. But she relaxed against Sean, knowing he would interpret that signal correctly as a thank-you.

Sylvia hung up at last. A black-haired female vampire with beautiful clear skin and dead eyes said, "Sylvia, we all know you're top dog. Put out the damn cigarette." The vampire waved her elegant hand at Sylvia imperiously.

"Abilene, tell me how you and Mustafa are doing," Sylvia

said, blowing out smoke, but then she stubbed out the cigarette.

A tall human with a full mustache, Mustafa had more muscles than any man needed, in Rue's opinion. He was very dark complexioned, and a slow thinker. Rue wondered about the dynamics of this team, since the vampire half was a woman. How did that work? Did she do the lifts? Belatedly, Rue realized that in Black Moon's form of entertainment, lifting was probably irrelevant.

"We're doing fine," Abilene said. "You got any comments, Moose?" That was her pet name for her giant partner, but no one else dared use it.

"The pale woman," he said, his voice heavily accented and deep as a foghorn. Moose seemed to be a man of few words.

"Oh, yeah, the last gig we did, the party for the senator," Abilene said. "The wife of one of the, ah, legislators... I don't know how she got there, why her husband brought her, but she turned out to be Fellowship."

"Were you hurt?" Sylvia asked.

"She had a knife," Abilene said. "Moose was on top of me, so it was an awkward moment. You sure I can't kill the customers?" Abilene smiled, and it wasn't a nice smile.

"No, indeed," Sylvia said briskly. "Haskell take care of it?"

For the first time, Rue noticed the sleek man leaning against the wall by the door. She seldom had dealings with Haskell, since the Black Moon people needed more protection than the Blue Moon dancers. Haskell was a vampire, with smooth, short blond hair and glacier-blue eyes. He had the musculature of a gymnast, and the wary, alert attitude of a bodyguard.

"I held her until her husband and his flunky could get her out of there," Haskell said quietly.

"Her name?"

"Iris Lowry."

Sylvia made a note of the name. "Okay, we'll watch for her. I may have my lawyer write Senator Lowry a letter. Hallie? David?"

"We're fine," David said briskly. Rue looked down at her hands. No reason to relate the incident, even though it had ended with a death…a death that hadn't even made the papers.

"Rick? Phil?" The two men glanced at each other before answering.

"The last group we entertained, at the Happy Horseman—it was an S and M group, and we gave them a good show."

They weren't talking about juggling. Rue tried to keep her face blank. She didn't want her distaste to show. These people had shown her nothing but courtesy and comradeship.

"They wanted me to leave Phil there when our time was up," Rick said. "It was touch-and-go for a few minutes." The two vampires were always together, but they were very different. Rick was tall and handsome in a bland, brown-on-brown kind of way. Phil was small and slim, delicate. In fact, Rue decided, she might have mistaken him for a fourteen-year-old. *Maybe when he died he* was *that young,* she thought, and felt a pang of pity. Then Phil happened to look at Rue, and after meeting his pale, bottomless eyes, she shivered.

"Oh, no," said Sylvia, and Phil turned to his employer. "Phil?" Her voice became gentle. "You know we're not going to let anyone else touch you, unless you want that to happen. But remember, you can't attack someone just because they want you. You're so gorgeous, people are always going to want you."

Sylvia braced herself in the face of that continued, terrifying gaze. "You know the deal, Phil," Sylvia said more firmly. "You have to leave the customers alone." After a long, tense pause, Phil nodded, almost imperceptibly.

"So, you think we need another minder, like Haskell? For

nights when we're double-booked on Black Moon shows?" Sylvia asked the group. "Denny's a great guy, but he's really just a lifting-and-setup kind of fellow. He's not aggressive enough to be a minder, and he's human."

"Wouldn't hurt to have someone else," Rick said. "It would've taken some of the strain off if there'd been a third party there. It looked like it was going to be me against all of them for a little while. I hate to injure the client base, but I thought I might have to. People who like that kind of show are ready for a little violence, anyway."

Sylvia nodded, made another note. "What about you Blue Moon people?" she asked, obviously not expecting any response. "Oh, Rue. Only a couple of the Black Mooners have seen you in your dancing clothes. Take off the other stuff, so they can see what you really look like. I'm not sure they could recognize you in a crowd."

Rue hadn't planned on becoming the center of attention, but there was no point of making a production of this request. She stood and unbuttoned the flannel shirt, pulled off the glasses and stepped out of the old corduroy pants she'd pulled on to cover her practice clothes. She held out her arms, inviting them to study her in her T-shirt and shorts, and then she sank down to the floor again. Sean's arms crossed over her and pulled her tightly against him. This was body language anyone could understand—"Mine!" The Black Moon people almost all smiled—Phil and Mustafa being the exceptions—and nodded, both to acknowledge Rue and to say they'd noted Sean's possessiveness.

Rue wanted to whack Sean across his narrow aristocratic face.

She also wanted to kiss him again.

But there was one thing she had to say. "We had some trouble," she said hesitantly. She could understand David and

Hallie's silence. They hadn't been on a professional engagement—*and* a man had died. But she couldn't understand why Megan wasn't speaking out.

Sylvia said, "With whom?" Her eyebrows were raised in astonishment.

"Guy named Charles Brody. He got mad when Megan wouldn't take money to meet him afterward. He mentioned your name, Sylvia, but he wouldn't…he didn't accept it too well when we told him we didn't work for Black Moon. He acted like it was going to be okay, that he accepted Megan's refusal, but when he turned to leave, he shoved her down."

"I don't recognize the name, but he could've hired us before," Sylvia said. "Thanks, I'll put him in the watch-for file. Were you hurt?" She waited impatiently for Megan's reply.

"No," Megan said. "Rue caught me. I would've said something, but I'd pretty much forgotten it." She shrugged. She clearly wasn't too pleased with Rue for bringing up the incident.

"I want to speak," Sean said, and that caught everyone's attention.

"Sean, I don't think you've spoken at one of these meetings in three years," Sylvia said. "What's on your mind?"

"Rue, show them your stomach," Sean said.

She rose up on her knees and turned to look at him. "Why?" She was stunned and outraged.

"Just do it. Please. Show the Black Moon people."

"You'd better have a good reason for this," she said in a furious undertone.

He nodded at her, his blue eyes intent on her face.

With a visible effort, Rue faced the group and pulled down the front of her elastic-waist shorts. The Black Moon people looked, and Abilene gave a sharp nod of acknowledgment. Phil's dark eyes went from the ugly scar to Rue's face, and there was a sad kinship in them that she could hardly bear. Mustafa scowled while Rick, David and Hallie looked absolutely matter-of-fact. Haskell, the enforcer, averted his eyes.

"The man who did this is out of the mental hospital, and he's probably here in the city," Sean said, his Irish accent heavier than usual. Rue covered her scars, sank to her knees on the floor and looked down at the linoleum with utter concentration. She didn't know if she wanted to swear and throw something at Sean or...she just didn't know. He had massively minded her business. He'd gone behind her back.

But it felt good to have someone on her side.

"I got a human to find a picture of this man in the newspaper and copy it." Sean began to pass around the picture. "This is Carver Hutton IV. He's looking for Rue under her real name, Layla LeMay. He knows she dances. His family's got a lot of money. He can get into almost any party anywhere. Even with his past, most hostesses would be glad to have him."

"What are you doing?" Rue gasped, almost unable to get enough breath together to speak. "I've kept all this secret for years! And in the space of five minutes, you've told people everything about me. Everything!" For the first time in her life, Rue found herself on the verge of hitting someone. Her hands fisted.

"And keeping it secret worked out well for you?" Sean asked coolly.

"I've seen him," a husky voice said. Hallie.

And just like that, Rue's anger died, consumed by an overwhelming fear.

If any of the dancers had doubted Rue's story, they saw the truth of it when they saw her face. They all knew what fear looked like.

"Where?" Sean asked.

Hallie crooked her finger at her partner. "We saw him," she

said to David. He put his white arm around her shoulders, and his dark, wavy hair swept over her neck as he bent forward.

"Where?" David asked Hallie.

"Two weeks ago. The bachelor party at that big house in Wolf Chase."

"Oh." David studied the picture a little longer. "Yes. He was the one who kept grabbing at you when you were on top. He said you were a bitch who needed to learn a lesson." Hallie nodded.

Tiny shivers shook Rue's body. She made an awful noise.

"Jeez," Hallie said. "That's what he said to you, huh, when he cut you? We just thought he wanted us to do a little, you know, play spanking. We did, and he chilled. The host looked like he was upset with the guy's outburst, so we toned it down. Please the man who's paying the bill, right?"

David nodded. "I kept an eye on him the rest of the evening."

Sylvia said, "You watch out for this guy. That's all. Just let Rue know if you've seen him. Nothing else."

"You're the boss," Mustafa said. His voice was low and rumbly, like a truck passing in the distance. "But he will not hurt Abilene."

"Thanks, Moose," said the vampire. She stroked his dark cheek with her white hand. "I love ya, babe."

"Getting back on track," Sylvia said briskly. "Rick, you and Phil didn't turn in your costumes for a week after that Greek party. Hallie, you can't have your mail sent here. If you keep that up, I'll start opening it. Julie, you left the lights on in the practice room last night. I've talked to you about that before."

Sylvia read down a list of minor offenses, scolding and correcting, and Rue had a chance to calm herself while the other employees responded. She was all too aware of Sean standing behind her. She could not have put a label on what she was feeling. She went to sit on the high pile of mats that they sometimes spread on the linoleum floor when they were practicing a new lift.

When the others began leaving, Rue started to pull her outer layer of clothes back on.

"Not so fast," Sean said. "We have practice tonight."

"I'm mad at you," she said.

"Turn out the lights behind you, whichever one of you wins," Sylvia called.

Sean went out into the hall and locked the front door, or at least that was the direction his footfalls took. She heard him come back, heard him over at the big CD player in the corner, by the table of white towels Sylvia kept there for sweaty dancers.

Rue began to warm up, but she still wasn't about to look at Sean. She was aware he began stretching, too, on the other side of the room.

After fifteen minutes or so, she stood, to signal she was ready to practice. But she kept her eyes forward. Rue wasn't sure if she was being childish, or if she was just trying to avoid attacking Sean. He started the CD player, and Rue was startled to recognize Tina Turner's sultry voice. "Proud Mary" was not a thinking song, though, but a dancing song, and when Sean's hands reached out for hers, she had no idea what he was going to do. The next twenty minutes were a challenge that left her no time for brooding. Avril Lavigne, the Dixie Chicks, Macy Gray and the Supremes kept her busy.

And she never once looked up at him.

The next song was her favorite. It was a warhorse, and the secret reason she'd decided to become a dancer, she'd told him in a moment of confidence: the Righteous Brothers' "Time of My Life." She'd worn out a tape of the movie *Dirty Dancing,* and that song had been the climax of the movie. The heroine had finally gained enough confidence in herself and trust in her partner to attempt a leap, at the apex of which he caught her and lifted her above his head as if she were flying.

"Shame on you," she said in a shaky voice.

"We're going to do this," he said.

"How could you take over my life like this?"

"I'm yours," he said.

It was so simple, so direct. She met his eyes. He nodded, once. His declaration hit her like a fist to the heart. She was so stunned by his statement that she complied when he put his hand on her back, when he took her left hand and pressed it to his silent heart. Her right hand was spread on his back, as his was on hers. Their hips began to move. The syncopation broke apart in a minute as he began to sweep her along with him, and they danced. Nothing mattered to Rue but matching her steps to her partner's. She wanted to dance with him forever. At every turn of her body, every movement of her head, she saw something new in his pale face—a glint of blue eye, the arch of his brow, the haughty line of his nose, which contrasted so startlingly with the grace of his body. When the song began to reach its climax, Sean raced to one end of the long room and held out his hands to her. Rue took a deep breath and began to run toward him, thinking all the way, and when she was just the right distance from Sean, she launched herself. She felt his hands on her hip bones, and then she was high in the air above his head, her arms outstretched, her legs extended in a beautiful line, flying.

As Sean let her down the line of his body very slowly, Rue couldn't stop smiling. Then the music stopped, but Sean didn't let her feet touch the floor. She was looking right into his eyes, and the smile faded from her face.

His arms were around her, and his mouth was right by hers. Then it was on hers, and once again he asked admission.

Rue whispered, "We shouldn't. You're going to get hurt. He'll find me. He'll try to kill me again. You'll try to stop him, and you'll get hurt. You know that."

"I know this," Sean said, and he kissed her again, with more force. She parted her lips for him, and he was in her mouth, his arms surrounding her, and she was altogether overwhelmed. It appeared that she was his, as much as he was hers.

For the second time in her life, Rue gave herself up to someone else.

"This is different," she whispered. "This is different."

"It ought to be." Sean said. "It will be." He picked her up in one smooth move. Their eyes were locked.

"Why are you getting into my life?" She shook her head, dazed. "There's so much bad in it."

"You fought back," he said. "You made a new life, on your own."

"Not much of one."

"A life with courage and purpose. Now, let me love you this way." His body moved against hers.

"I'm not scared." She was.

"I know it." He smiled at her, and her heart wrenched in her chest.

"You won't hurt me," she said with absolute faith.

"I would rather die." He was so serious.

"You know I can't have children," she said. She meant only to let him know he didn't need to use birth control.

"I can't, either," he murmured. "We can't reproduce."

If she'd ever known that, she'd forgotten it. She felt oddly jolted. She'd always supposed that her barrenness would be a terrible obstacle to forming another relationship, but instead it was a nonissue.

His tongue flicked in her ear. "Tell me what you like," he

suggested, his breath tickling her cheek. He walked over to the pile of exercise mats, carrying her as if her weight was nothing.

"I don't know," she said, partly embarrassed at her own ignorance, partly excited because she was sure he would find out what she liked.

"Light out, light on?"

"Out, please."

In the space of a second, he was back beside her. He had a few towels with him. He spread them on the mats, and she was glad, because the vinyl surface was unpleasant to the touch.

"My clothes?" he asked. He waited for her answer.

"Oh…off." Ambient light came through the frosted glass in the door of the studio, and she could see the gleam of his skin in the darkness. He was built smooth and sleek, as dancers usually are, and he was purely white except for the trail of red hair starting below his navel and going down. She followed that trail with her eyes and found herself gasping.

"Oh…oh. Wow."

"I want you very much."

"Yeah, I get that." Her voice was tiny.

"Can I see you?" For the first time, his voice was tentative.

She sat up on the pile of mats and rose to her knees. She pulled off her white T-shirt very slowly, and her bra was gone in an instant.

"Oh," he said. He reached out to touch her, hesitated.

"Yes," Rue said.

His white hands with their long fingers cupped her breasts with infinite gentleness. Then his mouth followed.

She gasped, and it was an urgent sound. His hands began tugging her shorts, gathering up her panties with them, and she lay down so he could coax them over her feet. He stayed down there for a minute or two, sucking her toes, which made her shiver all over, and then he began working his way up her legs.

She was afraid her courage would run out. She wanted him so badly she shook all over, but her only previous experience with sex had been short and brutal, its consequences painful and disastrous.

Sean seemed to understand her misgivings, and he eased his body up her length until his arms wrapped around her and his mouth found hers again.

"I can stop now," he told her. "After this, I'm not sure. I don't want to hurt you or frighten you."

Rue said, "Now or never."

He gave a choked laugh.

"That didn't sound very romantic," she apologized. His hips flexed involuntarily, pressing his hard length against her stomach, and he began to lick her neck.

"Oh," she said, reaching down to touch him. "Oh, please." His fingers touched her intimately, making sure she was ready. The delicate movement of his fingers made Rue shudder.

Then he was at her entrance, the blunt head pushing, and then he was inside her. "Layla," he said raggedly.

"It's good," she said anxiously. After a few seconds, she said again, in an entirely different tone, "It's so good."

"I want it to be better than good." His hips began to move.

Then she couldn't speak.

8

She had never imagined she could be so relaxed, so content.

His hair had come loose from its ribbon and trailed across her breasts as he lay on his stomach looking down at her. He had never seen anything so beautiful as her face in the faint glow of the city night that lit the room through the frosted glass.

She wondered how he could have become so important to her in such a short time. She loved every line of his face, the power of his sleek white body, the passion of his lovemaking; but most of all she loved the fact that he was on her side. It had been years since anyone had been on her side, unconditionally, unilaterally. She thought, *I should still be angry that he went to Pineville.* But she searched for the anger she'd initially felt and found it was gone.

"I'm a wimp," she concluded out loud.

"I know what that means," Sean said, his voice dreamy. "Why do you say that?"

"I'm glad you found out. I'm glad I don't have to tell you all about it. I'm glad you care enough to want to find…Carver."

The hesitation before she was able to say his name told Sean a lot.

"What did your parents do?" he asked. He hadn't had time to ask Will Kryder all the questions that had occurred to him.

"They didn't believe me," she murmured. "Oh, my brother, Les, stood by me. He saved me that night. But he's not a strong-willed, forceful kind of guy. See, my dad works for Carver's dad, and my dad probably couldn't get hired anywhere else now. He drinks a lot. I'm not sure he'd still have the job he's got if he wasn't my father. Dad knows Hutton's got to keep him on, or else he might talk. My mother…well, she decided to think it was a clever ploy on my part to get Carver to marry me. When she found out otherwise, she was…livid."

"She wanted you to marry him."

"Yes, she actually believed that I'd want to be tied to the man who raped me."

"In my time, we would have made him wed you," Sean said.

"Really?"

"If you were my sister, I would have made sure of it."

"Because no one else would have married me otherwise, right? Damaged goods."

Sean perceived he had made a massive error.

"And for the rest of my life I would have had to put up with Carver's little ways, like beating on me, because he'd raped me," Rue said coldly.

"All right, in my time, we would have been wrong," he conceded. "But we would have been on your side."

"I have you on my side," she said. "I have you on my side *now*. If this has meant anything to you."

"I don't get this close to anyone unless it means something to me."

"That come from being an aristocrat? In your time, were you like Carver?" There was an edge to her voice that hadn't been there before.

"The night we first make love, you can compare me to the man who raped you?"

She hadn't thought before she spoke. "After years of weighing every word I said to another person, all of a sudden I've gotten to be the worst—I'm so sorry, Sean. Please forgive me for the offense."

There was a long silence in the dark room. He didn't speak. Her heart sank. She'd ruined it. Her bitterness and mistrust had twisted her more than she knew. But she'd come by it naturally, and she didn't see how she could have existed otherwise.

After another unnerving two minutes of silence, Rue began to fumble around for her clothes. She was determined not to cry.

"Where are you going?" Sean asked.

"I'm going home. I've screwed up everything. You won't talk to me, and I'm going home."

"You offended me," he said, and his voice wasn't level or calm at all. He was saying, *You hurt me*. But Rue wasn't absorbing that. Before Sean could scramble into his own clothes, she was gone, wearing her flannel shirt tossed over her dance outfit. She'd thrust her feet into her boots without lacing them. She was out the door of the studio, then out the door to the building, before Sean could catch her. He cursed out loud. He had to check the studio and lock everything up; that was the duty of the last person out, and it was something he couldn't shirk. He could always catch up with Rue, he was sure; after all, he was a vampire, and she was human.

Carver was waiting for her in the third alley to the north.

Rue was walking very swiftly. She was trying not to cry; and not having much luck. She wanted to reach the next corner in time for the bus, which would be the last one running on a Sunday night. As she passed the alley entrance, Carver burst out with such astonishing suddenness that he was holding her arm before she could react.

"Hello, Layla," he said, smiling.

The nightmares she'd had for four years had come to life.

Carver had always been handsome, but his present look was far from his preppy norm. He'd spiked his dark hair and he was wearing ragged jeans and a leather jacket. He'd disguised himself.

"I have a score to settle with you," he said, still smiling.

Rue hadn't been able to make a sound when he'd grabbed her arm, but now she began to scream.

"Shut up!" he yelled, and backhanded her across the mouth.

But Rue had no intention of shutting up. "Help!" she screamed. "Help!" She groped in her bag for her pepper spray with her free left hand, but this one night she hadn't been prepared, mentally or physically, and she couldn't find the cylinder she usually carried ready to use.

Pinning her with his grip on her right arm, Carver began pummeling Rue with his fist to make her shut up. She tried to dodge the blows, tried to find the spray, tried to pray that help would come. Where was the pepper spray? Abandoning her futile one-handed rummaging through her big bag, Rue yanked it off her shoulder, since it was only an impediment. Then she fought back. She wasn't nearly as big as Carver, so she went for his genitals. She wanted to grip and squeeze the whole package, but he pulled back. All she managed was a vicious pinch, but that was enough to double him over. When he heard a woman shouting from across the street, he staggered away from Rue.

"Leave that girl alone!" a female voice yelled. "I'm calling the police!"

Rue sank to her knees, too battered to stand any longer, but she stayed facing him, her hands ready to defend herself. She would not give up what she'd worked so hard to maintain. Carver began to hurry down the alley as swiftly as his injury would permit—she was proud to see he was walking funny—and though Rue remained upright, but still on her knees, he vanished from her sight as he passed out of the alley and onto the next street.

"I won't fall," she said.

"Are you okay?"

Rue wouldn't even take her eyes from the alley entrance to examine the woman beside her. This woman had saved her life, but Rue wasn't going to be taken by surprise again, if Carver decided to return.

"Rue! Rue!" To her immense relief, she heard Sean's voice. Now Carver couldn't hurt her anymore; no matter how angry Sean was at her, he wouldn't let Carver strike her. She knew that. With profound relief, she understood she didn't need to stay vigilant any longer, and she sat back on the pavement. Then she was lying on the sidewalk. And then she didn't know anything else.

When she began to relate to her surroundings again, Rue knew she was in a strange place. Hospital? Nope, didn't smell like a hospital, a smell with which she was all too familiar. It was a quiet place, a comfortable place. She was lying on clean white sheets, and there was someone next to her. She tried to move, to sit up, and she found out she was sore in several places. Before she could gain control of herself, she groaned.

"You okay? You need a drink of water?" The voice was familiar and came from a few feet away. Rue pried her swollen eyes open. She could see—a little. "Is that Megan?" she asked, her voice a dry thread.

"Yep, it's me. Julie and I been taking turns."

"Who else is here? Where *is* here?"

"Oh, we're at Sean's place, in his safe room. That's him in the bed with you, babe. It's daytime, so he had to sack out. He wasn't going to leave you without someone to help you, though. He made us swear on a stack of Bibles that we wouldn't leave. So you won't think we're these wonderful people, I gotta tell you that he promised to help us out with the money we're getting docked for missing work. I mean, I want to help you, and I would've come, anyway. But I just couldn't, ah, skip telling you. Okay?"

Rue nodded. It was an effort, but somehow Megan caught the motion. "Water would be good," Rue managed to say.

In just a moment, Megan was sliding her arm under Rue's back and helping her sit up a little. There was a glass of cool water at her lips, and Rue sipped gratefully.

"You need to get up and go to the bathroom?"

"Yes, please."

Megan helped Rue rise. To her relief, Rue discovered she was in the T-shirt and shorts she'd worn the night before. She shuffled to the bathroom. When she was through, she washed her face in the sink and brushed her teeth with a toothbrush she found still encased in a cellophane wrapper. That made her feel a great deal better, and she made her way back to the bed with a little more confidence.

"Megan, I'll be okay now, if you need to get to work."

"You sure, girlfriend? I can stay. I don't want Sean to be mad at me."

"I'm good. Really."

"Okay then. It's four o'clock. Sean ought to be up in about two hours. Maybe you can get some more sleep."

"I'll try. Thank you so much."

"Don't mention it. See you later."

Rue had left the light in the bathroom on, and when Megan had gone through the heavy curtain at one end of the room, Rue turned to her silent companion. Sean lay on his back with his hair spread out on the pillow. His lips were slightly parted, his eyes closed, his chest still. The absence of that rising and falling, the tiny motion of life, was very unnerving. Did he know she was there? Did he dream? Was he truly asleep, or was he just held motionless, like a paralysis victim? She'd almost forgotten what they'd fought about. She stroked his hair, kissed his cool lips. She remembered what they'd done together, and a flush suffused her face.

What Carver had done to her, when he'd attacked her years before, didn't qualify as sex. It had been an assault, using his sex organ as the weapon. What she'd done with Sean had been real sex, making-love sex. It had been intimate and primal and wonderful. Carver had made her into a shell of a human being overnight. Over the course of a few weeks, Sean had helped her become a full person once more.

She wasn't going to chicken out just because he was dead part of the time.

So, when darkness fell, Rue made sure her arm was across his chest, her leg lying over his. Suddenly she knew he was awake. The next second, his body reacted.

"Good evening to you, too," she said, startled and intrigued by his instant readiness.

"Where is Megan?" he asked, his voice still a little fuzzy from sleep.

"I told her to go. I'm better."

His eyes widened as he remembered. "Show me," he demanded.

"You seem to be ready for anything," she said, greatly daring, her hand wandering down his abdomen in a tentative way.

"I have to see your injuries first," he said. "I shouldn't even be…it's your smell."

"Oh?" she tried to sound insulted, failed.

"Just the smell of *you*. Your skin, your hair. You make me hard."

Not a compliment she'd ever gotten before, but she could see the evidence of the sincerity of it.

"Okay, check me out," she said mildly, and lay down. Sean raised himself on one elbow, and his left hand began to turn her face this way and that.

"It's my fault," he said, his voice steady but not exactly calm. "I shouldn't have stopped to lock up the studio."

"The only fault is Carver's," she said. "I've played that blame game too many years. We don't need to start it all over again. For the first year after he attacked me, I thought, 'What if I hadn't worn that green dress? What if I hadn't let him hold my hand? Kiss me? Slow dance with me? Was it my fault for looking pretty? Was it my fault for treating him as I would any date I liked? No. It was his fault, for taking a typical teenage evening and turning it into the date from hell."

Sean's fingers gripped her chin gently and turned her face to the other side so he could examine her bruises. He kissed the one on her cheek, and then he pulled the cover down to look over her body. She had to stop herself from pulling it right back up. This level of intimacy was great and very exciting, but she sure wasn't used to it.

"This is the closest anyone's been to me in years," she said. "I haven't even seen a doctor who looked at this much of me." Then she told herself to shut up. She was babbling.

"No one should ever see this much of you," he said absently. "No one but me." His fingers, whiter even than her own magnolia skin, brushed a dark bruise on her ribs. "How much are you hurting?"

"I'm pretty stiff and sore," she admitted. "I guess my muscles were all tensed up, and then, when I got knocked around…"

He touched her side gently, his hand very close to her breast. "Will you be able to dance tonight? We need to call Sylvia and cancel if you will not be able. She can get Thompson and Julie to do it."

He was still hard, ready for her. She was having a difficult time remembering her sore muscles.

"I don't know," she said, trying not to sound as breathless as she felt.

"Turn over," he said, and she obediently rotated. "How's your back?"

She moved her shoulders experimentally. "Feels okay," she said. His fingers traced her spine, and she gasped. His hand rubbed her hip.

"Don't think I got bruised there," she said, smiling into the pillow.

"What about here?" His hand traveled.

"There, either."

"Here?"

"Oh, no! Definitely not there!"

He entered her from behind, holding himself up so his weight wouldn't press on her tender ribs. "There?" he asked, the mischief in his voice making something in her heart go all soft and mushy.

"You'd better…massage…that," she said, ending on a gasp.

"Like this?"

"Oh, yes."

After they'd basked in the afterglow for a happy thirty minutes, Rue said, "I hate to bring this up, but I'm hungry."

Sean, stung by his own negligence, leaped from the bed

in one graceful movement. Before Rue knew what was happening, he'd lifted her from the bed, ensconced her in a chair, and clean sheets were on the bed and the old ones stuffed in a hamper. He'd started the shower for her and asked her what kind of food she liked to eat. "Whatever's in the neighborhood," she said. "That's what I love about the city. There's always food in walking distance."

"When you come out of the shower, I'll be back with food for you," he promised.

"You haven't bought food in years, have you?" she said, and the fact of his age struck her in a way it hadn't before.

He shook his head.

"Will it bother you?"

"You need it, I'll provide it," he said.

She stared at him, her lips pressed together thoughtfully. He didn't say this like a wimp who was desperate for a woman. He didn't say it like a control freak who wanted to dole out the very air his sweetheart breathed. And he didn't say it like an aristocrat who was used to having others do his bidding.

"Okay, then," she said slowly, still thinking him over. "I'll just shower."

The heat of the water and the minutes of privacy were wonderful. She hadn't been around people on a one-on-one basis so much for some time, and to be precipitated into such an intimate relationship was quite a shock. An enjoyable one, but still a shock.

Having clean hair and a clean body did wonders for her spirits, and in the light of Sean's determination to provide for her, she found a pair of his jeans she could wriggle into. She rolled up the cuffs and found a faded pumpkin-colored T-shirt to wear. It was pretty obvious she wasn't wearing a bra, but she didn't know where her bra was. Rue had a terrible conviction that it was still in the studio, which would be a dead giveaway to the other dancers. She left the bedroom and went out into the living room/kitchen/office to wait for Sean. It was small and neat, too, and had a couple of narrow windows through which she could see people's feet go by. For the first time, she realized Sean had a basement apartment.

Shortly after, he came in with two bags full of food. "How much of this can you eat?" he asked. "I find I have forgotten." He'd gotten Chinese, which she loved, and he'd bought enough for four. Luckily, there were forks and napkins in the bags, too, since Sean didn't have such things.

"Sean," she said, because she enjoyed saying his name. "Sit down while I eat, please, and tell me about your life." She knew how his face looked when he came, but she didn't know anything about his childhood. In her mind, this was way off balance.

"While I was in Pineville," he said, "I looked in the windows of your parents' home. I was curious, that's all. In the living room, your father was staring into a huge glass case that takes up a whole wall."

"All my stuff," she said softly.

"The crowns, the trophies, the ribbons."

"Oh, my gosh, they still have all that out? That's just…sad. Did he have a drink in his hand?"

Sean nodded.

"Why did you tell me this when I asked to know more about you?"

"You're American royalty," he said, supplying the link.

She laughed out loud, but not as if he were really amusing.

"You are," he said steadily. "And I know you've heard Sylvia say I was an aristocrat. Well, that's her joke. My origins are far more humble."

"I noticed you could make a bed like a whiz," she said.

"I can do anything in the way of taking care of a human

being," he said. He looked calm, but she could tell he wasn't—something about the way his hands were positioned on the edge of the table. "I was a valet for most of my human life."

9

"You were a gentleman's gentleman?" Her face lit up with interest.

He seemed taken aback by her reaction. "Yes, my family was poor. My father died when I was eleven, so I couldn't take over his smithy. My mother was at her wits' end. There were five of us, and she had to sell the business, move to a smaller cottage, and my oldest sister—she was fifteen—had to marry. I had to find work."

"You poor thing," she said. "To have to leave school so early."

He smiled briefly. "There wasn't a school for the likes of us," he said. "I could read and write, because our priest taught me. My sisters couldn't, because no one imagined they'd need to." He frowned at her. "You should be eating now. I didn't get you food so you could let it grow cold."

She turned her face down to hide her smile and picked up her fork.

"I got a job with a gentleman who was passing through our village. His boy died of a fever while he was staying at the inn, and he hired me right away. I helped out his valet, Strothers. I went with them when they returned to England. The man's name was Sir Tobias Lovell, and he was a strange gentleman. Very strange, I thought."

"He turned out to be a vampire, I guess."

"Yes. Yes, he was. His habits seemed very peculiar, but then, you didn't question people above you in social station, especially since anyone could see he was a generous man who treated people well. He traveled a great deal, too, so no one could wonder about him for too long. Every now and then, he'd go to his country house for a while. That was wonderful, because travel was so difficult then, so uncomfortable."

"But how did you come to be his valet? What happened to Strothers?"

"Strothers had already grown old in his service, and by the time I was eighteen, Strothers had arthritis so badly that walking was painful. Out of mercy, Sir Tobias gave him a cottage to live in, and a pension. He promoted me. I took care of his clothes, his wigs, his wants and needs. I shaved him. I changed his linen, ordered his bath when he wanted, cleaned his shoes. That's why I know how to take care of you." He reached over the table to stroke her hair. "Once I was in closer contact with Sir Tobias, it became obvious to me there was something more than eccentricity about the man. But I loved him for his goodness, and I knew I must keep his secrets, as much for my own sake as for his. We went on, master and man, for many years…maybe twelve or fifteen. I lost track, you see, of how old I was."

That seemed the saddest thing she'd ever heard. Rue lowered her gaze to hide her tears.

"I realized later that he'd take a little from the women he

bedded," Sean said. "He pleased them very much, but most of them were weak the day after. In our small country neighborhood, he had the name of being a great womanizer. He had to go from one to another, of course, so no one woman would bear the brunt of his need. He seemed much healthier when we went to the cities, where he could visit houses of ill repute as much as he liked, or he could hunt in the alleys."

"What happened?"

"The village people grew more and more suspicious. He didn't age at all, you see, and people grew old very quickly then. But he lost money and couldn't afford to travel all the time, so he had to stay at the manor more often. He never went to Sunday church. He couldn't be up in the daytime, of course. And he didn't wear a cross. The priest began to be leery of him, though he donated heavily to the church.

"People began to avoid me, too, because I was Sir Tobias's man. It was a dark time." Sean sighed. "Then they came one night to get him, a few of the local gentry and the priest. I told him who was at the door, and he said, 'Sean, I'm sorry, I must eat before I run.' And then he was on me."

Rue had lost the taste for her food. She wiped her mouth and laid her hand over Sean's.

"He gave me a few swallows of his blood after he'd drained me," Sean said quietly. "He said, 'Live, if you have the guts for it, boy,' and then he was gone. The people at the front door broke in to begin searching the house for him, and they found me. They were sure I was dead. I was white; I'd been bitten, and they couldn't hear my heart. I couldn't speak, of course. So they buried me."

"Oh, Sean," she said, horror and pity in her voice.

"Lucky for me, they buried me right away," he said briskly. "In a rotten coffin, at that. Kept me out of the sunlight, and the lid was easy to break through when I woke." He shrugged.

"They wanted to be through with the job, so they hadn't put me in too deep. And they didn't keep watch at the churchyard, to see if I'd rise. Another stroke of luck. People didn't know as much about vampires then as they did a hundred years later."

"What did you do after that?"

"I went to see my sweetheart, the girl I'd been seeing in the village. Daughter of the dry-goods dealer, she was." He smiled slightly. "She was wearing black for me. I saw her when she came out to get a bucket of water. And I realized I'd ruin the rest of her life if I showed myself to her. The shock might kill her, and if it didn't, I might. I was very hungry. Two or three days in the grave will do that. And I had no one to tell me what to do, how to do what I knew I must. Sir Tobias was long gone."

"How did you manage?"

"I tried to hold out too long the first time," he said. "The first man I took didn't survive. Nor did the second, or the third, or the fourth. It took me time to learn how much I could take, how long I could hold off the hunger before it would make me do something I'd regret."

Rue pushed her food away.

"Did you ever see him again?" she asked, because she couldn't think of anything else to say.

"Yes, I saw him in Paris ten years later."

"What was that like?"

"He was in a tavern, once again the best-dressed man in the place, the lord of all he saw," Sean said, his voice quite expressionless. "He always did enjoy that."

"Did you speak?"

"I sat down opposite him and looked him in the eye."

"What did he say?"

"Not a word. We looked at each other for a couple of minutes. There was really nothing to say, in the end. I got up and left. That night, I decided I would learn to dance. I'd done village dances as a boy, of course. I enjoyed it more than anything, and since I had centuries to fill and no pride to be challenged, I decided to learn all about dancing. Men danced then, almost all men. It was a necessary social grace if you were at all upper-class, and I could go from one group to another, acting like Sir Tobias when I wanted to learn the ballroom dances of the wealthy, and like my own class when I wanted to pick up some folk steps."

They both unwound as Sean talked about dancing. Rue even picked up her fork again and ate a few more bites. Gradually Sean relaxed in his chair and became silent. When she was sure he'd recovered from his story, she said, "I have to feed the cat. I need to go to my apartment."

"But you can't stay there," Sean said stiffly.

"Then where?"

"Here, of course. With me."

She did her best not to glance around the tiny apartment. She could probably fit her books and clothes in somewhere, but she would have to discard everything else she'd acquired with so much effort. How could they coordinate their very different lives? How much of his feeling for her was pity?

He could read her mood accurately. "Come on, let's get your things. If I'm right, you've missed one day of classes. You'll need to go tomorrow if you're able. How is walking?"

She was moving slowly and stiffly. Sean put socks on her feet and laced her boots in a matter-of-fact way. There was something so practical and yet so careful about the way he did such a lowly task that she felt moved in an unexpected way.

"At least I don't have a wig you have to powder," she said, and smiled.

"That was a great improvement of the twentieth century

over the eighteenth," he said. "Hair care and shoes—they're much better now."

"Hair and shoes," she said, amusement in her voice. She thought that over while Sean got ready to go, and by the time they were outside in the night, she felt quite cheerful. She looked forward to lots of conversations with Sean, when he would tell her about clothes and speech patterns and so-cial mores of the decades he'd lived through. She could write some interesting term papers, for sure.

She loved to listen to Sean talk. She loved it when he kissed her. She loved the way he made her feel like a—well, like a woman who was good in bed. And she loved the way he han-dled her when they were dancing, the respect in which he seemed to hold her. How had this happened over the past few months? When had he become so important to her?

Now, walking beside him, she was content. Though her life had just been shaken to pieces and her body was sore from a beating, she was calm and steady, because she had Sean. She loved every freckle on his face, his white strong body, his quirky mouth, and his dancing talent.

He'd done wonderful things for her. But he hadn't said he loved her. His blue eyes fixed on her face as if she were the most beautiful woman in the world, and that should be enough. The way he made love to her told her that he thought she was wonderful. That should be enough. She had a strong suspicion any man would laugh at her for wondering, but she wasn't a man, and she needed to hear the words—without having asked for them.

The next second she was yanked from her brooding by an unexpected sight. She'd glanced up at her apartment win-dows automatically, from half a block away, and she'd gotten a nasty shock.

"The light in my apartment is on," she said, stopping in her tracks. "The overhead light."

"You didn't leave it on last night?"

"No. The ceilings are high, and it's hard for me to change the bulbs in that fixture. I leave on the little lamp by my bed."

"I'll see," Sean said, pulling away from her grasp gently. She hadn't realized she'd been gripping his arm.

"Oh, please, don't go to the door," she said. "He might be waiting for you."

"I'm stronger than he is," Sean said, a little impatiently.

"Please, at least go up the fire escape, the one on the side of the building."

Sean shrugged. "If it'll make you happy."

She crept closer to the building and watched Sean approach the fire escape. He decided to show off at the last minute and scaled the brick wall, using the tiny spaces between bricks as hand- and toeholds. Rue was impressed, sure enough, but she was also disconcerted. It was unpleasantly like watching a giant insect climb. In a very short time, Sean had reached the level of the window and swung onto the fire escape. He peered inside. Rue could tell nothing from his stance, and she couldn't manage to see his face.

"Hey, Rue." Startled, she turned to see that her next-door neighbor, a part-time performance artist who called herself Kinshasa, had come up beside her. "What's that guy up to?"

"Looking into my apartment," she said simply.

"What were you doing last night? Sounded like you decided to rearrange the whole place."

"Kinshasa, I wasn't at home last night."

Kinshasa was tall and dreadlocked, and she wore big red-rimmed glasses. She wasn't someone you overlooked, and she wasn't someone who shrank from unpleasant truths. "Then someone else was in your place," she said. "And your friend's checking to see what happened?"

Rue nodded.

"I guess I should've called the cops last night when I heard all that noise," the tall woman said unhappily. "I thought I was doing you a favor by not calling the police or the super, but instead I was just being a typical big-city neighbor. I'm sorry."

"It's good for you that you didn't go knock on my door," Rue said.

"Oh. Like that, huh?"

The two stood watching as Sean came back down the fire escape in a very mundane way. He looked unhappy, so far as Rue could tell.

Sean, though not chatty or outgoing, was always polite, so Rue knew he had bad news when he ignored Kinshasa.

"You don't want to go back up there," he said. "Tell me what you need and I'll get it for you."

Suddenly Rue knew what had happened. "He got Martha," she said, the words coming out in a little spurt of horror. "He got her?"

"Yes."

"But I have to—" She started for the door of the building, thinking of all the things she needed, the fact that she had to find a box for the furry body, the grief washing over her in a wave.

"No," Sean said. "You will not go back in there."

"I have to bury her," Rue said, trying to pull away from his hand on her arm.

"No."

Rue stared up at him uncomprehendingly. "But, Sean, I have to."

Kinshasa said, "Baby, there's not enough left to bury, your friend is saying."

Rue could hardly accept that, but her mind skipped on to other worries. "My books? My notes?" she asked, trying to absorb the magnitude of the damage.

"Not usable."

"But it's four weeks into the semester! There's no way—I'll have to drop out!" The books alone had cost almost six hundred dollars. She'd gotten as many as she could secondhand, of course, but this late in the term, could she find more?

At least she had her dancing shoes. Some of them were in a corner at Blue Moon Entertainment, and the rest were in the bag she'd taken to Sean's. Rue's mind scurried from thought to thought like a mouse trapped in a cage.

"Clothes?" she mumbled, before her knees collapsed.

"Some of them may be salvageable," Sean murmured, but without great conviction. He crouched beside her.

"I know some people who can clean the apartment," Kinshasa said. "They just came over from Africa. They need the money."

This was an unexpected help. "But it's so awful in there, Sean says." Tears began to stream down Rue's face.

"Honey, compared to the mass graves and the slaughter they've had to clean up in their own country, this will be a piece of cake to them."

"You're right to give me some perspective," Rue said, her spine stiffening. Kinshasa looked as if she'd intended no such thing, but she bit her lip and kept silent. "I'm being ridiculous. I didn't get caught in that apartment, or I would've ended up like poor Martha." Rue managed to stand and look proud for all of ten seconds, before the thought of her beloved cat made her collapse.

"I'll kill him for you, honey," Sean said, holding her close.

"No, Sean," she said. "Let the law do it."

"You want to call the police?"

"Don't we have to? He'll have left fingerprints."

"What if he wore gloves the whole time?"

"I let him get away with hitting me last night, and what does he do? He comes here and kills my cat and ruins all my stuff. I should've called the police last night."

"You're right," Kinshasa said. "I'll call from my place right now."

Sean said nothing, but he looked skeptical.

The police were better, kinder, than Rue expected. She knew what that meant. Her apartment must be utterly gory. Sean told the detective, Wallingford, that he'd be able to tell what was missing. "You don't need to go up there," Wallingford told Rue, "if this guy can do it for you." Sean and Wallingford went up to the apartment, and Rue drank a cup of hot chocolate that Kinshasa brought her. Rue found herself thinking, *I've had friends around me all the time, if I'd just looked.*

When Sean reappeared with a garbage bag full of salvaged clothes, he told Rue the only thing he knew for sure was missing was her address book. "Was my address in it?" he asked her quietly.

"No," she said. "Maybe your phone number. But I didn't even know where you lived until last night."

"The police say you can go now. Let's go back to my place." After an uneasy pause, he continued. "Do you think you can dance tonight? It's almost too late to call Sylvia to get a replacement team."

"Dance tonight?" She looked at him as they walked, her face blank. "Oh! We're supposed to be at the museum tonight!"

"Ballroom dancing. Can you do that?"

"If there's a dress I can wear at the studio." Though she had to wrench her thoughts away from her destroyed apartment, it would be a relief to think about something else. They would waltz a little, do a dance number to "Puttin' on the Ritz." They'd done the same thing several times before. It was a routine that pleased an older crowd, which the museum benefactors were likely to be.

"They asked for us specifically," Sean said. But then he scowled, as if there were something about the idea he didn't like.

"Then we have to do it," Rue said. She was so numb, she couldn't have put into words what she was feeling. When Sean unlocked the studio, he insisted she stand outside while he checked it out first, and she did so without a word. He led her inside, looking at her eyes in a worried kind of way, trying to gauge her fitness. "Besides," Rue said, as if she was continuing a conversation, "I need the money. I have nothing." The enormity of the idea hit her. "I have *nothing*."

"You have me."

"Why?" she asked. "Why are you doing this?"

"Because I care for you."

"But," she said, disgusted, "I'm so weak. Look at me, falling apart—like I couldn't have predicted this would happen. Why did I even get a cat? I should have known."

"Should have known you shouldn't love something because it might be taken away from you?"

"No, should have known he'd kill anything I loved."

"Come on," Sean said, his voice hard. "You're going to put on the pretty dress here, and I'm going to make some phone calls."

The dress was the palest of pinks. It was strapless, with a full skirt. In the trash bag she found some matching panties to wear under it, and a paler pink frothy half slip. There were panty hose in the costume room, and Rue pulled on a pair. Her shoe bag was there, thank God, since she'd walked out in such a huff the night before, and it contained the neutral T-strap character shoes that would suit the program.

Sean, who'd finished his phone calls, pulled on some black dancer's pants and a white shirt with full sleeves. He buttoned a black vest over that and added his dancing shoes to Rue's bag. While he was buttoning the vest, he felt a brush running through his hair.

"Shall I braid it?" she asked, her voice so small it was barely audible.

"Please."

With the efficiency born of years of changing hairstyles quickly, Rue had his hair looking smooth and sleek in a minute.

"Will you leave yours loose?" Sean asked. "It looks beautiful as it is." Rue seldom left her long hair unbound for a performance, but he thought its color was brought out beautifully by the pale pink of the dress. "You look like a flower," he said, his voice low with admiration. "You would be wonderful no matter what you looked like, but your beauty is a bonus."

She tried to smile, but it faltered on her lips. She was too sad to appreciate his compliment. "It's nice to hear you say so," she said. "We need to go. We don't want to be late."

10

They took a cab, which Sylvia would pay for; after all, they had to keep their clothes clean and fresh for the dancing. The Museum of Ancient Life had just opened a new wing, and the party was being held in the museum itself. All the attendees were patrons who'd donated very large sums toward the construction of the new wing. All of them were very well dressed, most of them were middle-aged or older, and they were all basking in the glow of being publicly acknowledged for having done a good thing.

The vampire and the dancer stood for a minute or two, watching limousines and town cars dropping off the well-heeled crowd. Then they made their way back to the entrance Sylvia had instructed them to use. The museum staffer at the door checked their names off a list. "Wait a minute," the heavy man said. "You're already here."

"Impossible," Sean said imperiously. "Here is my driver's license. Here is my partner's."

"Hmm," the man said nervously, his fingers drumming on the doorjamb. "I don't know how this happened. I shouldn't let you in."

"Then the Jaslows and the Richtenbergs will have to go without their dancing," Sean said. "Come, Rue."

Rue didn't have a clue what was happening, but she could tell Sean was quite indifferent that someone else had used his name, almost seemed to have been expecting it. If he was relaxed about it, so was she. "I'll call our employer on my cell," she said to the man. "You can explain to Sylvia Dayton that we're not being allowed entrance, so she won't blame us, okay?"

The man flushed even more, his eyes running up and down the printed list over and over, as if something different would pop up. When he glanced up at Sean and the vampire's eyes caught the guard's gaze, the man's face lost its belligerence instantly.

"I guess your names were checked off by mistake earlier. Come on in," he said.

Rue looked at Sean in awe. Vampire talents could come in handy.

It was lucky they'd dressed at the studio, because there wasn't a corner for them here. The back recesses of the museum weren't designed with parties in mind, as the Jaslows' home had been. The small rooms and narrow corridors were full of scurrying figures, and Rue realized that things were being handled by Extreme(ly Elegant) Events, Jeri's company, which had catered the Jaslows' party. The servers wore the traditional white jacket distinguished with the E(E)E logo on the shoulder. The halls were crowded with trays and trays of hors d'oeuvres, and cases and cases of champagne. Jeri was directing the staff, wearing the same serene smile.

And the man whose white jacket was straining across his

shoulders was surely Mustafa, aka Moose, who worked for Black Moon. As soon as she'd identified him, Rue realized that the short-haired woman opening a champagne bottle was Hallie, and her partner, David, was busy filling a tray of empty glasses. David looked quite different with his thick, wavy black hair pulled back and clubbed.

"Sean," she said, tugging on his hand to make him stop, "did you see Moose?"

He nodded, without looking around at her. They continued to make their way through the narrow maze of corridors to the door indicated on the little map Sylvia had left for them.

"Okay, this is it," he said, and they paused.

There was no place special to leave their bags, so they dropped them right inside the door, then changed into their dancing shoes on the spot.

"They're all here," he told her, when she was ready. "I called them. All of them who aren't working tonight, that is. Thompson and Julie have an early gig in Basing, and Rick and Phil have a very private engagement right after this for a few select museum patrons. But all the rest are here, even Haskell."

"Sylvia knows about this?"

"No. But that's so she can deny it."

"It's wonderful that they'd do this for you."

"They're doing it for you. Moose and Abilene gave our names to get in. The others came with the triple E people. When I heard the board had asked for us, specifically, I figured Hutton was behind it. We'll stop him tonight," Sean said, and then looked sorry he'd sounded so grim. "Don't worry, Rue." He kissed her on the check lightly, mindful of her lipstick.

Rue was too numb to grasp what Sean meant. Automatically, they checked each other over, Sean looked at his watch, and they swung open the door.

Since they were "on" the minute they stepped out of the

door, they walked hand in hand with a light, almost prancing walk, until they'd reached the center of a huge open area. The dome stretched upward for three stories, Rue estimated. She'd been to the museum before—when the new wing had been under construction, in fact—and she loved the wide expanse of marble floor. Wouldn't their music get lost in the huge space?

Sean and Rue reached the center of the floor, Rue trying not to stare at the glass cases of masks that lined the wall. The dancers stood there, smiling, arms extended, waiting for all the milling patrons to become aware of their presence and to clear the area for their performance.

"Aren't they lovely!" exclaimed a white-haired woman with sapphire earrings who wasn't standing quite far enough away. A scowling face seemed to disagree. Rue dimly recognized the obnoxious man from the Jaslows' party, Charles Brody.

Their music began over the public address system, and Rue had to fight to keep her face pleasant. Sean had another surprise for her. He'd switched routines. The music was "Bolero." This was their sexy number, the one they'd only performed once or twice at anniversary parties. Why had he picked that music for this night?

But as they began to twine together in the opening moves, Rue seemed to be able to feel the sensuousness in her bones. She felt the passion, the yearning, conveyed by the music.

Suddenly Sean lifted her straight up, his hands gripping her thighs, until they formed a column. She looked down at him with longing, and he looked up at her with desire. She extended her arms gracefully upward as he turned in a smooth circle. As he continued to hold her, changing his grip so she was soaring above him like a bird, her full skirt falling over his shoulders, the crowd began to applaud at their display of strength and grace. Sean let her down so gradually that her feet didn't jolt when they touched the floor. She was able to pick up her steps again smoothly. Then Sean leaned her back, back, over his arm, and put his lips to her neck. She felt her whole body come alive when she felt his touch, and she waited for the bite with the faintest of smiles on her face.

But in that second, she was aware of a difference. Her partner was far tenser than he'd ever been at the finale; in fact, he was like an animal expecting attack. His body covered hers more completely than it should, as if he were protecting her. The crowd was closer than it should be, and she distinctly saw Haskell's face turn sharply to the right, his mouth opening to shout, allowing a glimpse of his shining fangs. A woman screamed.

Carver, in a tux, stepped out of the polite circle that had formed around the temporary dance floor, then he reached in his pocket and pulled out a knife. He pressed a button in the hilt and a wicked blade leaped out. In the space of a second, he'd slashed Haskell, who faltered and fell. Megan grabbed for Carver's arm next, and she might have slowed him down if Charles Brody hadn't shoved her as hard as he could, just as he'd done that night at the party. Again Megan landed on the floor, and then Carver was in the center of the circle with them.

She knew what he would do. She was sure that Sean thought Carver would try to kill her, and he might—if there wasn't anything else he could do to her—but first, she knew, he would try to kill Sean. Their just-finished dance had shown clearly that she loved the vampire, and Carver would relish killing something else she loved. Because Sean wasn't expecting it, she was able to shove him off her just as the knife descended.

Black-haired Abilene tackled Carver from the rear. Carver couldn't make a killing blow that way, but he managed to sink the knife into Rue's abdomen and pull it directly back out to strike again. Then a wounded Haskell, bloody and enraged, piled on top of Carver. With a bellow of enthusiasm, as if he were on the football field, Moose threw himself on top of them all.

The pain wasn't immediate. Unfortunately, Rue remembered all too clearly when he'd done the same thing years before, and she knew in a very short time she would hurt like hell. She made a bewildered sound as she felt the sudden wetness. Amid the screams and shouts of the crowd, Sean was trying to get Rue to her feet so he could drag her out of the melee. "He may have hired someone to help him. You have to get out of here," Sean said urgently.

But Rue watched Karl take a second to deck Charles Brody before he joined the other vampires in pinning Carver to the marble floor. The trapped man was fighting like a—well, like a madman, Rue thought, in a little detached portion of her brain. Not all the museum patrons had seen the knife, and they were bewildered and shouting. There could have been twenty assassins in the confusion of staff, patrons and servers.

"Come on, darling," Sean urged her, holding her as he helped her clear the outskirts of the gathering crowd. "Let's get out of here." He could feel her desperation and assumed he knew the cause. His eyes were busy checking the people moving around them, trying to be sure they were unarmed. "I thought if we did 'Bolero' we might provoke him to attack when we were ready for him, but this wasn't what I had planned." He laughed, a short bark with little humor.

Rue reached her free hand under her skirt and felt the wetness soaking her petticoats. It had begun trickling down her legs. She staggered after Sean for a few feet. She put her hand against a pillar to brace herself. When she lowered it to try to walk, she saw her perfect handprint, in blood, on the marble of the pillar. "Sean," she said, because he was still turned away from her, still looking for any other assault that might be coming their way.

He turned back impatiently, and his eye was caught at once by the handprint. He stared at it, his brow puckered as if he were trying to figure it out. He finally understood the tang of blood that he'd barely registered in his zeal to get Rue to safety.

"No," he said, and looked down at her skirt. If his face could become any whiter, it did.

His eyes looked like the lady's sapphire earrings, Rue thought, aware that she wasn't thinking like a rational person. But she figured that was probably a good thing. Because in just a minute the pain would start up.

"You're losing too much blood," he said.

"She's going to die," Karl said sadly. He'd materialized suddenly, pulling off his white jacket as he evaluated Rue's condition. "Even if you call an ambulance this minute, they will be too late."

"What…" For once, Sean seemed to be at a loss as to what to do.

"You have to hide her," Haskell said without hesitation, coming up to join them. The ordinarily tidy blond vampire, now disheveled and smeared with blood, was still coolheaded enough to be decisive. "If you want to save her, this is the last chance," he said.

"Find a place," Sean said. He sounded…afraid, Rue thought. She'd never heard Sean sound afraid.

Karl said, "The Egyptian room."

Sean picked Rue up like a child. Haskell and Karl followed, ready to ward off any attack from behind. But only a museum guard ran up to them, making some incoherent comment on Rue's wound. Haskell, clearly not in any mood for questions and maybe a little maddened by the scent of blood, pinched the man's neck until he slumped to the floor.

The Egyptian room had always been Rue's favorite. She loved the sarcophagi and the mummiform cases, even the mummies themselves. She'd often wondered about the ethics of exposing bodies—surely once people were buried, they deserved to stay that way—but she enjoyed looking on the long-dead features and imagining what the individual had been like in life—what she'd worn, eaten…who she'd loved.

Now Sean carried her to the huge sarcophagus in the middle of the floor. Made to contain the inner coffin of a pharaoh, the highly carved and decorated limestone sarcophagus was penned in by hard sheets of clear plastic, preventing people from touching the sides. Fortunately, this pen was open at the top. A vampire could clear the barrier easily.

Sean leaped over lightly, followed by Karl, while Haskell held Rue. Though the lid must have weighed hundreds of pounds, Karl and Sean easily shifted it to one side, leaving a narrow opening. Then Haskell carefully handed Rue to Karl, while Sean climbed in the deep stone box, which came to his lower chest. Karl handed Rue in, and Sean laid her on the bottom. She was able to lie flat on her back, with her legs fully extended. She felt as if she was looking up at Sean floating hundreds of feet above her. He lay down beside her, and she felt the numbness wearing away.

Oh, God, no. Please. She knew the onset of the pain. As she began to scream, Karl moved the lid back in place, and then there was almost perfect darkness.

"Rue," said Sean urgently.

She heard his voice, but the pain rendered it meaningless.

"Rue, do you want me to end the pain?"

She could only make a small sound, a kind of whine. Her

fingers dug into him. There was hardly enough room side by side for them, and she had the feeling Sean couldn't straighten out, but that was the least of her concerns at the moment.

"You can be like me," he said, and she finally understood.

"Dying?" she said through clenched teeth.

"Yes. I wasn't quick enough. I didn't plan enough. And then you made sure he got you instead of me. Why, Rue? Why?"

Rue could not explain that she operated on instinct. She could not have borne to see the knife enter him, even though a moment's thought would have told her that he could survive what she could not. She hadn't had that moment. Her understanding was a tiny flicker in the bottom of a well that was full of agony.

"If I make you like me, you will live," he said.

This was hardly the best time to be making a huge decision, but she remembered the story Sean had told her about his master's sudden attack on him, the callous way the man had left Sean to cope with the sudden change. If Sean could survive such a metamorphosis, she could, because Sean was here to help her.

"Won't leave?" she asked. Her voice trembled and was almost inaudible, but he understood.

"Never." His voice was very firm. "If you love me as I love you, we'll weather the change."

"Okay." *Love,* she thought. *He loved her.*

"Now?"

"Now. Love you," she said, with great effort.

With no more hesitation, Sean bit her. She was already hurting so badly that it was just one more pain, and then she felt his mouth drawing on her, sucking her dry. She was frightened, but she didn't have the strength to struggle. Then, after a minute, the heavy grayness in her head rose up and took her with it.

"Here," said a voice, a commanding voice. "You have to drink, Rue. Layla. You have to drink, now." A hand was pressing her face to bare skin, and she felt something run over her lips. Water? She was very thirsty. She licked her lips, and found it wasn't water, wasn't cold. It was tepid, and salty. But she was very dry, so she put her mouth to the skin and began to swallow.

She woke again sometime later.

She felt...funny. She felt weak, yes, but she wasn't sore. She remembered vividly waking up in the hospital after the last time she'd been attacked, feeling the IV lines, the smell of the sheets, the little sounds of the hospital wing. But it was much darker here.

She tried to move her hand and found that she could. She patted herself, and realized she was a terrible mess. And there was someone in this dark place with her. Someone else who wasn't breathing.

Someone *else*...who wasn't breathing.

She opened her mouth to scream.

"Don't, darling."

Sean.

"We're... I'm..."

"It was the only way to save your life."

"I remember now." She began shivering all over, and Sean's arms surrounded her. He kissed her on the forehead, then on the mouth. She could feel his touch as she'd never felt anyone's touch before. She could feel the texture of his skin, hear the minute sound of the cloth moving over his body. The smell of him was a sharp arousal. When his mouth fell on hers, she was ready.

"Turn on your side, angel," Sean said raggedly, and she maneuvered to face him. Together, they worked down her panty hose, and then he was in her, and she made a noise of sheer pleasure. Nothing had ever felt so good. He was rougher with her, and she knew it was because she was as he was now, and his strength would not hurt her. Her climax was shattering in its intensity. When it was over, she felt curiously exhausted. She was, she discovered, very hungry.

She said, "When can we get out?"

"They'll come lift the lid soon," he said. "I could do it myself, but I'm afraid I'd push it off too hard and break it. We don't want anyone to know we were here."

In a few minutes, she heard the scrape of the heavy lid being moved to one side, and a dim light showed her Rick and Phil standing above them, holding the heavy stone lid at each end.

Other hands reached down, and Julie and Thompson helped them out of the sarcophagus.

"How is it?" Julie asked shyly when she and Rue were alone in the women's bathroom. The men were cleaning up all traces of their occupancy of the sarcophagus, and Rue had decided she just had to wash her face and rinse out her mouth. She might as well have spared the effort, she decided, evaluating her image in the mirror—delighted she could see herself, despite the old myth. Her clothes were torn, bloody and crumpled. At least Julie had kindly loaned her a brush.

"Being this way?"

Julie nodded. "Is it really that different?"

"Oh, yes," Rue said. In fact, it was a little hard to concentrate, with Julie's heart beating so near her. This was going to take some coping; she needed a bottle of TrueBlood, and she needed it badly.

"The police want to talk to you," Julie said. "A detective named Wallingford."

"Lead me to him," Rue said. "But I'd better have a drink first."

It wasn't often a murder victim got to accuse her attacker in person. Rue's arrival at the police station in her bloodstained dress was a sensation. Despite his broken arm, Carver Hutton IV was paraded in the next room in a lineup, with stand-ins bandaged to match him, and she enjoyed picking him from the group.

Then Sean did the same.

Then Mustafa.

Then Abilene.

Three vampires and a human sex performer were not the kind of witnesses the police relished, but several museum patrons had seen the attack clearly, among them Rue's old dance partner, John Jaslow.

"There'll be a trial, of course," Detective Wallingford told her. He was a dour man in his forties, who looked as though he'd never laughed. "But with his past history with you, and his fingerprints on the knife, and all the eyewitness testimony, we shouldn't have too much trouble getting a conviction. We're not in his daddy's backyard this time."

"I had to die to get justice," she said. There was a moment of silence in the room.

Julie said. "We'll go over to my place so you two can shower, and then we can go dancing. It's a new life, Rue!"

She took Sean's hand. "Layla," she said gently. "My name is Layla."

★ ★ ★ ★ ★

THE
DEVIL'S
FOOTPRINTS

AMANDA STEVENS

For Margie and Jeanie

Acknowledgments

As always, my deepest gratitude
goes to my wonderful editor, Denise Zaza,
and everyone at Harlequin MIRA for their encouragement and
support, and to my agent, Helen Breitwieser, for her expert guidance.

Many thanks, also, to Breathe
for their amazing friendship and inspiration.

PROLOGUE

The legend

On the night of January 10, 1922, a full moon rose over the frozen countryside near Adamant, Arkansas, a tiny community five miles north of the Louisiana state line. The pale light glinted on freshly fallen snow and spotlighted the oil derrick recently constructed in Thomas Duncan's barren cotton fields.

Despite the gusher that had been discovered on his property a few months after the Busey Number One had come in near El Dorado, Thomas refused to move to more comfortable accommodations in town, preferring instead to remain on the family farm he'd inherited from his father nearly half a century earlier.

Thomas liked being in the country. His nearest neighbor was nearly two miles away and he did sometimes get lonely, but the farm made him feel closer to his wife, Mary, who had passed away five years ago. She'd been laid to rest beneath a stand of cottonwoods on a hillock overlooking the river, and Thomas had tied bells in the branches so she would have music whenever a breeze stirred.

All day long, the chime of the bells had been lost in the icy howl of an Arctic cold front that roared down from the northeast. The gusts had finally abated in the late afternoon, but the weather was still bitter, even for January, and a snowfall—the first Thomas could remember in over a decade—blanketed his yard and fields in a wintry mantel. He watched the swirl of flakes from his front room window until dusk. Inexplicably uneasy, he fixed an early supper and went up to bed.

Something awakened him around midnight. The snow brought a preternatural quiet to the countryside, the silence so profound that Thomas could easily discern the pump out in the field as it siphoned oil from deep within the earth. Early on, the mechanical rhythm had kept him awake until all hours, but he was used to it now and that wasn't what had disturbed his rest.

Still half-asleep, he thought at first he'd heard a gunshot and he wondered if someone was out tracking a deer. Then he worried there might have been an explosion at the well; he got up to glance out the window where the wooden derrick rose like an inky shadow from the pristine layer of snow.

As he crawled back under the warm covers, he heard the sound again, a loud, steady clank, like something being dropped against the tin roof of his house.

Or like heavy footsteps.

The hair at the back of Thomas's neck lifted as a terrible dread gripped him. He scrambled out of bed, pulled on his clothes and grabbed a shotgun and coat on his way outside.

Using a side door to avoid the slippery porch, he trudged

around to the front of the house where he had a better view
of the roof.

The moon was bright on the snow, a luminous glow that
turned nighttime into a subdued twilight, and the air was
pure and so cold that his nostrils stung when he breathed. He
turned, looked up and what he saw chilled him to the bone.
Cloven footprints started at the edge of the roof, moved in a
straight line up the sloping tin and disappeared over the peak.

Slowly, Thomas turned in a circle, his gaze encompassing
the yard, the barn, the cotton fields and finally returning to
his house and then up the porch steps right to his front door.
He saw now what he had not noticed before. The footprints
were everywhere. He'd never seen anything like them. He'd
lived in the country all his life and he knew the tracks hadn't
been made by a four-legged animal, but by something that
walked upright. And the stride was long and at least twice as
wide as the footprints Thomas had left in the snow.

A terrible premonition settled over him. The farmhouse
had been his home since he was a boy, and on Sunday mornings when his neighbors headed into town for church services,
he had instead walked the fields alone. The peace he found
there was deep and profound, the clean silence of the freshly
plowed earth more suited to his idea of prayer and reflection.
But now, as he stood in his own front yard, Thomas Duncan
had the sense that a part of his heritage had been desecrated.

An urgency he couldn't explain prodded him, and he rushed
back to the house, avoiding the prints on the steps and across
the frozen porch as he flung open the front door. His heart
hammered against his chest as he stepped inside, expecting
to see melting tracks on the plank flooring. The only snow,
however, was from his own boots.

Quickly he bolted the door and strode down the narrow

hallway to the kitchen. As he opened the back door, his gaze dropped. The prints started at the threshold and continued down the steps and across the yard to the open field, as if something had come in the front door, passed through the house without leaving a mark, and let itself out the back way.

More afraid than he'd ever been in his life, Thomas moved back inside and clicked the thumb-lock on the door. He shoved a chair under the knob and sat down at the table, shotgun across his knees, to wait for daylight.

By morning, word of the footprints had spread throughout the town, and with it, speculation as to their source. One of Thomas's neighbors followed the tracks right up to the edge of the river where they continued in the same straight line on the other side.

For several nights after that, some of the men sat up with Thomas, waiting to see if the strange phenomenon reoccurred. When nothing happened, the community began to breathe a little easier—until a local preacher sermonized that the drillers, in their quest to strike it rich, had somehow punched a hole straight down to hell, unleashing the devil himself to run unbridled across the countryside.

The cloven footprints vanished with the melting snow and were eventually forgotten in the tiny Arkansas community.

Then seven decades later, they reappeared near the mutilated body of sixteen-year-old Rachel DeLaune.

1

She had no idea he was there.

Seated on the porch steps of the old Duncan farmhouse, the girl remained blissfully unaware of his vigil. If she had turned she would have seen him, but she didn't turn. Instead, she pulled her jacket more tightly around her slight body, as if stricken by a sudden chill.

In the distance, the ancient bells up in the cottonwoods tinkled in the shifting twilight. *Ghost music,* he thought. A serenade for the dead.

He listened for a moment, eyes closed, anticipation strumming the nerve endings along his spine. Then he crept a few steps closer.

And still she heard nothing.

Not surprising. He'd learned a long time ago the importance of a silent approach. No squeaking shoes. No snapping twigs. Not even an exhaled breath. He moved like a shadow,

like a stealthy predator bearing down with eagle-eyed precision on his prey.

Her head suddenly lifted, as if yanked by the invisible bond
that connected them, and he froze, heart hammering, until
the danger passed.

She settled back to her daydreaming as her dog played
nearby in the tall grass. Her back was to him; he longed to
call out her name, make her turn so he could glimpse her face,
stare deeply into those dark, dark eyes.

A shiver coursed through him. He wanted that contact more
than anything in the world, but it couldn't be today. It would
be night soon, and the longer he stayed out, the harder it became to control his natural urges. The demons driving him
sometimes made him careless and greedy and all too willing
to risk everything he needed to keep hidden.

But for her, it might be worth it.

Outwardly, she looked like a normal girl. Straight dark hair
with a fringe of bangs across her forehead. Pale skin. Deep
brown eyes. Nothing at all extraordinary about her appearance.

On the inside, though, where it counted the most, Sarah
DeLaune was anything but normal.

She was young, only thirteen, so he had to be very careful
with her. He was older, wiser and—in some ways—worldlier,
although he could shed his dreary veneer as easily as peeling
away the Goth persona he'd adopted. Unlike normal-look-
ing Sarah, he had embraced the trappings of darkness, because without the black clothes and heavy makeup, he became
someone else.

"Gabriel, you leave that squirrel alone. You hear me?" she
scolded her dog. "Don't make me cut a switch!"

He smiled at the idle threat. Sarah would never harm a hair

on that mutt's head. Until now, Gabriel had been her only companion. Until now.

The dog trotted over to the steps, and Sarah cupped his homely face in her hands, scratched behind his shapeless ears. Gabriel started to flop at her feet worshiping her, but a change of wind brought a new scent, a new excitement, and the dog whirled, his keen eyes searching the shadows at the corner of the house.

He started to step back out of sight, but it was too late. He'd gotten careless and now he'd been spotted.

As Gabriel bounded toward him, he reached into his pocket and snagged one of the treats he kept in a plastic bag. He'd learned early on that Sarah's dog had a weakness for bacon.

Skidding to a halt, the ugly mutt sniffed his hand, then greedily gobbled the morsel right from his palm. He dug out another, his gaze never leaving Sarah.

She'd risen from the steps and stood looking at him as if she didn't quite know what to do. Her instincts told her to run, but her curiosity urged her to stay. For a girl like Sarah, there really was no choice.

Slowly, she walked through the dead weeds toward the corner of the house, peering into the shadows.

He drew several quick breaths as he watched her. He'd been in her house on any number of occasions when the family was out. He'd drifted through the silent rooms, touched her things, absorbed her scent. He knew her so well by now. Her habits, her secrets, her innermost fears. Sometimes, it almost seemed as if she were a mirror image of himself. And yet for all that, he'd never before been this close to her.

A quiver of excitement vibrated through him as their eyes met for the first time. In that instant, he could feel her gaze penetrating the darkest recesses of his soul, probing the deepest corners of his mind, the way he'd searched every crevice of her room.

"Hey, you!" she called. "What the hell do you think you're doing?"

The intensity of her focus disconcerted him and he had to glance away as she approached. "I just wanted to have a look around. I didn't think anyone would be here this time of day."

"Well, you thought wrong." She gave him a scowling appraisal. "Who are you anyway? I've never seen you out here before."

"My name is Ashe Cain," he said, careful to remain in the shadows where she couldn't get a good look at him.

"Never heard of you, and I know everyone in town."

"I'm not from Adamant."

That caught her interest. "Where you from, then?"

"Does it matter? I'm not trespassing, am I?"

"Yeah, but nobody gives a shit about this place." She cocked her head as she continued to study him, apparently not the least bit afraid. He should have had more faith, he realized.

"Ashe Cain." She repeated his name slowly, as if testing the feel of the syllables against her lips. "Is that your real name or did you just make it up?"

The question startled him. "No, it's my real name. Why?"

"Because all the Goth kids at my school give themselves lame-ass names like Twilight and Shadow." She paused with a mocking smile. "And Ashe."

He scoffed at her suggestion. "Don't lump me in with those poseurs. I'm not like that."

"Why'd you come out here, then?" She nodded toward the old farmhouse behind him. "This is their hangout."

"I came to see the footprints."

Something darted through her eyes before she gave a derisive laugh. "That's just a stupid legend. The footprints don't really exist."

"Are you sure?"

She scratched the back of her knee. "I've been out here lots of times and I've never seen them."

"Just because you can't see something doesn't mean it's not real. Besides, I *have* seen them."

"You've seen the footprints? Where?"

"I can show you if you want."

A gust of wind ruffled her dark hair, the same breeze that stirred the bells in the distance. For the first time, he sensed her hesitancy. Not from fear, exactly, but from an instinctive resistance that would have to be slowly and carefully chipped away.

That same thrill of anticipation soared up his spine, and he turned his head so she wouldn't see his smile.

She thrust her hands into her jacket pockets. "Even if I believed you, which I don't, I have to get home. My old man hates it when I'm late for dinner."

"I hope you're not leaving on my account. You don't have to be afraid of me. I would never hurt you."

Her head shot up. "Do I look afraid? *Please.* Besides, you even think about laying a hand on me, my dog will kick your Emo ass."

He glanced down at the complacent mongrel at her side. "I can see that."

"He's a lot meaner than he looks," she warned.

He knelt and held out his hand, and Gabriel came over to sniff for more bacon. "Nah, he likes me. Don't you, boy? Good dog," he crooned, burying his hand in the soft fur. "I used to have a dog just like this. Maybe they came from the same litter."

The notion seemed to intrigue her. "Gabriel just showed up at my house one day. I always wondered where he came from." She paused as an unwelcome thought struck her. "You're not going to claim your dog ran away or something, are you?"

"No, he died. Someone poisoned him."

"On purpose? Man, that bites." She dropped to the grass beside Gabriel, dinnertime and her earlier reticence forgotten. "What kind of psycho would do something like that to a poor, helpless animal?"

"Someone evil," he said. "Someone without a soul."

Their gazes met and he saw her shiver. "My sister keeps bugging my folks to get rid of Gabriel. She hates him."

"Are they going to?"

"Probably. My dad takes her side every damn time. They both make me sick."

Her anger caused his heart to beat even harder. He had to take a couple of breaths to curtail his excitement.

Sarah wrapped her arms around Gabriel and gave him a squeeze. "They'll be sorry, though, won't they, boy?"

"What are you going to do?"

She lifted her thin shoulders. "I don't know yet, but I'll think of something."

"Maybe I can help you."

Her expression turned suspicious. "Why would you do that?"

"Because that's what friends do. They help each other out."

"News flash, retard. We're not friends. You don't even know me."

Oh, but I do, Sarah. Still he had to be careful, not push too hard.

"And anyway, I don't need your help and I don't want any

friends. Gabriel is all I need." Her tone was harsh and defiant, but he, and only he, could see the bereft shadow in her eyes.

His chest tightened; he knew that pain so well. They were so much alike, he and Sarah. Dark, sad, lonely. Her solitude drew him like a newborn baby grasping for its mother's breast.

She scrambled to her feet and dusted off the seat of her jeans. "Hey, I'm sorry I called you a retard."

He smiled. "That's okay."

"No, it's not. I hate when people call me that."

"Who calls you that?"

She answered with a shrug. If she noticed the edge in his voice, she didn't let on. "Are you coming back out here tomorrow?"

"I will if you want me to."

"Like I care one way or the other. I was just asking."

But that was a lie. She did care. Whether she knew it or not, she needed him as much as he needed her. She'd come back tomorrow, because she wouldn't be able to help herself.

Sitting cross-legged in the grass, he watched her cut across the edge of the field toward the road, Gabriel at her heels. The air chilled as the twilight deepened, and he knew he needed to be on his way, too. The voices inside his head were getting more desperate by the moment. He was out of time. He couldn't ignore them any longer.

He rose and stood listening to the bells pealing in the distance. *Death music.* He smiled. *A serenade for the doomed.*

2

Fourteen years later

Winter came late as it always did to the Deep South.

It arrived with only a whisper through the magnolia trees—a creeping shadow, an unwelcome presence easily ignored until a bitter cold front swept down from Canada, bringing freezing rain and record-breaking temperatures all the way to the Gulf of Mexico. Downed power lines, disrupted city services, massive pileups on the interstates—it was the kind of chaos New Orleans hadn't known since Katrina.

Even without the inconveniences, Sarah DeLaune hated the cold. Earlier, as she listened to sleet pelt against her windows, she'd been gripped by a strange anxiety, and she found herself wondering how she would cope if summer never came again. If the winter storm raging outside her house was not merely an anomaly, but a permanent shift in the subtropical climate of the Gulf Coast.

As she fantasized about being trapped in a frozen universe, she'd slipped so deeply into the gloom of her own thoughts that even the Valium she'd taken midmorning couldn't dig her out.

She'd recognized the early stages of cabin fever, and in spite of the incessant warnings issued by the weather service, she'd gone out, precariously negotiating the icy streets to the French Quarter, where she found the seedy bar that had been her hangout of late warm and inviting.

The party atmosphere, along with a few drinks and half a Xanax, had nudged her toward a mellower outlook, and at midnight she'd gone home to bed, eventually sinking into the kind of bone-melting sleep she hadn't known in months.

She'd been dreaming about her dead sister when the phone woke her up. She had no idea how long it had been ringing, because even after she opened her eyes, the sleep demons held her firmly in their grasp. Rachel's disembodied head floated above the bed, and the barest hint of sulphur hung on the chilly air, then another piercing ring sent the nightmare skittering back to the darker realm of Sarah's subconscious.

Her movements lethargic and dreamlike, she sat up in bed, willing her hand toward the receiver. But the caller had given up. In the ensuing quiet, Sarah could have sworn she heard the ghostly ticking of her alarm clock, even though she'd unplugged it days ago.

Leaning back against the headboard, she wondered how long she'd been asleep. She wanted to know the time, too, but not enough to get up and go find another clock. Nor did she check her phone to see who had been calling at so late an hour. A phone call after midnight was never a good thing.

Her first thought was that her ailing father had taken a turn for the worse. When she'd been there a week ago, the doctor had warned her that the old man had only a few months at best. The doctor had tried to break it to her gently, but he needn't have worried. Sarah would hardly be grief-stricken when the time came. She and her father had never been close. Sometimes, when he looked at her with the same old contempt, she wondered why she even bothered. She could have drifted along quite happily in their estrangement if Michael— Dr. Garrett—hadn't persuaded her to try and make amends before it was too late.

He liked to tell her that avoidance wasn't a solution, but Sarah wasn't so sure about that. Sweeping her problems under the rug had worked pretty well for her in the past. Might have continued to work, if the insomnia hadn't forced her back into treatment. And now, thanks to her visits back home, the nightmares had also returned.

Everything is connected, Sarah.

Well, no kidding.

She jumped, realizing that she'd drifted off again. Sitting upright in bed with her eyes wide-open. She hadn't been asleep, but the last few moments—or had it been hours?— had passed without her awareness. Now the phone was ringing again.

Someone really wanted to get in touch with her.

Sarah waited a moment, hoping the caller would give up again. When that didn't happen, she reached for the phone with a sigh, as she glanced out the window. Just beyond her tiny courtyard, the dead branches of an oak tree windmilled in a frigid gust.

"Hello?"

"Finally."

She recognized the voice at once, and his exasperated tone was like the prick of a needle against her spine. How like

Sean Kelton to think she had nothing better to do, even in the middle of the night, than wait for his call.

"Are you there?" he demanded.

"Yes, I'm here. What do you want?"

"What's wrong with you?"

Her hand tightened on the phone. "What do you mean?"

"It took you forever to answer and now you won't say anything. It's like you're there, but you're not."

"For God's sake, it's the middle of the night. I was asleep."

Sean fell silent. "I'm sorry," he said, after a bit. "I wouldn't have called if it wasn't important."

"It couldn't wait until morning?"

"I didn't know I'd wake you up," he said defensively. "You never sleep unless…" His voice trailed off with the slightest edge of accusation. "What are you taking these days?"

"That's none of your business. You gave up the privilege of poking around in my private life when you moved out."

Hang up, a little voice urged her. *Just press the button and make him go away.*

His voice was so familiar, the regret it stirred was still so deep that Sarah's free hand reached out for the pill bottle on her nightstand. Not finding it in the dark, her fingers scrambled across the wood surface.

"It may not be any of my business, but I still care about you, Sarah. I've been hearing things lately that worry me."

"What kind of things?"

"You've been hanging out in some pretty rough places."

"What, are you spying on me now?" The crablike hand searched through the nightstand drawer and closed, like a claw, around a plastic medicine bottle. She cradled the phone against her shoulder as she twisted off the cap, then dry-swallowed half a Xanax. The bottle was alarmingly empty.

"I'm concerned about you. I know how you get when you drink. Especially if you're still popping pills."

"Oh, and how do I get, Sean? Why don't you tell me?"

Another pause, one that seemed filled with his own regret. "You get reckless."

"You used to like that about me."

"There's a difference between being reckless and self-destructive. Took me a while to figure that out, but I see it pretty clearly now."

"Is that why you left?"

"You know why I left."

No, she really didn't, but her pride wouldn't allow her to ask any more than it would let her chase him down the morning he walked out.

Looking back, Sarah realized that he had been trying to tell her for weeks that it was over, but she hadn't wanted to hear it, so she refused to listen. She'd been out running errands that morning and had noticed something different about the house the moment she walked through the door. But she hadn't stopped to consider what it might be. Instead, she'd gone into the kitchen for coffee and that was when she found his note propped against the sugar bowl.

You're going to hate me for this, but I did what I had to do. If you want to talk, I'll listen, but I don't think there's much left to say at this point.

Sarah had folded the note and slipped it into her pocket as she walked calmly into the bedroom, then opened the door of the closet as if trying not to set off a bomb.

Sean's side was always a mess, but not that morning. His clothes were all gone. Suits, pants, shirts, everything. Nothing left but a couple of hangers dangling from the rod and a crumpled shirt on the floor.

He'd cleaned out the bathroom, too, and as Sarah walked through the house, she saw what her subconscious had noted earlier. Missing CDs and books. His laptop. Favorite pictures.

Everything of his—gone.

A big chunk of her life—gone.

And now here he was, nearly a year later, calling her in the middle of the night.

"How long can you just sit there and not say anything?" he asked angrily.

"You're the one who called me. I don't have anything to say to you."

"Sarah—"

"Just get to the point, Sean. I'd like to go back to sleep sometime tonight." Although she knew that wouldn't happen. She was wide-awake now.

"All right," he said in a resolved tone. "I'm calling because I need your help."

Sarah was instantly suspicious. "I'm not in a generous mood these days."

"It's not personal. I need your help with a case. We've got a body covered in ink, but no ID. I was hoping you'd come have a look, see if you recognize the artist."

Sarah clutched the phone, trying to ignore the surge of adrenaline that already had her heart thudding. She reminded herself that Sean Kelton never did anything without a motive. "Why me?"

"Because I couldn't get your partner on the phone," he admitted. "And because you know every tattoo artist in the city. Come on, you always loved working my cases with me. You were good at it, too."

She smiled, in spite of herself.

"So will you do it? I really *could* use your help."

"Would I have to come to the morgue?"

"We could wait and do it there, but I'd rather you come now. The body hasn't been moved yet, and I'd like to get your take on something at the crime scene."

"I'm a civilian, Sean. They're not going to let me waltz through a police barricade without some kind of credentials."

He hesitated. "Yeah, that could be a problem, but I'll take care of it. I'm sending a cruiser to pick you up. It's getting nasty out here. I haven't seen an ice storm like this since I was a kid."

In spite of her protests, Sarah was already scrambling out of bed, reaching for a pair of clean jeans from the stack on her dresser. An urgency she couldn't explain drove her, but her movements were still sluggish and it seemed to take forever to locate a shirt.

"How long until my ride gets here?"

"A couple of minutes."

A couple of minutes.

Which meant he'd dispatched the car before he called…or else the crime scene was *that* close to her house.

"Sarah DeLaune?"

The uniformed officer standing on her porch was young, probably around twenty-five, with a broad, pleasant face and twinkling blue eyes. He touched the brim of his cap. "Lieutenant Kelton sent me to pick you up, ma'am."

"I'm almost ready—" She glanced at his name tag. "Officer Parks. Just give me a second to grab a coat and find my keys. You can come in out of the cold if you want."

"Thanks just the same. I'll go wait in the car, keep the heater running."

"Suit yourself."

Sarah left the front door open as she shrugged into the wool jacket and gloves she'd dug out of the back of her closet when the cold front hit. A frigid wind blew through the room, lifting the edges of the newspaper on the coffee table.

The paper had been there for a couple of days now, turned to an article about a missing Shreveport woman named Holly Jessup. Sarah didn't know her, but for some reason, she couldn't get the name out of her head.

Holly...Jessup.

Grabbing her keys from the hall table, Sarah stepped out on the porch. The icy wind cut through her blue jeans as she struggled with the lock. Then she turned and hesitated at the edge of the porch before negotiating the frozen steps.

Snow flurries whirled over the street and drifted like feathers down to the lawn. Her tiny front yard was white and glistening, a winter wonderland that would vanish as soon as the sun came up.

Sarah hated the cold, but even she could appreciate the rarity of a snowfall in New Orleans. It happened maybe once every thirty years. She wanted to take a moment to enjoy the pristine tranquility of the night, but instead she found herself scouring the icy darkness, searching for the evil that had been awakened by her nightmare.

Ashe Cain.

No matter where she went or what she did, he was always there—watching, waiting, creeping so close at times she could smell the death scent he wore like cologne.

He'd gone away after Rachel's death, but Sarah's dreams always brought him back. He was out there tonight. She could feel him.

A shudder gripped her, a cold, black terror. Sarah wanted nothing more than to retreat into her house, to lock herself inside until the nightmare faded, until Ashe Cain had crawled back into the shadows of her past.

Shivering, she forced herself down the porch steps and across the frozen yard to the curb. Officer Parks got out of the car and came around to open her door.

"You didn't have to get back out," she said. "I'm perfectly capable of opening my own door."

"Detective Kelton made it real clear I was to take good care of you."

"Oh, he did?"

Parks grinned at her tone. "If it's all the same to you, I'd just as soon not get on his bad side."

He waited for her to climb inside, then closed the door behind her. A moment later, he slid behind the wheel and flashed another grin. They were probably close in age, but the cop's boyish looks and reverent demeanor made him seem much younger.

Sarah tugged off a glove and placed her hand over the heater vent. "Are you sure this thing is working?"

"Yes, ma'am. It's going full blast."

Then why was she still so cold?

Maybe because the bone chill had nothing to do with the weather and everything to do with her ultimate destination.

An icy sludge crawled through Sarah's veins. She was on her way to a crime scene to examine tattoos on a dead woman. The newspaper article suddenly came back to her, and she wondered again at the familiarity of the missing woman's name.

Holly Jessup.

Where had she heard it before?

"Ma'am?"

She turned. "Yeah?"

"You okay?"

"Why do you ask?"

"You seemed a little out of it there for a minute."

"Did I?" Sarah shrugged. "I was just thinking how much I hate the cold."

He gave a low chuckle. "You call this cold? Trust me, you don't know cold until you've spent a winter on Lake Michigan."

"You're from Chicago?"

"Slidell. But I went north to stay with my grandma when I was a kid."

"Why'd you come back down here?"

"Why do you think? I couldn't stand the cold."

He was smiling at her again, and there was enough ambient light in the car that Sarah could see the brief flare of attraction in his eyes. She wondered how long his interest would hold once he got to know her. She'd always had the ability to frighten off even the more ardent admirers.

Sean had been the exception. He'd lasted longer than most. But in the end, he couldn't take it, either. He could put up with the pills but not the secrets.

Parks nodded toward her seat belt. "You might want to buckle up. We're not going far, but the streets are like glass. If we skid into a light pole, I don't want you going through the windshield."

"I don't want that, either." Sarah fastened the shoulder harness, then put her hands back up to the vent. She couldn't seem to stop shivering. "Where exactly are we headed?"

"The body was found at a vacant house on Elysian Fields."

Just a few blocks from Sarah's place on North Rampart.

"Do you suppose that's the killer's idea of a joke?" she said dryly.

"I don't know what you mean."

"Greek mythology. Elysian Fields. The final resting place for the souls of the heroic and virtuous."

Parks gave her an uneasy glance. "Ma'am, I don't think that's the kind of thing this guy's into."

3

Esme Floyd prowled her tiny house, her arthritic knees pro-
testing every step. She didn't know why she was so uneasy
tonight, but she reckoned the weather had something to do
with it. Not a fit night out for man or beast, her mama would
have said.

But even on mild nights, Esme sometimes stayed up until
all hours. Came from all those years of waiting for her son,
Robert, to come dragging in at dawn, and then later, her
grandbaby, Curtis, although he'd never been as bad as his
daddy to lay out.

Not until that one winter…

Esme pursed her lips. She wouldn't study on that tonight.
What would be the point?

Whatever devil had been riding the boy all those years ago
was gone now. He'd turned into such a *fine* young man. A

doctor, of all things! Esme was so proud, she could strut. Not a single generation of Floyds had ever made it through high school, let alone college and medical school. Robert had quit in the ninth grade and by the time he'd turned twenty-one, he'd served time in Cummins.

Esme had no idea where her son was now. Dead, for all she knew. He took off right after he got out of the pen, leaving Curtis and the boy's mama to fend for themselves. Esme had ended up raising the child from the time he was twelve years old. He'd been a couple of years older than Rachel when he came here to live, but the two became thick as thieves once he let down his guard.

Thankfully, the DeLaunes hadn't minded him being around. Esme had been especially worried about James who was mighty particular about Rachel's friends. The family had been good to her, and she would have hated giving up her job. But Curtis had always been a quiet, easygoing boy, even when he was little, and he'd had enough sense to make himself scarce when he needed to.

Except when it came to Rachel.

That trouble had started brewing right from the get-go, but Esme hadn't the heart to take away the one good thing in her grandbaby's life. So she'd sat back and watched his friendship with Rachel DeLaune turn into fierce devotion and later, heartbreak when the girl moved on to someone more suitable.

Esme had worried then, as she still sometimes worried on nights when she couldn't sleep, that Curtis's attachment to Rachel might have crossed the line into obsession.

But it didn't much matter now. Rachel was dead, God rest her soul; had been for fourteen years.

Her killer had never been caught, but most folks in Adamant had their suspicions. The body had been found at the old Duncan farmhouse where Buddy Fears's boy used to hang out. Esme had seen him out there herself, lollygagging about with that no-account bunch he ran with.

Smoking dope and God only knows what. Nothing but trouble, every last one of 'em.

Derrick Fears had been the worst of the lot. Not a lick of respect for his elders, or even his own body, what with all those piercings and tattoos. Marks of the devil, Esme thought with a shiver.

William Clay had been the county sheriff back then, and she'd heard him tell James once that he knew in his gut that pack of degenerates had killed Rachel, probably during some devil-worshipping ritual out at the farmhouse. And if it took him the rest of his life, he'd see them boys fry.

But it didn't work out that way. Sheriff Clay had gone to his grave beaten and weary, Rachel's murder the only black mark against an otherwise outstanding career.

And all these years later, the killer was still out there.

Esme tried to turn away from her dark thoughts. She got out her Bible, but she was too jittery to read. And her joints were starting to ache. The arthritis in her knees and shoulders was getting worse all the time.

Curtis had been after her to retire ever since he'd come back home to work at the hospital in El Dorado, but to Esme, retirement was one step away from the old folks' home. She wasn't so stove up yet she couldn't make herself useful.

Setting aside the Bible, she got up and padded on bare feet to the bathroom to get a glass of water. She wouldn't take her medicine just yet. Not until the pain got so bad she couldn't stand it. She was too afraid of getting hooked on the pills.

She went into her bedroom, but instead of crawling under the warm layers of blankets, she shuffled over to the window to look out. The night was clear and cold, the moon so bright she could see ice glistening on the barren tree branches.

Her cottage window faced the back of the DeLaune house, and she stood for a moment admiring its graceful lines through the tree branches. Oh, how she loved that place. Over a hundred years old and still just as regal and elegant as she remembered it from her childhood.

Thomas Duncan's daughter had lived in the house, and Esme remembered when the old man had moved in with her. By then, his hair had been as white and wispy as cotton, his eyes frosted with cataracts. He'd sit in a cane rocker on the veranda for hours, mumbling to himself, paying no mind to the taunting neighborhood children who called him Crazy Ol' Tom.

Esme used to see him out there on Sunday mornings when she and her mama walked home from church. Sometimes his two little granddaughters would be playing in the yard and Esme would stop to watch.

"Stop that gawkin', Esme Louise," Mama would scold with her lips pooched out in stern disapproval. "You act like you ain't never seen old folk before."

But it wasn't Thomas who fascinated Esme; it was the two little girls who always seemed to be dressed in white.

"How come they don't never get dirty, Mama?"

"They do get dirty, child, what a foolish notion. They get dirty same as the rest of us. Only difference is, they got somebody to wash up after 'em."

"I wanna live in a house like that, Mama."

"Esme Louise, the only way you ever gonna live in a house like that is if you the one doin' the washin' up. And that ain't in the cards for you, baby girl, 'cuz I mean for you to get an education. Then you can go to Little Rock or Memphis and get yourself a *real* job. Make your own way. I don't want you havin' to do for nobody but yourself."

Esme hadn't said anything, but she'd thought to herself that it wouldn't be so bad washing clothes and scrubbing floors if she could live in a place like that. She didn't mind housework, not even the ironing that her mama took in.

Anything was better than fieldwork. Chopping cotton under a blistering sun in the summer and picking up pecans in the fall and winter when the ground was cold and wet and cockleburs stuck to your hair and clothes like prickly brown leeches.

Spring was the only time Esme enjoyed being outdoors, before the cloying heat of summer settled like a wool blanket over the countryside, while the air was still drowsy with roses and lilacs, and strawberries lay hidden like Easter eggs in lush, dewy vines.

Her mama had died in the springtime.

Esme had just turned thirteen, and she'd left school to take care of her younger brother and sisters. She'd married at sixteen, had a baby at seventeen and was widowed by the time she turned twenty.

When James and Anna DeLaune moved into the house as newlyweds, Esme had already been working there for years. James had paid her a visit, hat in hand, one Saturday afternoon and asked if she would please stay on and help them out. His young wife was frail and couldn't handle that big place all by herself. Esme had been there ever since.

Forty years she'd spent taking care of that house, and for the most part, she'd been content with her work. But after Rachel's death, everything changed. A terrible darkness had settled over the place.

James had doted on that girl—everyone did—and once she

was gone, he couldn't bear to step foot inside. He'd spent most of his time holed up in his chambers at the county courthouse, ignoring the needs of his troubled child and heartsick wife.

Anna hadn't been strong enough to carry the burden of her grief alone. She'd died a few months later. They said it was heart trouble, but Esme had her doubts. Anna had been a young woman, only thirty-six, and Esme suspected that Doc Washington had fudged the death certificate out of compassion for a family already broken by grief and guilt.

Esme had wondered then—and she would wonder until the day she died—if Anna DeLaune had deliberately taken her own life, leaving her youngest behind to deal with the sorrow in the only way she knew how.

Poor child.

Sarah had always been such a puzzle to Esme. She'd never had any friends to speak of. Didn't give a hoot about parties and sleepovers the way Rachel had. Instead, she'd spent her time roaming the countryside by herself, sometimes at all hours.

And those eyes…

Lord have mercy, the way that girl could look at you would lift the hair right up off the back of your neck.

But for all her peculiar ways, Sarah had been Esme's favorite. Maybe because of the way her daddy treated her.

Never made any bones about who his favorite was.

After the funeral, Sarah had closed herself off. Wouldn't talk to a soul about what happened. Even the special doctor called in by Sheriff Clay couldn't unlock the secrets trapped in that child's memory. But there were nights, while in the grip of a nightmare, that she would whisper a name.

Sometimes it seemed to Esme that, if she listened closely enough, she could still hear that name in the wind.

Shivering from the cold seeping in through the window, she lifted her gaze to the roof where moonlight glinted off a thin layer of snow. For a moment...

She blinked and looked again. *Jesus Lord.*

Someone was up there.

She could barely see him against the backdrop of night sky, but he was there, a nebulous form moving quickly up the slanting roof.

The glass slipped from Esme's hand and shattered against the cold, tile floor. Shards bit into her bare feet, but she paid scant attention to the pain. Her focus was still on the roof.

He must have been stooped over before, because now he rose up against the moonlight, a towering silhouette with a pale face and dark-rimmed eyes.

Esme tried to scoff at herself. She couldn't see that kind of detail in the dark. It was nothing more than an old woman's superstition.

But he was there. No matter how much she wished to deny it.

And in the split second before he bounded over the peak and disappeared on the other side of the roof, Esme could have sworn he'd seen her, too. She could feel the heat of his eyes burning into her soul.

4

Sarah spotted the glow from the pulsing lights even before they turned onto Elysian Fields. The street was the main thoroughfare through Faubourg Marigny, a neighborhood that had become increasingly hip and trendy as refugees from the French Quarter fled across Esplanade Avenue to escape the tourists.

As they made the corner, she saw the police cars and emergency vehicles lined up at the curb. She counted three patrol cars, a crime-scene van and a vehicle from the Orleans Parish Coroner's Office. A grim motorcade that almost always signaled a violent crime.

Even at this hour, lights burned in some of the pastel-painted bungalows and guest cottages along the street, and the curious had begun to gather. A few worried neighbors had thrown coats over their pajamas and hurried out to investigate the commotion. They stood in a tight cluster, breaths frosting on the cold air as a procession of cops marched in and out of the house.

Crime had never been a stranger in New Orleans. A brief calm had settled over the city after the flood, but once the state police and National Guard moved out, the local authorities had been overwhelmed by the escalating violence. Longtime residents already knew to keep a constant vigil. There were places you did not go alone and at night, but the Marigny had never been one of them.

Now, with so many neighborhoods still unlivable, a new breed of criminal—bolder and more violent than ever before—had moved into the upscale safe havens. Once the sun went down, everyone but the very brave or the very foolish was already home, sequestered safely behind locked doors and windows until daylight.

As Sarah got out of the car, a blast of cold air blew down her collar and jolted her from the lingering effects of her Xanax haze. Parks came around to her side and they crossed the street together. She could feel the curious eyes of the neighbors on them, and when she glanced back, a silence settled over the crowd. They shifted uncomfortably and looked away, no doubt wondering about her relationship to the victim.

Parks said something to one of the officers guarding the perimeter, and then he motioned for Sarah to follow as he ducked under the police tape and started up the walkway. Like most houses in the area, the Creole-style cottage was elevated from the ground with steps leading up to a narrow, gingerbread-trimmed porch.

Before they reached the top, the front door opened and Sean came out. Sarah paused with one foot on the next step, her gaze lifting. Someone pushed past her and clambered up to the porch, spoke briefly to Sean, then hurried into the house. Behind her, Parks gently nudged her forward, but Sarah ignored him. Her focus was only on Sean.

He was tall, trim, a commanding presence even at the age of thirty-three. At one time, he'd been the youngest homicide detective on the force, but no one who knew him had been surprised by his rapid ascension. Sean had always been quick to take advantage of an opportunity.

His black wool overcoat was unbuttoned and flapping in the wind. Sarah was surprised he even owned one. The cold front had caught most people unprepared and they'd had to make do with layers of sweaters and jackets.

The coat, however, was his only concession to the frigid temperature. His head was bare, and when he moved from beneath the porch roof, snowflakes settled in his black hair. He brushed them away as he stood gazing down at Sarah.

She'd told herself after his phone call that she wouldn't do this. She wouldn't let him see how much he'd hurt her. How much seeing him bothered her. Driving by his house in the middle of the night was one thing, but here she had nowhere to hide.

And yet she found herself clinging to his gaze, remembering the intimacy, remembering every nuance and gesture, every whisper, every promise.

She caught herself then and glanced away, but almost immediately her gaze came back to him. *He'd* called *her* tonight. He'd asked for her help. She didn't have to hide or pretend. She had every right to be here.

He came down a step or two and gave Parks a curt nod. But his gaze never left Sarah's. "Got her here in one piece, I see."

"Yes, sir."

"Thanks for that."

"No problem."

Parks headed back down the stairs as Sean waited for Sarah.

When they reached the porch, he pulled her away from the congestion near the front door.

"Sarah," he murmured.

She glanced away, unnerved by her reaction to him.

His voice turned gruff. "What the hell have you been doing to yourself? You look terrible."

Anger tightened her jaw muscles. "It's good to see you, too, Sean."

"I'm serious. You look like you haven't slept in days."

"I was sleeping when you called."

She could see skepticism in his face. "And how long had it been before that?"

"Why are you doing this?" she asked in exasperation.

"Doing what?" He sounded genuinely puzzled. "I told you earlier, I'm worried about you."

"Why?"

"Sarah—"

She pulled away when he tried to touch her. "You said you wanted me to look at the victim's tattoos. That's the only reason I'm here."

His features hardened, and that, too, was familiar. Sean didn't deal well with rejection, not even the mildest rebuke. "Damn it, why do you always have to act like this?"

"Like what?"

"Misunderstood. Put upon. Like you were the only one who got hurt when we split up."

"You know, Sean, that argument might be a little more convincing if you'd waited longer than four months before getting married. How is Catherine, by the way? Does she know you called me?"

He sighed. "I'm not doing this with you. Not here."

"Fine. Why don't you show me what you want me to see and then let me get the hell out of here?"

He ran his hand through his dark hair. It was longer than Sarah remembered, brushing the collar of his overcoat. He could use a shave, too, and his eyes were ringed with dark circles. She wasn't the only one who needed a good night's sleep.

The front door opened and a young officer hurried onto the porch. He stumbled down the stairs, took a few shaky steps into the yard, then bent over and vomited into a row of frozen camellia bushes.

A wave of nausea rolled through Sarah's stomach. She tried to tell herself the sound of the cop's retching had triggered the response, but deep down, she knew it was panic. Not for what she was about to see, but for the way Sean still made her feel.

"This is a bad one, Sarah."

His voice caused her to jump.

"I don't have any right asking you to do this. Lapierre would probably have my badge if she got wind of it," he said, referring to the female lieutenant.

Sarah had heard Sean talk about Angelette Lapierre before. She was a tough, thirtysomething Cajun who had come up through the ranks of the detective bureau. In spite of her age and gender, she'd been recently appointed the Homicide Division commander following a scandal that had claimed badges all the way to the top, decimating an already undermanned police force.

In the wake of her promotion, rumors abounded about her past, her affiliations and an affair with the newly elected mayor. According to Sean, Angelette Lapierre had visions of grandeur and was out to make a name for herself no matter who she had to take down—or sleep with—to get what she wanted.

He rubbed the back of his neck, frustration and weariness settling into every line and groove of his face. "She's on a tear about crime-scene contamination, which, ask any cop out here, is a joke. It's always been a problem, but nowadays we get people walking in off the damned street to gawk. Half the time we're so exhausted, we don't even notice."

"If you know you'll get in trouble, why did you ask me to come here?"

He flexed his fingers, anxious to get back to the action. "Because I want to catch this son of a bitch. And you've got more insight into this kind of thing than any detective I know. The rest is just bullshit."

That was Sean. If he had to break a few rules, exploit an old relationship, he didn't much care so long as he got results. He was probably more like Angelette Lapierre than he wanted to admit.

"I have a bad feeling this guy is just getting warmed up," he said. "We find another body, and all hell's gonna break loose. You can bet your ass, Lapierre will start showing up for some face time. The chief of police, the FBI…they'll all want a piece of the glory. This may be my only chance to show you a crime scene while it's still fresh. If you're willing."

"I'm here, aren't I?"

But he still hesitated. "It's more than just the tattoos. He drew this all over the walls." He took a piece of paper from his coat pocket and showed her the sketch he'd made. "You know about this stuff. Can you tell me what it is?"

A tingle shuttled up Sarah's spine. "It's an *udjat*. Some people call it the Eye of Lucifer."

Sean sucked in a breath. "It's satanic, in other words."

"It sometimes has that connotation. It's also called the all-seeing eye. Maybe the killer is trying to tell you that he's watching you."

"Or watching someone."

The dread deepened, lifting the hair at the back of Sarah's neck. "Did you find anything else?"

"The victim has a pentagram tattooed in her palm."

Oh, God... "Nothing out here?"

"You mean footwear evidence?"

She turned, searching the darkness. "Any unusual prints around the house?"

"Define unusual."

She hesitated. "You'd know them if you saw them."

"That's all I get?"

"For now. Are we going inside?"

He gave her an assessing look. "Yeah," he said. "Let's get this over with."

5

The front door was glossy with heavy coats of black enamel and was trimmed with a brass knocker and doorknob. Sarah paused, the metal numbers hammered into the wooden door frame catching her attention.

She put out a gloved finger to trace them, but Sean stopped her. "The crime scene techs have been out here, but once we're inside, it's better if you don't touch anything."

A draft of cold air followed them into the house and Sarah stood in the small foyer, shivering, pulse pounding as she took a quick glance around.

Like a lot of residences in the area, the cottage had been gutted and was now in a chaotic state of renovation. Paint cans and drop cloths littered the living room floor, and Sarah could smell varnish, sawdust—and another scent that didn't belong there.

Sulphur.

Her stomach jolted as the metallic taste of fear coated her

tongue. Sean hadn't told her where the body was, but she knew. Maybe it was the muted voices echoing down the stairwell or the swish of shoe covers in the hallway above her. Or maybe she had innate radar when it came to death and violence.

Sean handed her a pair of plastic booties and she slipped them over her shoes. He put his hand on her elbow, guiding her toward the stairs. Sarah wished she could grab the banister to steady herself, but she remembered his warning not to touch anything.

"Who owns this place?" she asked, trying not to think about what waited for her upstairs.

"Alain and Juliette Fontenot. They started the renovations just before Christmas and were hoping to move in by spring. I have a feeling this is going to put a damper on their enthusiasm."

"Were they the ones who found the body?"

"No, one of the workmen did. They shut down the job on Friday for the weekend, and then when the ice storm hit early this morning—yesterday morning now—the foreman called and gave the crew an extra day off. This guy says he came by to pick up some tools he left here."

"At this hour? How did he get in?"

"He has a key, but he claims the back door was open. He didn't think anything of it at first, just figured someone had forgotten to lock up on Friday. Then he found a broken window and decided to have a look around to see if any of the tools and equipment had been stolen. That's when he discovered the body. He called 911 from his cell phone."

"You think he's telling the truth?" They were almost at the top step now. Sarah paused, paralyzed for a moment by the unknown.

"First door on the right," Sean said behind her. "To answer your question, I don't think he's our perp. But I also doubt that the tools he came by for tonight were his."

"At least he called the police."

The wooden stairs creaked beneath their feet, and as they stepped onto the landing, two men talking in the doorway glanced over their shoulders. One of them was Danny LeJeune, Sean's partner. The other man was tall, slender, ridiculously handsome with dark hair and eyes the color of good jade. Sarah recognized him from a party she'd gone to once with Sean. He was Tony Vincent from the coroner's office.

He'd been a big hit at that party, she recalled. In spite of his reserved nature, his looks had attracted most of the single women in the room and at least half the wives. Sarah had watched from a distance, amused by the outrageous flirting, a bit smug in the knowledge that one Sean Kelton was probably worth a dozen Tony Vincents. Now she would have to reevaluate that assessment.

"We're ready to get her bagged whenever you're done," Vincent said.

Sean nodded. "Give us a minute. I've brought in someone to have a look at the tattoos."

Vincent's gaze flicked briefly over Sarah as he headed for the stairs. "No problem. Just holler when you're ready."

After he was gone, Danny LeJeune came over and gave Sarah a quick hug. "Hey, gorgeous. Long time, no see."

"How are you, Danny?"

"Can't complain." He gave her a weary smile. "No offense, hon, but you're just about the last person I wanted to see walk up those stairs. I was hoping you'd finally wise up and tell this guy to go to hell."

"Easy," Sean warned, and Sarah was surprised by the tension in his voice. She'd never known him to be at odds with his partner. They'd always been close.

Danny shrugged. "She's got no business being here, and you damn well know it. I wouldn't let a dog of mine go near that room, much less…" He trailed off, obviously not knowing what to call Sarah these days.

She flinched and she felt Sean stiffen beside her.

"Lapierre is going to shit a brick when she hears about this," Danny said.

Sean shrugged. "Who says she has to know? If anyone asks, we brought in an expert consultant."

"Oh, yeah, that's convincing."

"If there's trouble, I'll make sure it doesn't touch you," Sean said. "This is on me."

"You're damn straight, it's on you. But that's not my only concern here." Danny glanced down at Sarah and his voice softened. "You don't have to do this. Just turn around and head back down those stairs. Walk out the front door and keep going."

Sarah knew there was a double meaning in his advice. He was warning her to stay away from Sean.

She appreciated the sentiment. Danny was a good guy and she liked him. She'd even found herself wishing at times that she'd met him first.

He was a couple of inches shorter than Sean, but wider in the shoulders and broader in the chest. After a few drinks, he liked to reminisce about his glory days as a linebacker for the LSU Tigers. Sarah thought that he probably hadn't changed much since then. In spite of his wife's efforts to keep him on the straight and narrow, he could still party with the best of them. He'd just become more adept at hiding that part of his life.

Sarah put her hand on his arm. "I'm okay with this, Danny. I want to help if I can."

"You're both nuts if you ask me." But he fished a jar of Vicks from his pocket and opened the lid. "Smell's not as bad as some. The cold helps, but you might want a dab of this just the same."

Sarah smoothed some underneath her nostrils as Sean took her elbow. She walked ahead of him, pausing only briefly at the threshold before she entered.

She tried not to look at the victim, but she saw immediately that the woman was Caucasian with light brown hair and a slim build. She was lying facedown on the floor, so it was difficult to judge her age. Sarah had the impression that the victim was young, though.

She tried to keep her eyes averted, but it was impossible to ignore the blood. Large puddles near the body. Arterial spurts on the walls. It was as if the poor woman had been bled dry.

Sarah couldn't see any wounds. The damage was hidden by the position of the body, and she was suddenly very glad that the victim hadn't been turned over.

She put a hand to her mouth. "What did he do to her?"

"It's probably best if you don't know," Sean said.

Sarah forced herself to take a deep breath and the vapor made her eyes water. She glanced around the room. It was large with high ceilings and ornate molding that had recently been restored. Two long windows faced the neighboring house, but the glass had been covered with cardboard and taped securely at the edges, allowing no light to show through to the outside.

Sean hadn't been exaggerating earlier. The *udjats* were everywhere, even staring down at them from the ceiling.

"Did he use her blood to draw them?"

"We don't know that yet, but I'd say it's a pretty safe bet."
He paused, gesturing with a gloved hand. "Have you ever
seen anything like this?"

She had. A long time ago.

A full-length mirror had been propped against the wall opposite the doorway and positioned so that the body could be
viewed from certain angles. But Sarah's gaze was riveted, not
on the reflection of the victim, but on the wall behind her.

She glanced over her shoulder at the words that had been
scrawled backward in blood.

uoy ma I.

She turned back to the mirror and read them again in the
reflection.

I am you.

A rush of panic blindsided her, and she took an involun-
tary step back, right into Sean. His hands gripped her arms
to steady her. "You okay?"

"Yeah, I just… I don't know. That message on the wall
kind of threw me." She nodded toward the mirror. "Was that
already here?"

"Not according to the workman. He said this room was
empty when they knocked off work on Friday."

"Why would the killer bring such a large mirror with him?
Just so you'd be able to read his message?"

"I don't think so," Sean muttered. "I think the son of a
bitch wanted to watch himself."

Sarah moved toward the mirror, catching a glimpse of her
own reflection. Dark, sober eyes stared back at her. Black hair
tangled from the wind. Pale skin. Dry lips. No wonder Sean
had commented on her appearance. She did look like hell.

From where she stood now, she could still see the strange
message on the wall behind her reflection. *I am you.*

"Maybe I was wrong earlier when I said he wants you to know he's watching. Maybe he's trying to tell you that someone is watching him." Sarah could see her lips move in the mirror, but it seemed as if someone else had spoken. She felt an odd detachment from her own reflection.

"What are you talking about?"

She shook her head, not really understanding her own thoughts. "Maybe I should just look at the tattoos."

Sean took her arm and circled her around to the other side of the body, careful to avoid the blood on the floor. The victim's pale, waxy skin provided a macabre canvas for the ink on her arms and legs.

Her head was turned to the side, but her blood-matted hair concealed her face. All Sarah could see was one eye, open and staring. Like the painted *udjats* on the walls and ceiling, it seemed to follow her as she knelt on the floor beside the body.

"Do you know who she is?"

"No, not yet. We're checking with the neighbors, but so far no luck."

"When did it happen?"

"According to the coroner, she's been here at least forty-eight hours."

It had probably happened on Saturday night, then, only a few blocks from Sarah's house. She found herself wondering what she had been doing at the exact moment of the woman's death. Had she experienced any kind of premonition, some inexplicable sign that evil had been that near?

She bent her head and tried to concentrate on the tattoos. Skulls, dragons, serpent-entwined crosses. Nothing creative or unique about any of them. The designs were typical of the flash found on the walls of tattoo parlors all over the city.

But the red-and-black symbol on the victim's back...that

was unusual. And it was fresh. Scattered on the floor beside the body was the familiar paraphernalia of Sarah's art—thimble-sized ink cups, Vaseline, soiled paper towels. The killer had tattooed his victim at the murder scene. And he'd taken care to do it right.

That explained the barricaded windows, Sarah thought. He knew he'd be a while and didn't want to worry about discovery.

She leaned forward, studying the blood that had oozed from the needle stippling and dried on the woman's skin.

Behind her, Sean said, "She was still alive when he did that one."

"Looks like it bled quite a bit. She may have been drinking before he brought her here." The danger of excessive bleeding was why they never tattooed drunks at the shop. That and the morning-after regrets.

"We'll find out when we get the toxicology report."

Sarah paused, struck by something he'd just said. "What did you mean, she was alive when he did that one? The tattoos on her arms and legs are old. You can tell by how badly most of them are faded."

"I was talking about the pentagram in her right palm. See here? Ink smears, but almost no blood."

Sarah stared at the tattoo for a moment. Sean had called it a pentagram, but he was wrong. She started to correct him, but his attention was still focused on the victim's back.

"That's a pretty big tat. How long would it take to apply a design like that?"

Sarah shrugged. "Several hours, depending on the artist. But this guy's no scratcher. He knows what he's doing. Look how clean and sharp the edges are."

"What about the ones on her arms and legs? Any chance you recognize the artist?"

She shook her head. "Nothing stands out about the style, and the designs are pretty run-of-the-mill. And like I said, they're old. She's had most of them for years."

The creak of a footstep made them both turn. Danny came into the room and stood looking down at the body. He cocked his head, studying the strange design on the victim's back. "Hey, I never noticed before, but from this angle, it looks like a pair of naked women." He tilted his head the other way. "With really big breasts."

"Very helpful," Sean said. "It doesn't look like much of anything to me."

"That's because you've got no imagination." Danny squatted at the dead woman's feet. "You know what it reminds me of? No, seriously. It looks like one of those inkblots that shrinks use to analyze their patients."

Sean started to say something, but Sarah turned excitedly. "No, he's right. That's exactly what it looks like. A Rorschach inkblot."

"What does it mean?"

"It means something different to everyone who looks at it. That's the whole point. A patient's spontaneous response is supposed to reveal deep secrets or significant information that can be used in a psychological evaluation." Sarah turned back to the body. "There are only ten true Rorschach inkblots. Five black-and-white, two red-and-black and three multicoloreds. They're kept secret to protect the integrity of the test. The inkblot cards you see on TV and in movies are most likely fakes."

"What about this one?"

"I can't say for sure. You'd need to show it to someone

who's an expert in Rorschach inkblot therapy, but that might be difficult. The cards aren't used much anymore."

"How is it you know so much about these inkblots?" Sean's voice was deliberately casual.

Sarah met his gaze. *You already know the answer to that.* Aloud she said, "I read a lot."

"I still say it looks like two women with big breasts," Danny said. "What deep, dark secret does that reveal about me?"

"That you've got a one-track mind," Sean said. "But I didn't need an inkblot to tell me that."

Sarah's interpretation was very different from Danny's. Instead of two bodies, she saw faces—one light, the other dark.

Her gaze lifted to the mirror propped against the wall. She wanted to glance away, but she couldn't. This was the view the killer would have had when he looked up from his work. His own reflected face with the disturbing missive scrawled on the wall behind him.

I am you.

"Say it is real," Sean said. "If these inkblots are secret, the perp would need insider knowledge about them, right? Either as a patient or a doctor, and judging by his handiwork here, I'm pretty sure I know which one. But we can start by checking with some of the therapists in the city who still use these inkblots in their evaluations. Who knows? We might get lucky and find one who likes to talk."

"Shit," Danny said in disgust. "Do you have any idea how much I hate dealing with those condescending assholes? Never met one yet who didn't give me the creeps."

Their voices faded as Sarah continued to stare at the mirror. Suddenly she knew why the message had hit her so hard. It reminded her of something that had been said to her a long time ago.

We're the same, Sarah. Not outwardly, of course. But inside, our souls are mirror images.

No, she thought. *It can't be him.*

Her throat constricted and a film of sweat coated her skin. She told herself to relax, breathe deeply, but it was too late.

The darkness was coming for her.

A little while later, Sarah stood shivering on the front porch as two beefy men negotiated the slippery steps with the stretcher. She didn't want to stare at the body bag, but she couldn't seem to look away. The victim had been someone's sister or daughter or mother, and now she was gone, murdered by a psycho with a very dark compulsion.

Leaning her head against a newel post, she closed her eyes. Sean had asked her to wait while he finished up, but she was desperate to get home. She'd been outside for too long, and her face and hands were numb from the cold. But the frigid air had done nothing to dispel the dread still hammering at her chest. She recognized it for what it was—a memory trying to force its way out.

A therapist had once told her that every subconscious contained a special place—a vault—where lost memories were stored. Usually, those memories stayed locked up tight, but every once in a while, a song, a face or a seemingly random event could crack open the safe and provide a tantalizing, sometimes terrifying glimpse into the past.

The room upstairs had done that for Sarah. But the tumblers hadn't been turned by the puddles of blood on the floor or even the tattoos on the victim. The vault *had* been breached by the killer's message. And by the sight of her own pale face staring back from the mirror.

The door opened and Sean stepped out on the porch.

He moved up beside her. "Are you okay? You had me worried when you ran out like that."

"Yeah, I was kind of surprised by that, too," Sarah said. "I thought I had a strong constitution. Never considered myself the squeamish type."

"Sometimes it hits you all of a sudden. I've seen it happen to guys who've been on the force for years." Sean hesitated. "But maybe in your case, there's a little more going on than a weak stomach."

"What do you mean?"

"You were thinking about Rachel, weren't you? Damn it, I could kick myself for dragging you over here like this. I should have thought about how it would affect you."

She shrugged. "Don't worry about it. It's not a big deal."

"It's a very big deal. I saw your face when you ran out. It was like you'd seen a ghost. Do you want to talk about it?"

"Here?" She glanced around. The professionals and onlookers alike were starting to disperse, but Sarah still had no intention of getting into something so private. "I'm sure you've got better things to do with your time."

"I can spare a few minutes. Besides..." Sean sighed. "It's the same old story. Nobody saw or heard anything. Not a lot more we can do tonight except file the report and wait for the autopsy. And it might help if you told me what happened upstairs."

He put his hand on the railing next to hers. Not quite touching. Just close enough for her to know it was there.

"I don't think so, Sean."

"Why not? You always refused to talk about Rachel because you didn't want to drag your past into our relationship. At least that's what you said. What's stopping you now?"

"Why do you even care?"

"Sarah."

The mild rebuke sent a shiver up her spine. She could feel his eyes on her in the dark and she wanted to move away, but not nearly as much as she wanted to stay.

She looked out over the darkened street where moonlight softly illuminated frozen treetops. The flashing police lights reflected off tiny icicles, turning them into sapphires and rubies and in the distance, the palest of amber. The glistening neighborhood looked clean and beautiful and deceptively peaceful in the dark.

Sean shifted restlessly, impatient as always to cut to the heart of the problem. "After you and I got together, I read every newspaper account of the murder I could get my hands on. I even put in a few calls, tried to convince the local authorities to let me have a look at the police report. The one thing that seemed consistent in every account was the county sheriff's conviction that it was a ritual murder. They found satanic symbols at the crime scene, just like upstairs. Is that what hit you so hard?"

Sarah pushed damp strands of hair from her face. "Just leave it alone, okay? I've told you a million times I don't like dredging all that stuff up. It doesn't do any good. I don't remember anything about that night, and at this point, I doubt I ever will."

"But you do remember. You're just not letting those memories come out. That's why you still have nightmares. It's possible you know who the killer is. And you know he's still out there."

Sarah tried to muster an indignant response that would end this. "Oh, so you're a shrink now?"

"It doesn't take a shrink to figure this thing out. You were found near the crime scene covered in your sister's blood.

Whatever you saw that night traumatized you so badly you decided to forget what happened. But those memories are still buried in your subconscious. They come out when you dream. So you don't sleep until your body shuts down from exhaustion because you're desperate to keep them at bay for as long as you can." Sean leaned down and said in her ear, "Why won't you let them out, Sarah? Who are you trying to protect?"

Startled, she moved back, away from him, trying to put distance between herself and the past. But it was too late. She could feel herself slipping into that dark void of paranoia and guilt that had stalked her through most of her teenage years and followed her into adulthood. She found herself scouring the icy darkness, searching for the evil that she knew would sooner or later come back for her.

Sean touched her arm and she jumped.

"You remembered something earlier, didn't you?"

Slowly she turned to face him. "Is that why you asked me to come here? Because you thought the crime scene would jog my memory?"

It seemed to Sarah that he couldn't quite meet her gaze. "I called you because I want your help."

She wasn't convinced. There was something else at play here, something that Sean might not even be completely aware of himself. Somewhere along the way, he'd become obsessed with her sister's murder. It was no longer about Sarah's peace of mind. It wasn't even about justice. Sean had convinced himself—knowingly or otherwise—that he was the one person who could catch Rachel's killer.

"If you really want my help, why are you badgering me about something that happened fourteen years ago? Maybe you should try focusing on a crime you might actually be able to solve."

He winced and she could tell he was on the verge of a retort, then he changed his mind and shrugged. "Okay. Maybe
you're right. Maybe this isn't the right time to get into all that.
But there's something I need to know before I have Parks take
you home." His face looked both dark and pale in the light
spilling out from the windows. "What did you mean earlier
when you asked if we'd found any unusual prints around the
house?"

Sarah glanced up at the sky. The swirling snowflakes reminded her of tiny, dancing angels. She put out a hand to
catch one in her palm.

"What kind of prints were you talking about, Sarah?"

She remained silent as her fingers closed over a snowflake.

6

Adamant, Arkansas
Christmas Eve

The temperature dropped after dark and it had started to mist. Ashe shivered in his lightweight jacket as he glanced yet again over his shoulder, making sure he couldn't be spotted.

An unnecessary precaution, because the house was on a two-acre lot at the end of the street. Even if the closest neighbors should glance outside, they would see only a shadow beneath the DeLaunes' living room window.

Nor was there any need to worry about passing cars. The streets were deserted. He couldn't see anything but the kaleidoscopic blur of twinkling lights in the distance. On Christmas Eve, the good citizens of Adamant were home celebrating with their families.

But the night was like any other to him. He felt nothing more than a fleeting twinge of regret that no one knew or cared how he spent his

Christmas Eve. He didn't dwell on his loneliness, because being invisible had its compensation.

Shrugging off the disquiet, he turned back to the window. It was nearly midnight. Everyone except Sarah's father had gone up to bed, and he sat dozing in an easy chair in front of the fireplace. Blissfully unaware.

Earlier, the family had gathered around the Christmas tree to exchange presents. The window was open a crack to allow the smoke from the old man's pipe to escape, and Ashe had been able to hear their voices so clearly it was almost as if he were a part of the celebration. He'd followed the conversation with avid fascination, even though his eyes had been riveted on Sarah.

Dressed in jeans and a pale yellow sweater, her dark hair pulled back into a ponytail, she'd sat cross-legged on the floor, opening her gifts with a brooding scowl that had irritated her father. The contrast between her sister's girly squeals as she tore into one package after another had finally become too much for him.

"I've had enough of this." He got up and strode over to Sarah, grabbed her by the arm and yanked her to her feet. "If you want to sit there and sulk, you can damn well do it in your room. You're not going to ruin the evening for the rest of us."

Her mother nervously rose to her feet. "James—"

"Stay out of this, Anna. I should have taken care of this at dinner when she was being so rude and aggressive with her sister. She's an ungrateful little brat, and I'm not going to sit here and tolerate this surly behavior any longer."

Still clutching her arm, he marched Sarah out of the room and up the stairs. He was gone for a long time, and when he came back, he looked flushed and angry.

"Daddy, are you okay?" Rachel asked softly.

He smiled, his anger melting when he looked at her. "I'm fine, princess, don't you worry. I've got something that'll make us both feel better." He plucked a tiny package from his jacket pocket and placed it on the table beside his chair. "Come have a look."

"Another present?" She gave a little laugh as she tore away the ribbon and paper with frenzied excitement. From Ashe's place at the window, he saw a flash of fire from the open box before Rachel threw her arms around the old man's neck. "Daddy! Diamonds? Are they real?"

"Of course they are. Would I give my princess anything but the real thing?"

"But I thought…Mama said I should wait until next year and get them for graduation."

"And I say you should have them now."

"Thank you, Daddy. Thank you…thank you…thank you!" She planted a kiss on his cheek after each thank-you, then hugged him tightly. He clung to her for a moment before she got up and ran over to show her mother.

"Mama, look! Have you ever seen anything so beautiful? Isn't Daddy just the sweetest thing?"

Her mother murmured something Ashe couldn't hear, and then she watched her oldest daughter gather up all her presents and rush upstairs to try on her new earrings.

After she was gone, Anna walked over to the fireplace. "Why didn't you tell me about the earrings?"

"Since when do I need your permission to get my own daughter a gift?"

"Sarah's your daughter, too, James. Why didn't you give her something special?"

"Because it would have been a waste. Nothing we do is ever good enough for that girl."

"That's not true. She's just going through a difficult stage. I wish you'd try to be a little more understanding—"

"A stage?" He gave a bitter laugh. "Don't kid yourself, Anna. She's always been like this. That girl has always had problems. She's a liar and a thief, and I should have done something about it a long time ago."

Sarah's mother sat down on the hearth and folded her hands in her lap. "You've always been so hard on her."

"She's out of control and you damn well know it. I'm sick to death of dealing with her problems. I hate to think what she'll be like in a few more years. I see kids like her come through my courtroom all the time. Something needs to be done, and soon, or we may all live to regret it. I'm beginning to think Lydia Mason was right. St. Stephen's is the best place for a girl like Sarah."

"I hardly think Lydia Mason is an expert on what's best for our daughter. I can't believe you took her to see that woman behind my back."

"She's the only therapist in town."

"You could have talked to the counselor at school or consulted with someone in El Dorado. Why did it have to be her?"

"What's really got your goat here, Anna? The prospect of sending your daughter away to school, or what Lydia might tell that preacher husband of hers about you? I know how highly you value his opinion."

"This has nothing to do with Tim. I'm not sending Sarah away. I don't care what anyone says. She's only thirteen years old!"

"Will you calm down? It's not like we're abandoning her. St. Stephen's is only an hour's drive from here. You can visit her whenever you want."

"I'll never agree to this. She needs me."

"And what about your other daughter? What about her needs? I swear to God, the way that girl looks at Rachel sometimes makes my blood run cold."

"She resents Rachel because of the way you treat her. She knows Rachel is your favorite. Everyone knows it. You don't even try to hide it."

"Rachel is a beautiful young woman with a brilliant future ahead of her. I'm proud of her. Why should I have to hide it?"

Sarah's mother stared down at her hands. "If I'd known it was going to be this way—"

"What would you have done differently?" he goaded. "Go on, say it."

"She's just a child. What I did is not her fault."

"Maybe not. But I can't help how I feel."

"Yes, you can. Why won't you just admit it? This isn't about Sarah. It's about punishing me."

Ashe's blood pumped fiercely as he watched Sarah's mother rise and rush from the room. His curiosity was at a fevered pitch. He thought he knew everything about Sarah, but here was a new morsel, a secret that would need to be uncovered then studied and savored.

He returned his attention to Sarah's father and felt something dark gathering inside him. The old man had no idea what waited for him as he stared broodingly into the flames.

After a while, he nodded off, and Ashe thought how easy it would be to slide up the window, slip into the house and take a stick of firewood to the old man's skull. Or a knife to the thick, beefy neck. He could almost feel the warm blood spew over his hands, and for a moment, the desire was almost too much to resist.

But vengeance was worth waiting for and the time had to be right.

After all, the worst punishment wasn't death. It was losing the thing prized above all else.

7

By midmorning on Tuesday, the temperature had climbed twenty degrees, and the trees around Esme Floyd's house were dripping from the melting ice. The sun was finally out, but the wind still carried a sharp bite.

Shivering, Lukas Clay reached back inside the squad car to grab his heavy jacket. A cup of coffee would have hit the spot, but he wasn't about to turn around and drive back downtown. The sooner he got this over with, the sooner he could head home and catch a nap.

His job as chief of police in a town of barely three thousand people was normally uneventful, but the past thirty-six hours had been intense. An ice storm in this part of the country was always serious business. Very few drivers or vehicles were equipped to handle the treacherous roadways, and overhead power lines were always susceptible to falling tree branches.

As soon as the bad weather set in, Lukas had mobilized a task force consisting of two full-time and four part-time officers to patrol the outlying areas to make sure no one, especially the elderly, got stranded in the freezing temperatures. He'd been out all night himself and had just been on his way home when Esme Floyd's call came in. There'd been a disturbance at the DeLaune place the night before.

Lukas folded his sunglasses and slipped them in his pocket as he glanced around. Backed up to an old pear orchard, Esme's cottage was raised off the ground on brick pillars and underpinned with weathered latticework. Eyes gleamed from the darkness beneath the house, and a second later, an orange tabby shot through the slats and leaped to the top of a woodpile, where a black-and-white tomcat lay sunning.

Smoke curled up from the brick chimney, and as Lukas tracked the wispy stream, he spotted a buzzard circling the woods behind the orchard.

Something dead back there.

He watched for a moment, his eyes watering in the wind. As the vulture floated serenely on the air currents, a shotgun blast startled a flock of blackbirds out of the treetops and halted Lukas in his tracks.

The echo of gunfire vibrated against his chest. His heart jumped once, twice, three times before settling back to its normal beat.

Jesus, get a grip. Just somebody out hunting rabbits.

He'd been stateside for, what? Nearly two years and still the sound of gunfire—or a revving car engine—could propel him straight back to the war.

An army psychiatrist had assured him that it wasn't uncommon for the effects of PTSD to linger or even worsen over time, but Lukas had finally figured out for himself how he needed to deal with the aftermath. He'd have to find a way to compartmentalize his time in Iraq, the same way he had everything else in his life. It was just like cleaning house. A place for everything, and everything in its place.

Some of those memory boxes—like his childhood—were to be opened rarely and with great caution, although he supposed he hadn't had it any rougher than a lot of kids. Southern boys were raised with certain expectations. Once you accepted your place, once you mastered the pursuits deemed manly enough by a culture still mired in the past, you were rewarded for your trouble with jealousy and bitterness because your old man suddenly saw in you the passing of his own youth. Your triumphs became his failings, and he would do anything to prove he was still the better man even if it meant breaking you in ways you could never have imagined.

Sometimes the rivalry lasted well beyond the grave. How else could he explain his decision to come back here? Lukas wondered. Or even his career choice. Why follow in his father's footsteps if the idea of besting the old man's accomplishments didn't still hold some twisted appeal?

Not that it was going to be easy to live up to—let alone surpass—his father's reputation. William Clay had been a legend in Union County for as long as Lukas could remember. He'd served as county sheriff for the better part of twenty-five years, and in all that time, only one major case had gone unsolved.

Lukas glanced over his shoulder, a momentary spurt of adrenaline nudging away his fatigue. Fifty yards behind him, the DeLaune house rose like a stately specter, its pale walls and gleaming windows a constant reminder of the town's darkest secret.

Sixteen-year-old Rachel DeLaune hadn't just been murdered. Her body had been mutilated, the crime scene desecrated with satanic symbols. And in spite of his father's best efforts, the killer had never been caught.

Not yet, at least.

A thrill of excitement slid up Lukas's backbone even as he shuddered in dread. Something about that house always gave him the creeps. He couldn't explain it. It was a fine old place, beautiful in the spring and summer when the roses and crepe myrtle were in bloom. But in the dead of winter, surrounded by an army of skeletal trees with their limbs quivering in the wind, the house looked cold and bleak and abandoned.

Some said it was haunted. Some even claimed they'd seen Rachel's ghost at an upstairs window staring down at them as they passed by on the street.

But Lukas didn't believe in ghosts. Not the kind that came back from the grave anyway. The only thing that had ever haunted him was his past.

Which was why he'd locked it away.

Turning back to the cottage, he stepped up on the concrete porch and knocked on the door. As he waited for someone to answer, he watched the buzzard's spiral tighten over a spot in the woods where the quarry lay dead or dying.

After a moment, Esme Floyd drew back the wooden door and peered at him through the storm door. She was tall and thin with posture as straight as a yardstick and eyes that snapped with intelligence. The cotton dress she wore was crisp and spotless, her hair an improbable shade of silvery blue.

"Miss Esme, I'm Lukas Clay. I hear you reported some kind of disturbance at the DeLaune place last night."

"Lukas Clay? Well, Lord have mercy. I liked to not recognized you." She slipped on her glasses as she examined him through the door. "You used to take after your daddy, but I swear, you the spittin' image of your mama nowadays. Except for them eyes. Dark as muscadines. You got your daddy's eyes, all right."

She fumbled with the latch, then pushed open the door for him to enter. Stepping into her little house was like crawling into a blast furnace. The warmth was a welcome respite from the wind and cold at first, but after a few minutes, Lukas felt as if someone had cocooned him in a thick layer of wool. The cloying heat took his breath away, and he quickly peeled off his gloves and unzipped his jacket.

"Better take off that coat," Esme warned. "Else you freeze to death when you go back outside."

Lukas shrugged out of his jacket and she hung it on a hook near the front door.

"So you knew my mother?"

"I was acquainted with her," Esme said. "She was a real fine woman."

His mother had died when Lukas was eight, and he'd always been fascinated to hear about her through others. The box that held his memories of her had been put away for so long, he couldn't seem to find them anymore.

"Your daddy and Mr. James used to be big fishing buddies," Esme reminisced. "They'd go off on trips, sometimes stay gone for a week or more at a hitch. Your mama'd come by the house to pick him up when they got in. You'd always stay in the car, but I'd see you out there now and then, peeking out the back glass."

Lukas smiled. "I can barely remember those days."

"You were just a little thing, real quiet and shy. After your mama died, God rest her soul, your daddy quit coming around so much. I guess he had his hands full raising you."

Or maybe he'd found other pastimes besides fishing, Lukas thought. Because being a widower, much less being a father, had never changed the old man's behavior one whit. He'd always done as he damn well pleased.

Lukas followed Esme into the tiny living room where she'd set up her ironing board in front of the television. A soap opera was on, and she watched the story for a moment before she reached down and switched off the set.

"Tell me what happened last night," he said.

"It's like I told that lady on the phone. I saw something out my bedroom window." Esme picked up the hot iron and plowed it into a shirt. A cloud of steam rose as the iron hissed against the freshly starched fabric.

The smell of ironed cotton brought back an unexpected memory. Lukas suddenly had a vision of his mother standing behind an ironing board pressing one of his father's khaki uniforms as tears rolled down her cheeks. Lukas had been maybe four or five at the time.

"What's wrong, Mama?"

"Nothing, son. I'm just tired, that's all. You run along and play. I have to get these shirts done so I can get supper on the table by the time your daddy gets home."

Strange to be remembering that now, Lukas thought, as he sat down in a chair near the ironing board. "What did you see, Miss Esme?"

She glanced up, her eyes flickering with something Lukas couldn't define. "Somebody on top of Mr. James's house, that's what."

He stared at her in surprise. "On top of the house? In the middle of an ice storm?"

"The sleet had stopped by then. And the moon was out. I could see him up there plain as day."

"You could tell it was a man?"

She guided the point of the iron across the shirt collar. "Only thing I could tell for sure was that he was up to no good. Why else would somebody be up there that time of night?"

"What time was this?"

"After midnight. More like one o'clock."

"Are you always up that late?"

"My old arthritis bothers me at night. Sometimes it helps to get up and walk around."

"So you looked out the window and you saw someone on the roof of the DeLaune house. Why didn't you call the station?"

"I didn't want nobody out on those slick roads because of me. Somebody get killed driving over here, I got that on my conscience."

"Yeah, but we might have been able to catch him last night. It was probably just someone trying to find a way in out of the cold, but if it happens again, you call us. Hear?"

She went back to her ironing. Lukas watched her for a moment, mesmerized by her strong strokes.

"Have you seen anything like that before? Anyone coming around the house acting suspicious? Any strange cars parked out on the street?"

"Not lately, I ain't."

"But you have seen something?"

The iron faltered and another cloud of steam rose up from the shirt. "It was a long time ago. Before they sent him to the pen."

"Who?"

"That ol' Fears boy." Her tone was pure contempt.

"Are you talking about Derrick Fears?"

She nodded, her eyes gleaming with scorn. "I'd see him out on the sidewalk sometimes, watching the house. I'd try to run him off before Mr. James catch him, but he wouldn't budge. Just stand there and mock me. Sometimes he'd cup his hands to his mouth and squeal like he was real bad hurt. You ask me, there's something bad wrong with a body who'd do something like that after what this family went through. Something done took that boy's soul a long time ago."

"Did you ever call the police when you saw him out there?"

"Nothing the police could do about it. Ain't no law against standing on the sidewalk actin' a fool, is they?"

"Do you think it could have been Derrick Fears you saw on the roof last night?"

"They still got him locked up, last I heard."

"No, he's out."

"Out?" She said the word as if she couldn't quite comprehend its meaning.

Lukas nodded. "He paid his debt to society and they set him free."

She slammed the iron down so hard on the board, the rickety legs threatened to fold. "Now, don't that just beat all? He slices somebody up in a knife fight and don't get as much time as my boy, Robert, did for stealing some blamed old car. That don't seem right to me."

"It doesn't seem right to me, either, but I'm not here to argue the shortcomings of our judicial system," Lukas said. "I'm trying to figure out who was up on that roof last night and why." He walked over to the window and glanced out.

The path from the cottage led straight up to the DeLaune house, but trees blocked the view. How well could she have seen the roof in the middle of the night, even if the moon had been out?

As Lukas studied the back of the house, a slight movement in one of the upstairs windows caught his attention. He kept his gaze on the same spot, but when he didn't see anything else, he wondered if he'd glimpsed the reflection of a bird or the play of sunlight in the glass.

He glanced over his shoulder where Esme was noisily putting away the ironing board. "No one's living in the house right now?"

"No one left but Mr. James. And he won't be coming back home, bless his heart."

"What about the daughter? Sarah."

"She lives in New Orleans. Her and Mr. James don't get along, but since he took sick, she's been coming around more than she used to." In spite of the overheated house, Esme plucked a sweater off a hook and draped it over her scrawny shoulders.

"Miss Esme, were you here the night Rachel DeLaune was murdered?"

Her gnarled hand clutched the sweater to her bony chest. "Why you asking me about that? It don't have nothing to do with somebody being up on that roof, does it? Besides, I don't like thinking about that night."

"But you do think about it, don't you? Everyone in this town thinks about it. Because no one ever paid for that girl's murder."

"Your daddy did everything he could to find out who did it. He went to his grave still looking for her killer."

"But he never found him, did he?"

Esme trained her penetrating gaze on Lukas. "And you think you can find him, I guess. You think you can do what your daddy couldn't?"

Lukas was surprised and a little unnerved by how easily she'd read him. "I just want to do my duty by this town."

"Humph."

He ignored her dismissive response. "Tell me about the night they found her body," he said. "Where were you?"

"I was right here at home, that's where."

"How did you hear about it?" When she didn't answer, Lukas said softly, "Look, I know this is hard for you. You've worked for the family for years. You helped raise those girls. It was a terrible thing that happened, and a dark cloud has been hanging over this town ever since. I've read all the police reports, been over them I can't tell you how many times. But right now, I'd really like to hear about that night from you."

She pressed her lips together. "It won't help you. Might even do more harm than good stirring up that mess. You ever think of that?"

"What I think is that Rachel DeLaune deserves justice. I don't care how long it's been. You were there that night, Miss Esme. You may be the only person in town who can still help me piece together what happened. Will you do that?"

She was silent for a moment. "I still say no good can come from digging up the past. Sometimes it's best to leave a body resting in peace. But I reckon you'll keep after me until I tell you what I know."

Lukas smiled. "I have been known to dig in my heels."

"Oh, I can see that stubbornness in your eyes. Your daddy had it, too." She sighed wearily. "I'll tell you what I can remember, but then I don't want to talk about it no more."

Lukas nodded.

Esme gazed out the window. "I was just fixin' to turn in when Miss Anna called me. She said something bad had happened to Sarah."

"To Sarah?"

"That's what she said. A neighbor had found the child walking down the side of the road, covered in blood. They didn't know if she was hurt bad or not because they couldn't get her to talk. Wouldn't say a word to nobody. Only thing they knew to do was bring her home. Mr. James finally got it out of her that something had happened at the old Duncan farmhouse. He grabbed his pistol and took off over there. Miss Anna called the doctor and then she called me."

"Was your grandson still living with you then? Where was he during all this?"

An infinitesimal pause before she lifted her chin and said haughtily, "My boy was right here in his bed where he belonged. I didn't see no need in waking him up. Nothing he could do."

"What happened when you got to the house?"

"Miss Anna had Sarah in the bathtub washing the blood out of her hair."

"Why would she do that? Didn't she realize she could have been destroying evidence of a crime perpetrated against her daughter?"

"She wasn't thinking about nothing like that. She just wanted to get her baby girl clean as fast as she can."

"What did she think had happened to Sarah?"

Esme pursed her lips. "Wasn't my place to ask questions. I just tried to help the best way I knew how."

"What did you do?"

"I gathered up the dirty clothes and took them downstairs. That's when I heard Mr. James come back. He'd found Rachel at the farmhouse and carried her all the way back home. Even if he cut through the orchard and came across the field, he still had to pack her close to a mile."

The blood on one daughter had been washed down the drain while the other daughter's body had been removed from the crime scene. Evidence hadn't just been tampered with in this case…it had been trampled on.

"Judge DeLaune knows the law as well as anyone. Why would he remove his daughter's body from the crime scene?"

"The doctor was already on his way to the house to see about Sarah. Makes sense Mr. James would want to get Rachel home as fast as he can, don't it? He was too late, though. I took one look at what they'd done to that poor baby and I knew she was dead. Nobody could live through that. Mr. James knew it, too. He took her into his study and laid her out on the divan. Told me to go call Sheriff Clay, tell him to come quick. As soon as he arrived, he went into the study with Mr. James and they stayed there for a long time. When they finally came out, I heard him say he was going over to arrest Derrick Fears."

"But Fears had an airtight alibi for that night," Lukas said.

Esme gave him a sidelong glance. "You think a mother won't lie to keep her boy out of that kind of trouble?"

"Is that what you think happened?"

"That's what your daddy thought."

"Maybe that was his problem," Lukas said. "He was already dealing with a contaminated crime scene and a witness who couldn't remember how she happened to be covered in blood. By focusing on Fears, he neglected to look for other suspects."

Esme studied him for a moment. "You would have done things different, I guess."

He smiled. "Put it this way. I'm not my father."

"Maybe not." She plucked at a button on her sweater as she turned to stare at the back of the DeLaune house. "But I still say you got his eyes."

8

Lukas didn't really expect to find anything at the DeLaune house. Footprints left on the frozen ground would have been lost once the ice started to thaw. And, too, he had to wonder if Esme had imagined the whole thing. She lived alone and was getting on in years. Her eyesight probably wasn't as good as it used to be, and the view from her cottage was obscured by all the trees. In the dark, the barren limbs whipping over the roof might have looked like someone running up the steep slope.

But Lukas searched the grounds anyway, because in spite of her advanced years and failing eyesight, Esme Floyd didn't strike him as the type prone to flights of fantasy. And if someone had been up on that roof in the middle of the night, he damn well wanted to know who it was.

He glanced back at the cottage, saw Esme in the window and gave a quick wave. Then he walked around to the front of the house and used her key to let himself in.

The house was cold and deathly still. Like a tomb, he

thought. An apt description, since the place had seen its share of grief and tragedy. And now the owner, the last of the De-Laune family save for the youngest daughter, was in the hospital with only weeks, possibly days, to live.

Lukas lingered in the foyer as he glanced around the silent rooms, taking in the shrouded furniture and the tightly closed drapes and shutters that blocked most of the sunlight. Esme had told him that she still came over every other day to clean and air out the rooms, but the house already had an abandoned smell even though Lukas suspected there wasn't a speck of dust to be found in the entire place.

The living room was to his left, the dining room and kitchen to his right. Straight ahead, an oak staircase with a polished banister led to a long, second-story gallery and the bedrooms.

Lukas began in the living room and made sure all the windows were secure before he slid back a set of pocket doors that led into a study. As he stepped inside, he sniffed the air. The scent of leather and pipe tobacco still hung heavy in the room.

The gloomy silence pecked at his nerves, so he opened the drapes. Sunlight flooded in and he turned, taking in the room in one sweep. Glass-fronted bookcases lined the wall behind a fine old mahogany desk, and a leather sofa and two armchairs were grouped around a brick fireplace.

In spite of the handsome furnishings, the room was nondescript, like a picture clipped from a magazine. It was understated and dignified, and yet there was a hint of something unpleasant that Lukas didn't understand until he remembered what Esme had said earlier. James DeLaune had carried his daughter's body back from the farmhouse and placed her in his study.

Lukas walked around the sofa, sliding his hand across the

cracked leather as his gaze lifted to the carved oak mantel above the fireplace. It was crowded with photographs and they were all of Rachel DeLaune.

And in every shot, her smile charmed and mesmerized, but there was something haunting in her eyes.

If she'd lived, she would have grown into a knockout. Already at sixteen, she'd had a smoldering innocence that could drive a man wild. Maybe even compel him to kill.

Was that why she'd been murdered so viciously? Had she been the victim of a boyfriend's jealous rage…or the target of a madman's fantasy?

There wasn't a single photograph of James DeLaune's youngest daughter. Esme said that Sarah and her father had never gotten along, and as Lukas studied the shrine to James's dead daughter, he began to understand what his youngest must have faced. Here in this room, Rachel's presence was almost tangible. Here in this room, the old man had tried desperately to keep his favorite daughter alive, but the only way he could do that was by shutting everyone else out. Including Sarah.

Lukas reached for one of the photographs, then froze when he heard a noise over his left shoulder.

He turned, almost expecting—dreading—to see Rachel DeLaune's ghost slipping up behind him. When he found the room empty, he let out a quick breath.

Exiting the study, he walked back through the living room to the foyer where he stood listening to the house. The noise was coming from upstairs. Someone was moving about on the second floor.

He unzipped his jacket to make his weapon more accessible as he quietly climbed the stairs, his gaze lifted to the shadows above him.

The rooms on the second floor opened onto the gallery,

and as he neared the top of the stairs, he zeroed in on the door to his far right. It was slightly ajar and he could tell the sound was coming from inside that room.

Keeping his shoulder pressed to the wall, he drew his gun and gripped it with both hands, barrel pointed at the floor, so anyone waiting inside the room wouldn't be able to knock it from his hands.

Pushing the door open with the toe of his boot, he flattened himself against the wall and waited a heartbeat before easing around the doorjamb and through the bedroom doorway. Crouching, he quickly shifted his gaze from one corner to the next, noting the position of the bed, nightstand, dresser and desk.

No one was there. The room was empty.

And it was freezing inside. Colder than anywhere else in the house. Someone had cracked a window and frigid air rushed in. Lukas hadn't noticed the open window from the outside, but now he realized it was the source of both the cold and the sound. When the wind gusted a certain way, a tree limb scraped across the glass panes, like a bony hand trying to find a way in.

Lukas wondered if Esme had left the window open the last time she'd come over to air out the house.

Holstering his weapon, he took a quick look out the window. The tree grew right up against the house. Someone could easily scale the branches and climb onto the roof. And maybe that same someone had found a window unlocked and crawled in out of the cold last night.

Better have another look around outside, he decided. Maybe he'd missed a footprint.

As he started to turn away from the window, he saw a reflected movement behind him in the glass; his heart jumped

as he whirled. His arm came up, but complacency and exhaustion slowed his reflexes. He barely deflected the blow as
the lamp connected with his skull and his knees folded like
the flimsy legs on Esme's ironing board.

Ears ringing, he fell back, unable to catch himself. He
sensed a motion toward the door, heard a rush of footsteps,
but he couldn't seem to focus as he crashed into the wall and
slid down to the floor.

Cold air rushed over Lukas's face, rousing him. He smelled
damp earth and more faintly, the scent of something burning.

Someone leaned over him and said something, and he came
alert then, throwing up a defensive arm as he reached for his
gun with the other hand.

"Hey, take it easy. I'm trying to help you."

Slowly the face floating over him came into focus. It was
Esme Floyd's grandson. Lukas barely knew the man, but he
had no trouble placing him. He'd seen Curtis around town a
lot lately. He had a tendency to stand out, not because of his
race, but because of his looks. Handsome and graceful with
the light skin and green eyes of a Creole, he also had hints
of his grandmother in his features. The wide nose and high
cheekbones, the quiet dignity and keen intelligence. The way
his eyes seemed to size Lukas up with one sweep.

"What happened?" he asked. "Do you remember?"

Lukas put a hand to the back of his head and tentatively
touched the egg-size lump. "Somebody slipped up behind me
and coldcocked me good, that's what. I didn't hear a damn
thing until he was right on me. It'll be hell living that down."

"If I were you, I'd be more concerned about the damage to
my brain than my ego. You took a nasty blow to the head."

"I've had worse. Nothing a couple of aspirin won't take

care of." Lukas pushed himself up and tried not to react to the pain that shot through the base of his skull.

But Curtis saw the wince and said sternly, "We need to get you to the hospital. You probably have a concussion."

"I appreciate the professional opinion, Dr. Floyd, but like I said, I've had a lot worse." Lukas glanced at the smashed lamp on the floor, then his gaze slowly lifted. "What are you doing here anyway?"

Curtis sat back on his heels and stared at Lukas for a moment before getting to his feet. Something flared in his eyes, an icy disdain for any real or imagined innuendo in Lukas's question. "So that's it. You come to, see a black man standing over you and your first instinct is to assume I'm the one who hit you."

"I never said that."

"That was the implication, though, wasn't it?"

"It was just a simple question, Dr. Floyd. No offense intended."

Curtis shrugged. "Not that there's any reason I should have to justify myself to you, but my grandmother sent me over here. We're going out to lunch, and she wanted to know if you'd found anything before we go."

Lukas sniffed the air. "You smell something burning?"

"No, but it's probably someone down the street burning leaves."

"It's too wet to burn leaves." Lukas was sitting upright now. His gaze went back to the window as a gust of wind blew away the scent, bringing a fresh chill into the room. "Damn, that air's cold."

Curtis had retreated to the door and stood with one shoulder propped against the jamb. His professional concern had dissolved, and now he made no move to close the window or offer assistance to Lukas as he struggled to his feet.

Lukas went over to the window and glanced out. A tree limb scraped against the panes, reminding him that he'd been standing in that same spot when his attacker had slipped up behind him.

Now as he shoved the window down, he saw only his own reflection in the glass. But he had a feeling he was missing something. He'd seen something, heard something that now seemed to elude him.

He turned. Curtis was still in the doorway, watching him through narrowed eyes. Beneath a brown leather jacket, he wore a crisp white shirt that brought to mind Miss Esme at her ironing board.

For some reason, a snippet of their conversation suddenly came back to Lukas. *"You think a mother won't lie to keep her boy out of that kind of trouble?"*

"Did you see anyone on your way over here?" he asked. "Somebody out on the street maybe?"

"Not that I noticed. Of course, you have only my word on that." Curtis's expression was inscrutable except for the glimmer of contempt in his eyes. That was all too easily discernible.

He straightened, his every move elegant and unhurried in spite of the simmering hostility. He looked to be a man who knew exactly where he was going and how he intended to get there. And Lukas had a feeling he wouldn't let anyone stand in his way.

"I need to get back before my grandmother starts to worry," Curtis said. "Are you sure you won't let me take you to the hospital? If you were my patient, I'd order a CAT scan, an MRI and depending on the results, an overnight stay in the hospital."

"For one little bump on the noggin?"

"It's always best to eliminate unpleasant possibilities."

"On that, we agree," Lukas said. "Which is why the only place I'm headed at the moment is out to my car for my fingerprint kit." He squatted beside the broken lamp. "You didn't touch anything in here, did you?"

"You mean anything other than your pulse? I'm afraid I did." Curtis folded his arms. "I had to move the lamp out of the way to examine you."

"Then we'll need to get a set of your prints for comparison. Assuming, of course, you're not already in the system."

Lukas had meant it as a joke, but when he glanced up, he could see Curtis's nostrils quiver as he let out a sharp breath.

"Sorry. I guess that wasn't so funny."

The skin on Curtis's face was suddenly as gray as the winter sky, and when their gazes met, he had to look quickly away. In the space of a heartbeat, the elegant facade had crumbled, and behind those green eyes, vulnerability weakened his contempt.

"Is there something you need to tell me?" Lukas asked softly, taken aback by the man's swift change.

Curtis lifted a hand and wiped it across his face, as if he could somehow scrub away the cracks and restore his stoic demeanor. "I was in some trouble in college," he finally said. "Everything eventually got cleared up and the charges were dropped, but I was booked, processed, whatever you want to call it. I don't know whether my fingerprints ended up in the system or not."

"You want to tell me what happened?"

"No. It's in the past." He wore a pinkie ring on his right hand and the fingers of his left hand kept tugging at the gold. "My grandmother doesn't know about any of this and I'd like to keep it that way. My father's put her through a lot over the years. I don't want her worried about me."

"I can understand that. But you know what they say about secrets. They have a way of coming back to haunt you when you least expect it."

"You sound as if you've had some experience."

Lukas shrugged. "We all have secrets. Just take a look around this room."

Curtis's gaze wandered over Lukas's face. "What are you talking about?"

He waved a hand, encompassing the blue walls and white linens. The posters of rock stars and screen idols. The dressing table strewn with makeup, perfume bottles and corsage ribbons. "This was Rachel DeLaune's room, wasn't it?"

Curtis pressed his lips together. "You ask that as if you assume I should know. But I was never allowed anywhere in this house except the kitchen."

"But you knew this was Rachel's room. How could you not? Even I know it's hers. All you have to do is take a look around. I doubt anything's been changed since the night she died." Lukas paused, letting a long silence settle between them. "You can still feel her presence in here, can't you? Tell me what she was like."

The green eyes deepened angrily. "That's not really what you want to know, is it?"

So he had more than just his grandmother's nose and cheekbones, Lukas thought. He'd also inherited her insight. "No, you're right. What I really want to know is if she was seeing anyone when she died. I can't find a mention of a boyfriend in the police report. But a beautiful girl like that? She must have had plenty of guys sniffing around." He walked over to the dressing table, and for a moment, swore he could still smell her perfume. After fourteen years.

"She dated," Curtis said. "I don't think there was anyone special."

"Did she date you?"

Surprise flashed over his handsome features, and then he laughed, an ugly sound that didn't suit his suave veneer. "You're joking, right? You think James DeLaune would have allowed his precious daughter, his *princess,* to go out with someone like me?"

"Why not? Look how you turned out. I bet you were always smart and ambitious."

"That wouldn't have mattered to James DeLaune. As far as he was concerned, I was never anything but the housekeeper's mulatto grandson."

Lukas glanced up. "That's not a word you hear much these days, even around here."

"Maybe you just haven't been listening," Curtis said bitterly. "This town hasn't changed as much as you seem to think."

They were getting into some uncomfortable territory, Lukas decided. *Might even be a little dangerous.*

"Men like James DeLaune and my father grew up in a different era. Some of them have a hard time rising above their upbringing."

Curtis gave him a cynical look. "Are you making excuses for racism?"

"No. I'm just stating a sad fact. Times change, but sometimes that change is slow to take hold in a small town like this. But at least nowadays you won't get lynched for dating a white woman."

"And that's your idea of progress?" Curtis's lips curled into a sneer. "You know as well as I do it doesn't take a rope to lynch a man. All you have to do is trump up some charges against him, threaten his scholarship, ruin his reputation so that you can destroy his future and keep him in his place."

Lukas cocked his head. "Is that what happened to you? Is that why your prints may or may not be in the system?"

"Like I said, it's all in the past. And I think you and I are finished here." Curtis turned to leave.

"Dr. Floyd?"

He paused.

"Were you in love with Rachel DeLaune?"

He lifted his gaze to the ceiling, his expression a mixture of anger, resolution and sorrow as he stared at some distant point. Then he closed his eyes. "Why are you dredging all this up now? Why can't you let her rest in peace?"

Lukas shrugged. "I guess I just don't like mysteries. They eat at me. Keep me awake at night." He drew in a breath, letting the lingering scent of Rachel DeLaune's perfume strengthen his resolve. "And call me crazy, but I don't like the idea of a killer walking around loose in my town."

9

Sarah could lose herself in a beautiful tattoo. She'd always loved to paint and draw, but there was nothing so rewarding as working on a living canvas. The black work laid the foundation, but color brought the image to life.

"No scratching, no picking, no peeling," she warned as she carefully applied a bandage to her client's fresh tattoo. "Leave the gauze on for at least four hours. You can clean it with soap and water, but don't use a washcloth. That's too rough."

"Should I put Vaseline on it to keep it moist?" the client asked. It was her first tattoo and she was still a bit anxious.

"No Vaseline. You can apply a little medicated ointment for the first couple of days. After that, a good moisturizer. Very important to keep it moisturized. But don't worry about remembering all this now. I'll give you a sheet of instructions to take home with you."

Sarah walked the client out, then returned to her station to clean up. She heard the front door open and, glancing around the partition, she saw Sean walk in. The sight of him threw her, just as his phone call had the night before. They'd gone for months without any contact and suddenly here he was, pushing his way back into her life.

But that was Sean. His arrogance allowed him to believe he could come and go as he pleased, with little regard to the emotional toll on those he left in his wake. Sarah supposed in some respects he wasn't so different from her. She'd gone through most of her life with her armor firmly in place. It was the only way she'd known how to survive, growing up in the shadow of a worshipped older sister.

Even now, she could remember when the revelation hit her that she and Rachel were far from equals in her father's eyes. It wasn't so much the expensive presents he lavished on Rachel or the amount of time he spent with her. It was the way he looked at her, the way his voice softened when he spoke to her. And nothing Sarah did or said could ever elicit that same kind of affection.

So the defenses had come up, the emotions were turned off, and she'd spent the remainder of her childhood and adolescence convincing herself and those around her that she didn't need anyone. She was a loner, a misfit, a girl who didn't belong anywhere except in the shadows of her own imagination.

And then Sean had come along, and she'd been tempted to let him in. He'd gotten closer to the real Sarah than anyone had in years, but there was still a part of her she couldn't let him know. A part of her she needed to keep hidden even from herself.

Maybe it was inevitable, then, that he'd turned to someone else, a woman who didn't have Sarah's emotional baggage. She wanted to be philosophical and pragmatic about their breakup, but what she still felt all these months later was hurt and confused, like the little girl who'd once tried to bully her way into her father's good graces.

Sarah wiped down the barber's chair and cleaned her station until it was spotless. The used gloves, needles and ink were tossed into the proper waste receptacles, and everything that needed to be sterilized went into the autoclave.

Once she had everything organized, she walked up to the front of the studio where Sean sat looking through an issue of *Tattoo*. As she approached, he flipped back through the pages to the picture of her that he'd found.

She'd been shot with her back to the camera so that the tattooed wings on her bare shoulders were the focus of the frame. Her face was in profile, her expression pensive, mysterious and, from certain angles, almost sinister. Like a fallen angel, the photographer had coached her.

"So you're famous now," Sean said.

"Hardly." Sarah was only one of a dozen female tattoo artists featured in the layout, most of whom were much better known within the ink-slinger subculture than she. But it took time to build a reputation, and she was both patient and passionate about her art. Notoriety would come in due time.

What she didn't have patience for were Sean's games.

"What are you doing here? I'm guessing you didn't come in for a tattoo."

"As tempting as that sounds, no." He tossed the magazine aside and stood. "I was hoping you could spare a few minutes. I need to talk to you about last night. I'm still puzzling over some of the things we saw at the crime scene."

"What's that got to do with me? I've already told you everything I know about the victim's tattoos."

"It's not just the tattoos I need your help with," he said. "That room was loaded with symbolism."

Sarah shrugged. "Anything I could tell you about those symbols you can just as easily find out on the internet."

"Then be an ear. Let me talk it out. Sometimes that helps as much anything."

"Why me?" *Why not your wife?* she wanted to ask him.

Sean smiled. "Because this is what we do, Sarah. I talk, you listen."

His eyes were so penetrating, she felt herself slipping into a dangerous lethargy, and for a moment, it seemed as if every nerve in her body had gone crazy.

It wasn't healthy, the effect he still had on her. It wasn't right that a man like Sean Kelton—a man with the propensity to cause so much pain—should be so attractive and charismatic.

Sarah had known men like him before. Moody, intense, careless. The description probably fit her, too, but she'd always been more of a danger to herself than to anyone else. Not Sean. Sean didn't disappear from your life without first leaving a mark on your heart.

"I don't think this is a good idea," she said.

Something flared in his eyes and she could see how hard he had to work to suppress his impatience. "Anything that can help me find the whack-job responsible for slaughtering that woman is a good idea. Nothing else matters."

"Right. Nothing else matters. Because you live to catch killers, don't you, Sean?"

"Yes, I do. Is there anything wrong with that?"

"No, it's admirable. What I don't understand is why you keep trying to drag me into it. Why don't you go do your job and leave me out of it? I can't help you."

"Sarah." He took her arm when she would have turned away. "Don't make this personal. This isn't about us."

She pulled her arm from his grasp. "Don't kid yourself. Everything between us is personal."

His sigh was heavy. "I know we still have unfinished business, but I'm asking you to put that aside for now. This guy is out there somewhere and for all we know, he already has his next victim in his sights. You know about those symbols. You know about tattoos. You even know about Rorschach inkblots, so you tell me who else I should be talking to about this?" He leaned toward her, his gaze deep and probing. "You can help me find him. You may be the only one who can."

Even after living with the guy for two years, his intensity could still overwhelm her at times. Sarah had forgotten how unsettling his focus could be, and she tried her best to shake off the feeling of inevitability that his presence always evoked.

"Come on," he coaxed. "Let's just go down the street and have a cup of coffee. That's all I'm asking."

She stared at the flash on the walls for a moment, then let out a slow breath. "All right. But I can't stay long. I have a client coming in at five."

"Plenty of time," he said with a smile. "Grab a coat. It's warmed up outside, but the wind off the river's still plenty chilly."

Sarah and her partner's studio was located on Decatur, not far from the French Market, but they bypassed Café Du Monde for a smaller, quieter coffeehouse a few blocks away. She buttoned her coat as they walked along. The sky was blue and cloudless, and the weak touch of sunlight in her hair made her long for summer.

There wasn't much foot traffic on the street. The ice storm had kept most of the out-of-towners away, but by the weekend, if the temperature kept rising, the tourists would come back, perhaps not in droves, but enough to make life interesting again.

They walked side by side, hands in coat pockets, and Sarah couldn't help noticing how careful Sean was not to brush against her, even when they had to move aside for the occasional pedestrian. She understood why. He was a married man now and appearing too chummy in public with an ex-lover wouldn't be particularly helpful to his career or his marriage.

She knew she shouldn't be bothered by his caution or his distance. She told herself it was understandable and all for the best. But as they entered the coffee shop and she caught him casting a wary eye around the booths and tables, as if to make certain the patrons were all strangers, she felt the weight of regret settle in the deepest part of her heart. Regret…and a fair amount of resentment.

She'd spent two years of her life on a man who'd walked out on her without a backward glance. She wasn't going to kid herself about it, either. The only reason he was here now was because he wanted something from her. Needed something he felt he couldn't get anywhere else.

Ever since he'd moved out, a part of Sarah had been living in denial, nurturing a tiny hope that, in spite of his hasty marriage—or even because of it—he would someday wake up and realize they were meant to be together.

That hope was gone now, and as she slid into the booth across from him, she felt herself slip almost seamlessly from denial into anger—as much at her own stupidity as at anything Sean had done to her.

"You okay?"

She gave him a hard glance that seemed to take him aback for a moment. "Why wouldn't I be okay?"

"I don't know. You seem—"

"What?"

He shrugged. "Tired, I guess."

"Which is code for 'I look like shit,' right?"

"I didn't say that." His gaze moved over her face, searching for something he couldn't seem to find. Sarah took some satisfaction in knowing that her refusal to play the role in which he'd tried to cast her had left him bewildered. "You didn't get much sleep last night and that's my fault."

"Don't worry about it. I'm used to getting by on very little. Besides, I'm sure you were up all night yourself."

"You know me. I run on caffeine and adrenaline. We've always had that in common."

Which explained why their relationship had been so volatile at times. They were both wired too tight. Neither of them was the type to unwind with a glass of wine in front of the television, because for people like them, relaxation came at too high a price. You had to let down your guard for that.

The waitress came over, and Sean ordered coffee while Sarah asked for hot tea. When the cup was in front of her, she concentrated on the tea bag so that she could avoid Sean's gaze.

"There's something I'd like to ask you," she finally said.

"What is it?"

She looked up, expecting to find his eyes on her, but instead he was staring out the window, his mind seemingly a million miles away.

He barely knows I'm even here, Sarah thought. She could have been anybody.

"What does Catherine think of your tattoo?"

That caught his attention. His expression turned wary and anxious, like a soldier confronted by a potential minefield he knew he had to somehow navigate. "She doesn't like it much."

"Does she know what it means?"

"She knows it's an infinity symbol over my heart. So, yeah, I'd say she's probably worked it out. But if you're asking whether she knows what it meant to us...why I got it... no, I've never talked about it. That's just between you and me." His gaze burned into Sarah's until she had to look away.

"Well, I guess whatever it once meant really doesn't matter anymore, does it?"

"It matters," he murmured.

Sarah glanced away. It was all well and good to tell herself she'd finally accepted their breakup, that she could now even admit that it was all for the best. But when Sean looked at her as if she were the only woman in the world, when he made her remember the good times—and there had been quite a few—moving on wasn't so easy.

A man came into the shop and the frosty air that followed him in chilled Sarah. She thought about putting her coat back on, not so much to ward off the cold, but because she wanted to use it as another layer of armor between her and Sean.

"I don't know why I even asked," she muttered. "That's not why we're here, is it? You want me to help you find a killer. Should I be flattered that you think I have some sort of insight into a psychopath?"

He smiled. "Well, we all have our talents."

He was trying to use humor to defuse the tension, but he'd sadly misjudged Sarah's mood. All he'd done was piss her off even more. "And we both know what *your* talents are, don't we, Sean?"

"Do we?" He sounded amused.

"You're a master at avoiding confrontations. Leaving me a note when you moved out. Sending Danny around to tell me that you'd gotten married. I think the term I'm searching for here is emotional coward."

His smiled vanished and he gave her a cynical look. "That's pretty harsh coming from the queen of denial."

"Go to hell."

Her retort was punctuated by his angry silence. "Feel better?"

"No," she said bitterly. "Not even close."

He sat back against the booth and watched her. "Then by all means, continue. Let's get this over with."

"That's all this is to you, isn't it? A nuisance. An inconvenience. Something to be dealt with so we can move on to your agenda. I don't know why I never noticed before."

"What?"

"How easily you can switch gears. The looks, the smiles, even that poignant little revelation about your tattoo. *It matters*," she said in a mocking tone. "It's all very calculated, isn't it? But once in a while, the real you slips in. Like now."

He shook his head. "You've lost me. But if you want me to admit that I handled things badly when we split up, then fine. Yes, I did. I went about it in just about the worst possible way. Sending Danny to tell you about my marriage… that was a shitty thing to do and I've regretted it ever since. But believe it or not, at the time, I thought it would be easier coming from him."

"Oh, I'm sure it was easier—for you." She folded her arms on the table.

"I thought it would be easier for you, too. In case you haven't noticed, you and I have a hard time even being in the same room together."

"Luckily, that's not something we have to worry about anymore. Or it wouldn't be, if you'd just leave me alone."

"I didn't have to twist your arm to get you to come here."

The smug note in his voice made her want to slap him.

"That's a lapse in judgment I can easily fix." She picked up her coat.

"Sarah, wait."

He put his hand over hers, and his fingers were warm and strong and reassuring. An unexpected gentleness that jolted Sarah to her very core. She wanted to cling to his hand, draw his fingers to her lips, hold on to his warmth for as long as she could. The intensity of her longing both shamed and repulsed her, and she snatched her hand away.

"I'm sorry," he said. "Please don't go."

She drew a breath.

"Look, I realize under the circumstances this is asking a lot. I don't have any right to expect your help." He glanced down at his coffee, frowning, as if he didn't quite know how they'd gotten to this point. "But it's like I said earlier. This isn't about us. It's about finding this guy before he kills someone else."

"How can you be so sure that he will? You've only found one body."

"Call it instinct. Hell, call it paranoia, but I have a very bad feeling about this one. What he did to that woman wasn't rage or passion. It was a compulsion."

"And you think I can somehow help you figure out what it is that's driving him? I'm a tattoo artist, Sean, not a psychic."

"But you also know about the occult. I remember all those books you had lying around the house. Some of them un-nerved the shit out of me."

She glanced up. "Really? You never said anything."

"What was I supposed to say?" His fingers drummed an impatient staccato on the tabletop. "He's into that stuff, too, only he's twisted it somehow. I can't explain it, but I know this guy is deeply fucked-up in the head. And I know he's not finished."

His words filled Sarah with the kind of dread usually reserved for her nightmares. She suddenly remembered the feeling she'd had standing on her frozen porch the night before, watching the snow. She'd had the distinct impression that her dream had somehow unleashed Ashe Cain. And that he might be coming for her again.

She glanced at Sean, her stomach knotting in sudden agitation. "What do you want me to do?"

"Just tell me what you saw last night, what you felt. Your first impression, your gut instinct. Anything you can remember."

"I thought you only wanted me to listen."

"No. What I want is for you to help me get inside this creep's head."

But that wasn't a place she should go, Sarah thought. She didn't even know how to fight the demons that resided inside her own head. The very last thing she needed was a connection to another killer.

Yet, even as she tried to block her focus and strengthen her defenses, her mind was already racing with images from the night before. The house, the steps, the porch, the brass numbers hammered into the door frame. It was like she was back there again, moving through the empty rooms.

"I do remember something," she said hesitantly.

"What?"

"It may not mean anything. It could be just a coincidence."

"I still want to hear about it."

"You have to consider it along with everything else we saw last night. Keep it in context. Taken alone, it doesn't sound like much."

He nodded. "Let's hear it."

"When we were going inside the house, I noticed that the

number by the door started with a one and an eight. Eighteen is three times six. Six-sixty-six. The number of the beast mentioned in the Book of Revelation."

She half expected Sean to blow off her observation as a stretch and she really wouldn't have been all that sorry if he had. She didn't like talking about this stuff. It unnerved the shit out of her, too.

"I don't think anything about that crime scene was a coincidence. He seems to be heavily into symbolism and hidden meanings. It could be that he scoped out locations ahead of time, maybe even used the phone book to check for street addresses containing the right numbers. All he had to do was search until he found an empty house. He's not necessarily someone who's familiar with the area, just someone who knows how to find what he needs."

Sean looked at Sarah and nodded. "Good. What else?"

The waitress had brought glasses of ice water along with their tea and coffee, and Sarah absently traced her finger in the condensation. "I thought I smelled sulphur when we first entered the house."

"Sulphur? That's a pretty hard odor to miss. I didn't smell it, and no one else mentioned it."

Sarah shrugged. "Maybe it was just my imagination, then. I was dreaming about it earlier when you called."

"You were dreaming about sulphur? Jesus Christ, Sarah." He looked worried. "You're still having the nightmares, then."

"Yeah, when I can get to sleep."

"Are you still seeing that shrink?"

Her gaze dropped. "I really don't want to talk about that right now, and anyway, I need to be getting back to the studio."

"Don't go yet. You still have some time, and I think we're

making progress. I might never have known about the significance of the house number without you." He paused. "What
else can you tell me about the symbol he left upstairs? You
called it an *udjat,* right?"

"Like I said, you can get all this off the internet. More, actually. But what I do remember is that it's usually depicted as
the right eye, which represents the sun. The left eye—or the
mirror image—represents the moon. The killer drew both
in that room."

"Any idea why?"

She didn't answer at first. Her attention was caught by what
she had unconsciously traced on the side of the frosty glass.

I am you.

"Sarah?"

With the tip of her finger, she obliterated the killer's message, wondering if Sean had noticed the spidery script. "Sorry.
I was just thinking. If I had to guess, I'd say the killer is in
some sort of conflict with himself."

"The truly fucked-up ones usually are," he agreed. "Which
would go a long way in explaining his knowledge of Rorschach inkblots, wouldn't it? At some time or other, he's probably been in treatment. Now, if we could just figure out what
that particular inkblot means to him, we'd be in business."

"I don't think you'll ever know that," Sarah said. "But his
compulsion to tattoo his victim may tell you something. How
familiar are you with Leviticus?"

He gave her a bemused glance. "I know it's from the Bible."

"There's a verse that goes something like this: *Ye shall not
make any cuttings in your flesh nor print any marks upon you.* Some
people interpret the passage to mean that piercings and tattoos
are marks of the devil. I get that a lot from the true believers
who come into the studio hell-bent on saving my soul." In

spite of its notorious decadence, New Orleans was still, at its heart, a very spiritual city.

"And you think that's what he was doing…marking his victim for the devil?"

"I don't know. It's a possibility, I guess."

"But she already had tattoos," Sean said.

"They were old and faded. She didn't take care of them. Maybe he took that to mean she'd repented."

Sean ran his thumb back and forth across his bottom lip. "So he had to mark her again. First with the inkblot on her back and then with the pentagram in her palm."

"It wasn't a pentagram," Sarah said. "I meant to tell you last night. It was a triangle enclosed in a circle."

"What's the difference?"

She hesitated, not certain how deep of an explanation she wanted to get into. "Thaumaturgic triangles are used for casting spells and summoning demons. The triangle is the door through which the demon passes and the circle is used to protect the conjuror from possession."

Sean gave a low whistle. "So he tattoos her, kills her and inks a triangle in her palm to summon a demon. Just a normal day at the office for this guy."

"I noticed something else about that triangle," Sarah said. "It was a mess. The lines were scratchy and inconsistent, which means the needle didn't go in deep enough. That's the sign of an amateur. Nothing at all like the quality of the tattoo on her back."

Sean thought about that for a moment. "The adrenaline was still pumping from the kill. He probably had the shakes."

"No, I don't think it was that. The styles are completely different. And think about everything else we've talked about.

The symbolism of the left and right *udjats*. The inkblot with two distinct but identical images."

"Twins?"

"Not just a twin. A mirror image. Two sides of the same person."

"Identical twins, then."

"Maybe."

Sean sat back. "I never even considered that, but damn, Sarah, you may be onto something."

She could see the excitement building in his eyes, and the air around him seemed to crackle with electricity. He always got like this when a case started to break his way.

"You don't think I've lost my mind, then?" Her tone was light, but she was only half joking.

"Do you really want me to answer that?"

"Sure. Why not?"

He studied his coffee for a moment, and when he finally looked up, Sarah's heart thudded against her chest. Something had shifted...changed. There was something in his eyes that hadn't been there before. Something that made her react with an almost-violent start.

"You really want to know what I'm thinking?" He leaned into the table. "I'm wondering how I've managed to solve a damn thing without you. I've missed you, Sarah."

She jerked back as if he'd tried to physically assault her. "Why would you say that to me now?"

His eyes flashed. "Because it's how I feel. And no matter what you might think, it wasn't calculated. I told you because it's the truth, and because there's something else you should know. No, let me put it a different way. There's something I want you to know." His gaze held hers until she finally broke the contact. "Leaving you was the biggest mistake of my life."

Sarah could scarcely breathe she was so angry. He had no right saying any of this to her now, and the fact that he thought he could, without consequences, infuriated her.

"You're unbelievable."

He rubbed a hand across his face. "I know how this sounds. And I know there's no way I can possibly explain why I did what I did without making myself sound like a complete asshole."

"Oh, do go on. That's never stopped you before."

He dropped his hand to the table. "You're not going to cut me an inch of slack, are you?"

"Why should I?"

"God, you can be—"

"What?" she cut in. "A bitch?"

"No, not a bitch. That's not you. But you are a hard person to live with. You have to know that. The insomnia. The night terrors. Those damn pills you take. You're still letting the past eat you up inside, and all that anxiety takes a toll on those around you. And it's not like I don't have a shitload of misery of my own to deal with. Some of the things I've seen since Katrina…" He trailed off, his eyes bloodshot and haunted. "Day in and day out. That takes a toll, too, and I needed some downtime. I needed to be with someone I didn't have to worry about twenty-four hours a day."

"You wanted someone safe," she said.

"Yeah, maybe."

"And that was Catherine."

He glanced around without answering. "Christ, I need a cigarette."

"You quit smoking a long time ago."

"Old habits are hard to break," he muttered. "Sometimes the cravings come back when you least expect them."

Sarah was scarcely hearing a word. Her head was filled with confused, angry clatter, like a trapped bird flailing helplessly against a wire cage. "Tell me about her."

He gave her a doubtful look. "I don't think that's a good idea."

"Why not? Like you said, let's get it all out there so we can be done with this."

He waited a moment, as if sensing a trap. When she didn't say anything else, he shrugged. "All right. We grew up together. We dated all through high school. We even talked about getting married when we graduated."

Shit.

Maybe she didn't want to hear this after all, because every word that came out of his mouth twisted the knife in her gut a little deeper.

"So what happened?"

"Different colleges, different cities, different ambitions." He shrugged. "We drifted apart and eventually lost touch. I didn't see her for years. And then, there she was one day in the same restaurant, seated a few tables over. We got to talking, reminiscing about the old days, and it made me realize how easy life had once been."

"With her."

"That's the connection I made in my mind, I guess."

"So you rekindled the old flame," Sarah said scathingly. "Was this meeting before or after you moved out of my house?"

He was silent.

"I see." She glanced down at her hands. "Were you sleeping with her before you left?"

"No. But to be honest, that's why I moved out. I knew we

were headed in that direction and I didn't want to cheat on you. I didn't want to play around behind your back."

"What a fucking hero you are. So you moved out and four months later you were married."

"And that was the second biggest mistake of my life."

His words fell like tiny bombs between them. His eyes were on her, and Sarah knew he was waiting for her to say something, but she was utterly speechless.

"Well?" he prompted.

"You've only been married a few months. How can you already feel that way?"

"I felt that way after the first week."

"Instant regret?" She shook her head. "I would have hoped for a little more maturity from someone your age. You know, like giving your marriage a fair shot and all."

He frowned. "This isn't exactly the reaction I expected from you."

"Then what the hell *did* you expect?"

He glanced around. "Lower your voice, for Christ's sake."

She ignored him. "Did you think that you and I would just pick up where we left off? That's not going to happen. I've moved on."

"With someone else?"

"None of your business."

"Oh, *that's* mature." He started to say something else, but his phone rang and he snatched it out of his pocket to check the display. "Shit."

"Go ahead and take the call." Sarah grabbed her coat. "We're done here anyway."

"I'd like to walk you back to the studio. Will you wait a minute?"

"For you, Sean?" She gave a bitter laugh. "I don't think so."

IO

Autopsies and hangovers were never a good way to start the day, Sean decided on Wednesday morning as he suited up in the changing room at the morgue. He shook out a couple of aspirin from the bottle he carried in his pocket and washed them down with the last sip of his lukewarm coffee.

Crime scenes he could handle, but postmortems left him queasy for hours, even on good days. Already, the coffee was churning in his stomach.

If he ever bothered to analyze his aversion, he might conclude that it was the inhumanity of the procedure that bothered him. After all that cutting and sawing, the body was, in the end, just a slab of meat not so different from what he might see at the butcher's.

But Sean didn't spend too much time thinking about any of that until the moment was upon him. Like now. And then he had to work very hard to convince himself that he didn't have a good reason to skip out on this autopsy. He needed to be here. No matter how efficient the pathologist or how thorough the postmortem, certain details were almost always left out of the report.

And, as strange as it sounded, he'd found that being present for the final procedure had a way of reinforcing his bond with the deceased. That tenuous connection between investigator and victim that could sometimes get lost in the morass of cases that crossed a homicide detective's desk every single week.

Unlike a lot of cops he'd worked with over the years, he'd never mastered the ability to use humor or indifference to inoculate himself from the more grisly aspects of the job. He felt for the victims. He remembered their faces in his sleep.

Pushing open the door with his shoulder, he stepped into the autopsy suite. The room was spotless now, but Sean had no trouble imagining what it would look like once the procedure got under way. Autopsies were messy. Blood splashing onto the floor and equipment, dripping from the pathologist's hands and from the scales used to weigh the internal organs. In two hours' time, the area around the table would look like something from a slasher movie.

Dr. Frank Canard, the Orleans Parish coroner, was already inside, studying an X-ray in the viewer. He glanced over his shoulder when he heard the door close and gave Sean a brief nod. "Good. You're here. We can get started."

Louisiana law required that all coroners be physicians, and Dr. Canard was also a forensic pathologist who had served in the position for over twenty years. He'd seen it all during his tenure as coroner in a city with one of the highest murder rates in the country. He'd performed autopsies in some of New Orleans's most sensational cases. The grisly, sordid slaying of a beloved priest back in the eighties. The serial murders of a dozen prostitutes during the nineties. He'd once said, though, that nothing in his career had prepared him for Katrina and the hundreds of bodies that had passed through his makeshift morgue in the aftermath.

He was tall, wiry and grizzled, a once ruggedly handsome man with the nose and dogged determination of a prizefighter and the dignified demeanor of old Southern gentry. Even up to his elbows in blood and gore, he never lost that air of elegance and refinement that made him at home in some of the most fashionable salons in the state.

"Detective LeJeune should be here any minute, but we don't need to wait," Sean said. "I can fill him in later." He walked over to the foot of the table, carefully averting his eyes from the corpse. He focused instead on the X-ray Dr. Canard had been studying when he first came in. "Find anything interesting?"

"In the film? Nothing surprising."

Before he could elaborate, the door opened and Danny hurried into the room. He was gowned and gloved, but his mask still flopped around his neck. "Sorry I'm late. Kayla's car wouldn't start again. She had to drop me off at the motor pool and it took forever to check out a car." Fumbling with his mask, he walked over to the foot of the table and stood beside Sean. "What'd I miss?"

Unlike his partner, Danny had no qualms about attending autopsies. Like everything else about the job, he took postmortems in stride. "Man, oh, man." He shook his head as he stared down at the slab. "I thought she looked rough the other night, but *damn*."

"The condition of the body has nothing to do with who she was as a person," Dr. Canard gently chided him.

"I know that, Doc, and I don't mean any disrespect. But

thirty-six hours in the cooler sure didn't do her any favors, did it?"

Sean's gaze dropped to the table and his stomach lurched to his throat. He had to swallow very hard to keep that second cup of coffee down.

Jesus.

He looked away, drew in a gulp of filtered air, then glanced back. Danny was right. Even in death, time was never on a victim's side. Refrigeration couldn't stave off the inevitable bacterial decomposition forever, and the harsh overhead lighting made the gashes in her face and neck stand out even more ghoulishly against the chilled pallor of her skin.

But the natural breakdown of tissue and organs was the least of it. The killer's alteration of his victim's features would haunt Sean for weeks.

The corners of her mouth had been sliced in upward curls, creating a macabre imitation of a grin. Her eyelids had been removed, leaving a wide-eyed, waxy stare that sent a chill down Sean's spine.

Whatever beauty the woman once possessed had been stolen from her. All that was left of her face was a ghastly death mask carved by a psycho's deft hand.

"The throat wound was mortal," Dr. Canard was saying as he pulled the magnifier toward him and bent over the body. "The cut begins at the left carotid and extends to the right, severing the left artery, the left jugular and the sternomastoid. The trachea is partly severed. The right internal and external carotid and jugular are also severed." He glanced up. "Pretty much the only thing left intact is the spinal column."

"In other words, he damn near cut off her head," Danny said. "What about her face? Any chance he did that after she was dead?"

"No, I'm afraid not. But she suffered a severe blow to the head. It's entirely possible she was unconscious before he started cutting." Dr. Canard picked up a marker and pointed to an area on the skull X-ray that looked like a small spider-web. "You can see the fracture here on the film. The depression in the skull is a little bigger than a quarter. About the size of a hammer, I'd say. The bone directly under the impact point is driven in, toward the brain, leaving an imprint of the weapon." He demonstrated an air blow with an invisible hammer.

"And you think the blow was hard enough to render her unconscious?"

"I'd say so, but we won't know the extent of brain damage until we open up the skull."

"Is there anything about the pattern or position of the wounds to suggest there was more than one attacker?" he asked.

Danny turned to stare in surprise at the question.

Sean shrugged. "Doc?"

He was looking through the magnifier again. "The cuts appear to have been made by the same knife. I don't see any unusual striations or marks in the tissue and cartilage so I think the weapon had a smooth blade. A very sharp one." He glanced up. "Is there a particular reason you think there may have been more than one attacker?"

"The tattoos on her back and palm are both fresh, but I think they were made by two different artists. The needle didn't go in deep enough in her hand, which caused that scratchy, feathery appearance. I'm told that's the mark of an amateur. The one on her back was put there by a pro. Or at least someone who knew what he was doing." Sean could still feel Danny's eyes on him, but he didn't turn.

"I don't see anything in the cuts to substantiate multiple at-tackers, but I've found something on the torso that has me a bit puzzled." Dr. Canard moved the light down the body. "The purplish discoloration on the lower abdomen is postmortem lividity. The victim was found lying on her stomach so that's where the blood pooled. But notice the fainter discoloration on her upper abdomen and chest." He used the marker to point to an area just under the right breast and another on the left side of her chest, just below the shoulder blade.

"It looks greenish," Sean said. "Putrification?"

"No, it's bruising," Dr. Canard said. "As you know, bruises on a corpse, especially when they don't show up at first, can be tricky. The first thing we have to do is determine whether they were made before or after death. Size, color change, the presence of swelling and coagulation are all indications of an-temortem bruises, which is what we have here."

"Can you tell what made them?" Sean asked.

"We can make an educated guess. Bruises are caused by blunt trauma that damages blood vessels beneath the skin sur-face, allowing blood to leak out into the surrounding tissue. The characteristics of the object causing the bruise are usually obscured because blood tends to spread out or diffuse from the point of impact. That's why scalp injuries can sometimes result in black eyes. But if the injuries are inflicted immedi-ately prior to death, the loss of circulatory blood pressure can limit diffusion and the pattern of the causative object may be retained. A hard kick, for example, might reproduce the pat-tern of the sole."

"So is that what we're looking at here?" Danny asked. "The imprint of a shoe?"

"Not exactly. The shapes appear more defined in the pho-tographs we took, but let me see if I can show you." He leaned over the body, one gloved hand carefully tracing the outline of the bruises with the marker. When he was finished, he pushed the light away and glanced up. "Now do you see?"

Danny walked over to the side of the table to get a better view. Sean stayed where he was, his gaze riveted on the roundish shapes Dr. Canard had traced. Each bruise was about three inches in diameter and had a wedge cut out of the top.

Danny drew back. "What the hell...?"

The realization of what they were looking at dawned on Sean at the same time and his blood went cold with shock.

"I'd say they look a bit like cloven footprints," Dr. Canard said.

Danny moved back to the end of the table where he could eye the bruises from another angle. "Are you saying...? What the hell *are* you saying? The victim was trampled by some kind of animal?"

Sean's mind flew back to the crime scene, to Sarah's question about unusual prints. How had she known? *How the hell had she known?*

Suddenly short of breath, he had an overpowering urge to rip off his mask and head for the nearest exit. But running away from the questions storming his head wasn't an option, and besides, peculiar behavior in front of Dr. Canard wasn't a good idea. Coroners in Louisiana had the authority to determine mental illness in the living.

Already Danny was looking at him curiously. "You okay?"

"Yeah, yeah. It's just..." Sean drew a quick breath. "I wasn't expecting that."

"Who was? What the fuck are we dealing with here?" Danny sounded as unnerved as Sean felt, and when his phone rang, they both jumped.

Danny grabbed the phone from his pocket and walked

quickly away from the table to answer. Sean turned back to Dr. Canard. "Did you find any unusual hair or fibers in the wounds or on the body?"

"Animal hair, you mean?"

"I've read goats are sometimes used in sacrificial ceremonies. That could explain the imprints."

"I haven't found anything like that. Which could indicate the killer is somewhat familiar with forensic evidence."

"Bastard knew enough to clean up behind himself," Sean muttered.

Danny came back up to the table. He didn't bother to put his mask back on as he slipped the phone into his pocket. "That was Lapierre. She wants us to make another scene ASAP. Says there's something we need to see."

"She didn't say what it was?"

Danny's gaze had gone back to the table and Sean saw him shudder. "They've found another body."

"Did you tell Lapierre we're in the middle of an autopsy?" Sean asked irritably as he and Danny peeled off their gloves and gowns in the changing room a few minutes later.

"I did, Sean, but you know the lieutenant. When she tells you to jump, the only thing she wants to hear you ask is how high."

"She didn't at least give you a heads-up on what we're walking into?"

"All I know is that Mosley and Grimes were first up this morning and they took the call. Something at the scene must have made them nervous because they called in requesting that we come out and have a look. That's it. That's all Lapierre said." Danny staggered a bit as he pulled off his shoe protectors. "Just between you and me, though, she sounded weird."

"How so?"

"You know how she's always so cool and collected. Nerves of steel and all that. Well, today I heard something in her voice. Kind of like…I don't know…quiet excitement."

"Quiet excitement? What the hell does that mean?"

"I think whatever Mosley and Grimes reported has her all keyed up only she didn't want to show it. If I were a betting man, I'd put money on it having something to do with our Jane Doe in there." He nodded toward the autopsy suite. "Looks like you called it right, Sean. Our boy didn't want to stop at just one."

"Let's not jump the gun. We don't have any details."

Danny fished the car keys from a side pocket of his jacket. His navy blazer was one of two sports coats he wore perpetually, regardless of the season or weather. The fabric was worn thin at the elbows and the lining had a tendency to droop past the hem in the back, but Danny never seemed to notice or care. If it wasn't for Kayla, he'd probably be one of those guys who showed up every day in mismatched socks, if not something more offensive.

He waited for Sean at the door. "You might as well ride over with me. No sense taking two cars, when we'll be coming back here once we're finished."

"What's the address?"

"Just at the edge of the Quarter. North Rampart and Governor Nicholls."

Sean grabbed his jacket and followed Danny outside. The sun was shining and the temperature had already climbed into the high fifties. It was one of those strange winter days on the Gulf Coast that, in spite of the temperature, seemed more warm than cold. The ice storm that had crippled the city two days ago was already a distant memory, and the green-gold light filtering down through the live oaks promised an early spring.

Sean turned his face to the sun and let the warm rays beat down on him for a moment. He didn't want to go to a fresh crime scene, nor did he want to return later to the unfinished business at the morgue. He didn't want to think about the hoofprint bruise on the body or why Sarah had asked about strange prints at the crime scene the other night. All he wanted to do at that moment was go home, crawl back into bed and pull the covers over his head so he wouldn't have to deal with what was coming.

And yet, he could already feel something building inside him—that curious mixture of dread, excitement and morbid fascination that signaled the onslaught of his peculiar obsession. Killers intrigued him. Killers were his raison d'être.

He climbed inside the car and wrinkled his nose at the rank odor coming from an unknown source. "Don't they ever clean these things?"

Danny grinned as he slipped on his aviator-style sunglasses. "That's a rhetorical question, right?"

"Smells like wet dog in here," Sean muttered.

Danny took a whiff. "Nah, that ain't it. Something's gone bad. You root around underneath the seat, you're apt to uncover somebody's half-eaten muffuletta."

Sean cracked a window, letting the cool air rush inside. "You didn't notice the smell on the way over?"

"I did, Sean, but I figured it was a good way to desensitize my olfactory glands before I got to the morgue."

"You might have warned me about it."

"That's a two-way street, partner."

Sean turned. "What are you talking about?"

Danny shrugged, his gaze on a group of teenagers in blue

athletic jackets hanging out on a street corner. He slowed the car and gave them a long, hard look as he drove by. "Cap bills to the left," he said in disgust, noting the preference of a certain gang affiliation. "What do you wanna bet the oldest one's not more than fourteen? And here they are out loitering on a school day. We oughta run 'em in, is what we oughta do."

"They'd be back out on the street in an hour's time," Sean said.

"And that right there is a prime example of what's wrong with this city. No discipline. No sense of purpose. Hell, we're all just like those kids. Drifting along, biding our time until the next big one hits because we already know we're fucked. Seventeen feet below sea level in places and the lower we sink, the higher the gulf rises. And you can forget using the wetlands and barrier reefs as a buffer because they're all but gone. So what do we do? We bump up the levees by a few inches and pray that the next storm hits elsewhere."

"That's life in the Big Easy," Sean said with a shrug. "What else is new?"

"Not a damn thing, and that's my point. We almost get wiped off the face of the earth and nothing changes. There's something truly messed-up about this place, Sean. Sometimes I wonder why we even bother. What the hell are we still doing here?"

Sean had heard that argument before, especially since Katrina. And he had to admit, some days it seemed as if they were fighting a losing battle. The crime rate had skyrocketed. Over a hundred and fifty people had been murdered the previous year, but the D.A.'s office had managed to secure only three homicide convictions. The system had clearly broken down, and there were sections of the city that even cops didn't dare enter. Lawlessness prevailed, the kind of mind-sick violence that left people on edge and afraid of their own shadows.

Sean wasn't immune to the pressure, but for him, moving away wasn't an option. He'd been born and raised in the city. New Orleans was in his blood. For better or for worse, he was here until the bitter end.

An ironic sentiment, he supposed, considering the state of his personal life.

"So what do you think?"

About the levees? About the rising water level in the gulf? Sean realized he didn't have a clue what his partner had asked him. His mind had wandered off on its own tangent.

The lapse aggravated Danny. "You didn't hear a word I said, did you? What's eating you this morning?"

"I guess my mind's still back at the morgue."

"That was some freaky shit. You ever see anything like those bruises?"

"No." Sean stared out the window at the passing scenery, his focus zeroing in for a moment on an old woman waiting to cross the intersection. Their gazes met briefly before she quickly looked away, as if making eye contact with a stranger—any stranger—might somehow reveal her vulnerability.

"How did you figure that out about the tattoos?" Danny asked.

Sean watched the old woman in the rearview mirror. She was staring after their car. "Sarah told me."

"Why didn't you mention it before today?"

"I only found out late yesterday. I haven't had a chance to talk to you about it before now."

"You saw Sarah yesterday?"

Sean turned. "Yeah. Why?"

"Nothing. But you could have called me at home about those tattoos."

"I didn't think it was necessary. Besides, I wanted to wait and hear what Canard had to say before I brought it up. You're not really sore about it, are you?"

"Nah, forget it." But Danny's tone implied that something was bothering him.

"Look, if you've got something to say, just say it. Don't sit there and sulk all day."

Danny frowned at the road. "I don't sulk."

"Like hell you don't. Just ask Kayla."

"All right then, screw it. How long we been working together, Sean? Couple of years?"

"Almost."

"Why didn't you tell me you and Catherine split up? That's a pretty big deal. Why didn't you let me know what was going on?"

"Because I didn't need you to hold my hand," Sean said. "It was done. Why talk about it?"

"As easy as all that."

Sean glanced back out the window. "How'd you find out anyway?"

"Cat showed up at the house last night looking for you. She said you packed a bag and took off a few days ago. You won't take her calls, you won't tell her where you're staying. I guess us being friends and all, she thought I'd know how to reach you."

"What did you tell her?"

Danny lifted a hand and rubbed the back of his neck. "I told her I'm as much in the dark about your living arrangements as she is."

"She shouldn't have come by your place like that," Sean said in annoyance. "No point dragging anyone else into our shit."

"Does that include Sarah?"

"Sarah has nothing to do with this."

Danny turned his head slowly and looked at Sean over the rim of his sunglasses.

Sean frowned. "What?"

"You didn't move back in with Sarah? That's not why you don't want your wife to find out where you're staying?"

"Where the hell did you get a notion like that?"

"From Cat."

Sean stared at him in shock. "What did she say?"

"She figured if you're not staying with Kayla and me, you must be with Sarah. I got the feeling she was heading over there last night to have it out with her."

"*Shit.*"

"You haven't talked to Sarah this morning?"

Sean's head was throbbing again. He took out two more aspirin and dry-swallowed them before he answered. "No, I haven't talked to her. Why would I?"

"So you're saying your separation has nothing to do with her?"

"That's what I'm saying," Sean snapped. "Not that it's any of your business."

"It is if it affects the way you perform your job."

"It won't."

"Ice water in the veins, huh?" The car listed to the right as Danny made a sharp turn. "You're so full of shit."

"Pot meet kettle," Sean muttered.

"Joke about it all you want, but you've got some serious issues, my brother."

"Oh, boy, here we go." Sean dropped his head against the back of the seat and closed his eyes.

"Probably started when you were a kid. Your mother runs off with some guy, leaves you and your old man high and dry, and then a couple years later, he gets hit by a semi on his way home from work. *Bam!* You're screwed again. You see what's going on, don't you? It's what they call a pattern of behavior. You leave people before they get a chance to leave you."

"Wow, that is fucking deep, man. I'm impressed. I hope you didn't strain yourself figuring all that out."

"I've always had a knack for reading people," Danny said lightly. "I could probably be the next Dr. Phil if I set my mind to it."

"Come to think of it, I do see a strong resemblance." Sean sat up and studied Danny's profile. "Yeah, you're a dead ringer for the guy, especially around the hairline."

For someone who ordinarily didn't give a shit about his appearance, Danny had become overly sensitive about his thinning hair. He checked himself out in the mirror and then gave Sean a dirty look. "Here's some more insight for you. You're an asshole. How's that for deep?"

II

Strange that Danny had brought up his mother, Sean thought a few moments later, as they neared the entrance to Louis Armstrong Park off North Rampart. Because Sean's most vivid memory of her had happened inside the gates of that very park.

Shaded by live oaks and weeping willows, the lush enclave had once been a place where tourists could stop and catch their breath after the hustle and bustle of the crowds in the French Quarter. Named for the famed jazz musician, it was also known for Congo Square, an area where slaves had once been allowed to stroll on Sunday afternoons.

To Sean, though, the park would always be the place where, at twelve years old, he'd caught his mother with her lover.

That he had seen her at all that day was one of those coincidences he had looked back on later and wondered if some strange radar had led him to that exact place at that exact point in time.

Mostly, though, he'd blamed it on Donnie St. Germain. It

had been Donnie's idea that he and Sean skip the second day of the new school year because the classes and schedules were still so chaotic no one would miss them. Sean hadn't exactly resisted the plan. In fact he'd thought it was a pretty damn good idea. He and Donnie hid out until after the first bell and then took off on their bikes for a day of forbidden adventure, ending up that afternoon in the French Quarter.

They'd sat in Jackson Square for the longest time, eating snow cones as they watched the street musicians perform for the tourists. And then tiring of the circuslike atmosphere, they'd begun an exploration of the Quarter's alleyways, where the homeless and the drunk lay sleeping on flattened cardboard boxes in the sweltering heat.

Somewhere along the way, they found a half-empty pack of Marlboros and, cigarettes dangling from their lips, they pushed their bikes along the colonnaded sidewalks of Bourbon Street, gawking at the transvestites, peeking through the darkened doorways of the strip clubs, grinning because they thought they were a couple of badasses who'd pulled a fast one.

Eventually, they made their way to North Rampart where they spent some time watching a tattoo artist through a shop window. Sean had turned—he didn't even know why—and caught a glimpse of his mother entering the park across the street. It never even occurred to him that he might be mistaken. He just knew it was her.

His first inclination was to slip inside the tattoo parlor before she saw him, but he didn't have to worry about that. She was too preoccupied by the man who waited on the other side of the gate. He was tall, handsome and well-dressed. Not the kind of guy who worked in the refineries like Sean's dad, but someone who probably had a cushy office job downtown.

When Sean's mother walked up to him, the man put his

arm around her shoulders and drew her close. A moment later, they disappeared into the park.

Stunned, his heart hammering against his chest, Sean waited until Donnie went inside a store for a Coke and then he ditched him. Tearing across the street, he hid his bike in some bushes and then went through the gate.

He knew the park well enough, having been there the previous year on a school trip. He'd had a crush on his fifth-grade teacher, Mrs. Chauvin, so he'd been uncharacteristically attentive that day as she'd guided them through the highlights. All that came back to Sean as he wandered past the famous statue and across the square to the far side of the park, where he finally found his mother in the arms of the stranger, kissing him in a way Sean had never seen her kiss his father.

As he stood watching them, a murderous rage had taken hold of him, a fury so deep and devastating he found himself trembling, his hands squeezed into tight balls at his sides. He wanted to step out of the shadows and confront them, scream at them. He wanted to punch someone so bad it was almost a physical ache.

Instead, he watched for a moment longer, then turned and raced out of the park. By the time he got home, his mother's car was already in the drive, but he didn't want to face her. He never wanted to see her again.

So he got back on his bike and rode to the deserted school playground, sat alone on the merry-go-round and smoked another cigarette, not caring who saw him. When he got home, long after dark, he caught hell from his father for causing his mother to worry, which Sean found so ironic he was sorely tempted to rat her out. He wasn't sure why he kept silent. Maybe he hadn't wanted to hurt his father, but more likely, he wanted to pretend that what he saw in the park hadn't really happened. That everything in his life was still as normal as it had been that morning when his mother woke him up for school.

Two weeks later, she was gone.

It had taken Sean a long time to get over her betrayal. Of all the people in his life, he had loved her the most, but now she was nothing more to him than a distant memory.

And on the rare occasions when he found himself in Louis Armstrong Park, he didn't view it through the eyes of the disillusioned kid he'd once been, but from the jaded perspective of a cop who had seen too much. And that was fitting, he supposed, because the park had changed, too. No longer a tribute to the city's rich heritage, it was now a dangerous place where the naive or unarmed should never wander after dark.

And on the even rarer occasions when Sean looked back on his childhood, he didn't remember his mother's smile or her twinkling eyes or the books she'd read to him when he was little or the nights she'd sat up with him when he was sick. Instead, he recalled the way she'd hurried to her lover in the park. The way she'd been able to leave a son and husband so easily for a handsome, well-dressed stranger.

What Sean saw now, when he looked back, was the tragic decline of a decent, heartbroken man whose only fault lay in his inability to make a restless woman happy. Sean had often wondered over the years if his father's grief had caused him to deliberately swerve into the path of the oncoming truck. The man didn't drink or take drugs, and the accident had occurred in broad daylight. Most people who'd known Tommy Kelton had concluded that he must have fallen asleep at the wheel. There was no other explanation. None that anyone wanted to name.

His father's frame of mind the day of his death would forever remain a mystery to Sean, just like his mother's where-abouts. He had no idea where she was, or if she was even still alive. He'd never tried to find her, because he didn't see the point. He already knew everything he needed to know about her. He'd known it since the day he'd watched her in the park.

But Danny's assessment about Sean's past was way off base. It had no bearing on Sean's failed relationships. He had only himself to blame for the pain he'd caused Sarah—and now Catherine—and if he'd learned nothing else, he at least knew enough to own his mistakes.

All this flashed through Sean's mind in the time it took to drive past the park. And then he brushed his thoughts aside, forgot them, as he focused his attention on the line of patrol cars and emergency vehicles he could see up ahead.

"Shit, I just thought of something," Danny said. "Lapierre mentioned the flat was behind an old voodoo shop. Do you remember that case a while back where the guy strangled his girlfriend and cut up her body in the bathtub? Son of a bitch put her head in a pot of water on the stove. That apartment was over a voodoo shop on North Rampart. You don't think it's the same place, do you?"

"It's not the same place," Sean said.

"You sure?"

"Positive."

Danny glanced at him. "Oh, Christ, what was I thinking? You worked that scene, didn't you?"

Sean said nothing. That case, more than any other, still kept him awake at night.

"Man, that place must have been a fucking nightmare. Body parts in the oven and freezer." Danny glanced at Sean. "I can stomach a lot. You know how I am at autopsies. Cool as a cucumber. But something like that…I don't know, Sean.

I think something like that could give a guy problems for a long time. Maybe mess him up in the head for good. Not that I'm suggesting there's anything wrong with you."

"No, of course not."

"Is it true you found potatoes and carrots cut up beside the stove?"

"Jesus, Danny, do you really need the details? Let's deal with one nightmare at a time, why don't we?"

"Yeah, you're right, but I can't help wondering what makes a man snap like that. Murder in the heat of the moment is one thing, but hacking up the body of a woman you once loved…" He shook his head. "Sometimes it makes you wonder what any of us are capable of, under the right circumstances. Look at what happened during Katrina."

"You're just bound and determined to blow sunshine up my ass this morning, aren't you?"

Danny grinned. "I'm doing my best." He pulled in behind one of the squad cars and parked.

The area around the shop had been cordoned off, but as usual, a crowd had gathered on the street. Unlike the aloof bystanders who had stood outside the Marigny crime scene in the wee hours of the morning, a handful of the curious here were more aggressively inquisitive. Daylight had emboldened them, and they stopped just short of the yellow police tape, craning their necks to get a look down the narrow alleyway where most of the action was taking place.

As Sean and Danny approached the sidewalk, the chatter quieted, and for one split second, the only sound Sean heard was the tinkle of glass wind chimes hanging in the window of the shop next door. It was as if time stood still, giving him a moment to shrug off the remnants of one horror show before plunging headlong into another.

And then the reprieve ended with a burst of static from an officer's radio and the raucous laughter of a homeless man as he shuffled past the crowd on the street.

Flashing their shields to one of the young patrolmen at the perimeter, Sean and Danny dipped under the tape and headed toward the back of the building.

The alleyway was like dozens of others that were in or near the Quarter. Dark, dank and reeking of filth. The brick walls on either side were tagged with graffiti, and among the broken beer bottles that littered the cracked pavement, Sean spotted the occasional discarded syringe.

The apartment was on the ground floor and the door opened directly into the alley; there was no stoop or porch. A couple of now-dead begonias in coffee cans had been placed on either side of the door in a feeble attempt to disguise the stench of urine that emanated up from the gutter.

Two cops searched through the trash along the buildings and a third stood talking to Tony Vincent, the coroner's investigator. Sean spoke to them briefly as he opened the door.

The smell hit him like a fist in the face.

"Fuck," Danny said, and took a step back. He fished the Vicks from his pocket and dabbed a healthy dose underneath his nose. "I love the smell of menthol in the morning," he said with a grimace.

He didn't offer to share because Sean never used anything. He didn't find the vapor all that effective, and he'd learned early on that the presence of smells at a crime scene could provide valuable clues. The trick was learning how to peel away the overpowering odor of decay in order to detect the more subtle scents beneath.

Stifling his gag reflex, Sean stood just inside the door and glanced around. The studio apartment had a galley kitchen and a tiny bathroom that opened off the living-sleeping quarters. Like in a lot of old buildings in the area, the ancient plaster and brick had been patched over the years to update the plumbing and wiring. The space was cramped and dingy, and on cold nights, probably drafty as hell.

Lance Mosley and Charlie Grimes stood with their backs to the door as Patrice Petty, the crime-scene investigator, collected evidence on and around the body and another officer shot video footage of the crime scene.

The temperature inside was several degrees colder than outdoors, and Sean found himself shivering as he slid plastic booties over his shoes.

Charlie Grimes turned and gave them a nod. "Glad you boys could make it. Come looky what we got here."

Charlie was in his early fifties, tall and thick around the middle, a big bear of a man with black hair going gray at the temples. He was a good detective, amiable and dependable, if not overly creative in his investigations. Mosley, his partner, was younger and far more ambitious, but his arrogance could sometimes be a problem and he possessed none of Charlie's innate good humor. He wasn't well-liked in the department, but Sean had never had a problem with him.

As he joined the semicircle that had formed around the body, Sean's gaze dropped. The victim, a young female Caucasian with dark hair and a slender build, lay facedown on the floor. Her head was turned to one side and the matted hair that fell across her cheek obscured her features. She was naked from the waist up, and the first thing that caught Sean's attention was the tattoo on her back. It looked identical to the one on the Jane Doe in the morgue.

But unlike the Marigny crime scene, there was no blood on the floor, no symbols on the walls and ceiling, no paraphernalia to suggest she'd been tattooed at the scene. She'd been killed somewhere else, her body dumped here for a reason they had yet to discover. The building number was 1204. No way could you get six-sixty-six out of that.

"Looks like she's been here at least four or five days," Mosley said after the crime-scene investigators had finished with the body and moved on to another area of the room.

Sean glanced up. "Do we know who she is?"

"Not yet. All we know for sure is that she didn't live here. The flat's been vacant for a couple of weeks."

"Who found her?"

"The shopkeeper...Alexandra Lacroix," Charlie said. "Calls herself Madame Lacroix. Claims she's a voodoo priestess descended from Marie Laveau."

"Don't they all?" Danny muttered.

"Said she started getting whiffs of something dead by the time she locked up yesterday. She's got some pretty rank stuff in that shop or else she might have noticed the stink earlier. Said she thought it was a dead rat in the wall and called the landlord as soon as she got home. He came over around eight this morning to let in the exterminator and that's when they found the body."

"Who's the landlord?"

"Guy named Finch. Leslie Finch."

"Who else has a key besides Finch?" Sean asked.

"The previous tenant ran out on his lease a couple of weeks ago, and Finch said he hadn't had a chance to change the locks."

And probably never would have, Sean thought. "When was the last time someone was in here before this morning?"

"Finch showed the apartment to a couple on Saturday afternoon. He's getting us the contact information, along with the file on the previous tenant." Mosley's gaze was on Sean. "So what do you think? Is this your guy or what?"

"Can't say for sure."

"But it could be, right?" Mosley seemed almost giddy with anticipation. "Look at the tattoo on her back. A Rorschach inkblot, just like the one you guys found."

"Listen to that," Danny said. "Junior here's been doing his homework."

Sean snapped on a pair of latex gloves and moved around to the other side of the body. Kneeling, he gently lifted the hair from the woman's cheek so that he could get a look at her face. What was left of it. The mouth had been cut in the same upward curl and the left eyelid had been sliced away, exposing most of the eyeball. Sean quickly dropped the hair back into place.

Danny had moved around and was staring at the body over Sean's shoulder. "Shit. *Shit, shit, shit.*"

"It is the same guy, then," Charlie said grimly. He obviously didn't share his partner's enthusiasm at the prospect of serial murder. "We need something like this about as bad as we need another hurricane. I don't think this city can take much more."

The victim's arms were pressed close to the body, her hands arranged with the palms up. No tattoo, Sean noted, but she had ligature marks around both wrists.

"He had her tied up."

Danny leaned in for a closer look. "That's different from the other one."

"Some of the abrasions look like they were starting to heal," Sean said. "He had her a while before he killed her."

"Petty found carpet fibers on the body," Mosley said. "Hundred bucks says the perp drove around with the vic in the trunk of his car."

"Wonder how long it took him to memorize the lingo?" Danny said in a voice low enough that only Sean could hear.

"She must have been missing for days," Sean said. "Has anyone checked the lists?"

"We've got a possible match," Charlie said. "The victim's description fits a Shreveport woman who disappeared from her home a couple weeks ago. Name's Jessup. Holly Jessup."

"Her husband is some kind of bigwig up there so the case has gotten more exposure than it normally would have," Mosley added. "We've faxed a photograph and a list of identifying marks to the Shreveport P.D. They're contacting next of kin, and with any luck, we'll have a positive ID by the end of the day."

"Then you'll have more than we've got." Sean stood and glanced around. The setup bothered him. The killer had taken great care to stage the last scene, right down to the street number of the house and the ritualistic triangle in the victim's right palm. Sean saw none of that here. The only patterns that had been repeated from one kill to the next were the inkblot tattoo and the facial mutilation.

"Be interesting to see if the autopsy turns up any bruises," Danny said.

"Yeah, won't it?"

Patrice was just coming out of the bathroom and Sean walked over to see what she'd found.

"No blood in the sink, nothing in the toilet or pipes."

"What about prints?"

"I found a couple on the fixtures, but the place was wiped down pretty good by the cleaning crew the landlord brought in after the last tenant moved out."

Sean glanced over Patrice's shoulder into the bathroom. The medicine-cabinet door over the sink was slightly ajar. "Was that already open?"

"Yeah. That's the way we found it."

"No prints on the edge of the mirror?"

She shrugged. "Sorry."

"This may sound a little strange, but did you find any animal hair on the body?"

"You mean as in cat or dog hair?"

"No, I'm thinking of something more unusual. Goat hair maybe."

She lifted a brow. "I'll let you know if anything turns up when we go through the evidence at the lab."

"Thanks." Sean moved around her to the bathroom door. "All right if I take a look inside?"

"I'm finished, so be my guest."

As Sean stepped inside the tiny space, he turned and caught a glimpse of himself in the mirror.

And saw something besides his reflection.

The cabinet door hadn't been randomly left open, he realized. It had been positioned so that someone standing right where he was could see the body in the other room.

He leaned forward and blew on the mirror. A tiny patch of fog appeared. He continued until most of the mirror was frosted and he could see the spidery script the killer had left on the glass.

I am you.

12

Michael Garrett glanced at his watch. As always, she was right on time. Not a minute before or a minute after, but straight up two o'clock. Sarah DeLaune was nothing if not punctual.

Unlike Sarah, though, the clock had gotten away from him, and he hadn't had much time to prepare for their appointment. Ever since he'd moved his practice from the Poydras office to the upstairs apartment of his Garden District home, he'd been finding that distractions came a little too easily.

Last semester, he'd accepted a full-time teaching position at the university and had cut his practice back to only a few sessions per week. Keeping the medical-center office open had seemed an unnecessary extravagance, and most of the patients he still saw had been with him long enough not to be disconcerted by the new arrangements. It helped that the office had a private entrance by way of an outside stairway at the back of the house.

Michael stood at the window now and watched as Sarah

came through the garden gate, pausing on the other side as if
to get her bearings. That brief hesitation had become her ritual, and Michael often wondered what went through her head
at that moment. What internal battle she had to wage before
she could continue across the garden to his office.

She was an attractive young woman, intelligent and artic-
ulate, but she wore her self-defense like a suit of armor. And
she was full of contradictions. A tattoo artist without any visible tattoos. A nonconformist whose past hung around her
neck like a noose.

Today she had on a lightweight jacket with black pants and
boots. A leather handbag was slung over one shoulder, and as
usual, her face was heavily made up. Kohl liner around the
eyes, dark red lipstick on the mouth. Her thick, black hair was
twisted up in the back, but the wind had whipped it loose and
she lifted a hand to swipe a strand from her face.

The gesture held a certain unconscious elegance that took
Michael by surprise. Sarah's hidden grace was yet another of
the many dichotomies he'd noted.

She reminded him a little of Elise, and Michael sometimes
wondered if that faint resemblance was enough to warrant
suggesting another psychologist. The last thing Sarah needed
was a distracted therapist, and he had to admit that her dark
eyes and full lips had caused his mind to wander on occa-
sion. Even more so now, with the anniversary of Elise's death
coming on. Some days his head was filled with so many bleak
thoughts he had a hard time concentrating.

But even more problematic was the way Sarah's therapy
had stalled. She'd been referred to him by her doctor when
medication had failed to alleviate her insomnia, but the walls
she'd erected since her sister's murder were proving formida-
ble. She'd told him something of her background, something

of her sister's death, but always she kept a distance. Always she kept some doors closed.

She'd once inquired about memory-regression hypnosis, but for Michael, that was a treatment of last resort. Far from a magic solution, hypnosis was often ineffective—even downright risky, with sometimes unexpected consequences. And, too, a therapist could inadvertently feed his patient leading or suggestive questions in order to produce a response that fit a preconceived theory.

Michael was not one of those psychologists who eschewed the entire concept of repressed memories. He did believe, however, that dissociative amnesia was extremely rare, and that in most cases—perhaps Sarah's as well—the inability to recall certain events was not the result of lost memories, but of a lost neural connection. In other words, something physical may have destroyed Sarah's memories of her sister's murder, and it was entirely possible she would never recover them.

Michael watched her move across the garden, and a few moments later, the door to the outer office opened and closed. He turned from the window a split second before she knocked.

"Come in, Sarah."

She opened the door and hesitated for another fraction of a minute before entering. "How did you know it was me?"

He smiled. "It's two o'clock on Friday afternoon. Who else would it be? Besides, I saw you in the garden."

"The banana trees are a mess from the freeze." She shrugged out of her jacket and tossed it on the floor with her purse. "You've got some serious work to do in that garden."

"I'm not too worried about the banana trees. They'll recover soon enough, but I'm afraid I may have lost most of the plumerias."

"You can't save everything, I guess." She sat down and

folded her hands in her lap as she waited for Michael to take a seat. "So," she said. "Here we are again."

"Yes. Here we are. How have you been sleeping since I saw you last?"

She shrugged. "I catch a few hours now and then."

"Are you still taking Xanax?"

"Only when I need to." She laughed softly.

"Any adverse side effects? Memory loss, blackouts…?"

"I had an episode of sleepwalking last week. I woke up and found myself sitting in the shower. Thank goodness the water wasn't turned on." She laughed again.

"Another drug might be more effective as a sleep aid," Michael said. "I can talk to Dr. Bayden about other options if you'd like."

"Maybe. I'll think about it." Her smile disappeared. "I don't really want to talk about my sleep disorder today."

"Okay."

She bit the side of her lip. "I want to talk about Sean."

Michael nodded. He knew who she meant. She'd talked about Sean Kelton before.

"I saw him the other night," Sarah said. "He called and asked me to meet him at a crime scene. The victim had a lot of tattoos and he wanted to know if I could identify the artist."

"Did you agree to go?"

Her gaze drifted to the window. "Yes. The body was found near my home. I suppose that's one of the reasons he called."

"How did it feel seeing him again?"

She took a moment to answer. "I've been surprised at how angry I still am."

"Why would that surprise you?"

"Because it's been months. I should be over him by now."

"According to whose schedule?"

"I know, I know." She ran her fingers through her bangs, ruffling them into a charming fringe above her winged brows. "I saw him again the next day and things really got ugly."

"Would you like to talk about that?"

"No, actually." She twirled a strand of hair around her finger, a gesture that reminded him of Elise. She'd done that, too, when she was nervous or anxious. When she was getting ready to go home to her husband.

A frown flicked across Sarah's face. "What I want to talk about is something Sean said to me at the crime scene. It's been bothering me ever since."

"What did he say?"

Her eyes turned pensive, as if she was still trying to work it out for herself. "He implied that the reason I can't remember what happened the night Rachel died is that I'm trying to protect someone."

"Why did that bother you so much?"

Her gaze went back to the window. She couldn't see anything from where she sat, except for treetops and sky, but the scenery seemed to fascinate her. "I guess because it made me think about that night in a different way. I've always thought I couldn't remember being at the farmhouse because of the trauma and shock of witnessing Rachel's murder. But what if Sean's right? What if I suppressed those memories, not because of what I saw, but because of *who* I saw?"

"The killer, you mean."

She sat up straighter. "Maybe the killer was someone close to me. Maybe even—" She stopped herself short and pressed her lips together, as if afraid she might blurt out more than she intended to divulge.

"You told me once that you believed someone named Ashe Cain was responsible for your sister's death."

"That is what I've always believed."

"Is there a reason you'd want to protect him?"

She looked away, closed her eyes. "I'm afraid there may be," she said very softly.

Michael waited for her to continue, but instead she got up and walked over to the window to stare down at the dead garden. "The camellias are still blooming," she murmured. "It's amazing how hardy they are. They look so fragile. Such a delicate shade of pink." She turned and smiled. "But I've gotten off track, haven't I?"

"It happens."

She leaned back against the window frame. "Did I ever tell you that I had an imaginary friend when I was little? Her name was Fay."

"Did Fay have a last name?"

"No, just Fay. I was maybe four or five at the time and I was alone a lot. Rachel was already in school, but even when she was home during the summer, she never paid much attention to me. It was more than the three-year age difference. There was just never much affection between us. At best, she tolerated me. Kind of like my father. Although looking back, I don't think he tolerated me at all. I think he despised me. Or maybe he despised himself for producing such a plain, mediocre child after the perfection of Rachel."

"What about your mother?"

Sarah was silent for a long time. "My mother loved me, but there was a distance in our relationship. Like her mind was always somewhere else when we were together. I never felt as if I really belonged in that house, to those people. That's how I thought of them. They were strangers and I was just someone who lived on the fringes of their lives. I guess that's why I needed Fay."

"You were lonely."

"Desperately so, I think." She came back over and sat down in the chair. "Am I boring you yet?"

"Why? Do I look bored?"

"No, you have too much of a poker face for that." She cocked her head, studying him. "It's a rather nice face, though."

Her moments of mild flirtation always took Michael aback. Not because he hadn't experienced it before, but because with Sarah, even a beguiling smile was never quite what it seemed.

"Where were we?" she asked.

"You were lonely as a child."

"I'm sure that's why I acted out. I wanted attention."

"How did you act out?"

She drew her feet up to the chair and wrapped her arms around her knees. "I broke things. My mother's antique vase. My father's new fishing rod. Rachel's favorite doll. And when someone confronted me, I always blamed it on Fay. Fay did it. It was Fay. Very convenient, wouldn't you say? The strange thing is, after a while I think I actually began to believe it."

"What happened to Fay?"

"She went away when I started school. I guess my subconscious decided I didn't need her anymore. But school was hell for me. Worse than home. I had a learning disability, a mild form of dyslexia, that wasn't detected until I was in the third grade. I wrote certain numbers and letters, even words, backwards. Mirror writing, they called it. By the time I finally caught up to my level, it was too late. I was already branded."

"Were you bullied in school?"

She rested her chin on her knees. "I was teased, but I never considered myself a victim. I was tough," she said with a faint smile. "I fought back."

"Good for you."

"But by the time I got to junior high school, I was in full-blown rebellion."

"How did you rebel?"

"Let's just say, I embraced my weirdness."

He smiled. "Meaning?"

"I liked being different. We had these Goth kids at our school. Ghost-white makeup, black clothes, satanic jewelry. The whole nine yards. I'm pretty sure that look was already passé in most parts of the country, but trends came late to us. I thought they were cool. I used to follow them around, hoping they'd notice me, but the ironic thing was, even the outcasts didn't want me. And then I met Ashe."

Michael saw her shiver and she reached down to pick up her jacket. Then she let it fall back to the floor as if realizing that her chill had nothing to do with being cold.

"Ashe was Goth, too," she said. "But he didn't dress that way to shock or get attention like the others did. He wore the black clothing and the white makeup because that's the way he felt inside. He was dark and troubled and lonely, just like me. And without the clothing and makeup, he couldn't be himself. He needed the trappings in order to *be* Ashe Cain. Does that make sense?"

"We all wear masks," Michael said.

She shook her head, as if impatient that he wasn't getting it. "It wasn't a mask. It was who he was."

"You never saw him without the makeup and dark clothing?"

"If I did, I didn't recognize him. He was older than me, and he wasn't from Adamant. At least that's what he told me. All I knew was that he was my friend. He understood me in a way no one else ever had. We understood each other. He told me once that our souls were like mirror images." She leaned forward, her gaze clinging to Michael's. "Maybe they were. Maybe the reason he understood me so well was because…I created him. He was a figment of my imagination."

"Like Fay, you mean."

"Are you shocked?" She sat back with a satisfied smile, but her eyes looked bleak and haunted. "Have you ever seen a movie called *The Crow?*"

"The Brandon Lee film? I've caught parts of it on television," Michael said.

"Then you probably know the gist of the plot. A tormented soul rises from the grave to avenge the brutal rape and murder of his girlfriend. When I was thirteen, I was obsessed with that movie. I can't even tell you how many times I watched it. I had the sound track, the poster, everything. I was completely in love with the notion of this dark avenger who couldn't be stopped even in death." She paused, her gaze meeting his. "You see where I'm going with this, don't you?"

"Why don't you tell me?"

"After I met Ashe Cain, things started happening to the kids who teased me and called me names."

"What kind of things?"

"Nothing really terrible. Not until—" She glanced away. "Flat tires. Stolen wallets and keys. Stuff like that."

"And you think Ashe was responsible?"

"I know he was. He showed me the things he took."

"What did you do?"

"Nothing, because I told myself those kids deserved it. And that's my whole point. Ashe did what I secretly wanted to do." Her eyes challenged him. "Now do you get it? If I'd wanted to create the perfect avenger, he would have looked exactly like Ashe Cain."

"That doesn't mean he wasn't real," Michael said.

"Then how do you explain why no one else ever saw him? Why no one else ever heard of him?"

"Maybe that's the way he wanted it."

"Maybe." She twirled another strand of hair around her finger. Distracted. Agitated. "Do you believe that we all have the capacity for evil?"

Sharing a personal opinion or philosophical conjecture with a patient was never a good idea, but Sarah's question was one Michael had wrestled with for years. "Yes," he finally said. "I do believe that. But I also believe that in most of us, there is the ability and the desire to vanquish that side of our nature."

"What if suppressing the memories of what happened to Rachel is my way of vanquishing the evil inside me? What if recovering those memories unleashes something I can't control?"

Michael took a long time before he answered. "You can't fight evil in the dark, Sarah. The only way you can truly defeat it is to bring it into the light."

"You mean by remembering?"

"If that's possible. But also by making peace with your past. It's the only way you'll ever be able to move on with your life."

She gathered her jacket and purse and stood. "Something to think about," she said in a tone that was deceptively lighthearted.

"We've still got some time," Michael said. "Why don't we finish the session?"

"No, I really have to go. I have a client coming in soon. We're doing a dragon on his back—a custom design and very elaborate. Did I ever tell you what an honor it is to be allowed to tattoo the back? It's the largest canvas on the human body."

Michael got up to walk her to the door.

"You didn't ask about my father," she said.

"I'm sorry. How's he doing?"

"Not well. The doctors say it's only a matter of time. Weeks, maybe." In the outer office, she tugged on her jacket before going outside. "Admit it. You think my father is somehow the key to all this, don't you? You think the way he treated me as a child has turned me into a neurotic. And here I thought it was always the mother's fault."

Michael opened the door and they walked down the steps together. He watched her disappear through the gate, and a few moments later, he heard her car drive away.

Turning, he surveyed his ravished garden. Sarah was right. Everything was a mess now, but in another month or so, when the weather heated up, the color would come back. The banana trees would shed their brown leaves like a snake sloughing off dead skin, and wisteria would hang like a heavy curtain over the garden walls, perfuming the evening air with a nostalgic scent that always took him back to his days in the seminary.

But that had been a long time ago. Before Elise. Before his fall from grace.

13

As soon as she let herself into the house that night, Sarah had the strangest sensation that something was wrong. Her purse in one hand and a bag of groceries in the other, she used her shoulder to flip the light switch, then glanced around.

The house was so still that even normal sounds—the furnace, the clock, even the whisper of her own breath—unnerved her.

Sarah was so attuned to every nuance of her home that she was sure she would have sensed if someone had been inside while she was out. It wasn't that, but she couldn't explain the disquiet nor could she make it go away. And as certain as she was that no one had broken in, she also knew that, for her own peace of mind, she would have to make the rounds through her house, a tense investigation she always dreaded.

Setting her purse and groceries on a kitchen counter, she walked through every room, checking all the doors and windows, looking inside closets and the shower, underneath the bed and behind every chair. Except for the two years with Sean, she'd lived alone for a long time, and a search through all the dark places was nothing new for her. By now, she knew herself well enough to accept that she wouldn't be able to relax until she made a thorough sweep.

Everything was exactly as she'd left it that morning. No one had been inside. She was sure of it. But even after the search, that nagging unease persisted, and the sound of a car engine in her drive caused her to jump. She hurried to the window and glanced out. Headlight beams swung across her tiny front yard as the car backed out and headed down the street.

Just someone turning around. Nothing to worry about.

But Sarah was still jittery as she walked back into the kitchen, her palms unaccountably moist as she put away the groceries. For the first time in a long time, she wanted to call Sean, and the urge caught her completely off guard.

A storm of emotions ripped through her. Even after all these months, after everything he'd done, there were times like this when Sarah keenly missed having him in the house. The sight of him seated at the kitchen table going through a stack of files would have been especially reassuring on a night when her nerves were so frayed. When the last thing she wanted was to be alone.

He would have glanced up when she came through the door, taken one look at her face and got up from the table to give her a hug. "Rough session?" he'd ask.

Sarah would bury her face in his shoulder and tangle her fingers in his shirt as she breathed in the subtle, spicy scent of his cologne. That was the thing about Sean. For someone who spent most of his day dealing with death, he always smelled good. It was one of the things she missed most about him.

The lingering scent of his aftershave in the bathroom, on his pillow. On her hands.

She stood in the middle of the kitchen, remembering his fingers in her hair, his voice in her ear, the comforting feel of his body pressed against hers.

"Better?" he'd say.

"Hmm, yes."

Sarah opened her eyes and the phantom voice vanished.

Sean was gone and it did no good to look back. Besides, she was a grown woman. She didn't need a man's presence to help her feel safe in her own home. The little house on North Rampart had always been her sanctuary, and she had Esme to thank for that. Without her sage advice, Sarah would have blown through the inheritance from her mother within six months of her twenty-first birthday. But Esme had sat her down one day and given her a piece of her mind.

"What would your mama say if she could see the way you been carrying on? All that partying and carousing and acting like you ain't got a *lick* of common sense. You waste your money on some ol' boy and what you gonna have left when he up and leaves you? Nothing, that's what. Now, you listen to me, Sarah June." She shook a bony finger in Sarah's face. "You use what's left of your mama's money and buy yourself a little house. That way when them ol' boys take off like they do, you got someplace to go home to."

It was the best advice anyone had ever given Sarah, and for once in her life, she'd had the gumption to follow it. But then, Esme had never steered her wrong. Sometimes Sarah thought Esme was the only one who had ever really cared about her.

Making another pass through the house, Sarah finally managed to convince herself that her edginess was just residue tension from her session earlier that day. She and Michael had gotten into some pretty heavy issues, and the exhumation of an old deep-rooted fear was bound to leave her feeling ragged. Sarah had never talked about that fear to anyone, not even to Michael, but Sean's question had dug it out of a very bad place and now Sarah couldn't ignore it.

What if Ashe Cain had only been a figment of her imagination? What if he was nothing more than an apparition she'd conjured at a time in her life when she'd desperately needed a friend—an avenger?

But if Ashe Cain wasn't real, then who had killed Rachel?

That was the question Sarah had been dancing around in Michael's office. Who *was* she trying to protect?

She glanced out the window over the sink, but she could no more determine shadow from darkness than she could separate the fantasies of her loneliness from the reality of her past. Sometimes Sarah wondered if she could trust any of her memories, if the unhappy details of her childhood had been manufactured simply to justify her bad behavior.

It was at times like these that she felt like a stranger in her own life and she realized that after all the years of searching, she still hadn't the vaguest clue of who she really was. Might never know, because she was one of those people who would always be defined by the way others perceived her.

Getting out a bottle of wine, she poured herself a drink.

Why the hell did she keep doing this? Why did she torment herself with unanswerable questions?

If she'd learned anything about herself over the years it was that self-doubt inevitably led to self-destruction.

Already she felt herself on the verge of spiraling out of control, and she quickly lifted the glass to her lips, downing the wine in one gulp.

Ashe Cain was real. She had to believe that. She needed to believe it.

He'd been a troubled, psychotic boy who had done a very bad thing. He'd murdered Rachel in cold blood, maybe to avenge Sarah, maybe to fulfill some dark passion of his own. His motive hardly mattered now. It had been fourteen years since Rachel's murder. If Ashe was coming back, he would have done so by now. Real or imagined, he was gone from Sarah's life for good. She needed to believe that, too.

Pouring a second glass of wine, she washed down a Xanax, then carried her drink into the living room and checked her messages. The hang-up calls both annoyed and unsettled her. There had been a lot of them lately, and when she checked the caller ID, the numbers were all unavailable. Telemarketers, most likely.

Or someone checking to see if you're home.

Sarah became aware of the silence again, and she switched on the television before curling up on the sofa to wait for the pill to take effect. Her muscles had just started to loosen when the phone rang, and feeling that first gentle tug of sedated relaxation, she answered without thinking.

"Hello?"

"We need to talk."

Sarah's gaze went to the clock in the bookshelf. Ten-fifteen.

"Sarah? Are you there?"

"I'm here," she said on a long sigh. "But I don't feel like talking tonight."

"I can tell," Sean said in exasperation. "But that's too damn bad because there's something I need to ask you. It's about the crime scene the other night."

Sarah rolled onto her back and threw a hand over her eyes. "You sound like a broken record."

"I'm serious about this."

"So am I. You're killing my buzz and that's very serious to me. Besides, I've already told you everything I know."

"What about the footprints?"

She blinked in bewilderment. "What footprints?"

"You asked about prints the other night at the crime scene, remember? You wanted to know if we'd found any unusual prints around the house."

A headache began to punch at Sarah's brain. *Shit.* A moment ago, she'd been on the verge of a perfectly comfortable numbness, and now Sean was dragging her back to a dark, spooky place. She tried to resist because she really, really didn't want to go back there. She'd already made that journey once today.

"What kind of prints were you talking about, Sarah?"

She pressed her fingertips to her temple. "What difference does it make? You didn't find anything, did you?"

"Around the house? No."

"Then why does it matter?"

"Because we did find them. Just not outside."

Sarah's mouth suddenly went dry. She reached for her drink, but her hand bumped the glass and she watched in fascination as the red stain seeped across the tabletop.

"There were bruises on the body in the shape of footprints," Sean said. "*Cloven* footprints."

Oh, Christ, not that.

"That's what you were talking about, wasn't it? How did you know about them, Sarah?" His voice was low and insistent. Edged with something Sarah didn't want to name.

Her heart drummed in her chest. How *had* she known about those prints? "I didn't know. How could I?"

"Then why did you specifically ask about unusual prints that night? It's not a random question. What triggered it?"

She took a deep breath, tried to steady her voice. "It must have been the *udjat* you showed me. It reminded me of something."

"What?"

She pulled in more air, drowning. "Sean, it's late and I'm tired. Can't we talk about this tomorrow? I just want to lie here and relax for a little while before—"

"Before what?" His voice sharpened. "Are you going out?"

"No."

"Then I'd like to come over."

"No. That's not a good idea."

"We need to talk about this, Sarah. We need to talk about a lot of things."

No, no, talking about this was the last thing she needed. What she needed was to push the button and make Sean's voice go away. What she needed was to get up and go grab a towel because the wine stain on the table kept spreading.

What she did, though, was lie there with her heart pounding and her mind racing. They'd found cloven footprints on the body. How was that possible? New Orleans was such a long way from Adamant.

"You already know about the satanic symbols in the farmhouse where Rachel's body was found," she said finally. "When you showed me the *udjat,* all that came back. We talked about it the other night."

"I understand why seeing those symbols upset you," he said. "But it doesn't explain how you knew about the footprints."

"After Rachel's murder, there was a rumor in town that something had been found near her body. Something other than the symbols. Everyone assumed it had something to do with the footprints."

"What footprints?"

"They were a local legend. The man who lived in the farm-house supposedly awakened one night to find his field and yard covered with cloven footprints. They were even on his roof. Some believed that all the oil drilling in the area had somehow unleashed the devil. The marks became known as the devil's footprints because no one could come up with a more plausible explanation. Every so often, usually after a violent death, someone in town claims to have seen them." Sarah paused. "I asked if you'd found prints at the crime scene because it was an automatic response to the *udjat*. My memory was triggered and I remembered that old legend. But I never really expected that you would find any."

"So those bruises on the body are just a coincidence?"

"Is it so surprising to find something like that in a case inundated with satanic symbolism?"

"Maybe not," Sean said, after a moment. "Actually, that's another reason I'm calling. There's been a new development in the case. You may have already heard about it on the news."

Sarah could tell from his voice that it was bad. "I've been avoiding the news. What is it?"

"We found another body."

She stared at the spilled wine, watched in fascination as it dripped over the edge of the table onto the wood floor. Almost laughably symbolic. "Where?"

"A vacant apartment on North Rampart. Just a few blocks from you."

No!

Sarah got up with the phone still to her ear. "Hold on a minute, Sean."

Heart still thumping, she made another quick search of her house. She rechecked all the doors and windows as that inexplicable disquiet crept over her again.

"Sarah?"

She jumped at the sound of her name. She'd forgotten the phone was still to her ear. "Just a second."

Crossing the room to the window, she stared out at the street. An unfamiliar car had been parked at the curb a few houses down when she got home earlier. It was still there, only now Sarah imagined she could see someone sitting behind the wheel. Watching her house.

She stepped back from the window.

Sean's voice cut into the silence. "What the hell is going on?"

"Nothing. I just… I needed to check on something, that's all."

"Are you okay?"

She inhaled and exhaled slowly. "Yeah, I'm okay."

His voice lowered. The tension was gone now, and all she heard was a hint of familiarity, a slight whisper of intimacy that rippled through her memories.

She closed her eyes. If she asked him to come over tonight, she knew what would happen. They both did. She was vulnerable and scared, and Sean was Sean.

The moment he walked through her door, she would be in his arms, tearing at his clothes like a wildcat. Stripping her own away without a moment's hesitation or inhibition. Because in bed, with Sean, her defenses had a way of imploding.

But she wouldn't do that. She wouldn't let herself be that weak. She'd played a lot of roles in her life, but the other woman was not one of them.

"Sarah." He said her name softly.

"You're married, Sean. Or have you forgotten?"

"I haven't forgotten. But I think we need to talk about that, too."

"No, we don't. Not tonight." Maybe not ever.

"Sarah, please."

"Don't come over, Sean. And don't call here again. Go home to your wife and leave me alone."

She hung up the phone before he could say anything else and tossed it aside. Collapsing back on the couch, she tried to relax, but it was a long time before she could get Sean's voice out of her head. She almost expected him to show up at her door in spite of her warning, and when he didn't, the loneliness of her silent house seemed more crushing than ever.

Finally, she began to drift, and she found herself sifting through memories she hadn't thought of in years. Unexpectedly, she thought of the bells in the cottonwood trees at the farmhouse.

When the wind blew from a certain direction, the bells chimed over the graves, and Sarah remembered being both intrigued and repulsed by the sound. Ashe had told her once that when she heard the bells, it meant that death was coming.

"I thought bells tolled *after* someone died."

He smiled. "Not these bells, Sarah."

A few nights later, she'd been awakened by that same melodic tinkle. She'd gotten out of bed and gone over to her bedroom window to look out. When she slid the sash up, the sound grew louder, and she realized that Ashe had tied bells up in the tree outside her window.

Sarah could hear those bells now, only the tolling was very distant.

She opened her eyes and lay still for a moment. She wanted to believe it was nothing more than a manifestation of her memory, but she was fully alert now and she could still hear the bells. Faint, but not imagined.

Following the sound into her bedroom, she stood at the

French doors that opened into her tiny courtyard, her heart beating hard and fast against her chest.

She wouldn't go outside to investigate. Not now. Not in the dark. She didn't have to. She recognized the sound and she knew what it meant.

Death was coming.

Sean dropped the phone back into his pocket, letting the call go to his voice mail the way he did all the other calls from Cat. He'd have to talk to her sooner or later, but after his earlier conversation with Sarah had ended so unpleasantly, he was in no mood for a confrontation with his wife. Besides, he already knew how the conversation would play out.

She'd demand to know where he was, and he'd get defensive and evasive, which would set her off even more. Then the tears would start, and she'd end up begging him to come home so they could talk things out, even though he'd made it clear the only reason he'd be returning to their apartment was to pick up the rest of his things. As far as he was concerned, the marriage was over. All he wanted was out.

Sean wasn't proud of his behavior. Any decent man would tough it out and give the marriage and his wife a fair chance. But the outcome would be the same no matter how long he and Cat stayed together. It was never going to work for one simple reason—Sean wasn't in love with her and probably never had been. And worse, he didn't even like her very much these days.

How he'd let things get this far, he had no idea. Rushing into marriage so soon after his breakup with Sarah had been stupid and reckless, and she'd been right to call him on it. He had been looking for someone safe. Someone who could give him sanctuary from the horror show his job had become.

At the time, he'd thought that was Cat. Seeing her in the restaurant that day had been like a breath of fresh air. The way she looked at him, the way she smiled, made him forget for a moment how ugly his life had become.

And the physical attraction had been off the hook. Even in high school, Cat had been a knockout, but in her thirties now, she'd grown into a stunningly beautiful woman. A tall, graceful blonde whose unwavering attention during those first few months had been extremely flattering. Embarrassingly so, looking back.

She was as different from Sarah as night and day, and it had been easy for Sean to convince himself that she was the one. That she was so much better for him. He and Sarah fed off each other's doom and gloom, and the angst had become exhausting.

It had gotten to the point where Sean had dreaded going home because he was afraid of what he might find.

But the problem was, Sarah was also the most fascinating woman he'd ever known. And she wasn't as easy to get over as he'd hoped.

Outwardly, she was no match for Cat. Sarah's beauty took time to sink in. You had to look past all the heavy eye makeup and outlandish hairstyles, and even then, you could never be certain whether the woman you found underneath the mask was the real thing or yet another intriguing facade.

Sean had latched onto Cat because Sarah overwhelmed him. More to the point, she scared the hell out of him.

Her sister's murder had done something to her. She'd never been able to move on. It ate at her even after all these years, and nothing that came before or after was ever going to be as important to her, not even Sean. Fine. He could have lived with that, but the secrets she kept locked inside were a different story. They worried him, those secrets. They sometimes kept him awake at night.

He'd once naively thought that by solving Rachel's murder he could somehow free Sarah of her demons. But the harder he looked and the deeper he dug, the darker his suspicions became until one day he'd stopped searching. Because he'd come to the very grim realization that the truth of what had happened that night in Adamant, Arkansas, might be a truth he didn't want to face.

Those suspicions were what had driven him from Sarah. On some level, he'd been trying to protect them both. Cat had been just a convenient excuse.

So why the hell couldn't he leave well enough alone? Sarah was out of his life now. If he still cared for her at all—and he did—he'd let this go and allow her to get on with her life the best way she knew how.

Let sleeping dogs lie, Danny would advise him.

But Sean had never been that great at taking advice.

He paid for his drink and left the bar on Decatur. The blast of cold air that blew off the river drew a deep shiver down his spine and he pulled his coat around him as he walked along the narrow streets like a weary soldier. It was after eleven and he was exhausted, but instead of heading back to his car, he crossed Jackson Square and turned up St. Peter, past St. Louis Cathedral and the Cabildo.

A trumpet player stood underneath the famous lamppost in Pirate's Alley serenading a handful of tourists. The mournful song touched something deep inside Sean, and he found himself hurrying away from the melancholy wail toward the driving rock beat that throbbed from the bars and clubs on Bourbon Street.

For him, this was the heart of the Quarter. Here, time

never mattered, because day or night, a party could be found somewhere, even in the middle of a hurricane. No other seven-block stretch in the world was more evocative of erotic indulgence than Bourbon Street.

Sean was always reminded of something he'd read in an Ian Fleming novel as a kid. He hadn't understood the sentiment at the time, but now he often thought that the soul-erosion excess Fleming spoke of was the perfect way to describe Bourbon Street. Sean's senses had been awakened to the decadence a long time ago, but instead of revolting, he found himself coming back night after night, especially on evenings like this when he could feel himself slipping into a strange restlessness.

He didn't want to go home to Cat and he couldn't go home to Sarah.

Disconnected from the music and crowds, he wandered the streets aimlessly, like a ghost drifting through a world in which he no longer belonged.

Solitude had never sat well with Sean. He wasn't a man comfortable with his own thoughts. He needed something or someone to fill up the empty hours because soul-searching wasn't his style. There were too many unanswered questions in his life. Too many loose ends.

Too many roads leading him back to a woman whose past frightened him almost as much as it intrigued him.

14

A cool breeze whispered through the sycamore tree outside Sarah's window. From one of the branches, Ashe could see right into her room. He'd spent a lot of time in that tree. Especially after dark, when the risk of detection was slight. Her room faced the backyard, so the tree was only visible from the cottage. That could be a problem, but Ashe was always careful to come on moonless nights.

Besides, he'd always thought it was a risk worth taking. Although observing Sarah through the window wasn't as satisfying—or as exciting—as the times he'd spent alone in her room, sifting through her things.

Those secret forays had taught him so much about her…the books she read, the music she listened to. He even knew her favorite movie, and as his eyes lifted to the poster above her bed, he wondered if she'd put it all together yet, if she realized the significance of the pale, familiar face that watched over her every night while she slept.

Overhead, dark clouds drifted across the winter sky, but through the occasional crack in the darkness, Ashe could see stars. He gazed at the pinpoints for a long time, mesmerized by the twinkling light. On a night like this, so dark he was like a shadow, his senses came fully awake and it was easy to ignore those persistent voices in his head that confused and infuriated him. He hated those voices because they took him away from his world and dumped him back into a place that for him had no meaning, no purpose. No Sarah.

He shifted his position, moving a little closer to the window, but still careful not to attract her attention. He never let her see him outside her window. For one thing, he didn't want to frighten her, and for another, their twilight meetings at the farmhouse were much safer... for both of them.

Tonight he would make an exception, though. He would break his own rules because he had something very important to show her.

A thrill raced up his spine as he tried to anticipate her reaction, but he had no idea what it would be. Sarah was nothing if not unpredictable and that was one of the things he admired about her. Only one of the many things that kept him tied to her.

He watched her now as her hand flew across the sketch pad on her desk. Head bowed, her forehead wrinkled in concentration, she was oblivious to his vigil, oblivious to the way her life would soon be changed forever.

Leaning forward, he tapped on the glass.

Sarah's head shot up, and when she saw him, her eyes widened and she seemed a little frightened at first. She rose and crossed the room quietly, checked the hallway, then closed and locked her door.

She hurried over to the window and slid it up.

"What are you doing here?" she asked in an excited whisper.

Ashe smiled at the sound. "I want you to come with me. I have something to show you."

"Really? What is it?"

"You'll see. It's a surprise."

Her eyes lit. "You mean like a present? I have one for you, too. I know it's after Christmas and all, but…do you want to come in and see it?"

Ashe hesitated. Breaking two of the rules might be asking for trouble, but Sarah looked so excited and eager. He glanced around. The cottage windows were all dark, and the moon was still covered by clouds. No one would see him, surely.

"Turn off the light first," he said. "Bright lights hurt my eyes."

"But…you won't be able to see your present in the dark," she protested.

"You can leave on the lamp."

She turned off the overhead light and switched on the lamp beside her bed. Once the room was dim, Ashe climbed through the window and sniffed the air, letting Sarah's scent wash over him.

The forbidden familiarity of her room excited him because he knew so many of her secrets. And it was almost time to share with her the darkest secret of all, but he had to prepare her first.

Tonight, it would begin.

Absently, he picked up a yellow porcelain bird from her desk and cradled it in his palm. He'd always wondered about that bird. Normally, she kept it in a glass case on her nightstand.

She saw his interest and smiled. "My grandmother gave that to me when I was little. She collected porcelain birds. She kept them in a locked case in her parlor and I found the key. I took one out and accidentally broke off a wing. I hid it so I wouldn't get in trouble. But when Grandma found it, all she did was make me help her glue the wing back on. And then she gave it to me to keep because she said a wounded bird needed someone special to care for it."

"That's true," he said. "Does your grandmother live around here?"

"Nah, she died a long time ago. Just a few weeks after she gave me that bird. Sometimes I wonder if she knew she was going to go and that's why she gave it to me. She wanted me to have something of hers. I used to pretend that her soul lived inside it. That's why I kept it beside my bed. So it was the first thing I saw when I woke up in the morning." Gently she took the bird from his hand and returned it to the glass case.

When she turned, her smile was unexpectedly shy. "This is kind of weird, isn't it? You being in my room and all."

"Do you want me to leave?"

"No. I haven't given you your present yet." She walked over to her desk and picked up her drawing pad. "It's not finished yet, but... ta-dah!"

She handed him the sketch pad with a flourish, and Ashe turned it toward the lamp, taking care, as always, to keep his face shadowed. As he stared down at Sarah's drawing, a slow tremor crawled through him. For a moment, he couldn't tear his eyes away.

For the first time, he saw himself...the way Sarah saw him. It was as if she'd gazed straight down into his soul. And what she'd found when she peeled back the outer layers was something dark and beautiful and terrifying.

"You don't like it," she said after a moment.

"No, I do..." He was so overcome with emotion, he could hardly speak.

"Some people don't like the way I draw them," she said quietly. "But it's like...I don't know...like I can peer inside them somehow. What I draw isn't always what they want to see."

"You have a gift," he said. "Your grandmother was right, Sarah. You are special."

"Yeah, sure. Try telling that to my old man." She laughed, but *for a moment, he swore he saw the glint of tears in her eyes before she turned away.*

"He already knows you're special," Ashe said. "And it threatens him."

"Why would that threaten him?"

"You'll figure it out one of these days. Maybe what I have to show you tonight will help you."

"What is it?"

"You'll see."

She followed him out the window and they climbed down the tree together. The night was dark, but they stayed among the shadows anyway until they were safely away from the house. Up the path to the cottage, through the orchard, across the cotton field. To their special place.

For the longest time, they didn't talk, and as they neared the farmhouse, Ashe could hear the bells in the cottonwood trees.

Tolling for what was to come, he thought.

"Ashe?"

"Yeah?"

"Where do you live?"

"Around."

"Around where?"

He shrugged. "What difference does it make?"

"I'm just curious. Do you live in a house?"

"Sure. But not like yours."

"What do you mean?"

"Mine's not big and fancy."

"I hate my house," she said passionately. "I can't wait to get out of there. And when I leave, I'm never coming back." She pulled her jacket tightly around her as the breeze picked up. "Can I ask you something else?"

"I guess."

"You heard those girls calling me names the other day, didn't you? Amber and the others. That's why you stole their stuff. You did it for me."

"What's the girl's name who was laughing so hard?"

"You mean Holly Jessup?"

"Holly Jessup. Holly...Jessup," he said slowly, committing her name to memory.

He stared straight ahead, into the night. He'd wanted to do more than steal from them, but he couldn't without giving himself away. One of these days, though, when it was safe, he'd come back.

"Why did you do it?" Sarah persisted. "Why do you care what they call me?"

"Because we're friends."

"But why do you want to be my friend? We're not even the same age. We don't go to the same school. You won't even tell me where you live."

"None of that stuff matters, Sarah. We're friends because we're the same. I knew it the moment I first saw you. It's like our souls are mirror images."

She thought about that for a moment and nodded. "I think you're right. I think we are the same."

They were approaching the farmhouse now. A place of shadow and legend. A place of death.

But I am the real demon, he thought.

It would be his footprints they would find in the blood. His mark that would be left upon the body. And after he was done, after he was gone, the town would live in terror for another seventy years.

15

On Friday afternoon, Lukas Clay got off work early so he could be at the house for a delivery of flooring he'd ordered. While he waited for the truck, he set to work stripping the wood molding in the parlor and kept at it until well after dark.

Then, tired but still a bit restless, he popped the top off a Turbodog and sat out on the front porch in the cold night air, listening to the freight trains in the distance and watching moonlight drift down through the trees and sprinkle across the surface of the pond.

As content as he was with the way things had worked out for him, Lukas was still sometimes amazed by how easily he'd settled into rural life. He'd left Union County after high school and had never considered returning until after his father died.

Even then, the only reason he'd come back was to settle the old man's affairs and sell off the property and the house where he'd grown up. He'd hoped for a quick turnaround so he could get back to the business of figuring out what he wanted to do with the rest of his life. But real estate could sometimes sit on the market for months or even years in the South Arkansas economy, and while Lukas impatiently waited for a bite, he'd been offered the position of chief of police in Adamant.

The offer had been extended, he was told, on the basis of his impressive service record and his prior experience on a midsize police force, but Lukas suspected his last name, more than anything else, had been the real catalyst.

Whatever the prompt, the proposition had intrigued him. Opportunities hadn't exactly come pouring in since his discharge, so after only a day of mulling over his options, he'd accepted the position and had immediately set about finding himself a little place in town that would be convenient to the station.

In the ensuing months, he'd sold off parcels of the old man's land, which had given him some start-up cash. But the old homestead had generated nary a nibble, and Lukas had started driving out to the country on weekends to try to spruce up the place.

At first, he concentrated on minor, cosmetic repairs, but when he discovered how much he enjoyed working with his hands, he tackled the bigger plumbing, wiring and roofing projects. Before he knew it, he was in the middle of a hardcore renovation.

The satisfaction he got from bringing the old place back to life surprised him, considering that his childhood home didn't hold happy memories. His father had seen to that. But it was a good house on a nice piece of ground that was far enough from the road to provide a little peace and quiet on weekends. All the privacy a man could want.

And the work agreed with him. Lukas had found a strange kind of nirvana in a place he'd once thought of as hell. He relished the prickle of the sun beating down on his shoulders and the ache from a long, hard day settling deep into his muscles. He liked dropping into bed at night, so tired that he was dead to the world until the sun woke him up the next morning.

After a while, he'd gone inside, showered and hit the sack. He had no idea how long he'd been asleep when the cell phone on the nightstand rang. No one from the station ever bothered him out here unless it was an emergency, so he didn't hesitate to answer.

"Yeah?"

"Sheriff Clay?"

"No, this is Lukas Clay." He put a slight emphasis on his first name.

"Sorry, my bad. Your daddy was the sheriff, right?"

Lukas rolled onto his back. "Who is this?"

"Somebody you been looking for, Luk-*ass*." The male voice drawled the name, mocking Lukas's pronunciation. "I hear you been asking around town about me."

Lukas sat up in bed. "Fears?"

"You still want to talk?"

"Yes, but I'd rather have this conversation in my office instead of over the phone."

"That's a problem, see, because then I'd have to check my book and my people would have to get back to your people…turn into a real hassle. Let's just do this now and get it over with."

"Where are you?"

"Look out your window."

Lukas got up and parted the curtain. An old blue-and-white pickup was parked in the drive and he could see someone sitting behind the wheel. He was surprised and a little unsettled that he hadn't heard the engine. He must have been sleeping pretty damn hard. Some nights it was like that.

"That you up there, Luk-ass?" An arm gave a wave out the window of the truck.

"Yeah."

"You alone? I hope I'm not interrupting something." Fears chuckled.

"I'll be right down."

"Hey, grab us a beer on your way out. I got a little parched on the drive over."

Lukas quickly dressed, then slipped his .38 into the back of his jeans. Shrugging into his jacket, he headed out the front door.

Derrick Fears had gotten out of the truck and stood leaning against the front fender with his arms folded and his feet crossed at the ankles. As Lukas crossed the yard, Fears spread his arms and grinned. "You wanted to talk, here I am."

Lukas could see his face clearly in the moonlight. It was thin and creased, the visage of a man who had aged quickly and not well. But beneath the jeans and insulated hunting vest, his body was still powerful and sinewy.

"Hey, where's my beer?"

"Sorry, fresh out," Lukas said with a shrug.

Fears's hair was clipped so short, his scalp gleamed in the moonlight. His head was lowered and the way he looked up through his lashes was both cagey and deliberate. "You never answered my question. You out here all alone?"

Lukas gave him a hard appraisal. "How did you know where to find me?"

"Oh, I got my ways, don't you worry about that."

He appeared sober, but his eyes were moving about ten times faster than normal, and Lukas detected a slight quiver in his voice that made him wonder what Fears had recently shot up or ingested. Crystal meth was the drug of choice in most rural areas because of the cost and the ease of procurement. But amping could produce some erratic and violent behavior, the prospect of which made Lukas grateful for the feel of his gun against his back. The house was miles from the highway.

"Who told you where I'd be?" he pressed.

"A little birdie I know says you've been spending a lot of time out here." Fears glanced around. "You've got the place looking pretty spiffy. Much better than the last time I was out here."

"When was that?"

"Long time ago. Back when your old man was alive. He gave me the scenic tour once." Fears nodded over Lukas's shoulder. "There's an old storm cellar back in those woods. Used to be a house out there, too, but it burned down. You ever go out there?"

"Not recently."

"Maybe you should check out that cellar sometime. No telling what you might find down there. Besides spiders and rattlers." He grinned.

"Maybe I'll check it out one of these days," Lukas said.

"Yeah, you do that." Fears gazed off into space. "That storm cellar was where your old man used to interrogate his prisoners. And by interrogate, I mean beat the shit out of." He turned and cocked his head as he studied Lukas's reaction. "What do you say we go down there right now, just me and you, and check it out? I've got a flashlight in the truck. Be like a stroll down memory lane."

"Maybe later." Lukas didn't like the sudden feral gleam in Fears's eyes. He'd seen that look before. "Where were you last Tuesday?"

"Home," Fears said.

"Just like that? You don't even have to think about it?"

"That was the day after the ice storm hit. I didn't have to go in to work, so I slept in."

"All day?"

"Well, you know how it is. Guy like me needs his beauty rest. You don't believe me, talk to my old lady. She can vouch for me. I've been staying out at the house with her ever since I got back to town."

"I've already checked," Lukas said. "Your mother was at the hospital on Tuesday. She pulled a double shift so she was there from early morning until late evening. Looks like she's not in any position to provide you with an alibi this time."

Fears wiped the corners of his mouth with his thumb and forefinger. "And just why the hell would I need an alibi?"

"Someone broke into the DeLaune house that day. When I went over there to check things out, I saw a reflection in a window right before I got a lamp bashed into my skull. That reflection looked a lot like you, Derrick."

Fears laughed. "No shit?"

"No shit. So why don't you tell me why you were there?"

The amusement faded. "You've got the wrong guy, Sheriff."

Lukas didn't bother correcting the title. "I don't think I do. I saw you pretty clearly in that window."

"Then why ain't you already got my ass sitting in a jail cell somewhere?"

"Maybe I'm waiting to hear your side of the story."

"Mighty big of you. It's more than your old man would do, that's for damn sure." Fears folded his arms and leaned back against the truck. "Let's just say, hypothetically speaking, it *was* me you saw in that window. Maybe I was there at the house looking for the same thing you are."

Lukas stared straight into his eyes. "And that would be?"

"You've been asking questions about that girl's murder, which makes me wonder if you're trying to find her killer. Maybe you and me want the same thing."

"That still doesn't tell me why you broke into the De-Laune house."

"I never said I was there. We're speaking hypothetically, remember?"

Lukas's eyes narrowed. "Do you know something about Rachel DeLaune's murder?"

"I know I didn't do it, so chances are pretty damn good that whoever whacked her is still around in these parts. And the son of a bitch was more than willing to let me take the blame." Fears shifted his stance, his gaze going back to the woods behind the house. "Everybody thinks your old man was such a great cop, but he really blew it on that case. He never even looked at anybody but me. It was too damn easy to blame the weirdo. He wanted a confession, so he took me down in that cellar and tried to beat one out of me. He left me lying down there in my own blood and shit for two days, and when I still wouldn't crack, he started in on me again. The way I see it, I've got some payback due me."

"And that's why you went to the DeLaune place? What were you hoping to find? Evidence? You don't think that house was searched after the murder?"

"Why would your old man order a search when he already had it in his head I did it? Just because he couldn't make the charges stick doesn't mean he ever seriously considered any of the other suspects."

"What other suspects?"

"Plenty of people had it in for that girl. She wasn't at all like what she pretended to be."

"Meaning?"

"She was a real pistol. She just knew how to hide her bad-ness, is all. So maybe instead of trying to figure out who wanted her dead, you ought to be asking yourself who *needed* her dead."

"And you think you know who that someone was?"

His smile was cagey again. "I've got a few ideas. My old lady used to work for Doc Washington when he still had his office on Pear Street. She said Rachel came in one day com-plaining of dizzy spells. She'd passed out in school that same day. Doc thought it was probably low blood sugar, but when he ran some tests, he found out she was knocked up."

Lukas tried not to show his shock. "She was pregnant at the time of the murder?"

"Unless she got rid of it, yeah."

"There was nothing about a pregnancy in the autopsy re-port."

"Judge DeLaune wouldn't have wanted anything like that getting out about his precious little girl, now would he? He and your old man were like *this* back then." He held up crossed fingers. "Between the two of them, they ran this county. They could leave out anything they damn well wanted from those reports."

"Why didn't your mother say anything about this when you were arrested?"

"She did. Nobody'd listen."

"Does she know who the father was?"

"No, but I've got a few ideas about that, too. Like I said, you gotta ask yourself who needed that girl dead. It had to be somebody with a lot to lose, right? Like a fancy scholarship maybe. Or a wife."

"Is this all just supposition or do you really know something?" Lukas said.

Fears shrugged. "Let's just say, I had a lot of time in the joint to do some thinking. And what kept running through my head was the way Judge DeLaune used to look at that girl when he thought no one else was around."

"You think he killed his own daughter?"

"It wouldn't be the first time, would it? Maybe things got out of hand. Who knows? He's the one who found her, right? I'm not a cop like you, but even I know that'd be a good way to explain why his prints and DNA were at the crime scene."

According to Esme, Judge DeLaune carried Rachel's body all the way back to the house while Anna DeLaune washed blood out of Sarah's hair. Why had they taken such pains to destroy evidence that could have led to Rachel's killer?

"When your old man took me down in that cellar, I was just seventeen years old," Fears said. "I was too scared to fight back then, but I'm not a kid anymore. Being locked up with a bunch of low-life scumbags teaches you a thing or two about survival. If you really want to find that girl's killer, more power to you. But if you're figuring on coming after me the way your old man did, then I'm not going to be so neighborly the next time we meet up."

Lukas felt the gun pressing into his back. "Is that a threat?"

"A *threat?*" Fears opened the truck door and climbed into the cab. "After I drove all the way out here just to do you a solid? No, man, that wasn't a threat. That there was just a friendly piece of advice."

16

Sarah had only been home from work a few minutes on Saturday when Sean showed up at her door. It had been raining when she left the studio, and her hair was still damp from the long walk to her car. When she got home, she'd barely had time to change her shirt and kick off her wet shoes before the doorbell rang.

"What are you doing here?" she said as she stood in the open doorway, her body language telling him plainly that she had no intention of inviting him in. "I told you last night I didn't want you to come here."

"I thought you meant last night," he said with an offhanded shrug. "You know, don't come here as in right now."

He wore a dark crewneck sweater over a white T-shirt and jeans, which either meant he'd had the day off or his watch had ended at five. He always dressed in a suit and tie for work. He'd told Sarah once it was a matter of intimidation, but she'd always thought there was probably a little ego involved. Sean looked good dressed up and he knew it.

"No, I meant, as in *never*," she said.

"Never is a long time."

"Yes, precisely."

He watched her for a moment, his face shaded by the darkness. She could see his eyes, but she couldn't read what was in them.

"You look a little tired tonight, kiddo."

She gave a bitter laugh. "Is that all you can ever say to me?"

"You haven't been sleeping, have you?"

She shrugged. "My neighbor's wind chime kept me up last night."

No bells in her tree, she'd discovered that morning. Just the wind chime in her neighbor's courtyard and an imagination triggered by a silent house.

She leaned a shoulder against the door frame and folded her arms. "How did you know I was home anyway?" She was usually at work until ten on Saturday nights.

"I went by the studio. They said you left early. I wanted to know you made it home all right."

"Why?"

"This neighborhood isn't as safe as it used to be."

Sarah was quiet for a long time. "Why do you keep doing this?"

"What?" He was the picture of innocence. "You know what they say about old habits."

"What do you want from me, Sean?" She hadn't meant to pour so much pain and anger into that one question. She sensed, more than saw, his wince.

"Jesus, Sarah. Do I have to want something? Can't we just talk?"

In the deepening twilight, he was hardly more than a silhouette on her porch, but Sarah's memory had no trouble
sketching his features. The piercing eyes, the slightly brooding mouth.

"I'd just like to know what point there is to all this," she said
wearily. "Every time we talk, we cover the same old ground."

"I know we do. And yet, here I am again."

She cast her eyes heavenward where a light rain still fell
from a black sky. Neither of them said anything for a long moment, and then Sean lifted his hands and blew on his fingers.
"It's cold out here, Sarah."

"You have a warm body to go home to, don't you? Or isn't
Catherine home?"

For an instant, he seemed stuck for a response, and then he
shrugged. "I don't know where she is tonight."

"Is that why you're here?"

"I'm here because I wanted to see you. It may be old ground,
but we do have things to talk about."

She waited a heartbeat, then backed away from the door so
he could enter. He walked into the living room, dominating
the space as he gazed around. "It still looks the same," he said.

"Well, not quite. Your stuff is gone."

"Right."

Sarah stood perfectly still, trying to ignore the pounding
of her heart. But seeing him here like this, with raindrops
glistening in his hair and uncertainty in his eyes, she couldn't
stop the stir of memories, the echo of emotions that should
have been long dead. His eyes met hers and she felt her nerve
endings sizzle.

Aggravated by her reaction, she let her anger slip out. "What
did you think, Sean? That I'd get rid of all my things because

they remind me of you? I like my house just the way it is," she said defiantly.

"I like your house, too. I always did."

"Just not enough to stay."

His silence spoke volumes. "You know it's not that simple. I never meant to hurt you."

"The problem is, you didn't try very hard not to."

His smile was tense. "I hate hearing you sound so bitter."

"Bitter is my middle name," she said. "Why do you think I'm so screwed up?"

"Don't talk like that. I don't like you joking about your mental state."

She stared at him in surprise. "Are you kidding me? Since when?"

He glanced away. "I just don't, that's all." His gaze lit on the small suitcase she'd carried from her bedroom into the living room before she left for work that morning. "Going somewhere?"

"I have a few days off. I'm driving up to Arkansas to visit my father."

"I thought you hated your father."

"No, my father hates *me*. There's a big difference."

"Then why are you going? Why don't you just let the old coot stew in his own juices?"

"Because Michael seems to think I need to make peace with my past."

Something flickered in his eyes as he said, very quietly, "Michael?"

"My therapist." The teakettle on the stove whistled, and Sarah quickly moved past him to the kitchen. "Excuse me."

When she came back, she found him in the alcove off the

living room that she used as an art studio. He stood in front of her drawing table studying one of her sketches.

He glanced up when she came in. "What's all this?"

She walked over to the table and they stood side by side. "It's the inkblot tattoo. I've been trying to recreate it from memory."

"Why?"

"I'm not really sure," Sarah said with a frown. "Something about it keeps bothering me. I thought if I looked at it long enough, I might be able to figure out what it means."

"You said we'd probably never know what it means."

"Not to the killer, no. I'm talking about what it means to me."

Sean reached in his pocket and pulled out a couple of photographs that he tossed on top of the drawing. "Maybe these will help."

Sarah picked up the pictures and examined them under the light. She thought at first they were of the same tattoo. "Wait a minute," she said. "These are different."

"They're from two different victims." Sean pointed to one of the shots. "This was taken at the first crime scene."

Sarah reached for a magnifying glass. "It still looks like two faces," she said. "But on this photograph, the right face is shaded, and on the other, the left face is shaded."

"You see faces, Danny sees breasts, and I don't see anything," Sean said. "God only knows what the killer sees."

"Maybe you should show these photos to Michael," she said.

"You're on a first-name basis with your shrink."

"So what? I just never think of him as Dr. Garrett."

"Seems a little chummy to me. Not exactly professional."

His obvious irritation amused Sarah. "He happens to be an excellent therapist, and I know he's used the Rorschach cards in his practice. He teaches full-time so he doesn't keep regular office hours. You'd have to call and make an appointment."

"You'd be all right if I saw him?"

It sounded like a casual question, but Sarah knew that it wasn't. "Why wouldn't I be? You're the one who has cause to feel awkward."

"Why? Oh, I see. My name has come up in your sessions, I take it."

"Once or twice."

"And what did you tell him about me? That I'm a cold-hearted bastard?"

"Among other things."

Sean turned to look at her, and suddenly they were so close, Sarah could smell his cologne, feel his breath. His eyes burned into hers. "What did you tell him about *us*? Did you tell him…everything?"

A thousand sensations stormed through Sarah. So many memories. The feel of Sean's lips, his tongue…the taste of him…

Her gaze traced the angle of his strong jaw, the sensuous line of his lips. She was suddenly acutely aware of his hard, perfect body only inches from hers.

He skimmed his knuckles down her cheek and Sarah shivered. "You don't tell him our secrets, do you, Sarah? Those are just for us."

She pushed his hand from her face and saw anger glint in his eyes before he glanced away. "Keep the pictures," he said. "Maybe they'll help you figure things out."

"Isn't that against regulations?"

"What, are you going to turn me in?"

Maybe she should, Sarah thought. Maybe that was the way to end this dance once and for all.

She stared down at the photographs, her breath still too shallow, her cheek tingling from where he had touched her. "Do you know who they are?"

"The victims?" He was suddenly all business again, his voice brusque, his eyes steely with determination. "Not yet. Not the first one. The second victim's name is Holly Jessup."

Sarah felt everything inside her go still.

Holly Jessup.

Sean saw her expression and frowned. "What? Don't tell me you know her?"

"No, it's not that…" Sarah left the drawing table and walked back into the living room. Sean followed her. "I know that name," she said. "I saw it in the paper the other day. They said she'd disappeared from her home in Shreveport."

"Yeah, that's right. Her abductor kept her alive for days before he killed her. Then he dumped her body in a vacant apartment. We didn't find blood or symbols like at the first crime scene. But the killer left a message in the bathroom mirror."

"The same one?"

"Yeah. 'I am you.' Looks like you were right about him. He seems to have a thing about mirrors."

"Or mirror images." Sean's gaze was so intense, a chill skated up Sarah's spine. "Why are you looking at me like that?"

"I was just thinking about something."

"What?" When he didn't answer, she dropped her voice. "Sean, what is it?"

"I don't mean to sound melodramatic, but where were you last Saturday night?"

Sarah just stared at him.

"Holly Jessup's neighbors reported seeing a strange car in the neighborhood the day she went missing. An old green sedan. The original crime scene and the dump site of the second body are both just blocks from here. If you were out late last Saturday night, it's possible you could have seen the car in this neighborhood."

Sarah's mind went instantly to the car she'd noticed parked at the curb the night before. It had already been dark when she got home and she'd been in a hurry to get inside. Could it have been the green sedan Holly Jessup's neighbors had reported?

"I worked until ten and then I came straight home," she said.

"You didn't go out later?"

"No."

His voice was flat, his eyes suddenly distant. "That's not like you to stay home on a Saturday night."

"I don't think I like what you're implying. What's this all about?"

"I told you. I thought you might have seen a dark green car in the neighborhood."

"I was home last Saturday night," Sarah said on a breath of anger. "Where were *you?*"

Sean glanced up. "Pardon?"

"Someone kept calling here and hanging up. When I called the number back, it was Catherine. She didn't say anything, but my guess is she was looking for you. So where were you, Sean?"

Irritation flashed in his eyes a split second before he gave her an enigmatic smile. "I always said you'd make one helluva detective."

17

The smoke curling up from the roach clip in the ashtray burned Catherine Kelton's eyes. She was sorely tempted to roll down her window to let in some fresh air, but she didn't want to mess up her hair and makeup. Now that she'd passed thirty, it wasn't so easy to achieve that dewy, fresh look from her pageant days, and she hadn't spent the past hour and a half in front of a mirror just to have the wind and rain smudge it all to hell.

Her short black dress crawled up her thighs and she kept tugging it down out of habit, even though she and her friend, Ginette Tenney, were the only occupants of the car. Cat wished for a moment that she'd dressed more casually—like Ginette, in skinny-leg jeans and a cute little top—but if she caught Sean out with his girlfriend tonight, she damn well wanted them both to see what he was missing.

"How long has it been, Kitty Cat?"

She turned to Ginette who was driving. "How long has what been?"

"Since you and me got wasted together. I don't mean a beer by the pool or a cocktail before dinner. I'm talking about a full-on, shit-faced, girls'-night-out drunk." Ginette reached for the roach in the ashtray, but by now it was nothing but smoldering ashes. She rolled down her window and tossed it out. "Damn," she said. "Burned my fingers."

"You should quit smoking that stuff, Ginette, you're not a kid anymore."

"Hey, you like the hooch, I like my weed. What's the diff?"

"The difference is, you're destroying your brain cells. After all these years, you probably don't have that many left."

"Preach it, sister," Ginette said good-naturedly. "My memory's not worth shit these days. But I'm not sure you've got that much room to talk, the way you've been knocking back the sauce since we left the house. How much you got left of that fifth?"

"Enough to get drunk if I want to."

"Well, Jesus, Mary and Joseph, what are you waiting for?"

Cat shook her head. "You haven't changed a bit since we were in high school. You're still a bad influence, just like Mama always said."

"Damn straight and proud of it." Ginette drew a hand through her short, black hair, pulling the bangs off her forehead. She wasn't a particularly attractive woman; her features were too sharp and her face too weathered from the Gulf Coast sun. But she still had a good body and a great smile and was always up for whatever.

The two women had been best friends since the eighth grade, and Cat had the sudden urge to tell Ginette how much she valued their relationship. But she was just lit enough that a sappy confession might turn into a crying jag, and then her mascara would run all to hell and back.

Instead, she turned to stare out the window. The neon lights over the bars and clubs looked soft and hazy, and the wet streets beneath the streetlamps shimmered like quicksilver. Even with the windows up, she could hear music drifting from the jazz clubs, and she thought to herself that New Orleans was beautiful in the rain.

She felt something well inside her—a wave of loneliness that was as uncharacteristic as it was unwelcome. So her home life had gone belly-up. It wasn't the end of the world. Hell, it wasn't even her first busted-up marriage. It was, however, the first time she had been the one left behind, and that didn't sit well with Cat.

Don't get desperate. Just find a way to make the bastard pay, was her motto.

Ginette turned onto North Rampart, and Cat, who had begun to feel a bit copacetic about her situation once her mind had turned to revenge, was suddenly hit square between the eyes with her husband's philandering. Sean's car was parked in front of Sarah DeLaune's house. A rush of indignation flushed Cat's cheeks. Well, that and the whiskey.

"That goddamn, motherfucking son of a bitch!"

Ginette's head whipped around and she gave Cat a wide-eyed stare. "Man, you must really be pissed. I've never heard you talk like that before."

"I've never been married to a cheater before, have I?"

"That's a good point." Ginette switched on the wipers to clear the windshield. "Is that her house?"

"Yeah."

"Is that his car?"

"Yeah."

"Goddamn, motherfucking son of a bitch." Ginette eased up on the gas. "What do you want to do? I say we go in there and kick some ass. I mean, lay some serious hurt on that shithead. Just say the word and I'll stop the car right now. Right in the middle of the street. I don't give a fuck."

"Just drive on by."

"What?"

"You heard me."

A light shone from one of the front windows and Cat peered through the drizzle, trying to catch a glimpse of Sean inside.

Ginette leaned forward to stare out Cat's window. "That's a nice little house. What did you say she does?"

"She's a tattoo artist."

"Shit, Cat, we're in the wrong business. We sure as hell won't make enough dough cutting hair to afford a place like that."

"She comes from money," Cat said.

"That *bitch*. So what do you want to do now?"

"Turn at the next corner and park behind that old pickup truck. That way we can watch the house, but if they come out, they won't spot the car."

Ginette made the turn and slid her compact car into the curb behind the truck. She killed the lights and turned off the engine. In the ensuing silence, Cat could hear the motor ticking down, and in the distance, the wail of a siren. It was a wet, gloomy night, and she suddenly wasn't having much fun. Cat didn't like it when she wasn't having a good time.

Ginette propped her arm on the steering wheel and peered at her in the dark car. "You okay?"

"Yeah, I just want to sit here for a while and contemplate what I'm going to do to that bastard."

"I say give him a Lorena Bobbitt."

"Nah, I don't like knives," Cat said. "How about I just shoot it off?"

Ginette suddenly sobered. "Listen, in all seriousness, don't get too carried away, okay? Bastard's not worth doing time over. No man is. I mean, I'm all for kicking his ass, don't get me wrong, but that Saturday Night Special you slipped in your purse before we left the house has me a little worried."

Cat shrugged. "It's just for protection."

"Against what? Or should I say who?"

"Don't you ever listen to the news? The police found two bodies in this neighborhood in the past week. Both of the victims were white women, about our age."

"Well, that's information I would have found useful…say… oh, I don't know…before I let you talk me into this. Do the police know who killed them?"

"No."

"So the killer's still out there somewhere."

"That's why I brought the gun. You can't be too careful these days. Not around here."

"Is it loaded?"

"Fuck, yeah, it's loaded."

Ginette picked a piece of lint from her sweater. "Would you not say that word? It's like hearing my mother say it."

"Well, that's too fucking bad, Ginette, because I'm going to say fuck as many fucking times as I fucking well please tonight. What do you think of that?"

"Well, fuck, don't let me stop you."

They started laughing and couldn't stop. Ginette clutched her stomach as she let her head fall back against the seat. "This is fun. I just wish I didn't have to pee so bad."

"I'm sure you can find some bushes around here somewhere."

"With an ax murderer running around loose? Thanks, I'll hold it."

"I don't think he used an ax."

"Whatever. Did I tell you about this recurring dream I have where a psycho drag queen chases me around my bedroom with a hatchet? I think it's a safe bet I'm not going to be peeing in any bushes tonight."

"Suit yourself," Cat said. "It's your bladder."

Ginette fiddled with the CD player. "What do you feel like listening to?"

"I don't care. Something old-school maybe."

"How about a little classic Southern rock for a couple of classic Southern broads?"

"Skynyrd?"

"Hell, yeah, Skynyrd." Ginette put in the CD and they listened for a moment. "Never gets old, does it?"

"Reminds me of junior high," Cat said. "They used to end every dance with 'Freebird,' remember? Then we'd go over to your house and play the *90210* drinking game. Take a drink every time Brandon asks someone out."

Cat laughed. "Maybe we should do that right now."

"What?"

"Take a drink every time someone says the F-word."

"No fucking way," Ginette said. "I'm driving, remember? If we get pulled over, I'm dead meat because I can barely walk a straight line even when I'm sober. You're just going to have to put out."

"Why me?"

"Because you're used to sleeping with a cop."

"Oh, like you're not? Does the name Eddie Jarvis ring a bell?"

"Fuck, I was hoping you didn't know about that."

Cat passed her the bottle. "Here, take a drink."

"Why?"

"Because you said f-u-c-k."

"No, I didn't."

"Yes, you did. Now take a drink."

"Well, fuck, maybe I did."

They sat with their heads resting against the cushioned seat backs, listening to "Simple Man" as they stared out the windshield, watching the rain.

"I still have to pee," Ginette said. "How much longer do we have to wait?"

Cat sat up. "There he is. There's Sean."

Her heart was suddenly pounding as she watched him step out on the porch. He didn't linger or look back like a man who hated to leave, but instead he strode out to his car like a man who was more than a little pissed. Cat knew that walk.

A moment later, he got in his car and drove off.

"Now what?" Ginette said.

Cat reached for the door handle. "I'm going in there and have a little talk with her."

"*What?* Why?"

"Why do you think?"

"What if she calls the cops on you?"

"Just for talking?"

"Something tells me you've got a little more in mind than just talking. Whoa, wait a minute. Looky there." Ginette nodded in the direction of the house. "Is that her?"

A woman had come out on the porch with a small suitcase. She set it down while she locked the door, then carried it out to the car in the driveway and loaded it into the trunk. The interior light came on as she opened the door and climbed behind the wheel.

"Girl's in serious need of a stylist," Ginette muttered.

The car backed out of the driveway and headed down the street in their direction. They both ducked until the headlights were by them, and then Cat opened her door.

"Where do you think you're going?" Ginette asked suspiciously.

"Now's my chance to have a look around, see if Sean's moved back in with her. I have a right to know, don't I?"

"Yeah, you have a right to know, but riddle me this, Cat Woman. Just how do you plan on getting in? You and me both saw her lock the front door."

"Maybe she left a spare key under the mat or something."

"And if she didn't?"

Cat shrugged. "I'll think of something."

"You mean something like breaking and entering? That's not just a night in jail, Kitty Cat, we're talking the state pen."

"I don't care."

"Well, I sure as hell do, because they'll haul my ass off right along with you. Clovis will have a shit fit if he has to come bail me out."

"Look, just call me on my cell phone if you see one of them coming back. Or if you see the cops. I'll get out before anyone catches me."

"Damn it, Cat—"

Cat turned. "Hey, remember what we always say? A friend is someone who will bail you out of jail, but—"

"A best friend is the one sitting next to you in the cell. Yeah, I remember."

"I need you to be my best friend right now, Ginette."

She sighed. "Why do I have such a bad feeling about this?"

"It'll be okay," Cat said as she climbed out. "I'll be back before you know it."

"Cat?"

She leaned down and peered through the window Ginette had lowered. "Yeah?"

"Are we having fun yet?"

Purse hooked over her shoulder, Cat hurried down the street, trying not to look too conspicuous in the wet dusk. The rain had let up, but a fine mist settled over the street and glistened like spun cotton from the treetops. Tires swished on the wet pavement as cars sped by, and a few of the drivers threw her an appreciative wave.

She pulled her trench coat tightly around herself as she glanced over her shoulder. Ginette was but a faint silhouette in the car, and Cat resisted the urge to motion for her. It was odd to be doing this alone; Ginette used to be the daredevil of the two. She was the one who always had to talk Cat into whatever harebrained scheme she cooked up. But Ginette had mellowed out on her. Probably from smoking all that damn pot.

No matter. Cat needed to go this one alone anyway, because this was her mess. Her mission. She didn't even know what the hell she would do if she did find a way inside, so it was probably best not to drag Ginette along. If she found Sean's clothes in that woman's closet, Cat wasn't sure how she'd react. She didn't relish the thought of anyone, even her best friend, watching her lose it.

And she *would* lose it. No use kidding herself about that. Most of the time, she managed to appear cool and collected, but that was an act. That was the facade that Sean had expected from her. And so that's what she gave him, because for as long as she could remember, her every waking thought had been geared toward hooking Sean Kelton.

Back in high school, he'd been hot for her, too. All those

nights in the backseat of his car. On the sofa in her parents' living room. He couldn't get enough of her.

Then he'd gone off to college in Baton Rouge, and almost immediately Cat had sensed a change in him. They were only a two-hour drive apart, but Sean found more and more excuses to avoid her, until she'd finally forced the issue and he'd told her flat out that it was over.

And now it was déjà vu all over again, Cat thought angrily. She slipped her hand inside her purse and fingered the .38.

But Sean didn't know who he was dealing with. She wasn't some lovesick fool who'd just roll over and play dead like she had the last time he did the fade. If he thought he could disrespect her and not live to regret it, he was sadly mistaken. She was Catherine Fucking Landry, goddamn it. That had once meant something. Still did, if she had anything to say about it.

As she neared the house, Cat gulped in cold air to steady her nerves. She didn't bother looking for a key under the front mat, but instead slipped along the side of the house to the back. The homes here were so close together that she could hear the neighbor's television. A soft breeze drifted through the trees, rousing a wind chime somewhere nearby.

There was something eerie and plaintive about that sound, and Cat found herself shivering as she opened the wrought-iron gate to Sarah's courtyard. The hinges squeaked and the lock clanked shut behind her as she stood gazing around the shadows. She could hear the trickle of a fountain and the paperlike stirring of the dead banana leaves in the breeze. And still, the ghostlike music of the wind chimes.

As she stood there contemplating her next move, Cat had the sudden feeling that she was being watched. She studied the darkened windows of the house, saw no movement inside, no telltale gleam of hidden eyes.

Just her imagination. Sean was gone. Sarah was gone. The house was empty. Now was her chance.

Another deep breath and she was across the courtyard and in front of the French doors. She bent, picked up a rock from a flower bed and steeled herself to smash a windowpane, but at the last moment, she tried the door. It was unlocked. It opened quietly when she gave it a soft push.

That was strange. Sarah had left with a suitcase. Surely she would have checked the doors if she planned to be away for a day or two. Unless she'd been too distracted. Unless Sean was planning on coming back here.

In which case, he was in for a very unpleasant surprise.

Cat pushed open the door and stepped into the dark house. Her eyes took a moment to adjust, and then she glanced around, realizing that she was in the bedroom. The thought of Sean in that room, in that bed with that woman, sent Cat into the kind of fury that took even her by surprise. She'd become adept at hiding her temper, but now anger and indignation exploded from her every pore, unleashing a kind of rage she'd never known before.

Cat stormed through the room like a madwoman, ripping clothes from hangers, dumping drawers onto the floor, breaking everything she could get her hands on.

Her fury finally spent, she found herself struggling for breath as she stood in front of the dresser mirror. Even though she hadn't turned on a light, she could see the outline of her reflection.

A movement in the mirror caught her attention. Her gaze lifted and she could just make out the silhouette of someone in the doorway behind her. Watching her.

Cat's heart banged against her chest as she whirled. "Who are you?" she gasped.

★ ★ ★

Shit!

Phone pressed to her ear, Ginette shivered as she hurried down the street.

Damn it, Cat, pick up!

What the hell was taking her so long?

At least no one had called the cops. Yet.

Glancing warily over her shoulder, Ginette left the sidewalk and slipped into the shadows along the side of the house. It was still misting and she still had to pee. Cat was going to owe her big-time for this one.

She found the back gate and let herself into the courtyard, then crossed to the French doors and peered through one of the panes. It was dark inside the house. She couldn't see a damn thing.

Ginette tried the knob, and when the door silently opened, she stuck her head inside.

"Cat?" she said in a loud whisper. "Where are you?"

No answer.

She took a tentative step inside. "Cat? You still here?"

She'd brought a flashlight with her, and now as she angled the beam around the bedroom, she gasped in horror.

Holy shit, Cat. What the hell did you do?

Everything was a mess, like a hurricane had blown through the place. The bedding ripped all to hell. Clothes tossed every which way. Broken glass underfoot. Furniture and lamps overturned.

And something slippery on the floor.

Ginette's feet slid out from under her, and she fell with a hard crash. She dropped the light to catch herself with her hands and screamed when shards of glass bit into her palms.

"Fuck!"

The light hit the floor and blinked out. Ginette lunged and grabbed it just before it rolled under the bed.

She whacked it on her thigh and the light came back on. Aiming the beam onto the floor, she saw what she had slipped in. What was now all over her hands and clothes.

Blood.

It seemed to be everywhere.

Oh, sweet Jesus.

She tried to get up, but her panic made her clumsy and she fell back into the grisly mess. The blood was all over her now. She could even taste it on her tongue.

Sobbing, gasping for breath, she scrambled on hands and knees away from the gore. She sat huddled against the wall, playing the beam over the room. But always she brought the light back to the bloody floor.

Dear God, what had Cat done?

And then she heard something on the other side of the room.

Still clutching the flashlight, Ginette crawled around the bed.

"Cat?"

She was lying on her side, facing the wall.

"Oh, Jesus, Cat, what happened? What did you do to yourself?"

Ginette was beside her now, and when she rolled her over, Cat's eyes were open and staring, gleaming in the light that Ginette shone down on her.

Dead. She was dead.

Oh, God, oh, God, oh, God.

For a moment, Ginette remained shocked and motionless. Then her mind clicked back into place.

Cell phone! Nine-one-one.

Where was her fucking purse?

She started to move away, but then she saw Cat's eyelids flutter. Her lips moved.

She was alive!

Oh, thank you, God, thank you, Jesus.

"Cat, what happened? Where are you hurt? God, there's so much blood on the floor..." Her words trailed off when she saw that Cat was looking, not at her, but at something behind her.

Ginette heard nothing more than a whisper of sound. Felt only a stinging sensation when the blade first dug into her throat.

She looked down and saw, in her last instant of life, the reflection of her killer in Cat's eyes.

18

Father Dominique Dagan patted his lips with a linen napkin and gave a contented sigh. "That was a wonderful meal, Michael. I'm sorry you didn't enjoy yours. Too well done?"

Michael glanced down at the cold steak and limp asparagus on his plate. He shrugged with an apologetic smile. "The rib eye was fine. I guess I'm just not hungry tonight."

Dominique studied him over the candle that flickered in the center of the table. "I think you forget how well I know you. I very much doubt your appetite is the problem. You seem to have the weight of the world on your shoulders tonight."

"I never could fool you, could I? You know me better than anyone."

In spite of the age difference—Dominique had just turned sixty, Michael had not yet hit forty—the two men had been close friends for years. Together they had weathered a lot of storms, spiritual and otherwise.

It was Dominique who had given Michael the benefit of

the doubt when rumors had first started to circulate about the younger priest and a married parishioner. And then, when the painful truth had finally surfaced, when the affair had ended so tragically, Dominique had been the first to offer his un-wavering support.

He'd never left Michael's side during the long hours of ques-tioning at the police station after the bodies were discovered, nor later, when the sordid details of the murder-suicide had hit the papers. He'd been friend, confidant and spiritual ad-viser to Michael as he struggled with the agonizing decision to leave the priesthood, when even his own mother hadn't been able to look at him, much less forgive him.

For so many years now, Dominique had been the one con-stant in Michael's life, and he sometimes wondered where he would be without the priest's unflagging support and accep-tance.

Dominique lifted his wineglass now and watched Michael over the rim. "So tell me what it is that's weighing so heavily on your mind tonight."

Michael waited until the table had been cleared, then he picked up his own glass and sipped, his attention caught for a moment by the flickering candlelight.

"I'm worried about one of my patients," he finally said.

"Is it something you can discuss with me?"

Michael's gaze was still on the flame. He wanted to talk about Sarah, but for some reason, he found it difficult to, even with Dominique. Perhaps *especially* with Dominique, consid-ering how much he knew of Michael's past. A line had been crossed once and lives were destroyed. Vows had been com-promised and two people were dead, because of Michael's moral failings.

He'd made a promise to himself and to whatever god he

still believed in that he would never make that mistake again. He would never give in to his weakness. And yet, long after Sarah had left his office yesterday, he had sat in his garden and thought about her.

Michael was no stranger to desire. After Elise, there had been others. Quite a few when he'd first left the church. But not because he'd been trying to make up for lost time, but because he'd been searching for something he'd still yet to find.

In some ways, Sarah was very much like him. Always searching. Always wanting. A fallen angel who belonged to neither heaven nor hell, but rather existed on the fringes of a world that didn't understand her, and therefore, would never fully embrace her.

"Do you know anything about dissociative identity disorder?" he asked Dominique.

"It's what they used to call multiple personality disorder, isn't it? At one time, demon possession might have been considered the cause of such an affliction."

"In which case, my past would hardly qualify me to be of much assistance," Michael said ruefully.

"Or perhaps it would make you uniquely qualified," Dominique said with a smile. "At any rate, I thought the disorder had been mostly discredited by the psychiatric community some years ago."

"Yes and no," Michael said. "It's a controversial diagnosis, no question, and there are some therapists who flat-out discount it as a valid disorder. But I try not to base my opinion on the latest fad or current debate raging within the pages of the psychiatric journals."

"So I take it you've witnessed firsthand these multiple personalities in a patient."

"I've noted three separate alters so far. The interesting thing is, though, I've yet to meet the host, which is usually the identity that most often initiates treatment. In this case, the dominant personality in the sessions is a young male who calls himself Jude. He claims he's the protector."

"Who is he protecting?"

"That's yet to be determined. I've also caught glimpses of a childlike alter, a young boy. I believe this identity represents the host as a physically or sexually abused child. At some point, the child was able to slip into a state of mind in which it seemed that the abuse wasn't really occurring to him or her, but to somebody else."

"The protector?"

Michael nodded. "And now the protector has returned, because he perceives—rightly or wrongly—that the host is in trouble."

Dominique leaned in, obviously intrigued. "What kind of trouble?"

"Possibly from another alter," Michael said. "A third personality. The appearance was very brief, but I had the sense that this identity is also male, perhaps a little younger than the protector. And he's the one with all the rage. I think that's why Jude came to see me. He's been able to maintain his dominance until now, but the anger may be getting too strong for him to control. The only way he can contain it and protect the host is to find a way to merge all the separate identities into one unified alter."

"Which is where you come in."

"Hopefully, yes." Michael polished off his wine as the waiter discreetly left the check. "There's another aspect of this case that I find particularly troubling. I've detected some inconsistencies in Jude's demeanor. I think he's become very adept at deception, probably because of his need not only to protect the host, but also to fool the abuser. It's also possible that I'm being played."

Dominique lifted a brow. "Are you saying the whole thing could be a hoax? Why would someone go to so much trouble?"

Michael shrugged as he signed the credit-card receipt. "A need for proof of an existing psychiatric disorder perhaps. It's happened before, believe it or not."

The check settled, they walked out to the parking lot together. Dominique paused before climbing into his car. "The rage you spoke of earlier...if there really is an identity that is filled with so much anger, would you consider such an alter dangerous?"

"Under the right circumstances."

"Then be careful, Michael. Whether the disorder is real or a deceitful performance, you may be dealing with someone extremely cunning and dangerous."

Michael thought about the warning as he drove home in the rain. He'd sensed danger, too, that day in his office, but he hadn't wanted to worry Dominique, so he hadn't told him about the eyes of the third alter. Seething with pent-up rage, almost glowing with hatred. That brief glimpse had almost been enough to make Michael believe in demons again.

He tried to put it out of his mind as he considered the possibility of stopping somewhere to buy flowers to place on Elise's tomb. But it was late and the cemeteries in New Orleans were places of danger after dark. Tomorrow was Sunday. He had all day to wallow in his penitence if he needed to.

He parked in the garage when he got home, and as he came through the side door, his attention was drawn to the garden. He always left a lamp on in his office, and in the light that filtered through the glass panes in the door, he saw someone sitting at the top of the stairs. Head bowed, arms hugging knees. Shivering in the cold, wet air.

Pausing for only a split second, Michael walked through the gate and quickly crossed the garden. At the bottom of the steps, he hesitated again.

"Hello," he said as he started up the stairs. "I didn't expect to see you tonight."

Silence.

The head lifted and was caught in the light.

Michael drew a quick breath. "So," he said softly. "Which one are you?"

19

Halfway between New Orleans and Adamant, the heavens opened up and the rain blew in heavy sheets across the freeway. Traffic slowed to a crawl as emergency flashers blinked from the shoulder of the road where drivers had pulled over to wait out the storm.

Sarah tried to keep going, but the rain came down so hard she could barely see past the windshield. Creeping along behind a line of cars, she took the next rest-stop exit and parked. She ran the heater for as long as she dared, but when the storm showed no sign of letting up, she had to shut off the engine. Huddling in her jacket, she put back her seat and tried to relax.

Somehow, she managed to doze off and when she awakened, the rain had slacked to a shower and the rest-stop parking lot had emptied. Only a few other cars remained, along with a couple of eighteen-wheelers.

Checking the dash clock, Sarah realized she'd slept for over two hours, unheard of for her. And now she felt groggy and out of it. She needed to wash her face and use the restroom, but she wasn't all that keen on getting out of the car so late at night.

But the call of nature was urgent. She didn't have a choice. And there were still a few other people around. She watched from the rearview mirror as a woman with two little girls came out of the restroom. They lingered underneath the cover near the vending machines while the woman dug in her purse for change.

Sarah got out of the car and hurried across the parking lot to the pavilion. Nodding at the woman, she pushed open the door to the ladies' room.

The place was a typical public restroom. Sarah chose the cleanest-looking stall and went in. After she was finished, she walked over to the sink to wash her hands and splash cold water on her face.

As she bent over the sink, she heard the outer door open and close. She thought at first that the mother or one of the little girls had come back in. She finished washing her face, and as she reached for a paper towel, she glanced in the mirror.

Slowly she turned. That was odd. Whoever had opened the door hadn't come all the way into the bathroom. Sarah's gaze went to the partition that separated the stall area from the outside door. Was someone behind that thin wall? Waiting? Listening to her every move?

Her heart started to pound as she stood motionless. Almost breathless with fear.

And then, very softly, the door opened and closed.

Hooking her purse over her shoulder, Sarah ran out of the bathroom and glanced around. The woman and little girls were gone. The covered pavilion was empty.

No reason to panic, she told herself as she headed toward

her car. A few vehicles remained in the parking lot. She wasn't alone.

Nevertheless, she dug her keys out of her pocket and clutched the remote, ready to sound the panic button if anyone approached.

When she reached her car, a gust of wind swept raindrops across the parking lot. Shivering, Sarah pressed the unlock button, her gaze scouring the shadows as she climbed in and locked the doors.

Once inside, her tension eased, but she continued to scan the area, searching, she realized, for a dark green sedan.

By the time she rolled into Adamant, it was well after midnight and the streets were deserted. Even in prime-time hours, the town didn't offer much in the way of excitement.

On a Saturday night, most of the teenagers who were old enough to drive made the twenty-minute trek into El Dorado, the county seat. Or else they spent the evening driving the main drag, the two-lane highway that ran straight through town, with only a handful of traffic lights to slow them down.

Adamant hadn't always been so dead. It had once been a thriving community. Dependent on the declining cotton and timber markets at the turn of the last century, the town's fortunes had reversed in the early twenties with the discovery of oil in the area.

When Busey Number One hit near El Dorado, the economy was blown sky-high. Geologists, speculators and wildcatters poured in from every corner of the country and wooden derricks rose overnight to mar the scenic vistas.

But the windfall soon played itself out. Wells that had run at full capacity during the peak went dry. Natural gas was allowed to escape into the air and spills contaminated the ground water. Within five years, the oil boom had gone bust and the skeletal remains of the oil derricks and the dark holes that burrowed deep into the earth were all that remained of prosperous times.

Adamant was now a ghost town, Sarah thought as she drove through the darkened streets. At least for her it was. Whatever charm the town once possessed had long since withered and died. All that remained now, other than an abundance of churches and gas stations, was a stagnant community that existed on memories.

The rain was still coming down when Sarah pulled into the driveway. She sat for a moment staring up at the house. Tall and imposing even in the dark, it was the kind of place that was envied and admired, the kind of house that strangers stopped to stare at, especially in the summer when the gardens were in full bloom.

Sarah's father had once employed a gardener in the warm months, but Esme was never satisfied with his work. She didn't trust him with her prized peonies, and donning bonnet and gloves, she'd chase him away every chance she got.

It was still a beautiful house. Still James DeLaune's showplace. But it wasn't Sarah's home and never had been.

Using the remote Esme had given her, she parked in the garage, and then grabbing her suitcase from the trunk, carefully navigated the slippery walkway to the house.

Kicking off her shoes in the mudroom, she set down her suitcase in the kitchen and turned on a light. Shrugging out of her wet jacket, she glanced around.

So, here I am again.

The first thing she'd noticed upon returning was that nothing much had changed since she'd been shipped off to boarding school. The kitchen was the only room in the house that had been touched, and here only the appliances had been updated. The layout was the same. The blue-and-white color scheme the same.

The memories were the same.

The kitchen had always been Esme's domain. Sarah's mother was often out when she got home from school, but Esme was always there, a calm, stoic presence in the midst of Sarah's loneliness.

As for Rachel, she barely took the time to change her clothes before she was off again to cheerleading practice or student council meetings or whatever it was that she did after school to keep her away from the house.

Sarah's father would get home at six and go straight to his study, where he would expect to relax without interruption until dinner. Then they would all sit down together, and for the next hour, time would creep for Sarah. If she'd had her way, she would have eaten all her meals in the kitchen or at Esme's cottage. Anywhere but at the same table as a man who could barely stand to look at her.

Sean was right, Sarah thought now as she carried her suitcase up the stairs to her old room. Why did she keep coming back here? Why couldn't she just let the old man die in his own bitterness?

Did she really think her sojourns back to Adamant were going to finally earn his love and approval? After all these years?

That's not why I'm here.

She'd come home, because the demons that had to be confronted were here. The evil that had to be vanquished...was right here in this house.

20

Sarah slept very little that night, but the next morning, she was up and dressed by nine. The rain had stopped sometime during the night, and the sun that slanted through her bedroom window looked warm and inviting. She stared out into the backyard, watching the spiral of smoke from Esme's chimney. Even though it was warm out, Esme still wanted her fire.

Halfway down the stairs, the smell of coffee hit Sarah, and as she walked out into the kitchen, she saw that Esme had already been there. She'd left a plate of frosted cinnamon buns, and Sarah nibbled on one as she waited for the coffee to finish brewing.

Fifteen minutes later, she was out the door. Esme would be in church by now so Sarah didn't bother stopping by the cottage. Instead, she cut through the orchard and headed across the field.

The ground was still wet from the rainstorm, and by the time Sarah reached the farmhouse, her shoes were caked with mud. She used a stick to clean them off, and then she stood there for the longest time staring at the house.

It was typical of a late nineteenth-century farmhouse. Two stories, a wide porch and a peaked roof. The whitewash on the siding had long since worn away, and the roof looked ready to cave in places. Weeds and brambles had taken over the front yard, and the pine forest was slowly reclaiming the cotton fields.

Sarah had been making the trip out here each time she'd returned to see her father. But as she stepped up on the porch, she realized this was the farthest she'd ventured. Her first trip out here had been just before Christmas. She'd parked at the end of the gravel road and sat for a long time. The next time, she'd walked over from the house, but had gotten no farther than the edge of the overgrown yard. The last time, she'd made it all the way to the steps and had even managed to sit for a moment.

Now she was actually standing on the porch. A few more steps and she would be at the door. Another step and she would be inside.

But she wouldn't take those extra steps today. Already her breath was coming too fast, and the tension in her chest was like a balled-up fist. She'd downed half a Xanax before she left the house, but it hadn't yet taken effect.

Or maybe, *maybe,* the anxiety gripping her was too powerful for any medication.

As Sarah stared at the old weathered door, panic rolled over her, making her palms sweat and her stomach churn.

Squeezing her eyes closed, she tried to remember what Michael had told her to do when she felt the onslaught of an attack. Take deep breaths. Nice and slow. In…out. In…out.

She opened her eyes, and the door seemed to waver, like

a mirage. Perspiration broke out on her forehead and she felt herself go weak at the knees. Sarah grabbed the nearest newel post and clung for dear life. She wouldn't black out. Not here.

Dear God, please not here.

The last time...

Mustn't think about that. *Couldn't* think about that.

Fumbling in her pocket, she found the other half of the pill and managed to work up enough saliva to get it down. Sinking to the steps, she dropped her head between her knees.

The sun had felt warm on the way over, but now the breeze was cold against her clammy skin. Shivering, Sarah kept her head down until the spell subsided.

She shouldn't have come out here. Obviously, she wasn't ready.

But if not now, when? Would she ever find the courage to confront what waited for her inside that house? Or was she destined to spend the rest of her life running from shadows? Running from the truth, and forever chased by a terrible fear? A hideous secret she couldn't even remember?

You can't fight evil in the dark, Sarah. The only way you can truly defeat it is to bring it into the light.

As quickly as the attack came on, the panic left her. Whether from her own resolve or the medication, Sarah didn't know or care. She was back in control now. That was all that mattered.

Feeling steadier, she lifted her head a split second before she felt his fingers in her hair.

21

The touch was phantom. Had to be. Or maybe the wind had ruffled her hair.

The floorboards on the porch creaked, and as Sarah lifted her head, she saw a shadow on the ground looming over her. Someone had come up behind her.

Startled, she scrambled down the steps and whirled, almost expecting to find a funereal face staring back at her. But the man on the porch wasn't Ashe Cain.

In the years since Sarah had last seen Derrick Fears, he'd undergone a drastic metamorphosis. Gone was the weird teen that had seemed so dark and mysterious and impossibly cool to the adolescent Sarah. The Goth Svengali who had claimed to walk in the devil's footsteps. In his place was a thirty-one-year-old man with a scarred and careworn face. Hard eyes and a cruel, taunting mouth.

Gone also was the corpse pallor and the dyed black hair. His head was peeled now, the hair buzzed so short that when he turned a certain way, Sarah could see the inverted-cross tattoo on the left side of his skull. One of the few remaining remnants of the boy who'd once called himself Azrael.

He wore jeans and an old flannel shirt over a gray concert T-shirt. Ink flames licked up his neck and kissed the line of his jaw. His sleeves were rolled up and his forearms were also covered in art, but Sarah couldn't make out the individual designs.

His eyes mocked her from the porch. "You don't know who I am, do you?"

"I know exactly who you are," Sarah said in a steady voice.

"After all these years?" He propped his hand on one of the newel posts, his gaze never leaving hers. "It's been a long time. How've you been, Sarah?"

"Not too bad. And you?"

"Can't complain. Not after where I've been." The smile disappeared and his gaze hardened. "I guess you heard I spent some time in the slammer."

"Someone may have mentioned it. I don't live here anymore, though, so I don't keep up with local gossip."

"I can't blame you for that. If I were in your place, I wouldn't want to be reminded of this shit hole, either. Although I can't help wondering what brings you out here."

"I was wondering the same thing about you."

A faint smile touched his lips. "Maybe I was hoping to run into you."

"How did you know I was in town?"

"Unlike you, I do keep up with local gossip."

"That still doesn't explain how you knew I would be here this morning." His perfectly timed arrival seemed too much of a coincidence to Sarah, and the notion that he had followed her sent a chill straight down her spine.

"I guess we just think alike, is all." He glanced over his shoulder at the house. "Have you been inside?"

"No, not yet."

"Don't tell me you're afraid. This place never used to scare you. You hung out here all the time."

That was before my sister was murdered in the front room. "This was your haunt, too. You and your friends. Did you ever see a strange boy hanging around here a few weeks before my sister was killed?"

That half smile again. "Strange is a relative term for people like you and me. What did he look like?"

"He was Goth. Except…"

"Except…what?"

She shook her head. "Nothing. You may have seen him with me."

He paused. "I never saw you with anyone. You always came out here alone. Just you and your dog."

Something in his eyes—and that slight hesitation—made Sarah wonder if he was lying. But if he'd seen her with Ashe Cain, he would surely have told the police.

"Back then, you were the only person I knew who'd come out here by yourself after dark," Fears said. "Besides me, of course. You had a real thing for spooky places, didn't you?"

"So did you, apparently."

"Nah, I did all that stuff to get under my old man's skin. I liked shocking people. But some of the spells we cast in the house were pretty damn convincing. I had a few of those idiot assholes believing we'd actually summoned the devil one night."

"You played your part well," Sarah said. "You had your own little cult."

"It wasn't difficult. People are stupid for the most part. They believe what they want to believe."

He stared down at her in amusement, the nightmare house behind him.

"Take those footprints," he said. "That shit never happened. It was just some old gomer with a wild imagination. Should have shipped him off to the loony bin, but instead people believed him. Got so worked up, they convinced themselves the devil climbed out of an oil well and danced his way across a cotton field."

His laugh was hard and mean. He folded his arms and leaned a shoulder into the post. "People used to believe a lot of things about you, too, didn't they? You know what we called you?"

"I can only imagine."

"Suicide Sarah."

Her reaction was visceral. "That's a terrible thing to call someone. Especially a kid."

"It fit you, though, didn't it? You were gloomy as hell back then."

"That's pretty ironic, coming from a guy who used to call himself the Angel of Death. Oh, yes," she said, when she saw his brow lift in surprise. "I knew what your name meant."

"I always did think you were smarter than most folks around here gave you credit for." He glanced toward the door. "Isn't there an old saying about the murderer always returning to the scene of the crime?"

Gooseflesh prickled at the back of Sarah's neck. He watched her as she watched him.

"What happened to your sister…must be hard to get over something like that. Especially if you were close. But you and Rachel weren't that close, were you? Least that's what I always heard. Maybe because she was your old man's favorite. Everybody in town knew how crazy he was about her. Didn't have much use for you, though, did he? Shipped you off the first chance he got."

Slowly, he came down the steps. Sarah resisted the urge to retreat. For some reason, he seemed determined to intimidate her and she was just as determined that he wouldn't.

He cocked his head, studying her. "You don't take after him much, do you? 'Course that's a plus in my book."

"Why's that?"

"Let's just say, I'm not one of the judge's biggest fans. Not after the way he used his pull to try and railroad me for that murder. Kind of surprising a man in his position would rush to judgment on such flimsy evidence. You'd think he'd want to make damn sure they got the right guy."

"Despite what my father did or didn't do, you were never charged with Rachel's murder," Sarah said.

"No, I wasn't, but that don't cut much ice in these parts. Most of the mullet crowd still believe I killed her. They believe it, because that's what they want to believe. It's easier than thinking someone else did it. A neighbor maybe. Or a close friend. Be hard living with that kind of suspicion in a town this small. So the self-righteous pricks just keep right on telling themselves I did it. They keep right on looking at me like I'm something they wouldn't want to scrape off their shoes."

"Why are you telling me all this?" Sarah said. "I'm not one of those people. I haven't even seen you in years."

"Because there's something you need to know about me. I may be a lot of things, but I'm not a murderer. I killed once in self-defense, and the only reason I did time was because the jury wanted to stick it to me for what happened to your sister. That way, they could tell themselves I got what was coming to me."

He crossed the space between them and planted himself in front of Sarah. His body was wiry, but she could sense the power of it. The pent-up tension in his hard muscles.

Sarah's heart pounded and her palms began to sweat. It was foolish to have come out here alone. Crazy to be standing here talking to a man who could probably snap her like a twig. She wasn't that fearless thirteen-year-old who refused to be intimidated by an old legend. Or by her father's contempt.

And yet something about Derrick Fears, about his anger, intrigued her.

He pointed to a scar on his right temple. "See this? Courtesy of Sheriff Clay's brass knuckles. And these?" He turned over his arms to show her the circular scars dotting his skin. "Cigar burns. Got 'em on my legs and all over my back. However much some people in this town wanted to believe I killed your sister, this is how bad the sheriff wanted to prove it."

"Sheriff Clay did that to you?" Sarah stared in horrified fascination at the scars.

"Hell, yeah, he did it. Kinda scary, ain't it, when you figure I'm probably not the one who took the brunt of his anger."

"What do you mean?"

"He was one mean son of a bitch and a guy like that can't just turn it off when he goes home at night. I reckon he and your daddy both had secrets they didn't want dug up."

"You keep implying you know something about my father. Why don't you just say it?"

"Because I doubt I'd be telling you anything you don't already know." He circled Sarah now like a predator. "Besides, you've got a few secrets of your own, don't you, Suicide Sarah?

You were here when it happened. You know who killed your sister, don't you?"

"No!"

"Oh, that's right. You lost your memory, didn't you?" His smile was grim and cruel as he kept circling. "That's what you claim, but maybe you're just flat-out lying. Maybe you saw something you've been keeping to yourself all these years." He stopped and stared down at her. His breath was hot on her cold face. "But let's say you really can't remember. Maybe seeing all those old bloodstains would jog something loose for you. I bet if you tried real hard, it'd all come back to you. You might even remember the screams. Think about it. She must have been carrying on something fierce when the cutting started. You're telling me you don't remember that? I don't see how you could forget it."

An icy dread pumped through Sarah's veins. She tried to back away from him, but his hand shot out and closed around her arm, trapping her. "People always wonder what it feels like to be cut like that, how much it must hurt and all, but I bet what really gets you is the sound. That wet noise the blade makes when it sinks through all that muscle and tissue and fat. You ever heard that sound, Sarah?"

"Take your hand off my arm," she said.

He grinned down at her, and for an instant his grip tightened. Then he glanced over her shoulder and something flickered across his face before he released her. He reached up and drew a finger across her throat before she could pull free.

A moment later he was gone.

Sarah watched as a squad car bumped along the gravel lane. It pulled to a stop at the edge of the yard and a man in a pressed uniform got out and came toward her.

No wonder Derrick had taken off so abruptly, Sarah thought. He must have spotted the car before she heard the engine.

The officer walked toward her through the tall weeds. Sarah was facing the sun and she put up a hand to shade her eyes.

"Was that Derrick Fears I just saw?" His voice held more than a hint of contempt.

"Yeah, that was him," Sarah said.

He stared down at her from behind dark glasses. "He's a pretty nasty customer. He didn't bother you, did he?"

"Put it this way. He didn't hurt me."

"Well, I guess that's something. Still, he's got no business being out here. Nobody does."

"Why? Who owns this place?" Sarah could feel the strength of his gaze through the mirrored lenses, and she found herself shivering in the cold breeze.

"The county's owned it for years, ever since the Duncan heirs stopped paying the taxes. And it's my job to run off trespassers."

"Meaning me?"

"Unless you've got official business out here, and I can't think what that would be."

Sarah glanced at the house. "I guess curiosity wouldn't be classified as official. I grew up around here. I just wanted to see what the old place looked like these days."

"Yeah, we get that a lot." He stood like a statue, watching her. "Believe it or not, people still come out here to search for the footprints."

"That's not why I'm here."

He peeled off his sunglasses and she saw that his eyes were darker than she expected. Cold and piercing. The intense focus was more than a little unnerving.

"If you didn't come to look for the footprints, then you must be here about the murder," he said.

A ghost drifted past Sarah. "What makes you say that?"

"Because that's the other reason people make the trip out here. They still want to see where it happened, even after all these years."

"It's personal for me. I knew the victim."

"It's a small town. Almost everyone knew her." For the first time, his gaze moved from Sarah and he stood staring at the house, a breeze ruffling his brown hair. "My father was the county sheriff when it happened. He headed up the investigation and the fact that he never could close the case really did a number on him. He was a proud man and a failure like that ate at him. I wasn't around toward the last, but I'm told he was obsessed with solving that murder right up until the day he died."

"Now I know who you are," Sarah said in surprise. "You're the new police chief, right? I've heard about you."

A faint smile touched his lips, reminding her of Derrick Fears's taunting smirk. "Well, you know what they say. You can't believe everything you hear."

"I'm Sarah DeLaune." She held out her hand.

"Lukas Clay."

Sarah could sense his interest in the way he looked at her, in the way he held her hand a moment longer than was necessary. But she wasn't on the market. She wasn't over Sean yet, and she didn't know if she ever would be. Which was why she found her jittery reaction to Lukas Clay so unsettling.

"I guess you do have a personal reason for coming out here." His tone warmed. "I heard you've been by the station to see me a couple of times."

"You were out. And no one else seemed able or willing to help me."

"I understand you wanted to get a look at your sister's case files."

"That's right. Is there any reason why I can't see them?"

"No. But I guess I'm wondering why you'd want to."

"I'm just trying to piece it all together," she said with a shrug. "Trying to make some sense of what happened."

He nodded. "I can understand how you wouldn't be able to let something like that go. It's hard for the family to move on when there's no justice."

"My motives may not be quite as altruistic as you seem to think," Sarah said. "I'm not after justice. I'm just looking for a way to chase away the nightmares. My shrink tells me that making peace with my past may do wonders for my mental outlook."

"Be careful. You can't trust everything a shrink tells you."

"What?"

The corners of his mouth twitched. "Don't you watch movies? The psychiatrist is always a twisted psychopath."

What an odd thing to say, Sarah thought. "I'll be sure and remember that."

"In the meantime, come by the station first chance you get, and I'll see that you get a look at those files."

"Thanks."

"I'm heading back in your direction," he said. "Can I give you a lift?"

"My shoes are all muddy. I wouldn't want to track up your car."

"That's what floor mats are for. Besides, with Fears out here traipsing about, I'd feel a lot better if you'd let me drive you."

"If you're sure it's not too much trouble."

"No trouble at all."

They got in the car, and he backed down the gravel drive to the main road, then turned the car toward town. The interior smelled like peppermint and another scent that Sarah couldn't identify.

He'd put the sunglasses back on, but Sarah could see his eyes through the corners as he watched the road.

"Has Miss Esme talked to you about what happened the other night?"

"I haven't seen her yet," Sarah said. "Is she okay?"

"As far as I know she is. She claims she saw someone on the roof of your house."

"On the *roof*? Why on earth would someone be up on the roof?"

He shrugged. "That's what I wondered. I chalked it up to her getting on in years and her eyesight not being what it once was. I figured she saw some branches whipping around in the wind. The thing is, though, someone was in the house when I went by there the next day. Whoever it was knocked me out cold before I could get a look at him."

Sarah stared at him in shock. "Were you badly hurt?"

"Just a bump on the head. What concerns me is that I couldn't find any sign of a break-in. I don't know how he got in." He pulled the car to the curb in front of her house and parked. "It's possible he came through a window. Miss Esme says she comes over to air out the house every so often. She could have left one open."

That didn't sound like Esme. Sure, she was getting older, but her mind was still as sharp as ever.

"Was anything stolen?"

"I had Miss Esme go through the house and she couldn't find anything missing."

"So why was someone in there?"

He paused. "I think it was Fears. He denied it, but he wasn't very convincing."

Sarah thought about the way those dark eyes had mocked her earlier. "If he didn't take anything, what was he after?"

"I don't know yet. Even if it was him, I doubt he'll be back. He knows I'm watching him now. But just to be on the safe side, make sure you keep all the doors and windows fastened. You should consider getting the locks changed, too."

"I won't be here long enough for that," Sarah said. "But thanks for the advice. And the ride home."

He fished a card out of his pocket and handed it to her. "You see anything suspicious, you give me a call—day or night. That's what I'm here for."

Sarah climbed out of the car and headed up the walkway without looking back. By the time she got inside, Lukas Clay had already driven away.

22

The antiseptic smell of despair engulfed Sarah as she walked down the corridor to her father's room. The sickly sweet scent was like no other, and every hospital she'd ever been in always had that same odor. Which was one of many reasons why she tried to avoid them.

The aversion was strange, she supposed, because she wasn't usually squeamish about such things. The disinfectant they used at the studio didn't bother her at all, nor did the sight of blood oozing from a fresh tattoo. She simply wiped it away, along with the excess ink, and that was that. Not a second thought.

Hospitals were different, though, and the end result of a trip here was never a beautiful piece of art on a living canvas.

Sarah paused outside her father's room. She didn't want to go inside. Facing him again was the very last thing she wanted to do. But he was still her flesh and blood, her only living relative, and she wouldn't wish on her worst enemy what the final stages of cancer had done to him. It was shocking to see him so feeble when he'd once been so vital.

Bracing herself, she pushed open the door and walked inside. He was lying on his back, sleeping. Or at least, his eyes were closed.

A man dressed in a dark suit and a clerical collar stood at his bedside gazing down at him.

Sarah's breath caught. "Is he...?"

"No, no, he's just sleeping."

She put a hand to her chest. "When I saw you standing over him like that..." She gave a shaky little laugh. "A minister at my father's bedside is about the last thing I expected to see."

His smile was apologetic. "I'm sorry my being here upset you."

"No, it's okay. And that's not exactly what I meant anyway..." She trailed off again as their gazes connected. She felt a flicker of recognition, but she couldn't place him.

He was around fifty, with ordinary features. Something about him—the way he'd stood over her father's bed when she walked in, the way his dark eyes held hers now with an intense curiosity—niggled at Sarah's own curiosity. Who the hell was he?

She glanced down at her father. "How's he doing?"

"Holding his own. One of the nurses said he'd rallied for a little while this morning."

"That's good."

The minister came around to her side of the bed. "You must be Sarah. I haven't seen you in years, but I knew you the moment you walked in. You're the spitting image of your mother."

He took her hand warmly in his, and Sarah felt the sting

of unexpected tears. No one had ever told her she looked like her mother.

"I'm Tim Mason." He put his other hand over hers, holding on for a long time. "You probably don't remember me."

"No, I'm sorry, I don't," Sarah said, slipping her hand from his. "I haven't lived here in a long time."

"Since you were thirteen, I believe. That's when you went away to school."

Sarah was taken aback. "That's right. I'm surprised anyone remembers that." She paused. "I hope you don't mind my asking, but what are you doing here? My father has never been much of a churchgoer. In fact, he has some pretty strong views on religion."

"Oh, I'm well aware of how James has always felt about *my kind*."

"You sound as if you've known my father for a long time."

"We go back." There was an edge of what sounded like regret in his voice.

"Did he ask you to come by?"

"No. But at a time like this, even a man who's lost his faith may feel the need to clear his conscience."

Sarah stared at him, still puzzled by his presence and his demeanor. "I'm not so sure my father would agree with you."

His expression turned troubled. "I'm more concerned about you at the moment. I hate that you're all alone at a time like this. If you find yourself in need of someone to talk to, come by the church. We're still on Oak Street. You don't need an appointment to see me, just drop by anytime. I'm almost always in my office."

"Thank you."

"I mean that," he said, his gaze holding hers. "I'm available anytime you need me."

He pushed open the door to leave, then held it for a nurse who was just coming in. She saw Sarah at her father's bedside and gave her a sympathetic smile. "I'm Judy," she said. "I don't think we've met. Are you Mr. DeLaune's granddaughter?"

"No, I'm his daughter," Sarah said.

"Oh, I thought—" She glanced at the door, then back at Sarah. "Busy day," she said with a sigh. "I'm here to give Mr. DeLaune his shot."

"Should I wait outside?"

"No, you're fine."

She gave Sarah another glance as she finished up and left the room. Sarah looked down at her father. The needle prick had awakened him. His eyes were already glassy from the previous dose of morphine as he stared up her.

"It's me, Dad. Sarah."

For a moment, she wondered if he'd lost his comprehension. He seemed not to recognize her. His breathing was labored and his skin pale and paper-thin. He'd once been a robust man, but the arms lying on top of the sheet were stick-thin and threaded with veins.

"What day is it?" he finally said. A cough rattled in his chest.

"Sunday."

"Sunday." He thought about that for a moment. "Don't you have work tomorrow?"

"I took a few days off so I could drive up here."

"You didn't get fired, did you?"

"No, Dad, I didn't get fired."

She didn't bother to remind him that she was part owner in the studio. She'd answered these same questions the last time she came to see him.

"All that money to send you to art school and you end up

in a goddamn tattoo parlor." He spat out his condemnation like a nasty taste in his mouth.

"Your money didn't send me to art school," Sarah couldn't help reminding him. "I used Mama's money for my schooling."

"And how do you think she had that money to leave you? Because I was there to put food on the table and keep a roof over her head. She didn't need to spend a dime of her own money because she had mine to squander on one damn fool thing after another."

"Dad."

"Maybe if she'd had to work a day in her life, she would have had a little more appreciation for how good she had it. And maybe if she hadn't had so much time on her hands, she wouldn't have ended up doing what she did." His fingers clutched at the covers. He seemed to be working himself up into a state.

"What did Mama ever do that was so bad?" Sarah said softly.

"Spent all of her time down at that church instead of home where she belonged. How much is a man supposed to put up with?"

Sarah said nothing.

"She expected me to just forget all about it. Put it behind us, she said. How was I supposed to do that, when I had a reminder of what she did looking me in the face every time I turned around?"

"I don't know what you're talking about," Sarah said. "What is it you think Mama did to you?"

He gazed at her stonily, his fingers still working the covers.

"Is that why you hate me? Because of something Mama did?"

"I don't hate you," he said on a raspy breath. "I just can't stand the sight of you."

Sarah glanced away, telling herself it didn't matter what he thought. She didn't need his love or approval. She didn't need anything from him. But as hard as she'd worked to inoculate herself from his contempt, his words still cut her to the quick. "Why? What did I do?"

"I should have protected her. It's a man's duty to take care of his family. Especially his child." Another cough racked his frail body and this time the strain seemed almost more than he could bear.

Sarah reached down and put her hand over his. "It's okay, Dad. Maybe you shouldn't talk. Just get some rest."

"Rest?"

"You need to keep up your strength."

"What for? I don't want to linger any longer than I have to. I'd rather get it over with. I've been dying inside for fourteen damn years."

"I know you have."

He seemed not to hear her. He was lost in his own misery. "It was my duty to protect her and I didn't. My little girl murdered and I couldn't do anything to stop it."

"What happened to Rachel wasn't your fault."

"Not my fault?" His voice took on a strange tone. "Then whose fault was it?"

"I don't know."

"You do know." Sarah's hand was still on his, but he turned it. Suddenly he was gripping her wrist. "You know because you did it. It was *you*."

The hate and fury in his voice was like a knife blade through Sarah's heart. She was so stunned by the attack, she couldn't utter a word. Couldn't muster a denial. For a moment, she could barely even breathe. "No!"

His fingers tightened around her wrist. "I knew it the moment they brought you home. The moment I saw all that blood on you. And you acting so strange, refusing to talk. I knew you hated her. You were so goddamned jealous and spiteful, something was bound to happen sooner or later. I told your mother, but she wouldn't listen. Even I never dreamed you'd go as far as you did. Your own sister. Your own flesh and blood. No one could have known. Who would ever think something like that could happen?"

Sarah was trembling all over, her heart a pounding piston in her chest. "I didn't hurt Rachel. How could you think that of me?"

"Your own mother thought it of you," he said with malicious triumph. "Why do you think she washed off all that blood? Had Esme burn your clothes? She knew it was evidence, that's why. She wouldn't let you get psychiatric help because she was too afraid of what they'd find out. One daughter dead, the other a murderer. She couldn't live with that."

Sarah tried to back away from the bed, but as weak as his grip was, she couldn't seem to break free.

"Don't you dare leave here until I'm finished with you. I've kept this inside me all these years, and it's eaten me alive, just like this damn cancer. I never did anything about it, because I made a promise to your mother. I told her I'd keep quiet, if she'd send you off somewhere so I didn't have to look at you. Didn't have to live with you under my roof. But Anna's gone and now here you are back. Wanting my forgiveness. Sniffing after my money. Well, you're not going to get either. Do you hear me? I don't forgive you and I'm not leaving you a cent."

Sarah wrenched her hand from of his grip and ran out of the room, his enraged accusations following her out the door.

All she could think was that she had to get out of the hospital, away from his voice, away from that smell. Away from the terrible dread building inside her. She had to have air before she threw up. She could already taste vomit in her throat.

In her blind rush, she collided with another body just outside the door. Muttering an apology, she tried to move away, but strong hands gripped her arms, steadying her.

"Sarah?"

She looked up in confusion.

"Are you okay?"

"I don't—" She blinked. "Curtis?" She couldn't seem to make her brain work. "What are you doing here?"

"I work here, remember?" His gaze lifted to the door behind her. "What happened in there?"

"Nothing."

"It sounded like something to me. I could hear the old man carrying on all the way out here."

"It was just an argument," she said. "You know how he is. I need a little fresh air, that's all."

"Okay. But I hope you're not planning on driving in this condition. Look how your hands are shaking. I'm off for the next few hours. I can take you home."

"No, I have my car here."

"Then I'll drive your car and have someone pick me up."

"That's way too much trouble," Sarah said. And really, she just wanted to be alone at the moment.

But Curtis was insistent. "It's no trouble. And anyway, you know what Gran would do to me if I let you get behind a wheel like this." His green eyes smiled down at her. "Just wait for me, okay?"

He was gone for only a few minutes, and then they rode the elevator down to the lobby and left the building.

Sarah was still trembling when she climbed into the passenger seat of her car. Curtis got behind the wheel.

"I still say this is too much trouble." She rubbed her hands up and down her arms. "How are you going to get back to the hospital?"

"A friend is coming by to pick me up. Don't worry about it. He owes me." He gave her a concerned glance as he pulled out of the parking lot. "Now do you want to tell me what happened?"

"I told you it was nothing. He's dying, and yet I still seem to bring out the worst in him."

"And you still think it's your fault," he said quietly. "Which is exactly what he's always wanted."

Sarah glanced at him. "You don't like him much, do you?"

"He's been good to my grandmother," Curtis said. "I guess even the devil should get his due."

"What did he do to you?"

He shrugged. "It was a long time ago. It doesn't matter anymore."

It obviously did matter, but Sarah could tell he didn't want to talk about it. She let the matter drop as she dug in her purse for her pill bottle.

"What are you taking?" Curtis asked.

"Xanax."

"Anxiety attacks?"

"Anxiety attacks, insomnia, night terrors. Take your pick."

"How long have you been on it?" He sounded worried.

"I don't know. A few months. It's legit. My doctor gave

me the prescription, and I'm seeing a shrink. I've got all my bases covered."

"You do know it's addictive, right? I hope your doctor covered all the bases when he prescribed it."

"I only take it when I'm feeling anxious." Which seemed to be a lot of the time these days.

"I've heard that before," he muttered, his gaze on the road.

Sarah studied his profile as he drove. Even as a kid, he'd been attractive, but now in his early thirties, he was a strikingly handsome man. And a doctor, to boot.

"I bet you have women swarming all over you," she said.

"What?"

She smiled. "You must be one of the most eligible bachelors in town."

"I don't have much time for a social life, I'm afraid."

"You do know how proud you've made your grandmother, don't you?"

"I hope I have. I owe her everything. I hate to think where I'd be if she hadn't taken me in."

"Is that why you came back here? So you could be near her?"

"Mostly. But I guess a part of me also had something to prove."

"Well, you've certainly done that," Sarah said.

"I'm not so sure." His expression turned pensive. "Sometimes I wonder if we can ever really overcome the past. It's what makes us who we are. One small thing done differently and we become someone else. It's like the butterfly effect. One moment can change history. One decision can change everything."

"Very philosophical," Sarah said. "I suppose my life changed the night Rachel died."

"Her death changed all our lives. We would all be different people if not for that one moment in our past."

"I know you loved her," Sarah said softly. "I've known it since we were kids."

She saw his hands tighten on the steering wheel.

"You don't have to talk about it if you don't want to, but I wish you would. I wish you'd tell me about her. I barely even knew her. We were sisters, and yet I don't know the first thing about her."

He was silent for a moment. "She wanted to be a doctor."

"Really? She always talked about being a lawyer. I thought she planned on following in our father's footsteps."

"No, that was *his* plan." His voice hardened. "It wasn't what Rachel wanted."

"Why didn't she tell him?"

A muscle twitched in his jaw as he watched the road. "It was a complicated relationship."

"What do you mean?"

He shot her a glance. "Maybe you shouldn't ask questions if you don't want the answers."

Something coiled in the pit of Sarah's stomach. "What are you talking about?"

"Are you telling me you really don't know?" He sounded almost angry.

"Know what? You're the second person today who's beat around the bush about my father. If there's something I should know, just tell me."

He hesitated, his hands gripping the steering wheel, his lips pressed together in a hard line. "All I really know is that Rachel didn't want to disappoint him. Her need to please him was almost a compulsion."

"They were always close," Sarah said.

"Close? Yeah." He suddenly looked indescribably weary. "This may be small comfort to you, Sarah, but sometimes it's just as hard being on that pedestal as it is being the one looking up."

While they waited for Curtis's ride, Sarah made a pot of coffee. She felt awkward from their previous conversation and was glad when Esme came in a little while later.

She planted her hands on her hips as she regarded Sarah from across the room. "Well, there you are. I'd about decided you hadn't made it home after all. 'Cause otherwise, you would have already come to see me."

"I'm sorry," Sarah said. "I meant to come by earlier, but then I decided to go to the hospital to see Dad." She got up from the table to give Esme a hug. "Believe me, I would much rather have been here with you."

Esme's scrawny arms held her tight for a moment. When she drew back, her gaze lit on Curtis. "What are you doing here?"

A horn sounded outside and he stood. "That's my ride. I'll let Sarah fill you in. I have to get back to the hospital, but you two ladies have a nice evening." He came over and dropped a kiss on the top of Esme's head. "Don't work too hard."

"I don't need you telling me how hard I can and can't work," Esme fumed. "You worry about your own affairs."

He winked at Sarah. "Take care. You need anything, give me a call."

As soon as the door closed behind Curtis, Esme went over to the table and began gathering up their cups.

"Here," Sarah said, as she tried to help Esme clean up. "Let me do that."

She received a glower for her offer.

"I reckon I can still wash a few dishes," Esme grumbled.

"I'm not ready for the old folks' home just yet, despite what some people around here seem to think."

"I don't think that at all," Sarah said. "I just want to help."

"If I need help I'll ask for it," Esme informed her.

Sarah threw her hands up. "Okay, you win. I give up. Will you at least come and sit with me a minute, so we can talk?"

Esme reluctantly came back over and pulled out a chair. Even though she'd worked in this kitchen for four decades, she was still hesitant to sit at the table with Sarah.

It was times like this that Sarah could feel a distance between them. She loved Esme more than anyone in the world, and she knew the older woman would lay down her life for her. But there was a wall between them, one that Esme chose to keep firmly in place. And as much as Sarah hated it, she knew that divider would always be there.

"What is it?" Esme demanded with no small amount of suspicion. "You ain't got yourself in some kind of trouble, have you? Is that why Curtis was here?"

"What? No," Sarah said. "He just brought me home from the hospital. I'm not in any trouble."

"Well, that's a relief. Way past time you stopped all that nonsense. You oughta be settled down having babies by now. First thing you know, you done wait too late."

"I think I have a few good years left in me. Besides, I'm not the motherly type."

"That's true," Esme said bluntly.

"Maybe I'm more like my father than I want to admit," Sarah said. "I'd hardly call him the paternal type."

"Lord have mercy, girl, what a thing to say about your own daddy."

"It's true, isn't it?"

Esme said nothing.

"You know what I'm talking about," Sarah said. "Don't pretend you don't."

Esme shook her head with mournful reproach. "Mr. James on his deathbed, and here you are talking about him like that."

"You mean even now we still have to worry about *his* feelings?"

She heaved a weary sigh. "Let it go, child."

"I can't let it go. If anyone knows what went on around here, it was you," Sarah said. "You know why he hates me, don't you?"

"I've done told you I don't know how many times before. He don't hate you. He's just got a way about him."

"It's more than that. He blames me for Rachel's death."

"Blames you? Why would he do a thing like that?"

"He's never said anything to you about it?"

"He says a lot of things these days, but you can't pay attention to half of it. The medicine they got him on makes him talk out of his head. You can't take it to heart."

Sarah leaned across table. "He thinks I killed her, Esme."

Her eyes widened. "No, he don't."

"That's what he said. He said Mama thought so, too. That's why she washed the blood off me that night. That's why she stopped taking me to see a therapist. She was too afraid of what she might find out. And now I'm thinking…maybe that's why she died. Maybe that's why her heart gave out. Because of me."

"Your mama may have died of a broken heart, but it didn't have anything to do with you, Sarah June."

"Mama had a broken heart?"

Esme hesitated. "One of her babies was murdered. 'Course she had a broken heart."

"Do you think I killed her, Esme?"

Esme reached across the table and grabbed Sarah's hand,

clutching it in both of hers. "Now you listen to me. You didn't have nothing to do with your sister's death. I don't know who killed that poor child, but it wasn't you."

"How can you be so sure?"

"Because nobody in the world knows you better than me. You didn't do it. It's not in you. I want you to put that notion clean out of your head, and I never want to hear another word about it."

"Esme, did you know about Curtis and Rachel?"

Her eyes flashed again with unexpected fire. "We don't need to be talking about that, neither."

"Why not?"

"Child, please."

"Did my father cause problems for Curtis?"

"If there was trouble, it was Curtis's own making. That boy knew better than to do what he did."

"What did he do besides love my sister?"

"She wasn't his to love."

"She wasn't a possession. She had a mind of her own. And I know she loved Curtis, too. I could tell by the way they looked at each other. What did Dad do to break them up?"

"I don't know," she said stubbornly.

"Esme…"

The dark eyes begged Sarah to drop the subject, but it was too late. She couldn't let it rest now.

"Did my father hurt Rachel?"

"Hurt her? He loved that child."

Sarah clung to her hand. "You know what I mean."

Esme's lips pursed. "What I know is this. You need to stop wallowing around in the past. No good ever comes of it."

"I can't stop. I have to know if he hurt her. It would… It changes everything, don't you see?"

Esme just went right on shaking her head.

"Did you ever see anything that made you suspicious?"

"No, child. It weren't my job to be suspicious."

Sarah walked out to the back porch and watched until Esme got all the way to the cottage. Then she turned and went back inside, that terrible question still churning inside her, making her sick and shaky. Making her wish she'd never come back here.

Maybe Esme was right. Maybe no good could come from digging up the past. Rachel was dead, her father was dying. How could the truth help any of them now? Especially when that truth might be harder to live with than the questions. When that truth might include Sarah's unwitting complicity.

Her bedroom had been next to Rachel's. If something had gone on behind that common wall, how could she not have known? How could she not have told?

Weighted down by the condemning silence of the house, Sarah wandered upstairs to try and find something to occupy her mind. Turning on the bedside lamp, she picked up the glass case that still rested on her nightstand. It was empty now. She'd taken her grandmother's little yellow bird to the funeral and placed it in her sister's casket. In her cold hands.

All these years, she'd thought of Rachel as the perfect daughter, the favored sister, someone she could never live up to. But Rachel had been more than that. She'd had hopes and dreams just like everyone else. And she'd had secrets, too. Terrible secrets.

Sarah wished she'd somehow found a way to bridge the distance between them before it was too late. Because now, she and Rachel were never going to be anything more than what they'd been before the murder…strangers living in the same house.

Maybe that was why she'd put the bird in Rachel's hands. Because she hadn't known how to give her sister the love and comfort that she must have so desperately needed.

A tremor coursed through Sarah as she walked over to the window and stared out at the gathering twilight. She'd always been afraid of the dark, although there was a time when she would never have admitted it to anyone. Not even to herself. Back then, she'd looked for ways to prove just how fearless she was. Like going to the Duncan farmhouse alone.

But in this well-lit room, the darkness was already closing in on her. Sarah had always felt alone here. Alone and isolated from the rest of the world.

How must Rachel have felt?

Why her and not me? Sarah wondered.

What would drive a man to do that to his own child?

Make him unnaturally love one daughter while shunning the other? Shun her as if she weren't his own.

The thought stopped Sarah completely. She tried to shove the suspicion away. Told herself she was grasping at straws. But the notion wouldn't be dismissed, because it explained too much.

It explained everything.

23

"Looks like somebody's finally claimed our Jane Doe," Danny said as he hung up the phone on Monday morning. He and Sean sat across from each other in a cubicle that was just large enough to accommodate two desks shoved against each other and an overflowing file cabinet.

Danny reared back in his chair and clasped his hands behind his neck. "Her name's Amber Gleason. She worked as a cocktail waitress at a dive on Airline Drive called the Neon Lounge. One of the other girls saw the article in the paper and called in. She said Amber hasn't been in since a week ago Saturday night."

Sean looked up from the report he was typing on the computer. "And they're just now missing her?"

"Hey, this is New Orleans, the Big Easy, remember? Eccentric behavior is the norm not the exception. A waitress blows off work for a few days, nobody's going to get all cranked off about it. And anyway, this girl says Amber had a pretty bad sauce problem. They just figured she'd tied one on and was holed up somewhere drying out."

"We'll need to get over there and talk to the people on her shift. Maybe somebody saw something." Sean hit the save button on the computer and picked up his coffee. "Is this girl willing to go down to the morgue and ID the body?"

"She's on her way. I'm heading over there to meet her. You want to ride along?"

"To the morgue? Thanks, I'll pass."

"Thought you might."

"Besides, I have an appointment with a shrink."

"Well, it's about damn time," Danny said as he grabbed his jacket. "Why don't you run my little theory by him while you're there? You know, the one about your issues."

"Yeah, Danny, I'll be sure and do that."

A few minutes later, Sean headed out for the Garden District. The address he'd been given was on Chestnut Street. The house was a two-story brick home with a wide veranda, ornate grillwork, and a narrow walkway that led back to a walled garden draped with wisteria vines. It was the kind of place the Garden District was famous for—lush lawns, shimmering swimming pools and hidden courtyards all wrapped up in the unmistakable air of Southern gentility.

Michael Garrett had told Sean when they spoke earlier to come through the garden and up the back stairs where he would be waiting in his office.

Sean let himself through the gate and glanced around, feeling vaguely resentful. At the top of the stairs, he knocked on the door, and when he didn't get an answer, he walked on in. He found himself in a small sitting area with leather chairs and important-looking artwork on the walls, none of which he recognized.

"Hello?"

"Come on in, Detective," the voice called from the next room.

Sean opened the door and stepped inside. A man stood at the window staring down into the garden. When he turned, the light streaming in behind him created a halo effect that vanished the moment he walked toward Sean.

"Detective Kelton? I'm Michael Garrett," he said, extending his hand.

He didn't look at all the way Sean had pictured him. His image of a middle-aged therapist in a cardigan and loafers was forced to give way to the reality of a sleekly dressed man in a dark suit, blue shirt and silk tie, all of which looked expensive. And when they shook hands, Sean noticed a gold watch.

"Thanks for making time to see me," he said.

"No problem." Garrett waved Sean toward a chair, then went around to sit behind his desk. "I'm happy to help you out in any way I can, but as I told you on the phone, I'm not sure how much I can tell you from looking at crime-scene photos. I'm not a forensic psychologist, and I assume the police department has their own consultants for such matters."

"We're on a pretty tight budget these days," Sean said as he sat down across from Garrett. "But that's not the only reason I'm here."

Garrett watched him impassively.

"I'm worried about Sarah."

"I can't discuss Sarah with you."

"I'm sure she's told you plenty about me," Sean said dryly. "Whatever she's said, it's probably true."

The therapist's implacable demeanor made Sean uncomfortable. He didn't feel in charge in this environment and he didn't like it.

"The thing is, I still care about Sarah. I'll do anything I can to protect her."

One brow lifted slightly. "Have you told her how you feel?"

"Yes, but I don't think she's in the right frame of mind to hear it right now."

Garrett sat perfectly still. His posture was remarkable, Sean thought. "You were recently married, weren't you, Detective?"

"Yes."

"Perhaps that's why Sarah feels a little reticent about discussing your feelings for her."

The guy's expression never changed, and yet Sean felt as if he'd been sucker punched. "You know about Sarah's past, right? The murdered sister?"

"As I said—"

"Yeah, yeah. You can't discuss her with me. Then just listen, okay? I'm beginning to have a bad feeling that Sarah's past may be connected to the cases I told you about earlier."

"Go on."

Sean scrubbed a hand across his mouth, hardly knowing where to start. "When Sarah and I first got together, I looked into her sister's murder. I was arrogant enough to think I could find something the local cops had missed."

"Did you?"

Sean hesitated. "I found a lot of things that disturbed me about that case, not the least of which was the satanic symbolism left at the crime scene. Because of those symbols, the police focused their attention on only one suspect, and they spent weeks trying to break his alibi. It occurred to me, as I studied the case, that if the killer's intent was to use that symbolism to misdirect the investigation, it worked like a charm."

"Is that what you think is happening with the cases here in New Orleans?"

Sean shrugged. "I don't know yet. What I do know is that the first crime scene was loaded with satanic symbolism, like that old house in Arkansas. And the victim had fresh tattoos. Two things that would lead me to think Sarah might be the one person who could help with the case. She's always been fascinated by the occult, and she's familiar with every tattoo artist in the city. So I get her over to the crime scene and the first thing she asks about is footwear evidence. She wants to know if we found any unusual prints around the crime scene. Two days later, the coroner shows me cloven-shaped bruises on the victim's torso. That has me wondering how Sarah knew about those footprints before we did."

The implacable eyes met Sean's across the desk. "Did you ask her?"

"She said there was an old legend in the town where she grew up about the devil's footprints. It was rumored that those marks were found near her sister's body. The symbolism at the crime scene triggered the memory, and her question about the prints was an unconscious response."

"Do you believe her?"

"I believe she wants to believe that's a plausible explanation."

"But you don't."

"To be honest, I'm not sure what to think. The similarities to her sister's case worry me."

"Do you think Sarah is somehow involved in these killings?"

It was Sean who stayed silent this time.

Garrett leaned forward. "If I were to determine that any of my patients provided a significant threat to others, I would be required by Louisiana law to report my judgment to the proper authorities. I've made no such report, Detective."

Sean nodded. "Okay. I hear what you're saying." He wanted to be relieved, but there was still too much about this case that he didn't understand. Too much about Sarah's past that kept niggling at him.

"The cloven-shaped bruises are interesting," Garrett said. "Did you find similar marks on the second victim?"

"No, and that bothers me, too," Sean said. "The killer went out of his way to stage everything about the first crime scene, right down to the numbers in the street address. The symbolism was almost overkill. Everything he did was precise and full of meaning. But there was very little of that at the second scene. It was like he'd already made his point. He killed the second victim somewhere else and then dumped her where he knew the body would be found. But he still tattooed her back and carved up her face to make sure we'd know he did it."

"Carved up her face?"

"That's another one of his calling cards. He slits the corners of the victims' mouths and removes their eyelids. It distorts their features into a macabre death mask." Sean removed photographs from an envelope and walked over to Garrett's desk. "These are from the first crime scene. The symbols on the walls are called *udjats*. The eye of Lucifer. You can see he drew both the right and left eye, which I'm told is rare. The right eye represents the sun, the left eye, the moon. Day and night. Good and evil. The symbol in the palm is a thaumaturgic triangle, which is used to summon demons. Like I said, overkill. He wanted to make sure we got his point."

"You think the symbolism is misdirection?" Garrett turned on the lamp and reached for a magnifying glass.

"I don't know yet. Sarah suggested the tattoo on the palm and the one on the back were made by two different artists. The triangle is noticeably inferior to the inkblot. But it's easy to buy a tattoo machine off the internet. With a little artistic talent and some practice, he could probably create a pretty decent tattoo, especially if he took his time. But if he was in a hurry or if he got nervous, his inexperience could cause the quality of the second tattoo to slip." Sean stared down at the images. "What I need to know from you is whether the tattoo on her back is based on a genuine Rorschach inkblot. That could indicate he's had a psychological evaluation at some point in his past."

Reaching into a desk drawer, Garrett pulled out a leather portfolio, then removed a set of Rorschach prints which he shuffled through like a deck of cards. Finding the one he wanted, he placed it beside the crime-scene shot and studied them together.

"Do you have the photograph from the second victim?" he asked.

Sean took it out of the envelope and tossed it onto the desk. "The tattoos look identical at first glance, but they're not."

"I can see that." Garrett took his time examining the photographs. "Both tattoos are definitely inspired by the same Rorschach image." He pointed to the card he'd removed from the portfolio. "He's modified the design, however, to represent something specific to him."

"Can you tell what that is?"

"It could be anything. The inkblots are ambiguous. They mean something different to everyone who looks at them, because each individual brings his or her own set of unique circumstances into the interpretation." Garrett looked up. "The only thing I can tell you is what the killer seems to want us to see."

"Which is?"

"Faces." He pointed to the photograph. "In his modification, the face on the right is in the light, while the face on the left is shaded. The left side, just like the left *udjat,* is the night side, the dark side. Let's say it represents the mirror image. But the tattoo on the second victim is the opposite. The face in the light is the mirror image. The hidden side."

"So what the hell does any of this mean?" Sean asked impatiently.

"He's using these images to communicate. To send a message. But that's actually not the salient point here. With whom is he trying to communicate?"

"The police, I guess," Sean said. "These guys like to flaunt how clever they are. And the tattoos aren't the only messages he left for us. At the first crime scene, he wrote something backwards on the wall so that it had to be read in a mirror. At the second scene, he left it *on* the mirror."

"What did he write?"

"'I am you.' Maybe he's trying to tell us he's one of us. A cop."

Garrett frowned. "I am you," he murmured, and then his expression subtly altered. "I...am...you."

"Does that mean something to you?"

"He may not be trying to communicate with you at all, Detective Kelton." Garrett's voice sounded deeply troubled. "It's entirely possible the killer is leaving these messages for himself."

"How'd it go at the morgue?" Sean asked Danny, who had beat him back to the office.

"We got a positive ID, so at least now we can start checking for a connection between Amber Gleason and Holly Jessup."

"Well, that's progress. Don't you want to know how it went with the shrink?"

"Yeah, but I need to tell you something first."

For the first time, Sean noticed Danny's worried expression. "What's going on?"

"Do you know a guy named Clovis Tenney?"

"He's married to a friend of Cat's. Why?"

"Morales says he called here while you were out. He was pretty anxious to talk to you. He says his wife's gone missing. Says she went out on Saturday night and he hasn't seen her since."

"Did he file a missing persons?"

Danny nodded. "A patrol officer located her car parked on a side street just off North Rampart." He handed Sean a piece of paper with the address. "That's a bad location these days."

"Any sign of foul play?"

"One of the officers noticed a small amount of blood on the driver's side door." Danny paused. "That's not all. Tenney says he thinks Cat was with his wife on Saturday night."

Sean stood on the street and watched as the crime-scene unit went over the car. Once they were finished, a crowbar was used to pop open the trunk, but nothing was found inside. Except for the blood on the door, the car appeared to be clean.

But that spot of blood worried Sean a great deal, as did the location of the car—less than a block from Sarah's house. He remembered what Danny had told him the other day about Cat's intention to confront Sarah and he was starting to get worried.

Sean had been at Sarah's house on Saturday night. If Cat had seen him there, she would have probably jumped to the wrong conclusion. And it was very possible she'd showed up at Sarah's door to have it out with her before Sarah left for

Arkansas. If that were the case, Sarah might well have been the last one to see Cat.

While he waited for the car to be searched, Sean called Sarah's cell phone and left a message when she didn't answer. He had a feeling, though, that voice mail from him would go unopened.

He called anyone else he could think of who might know of Cat's whereabouts. One of her friends had seen her with Ginette early Saturday evening, so it seemed that Clovis Tenney was right. The two women had been together. And now they were both missing.

After the wrecker hauled the car to the impound and the scene was cleared, Sean walked up the street to Sarah's house. He still had his key and he let himself in.

Standing just inside the door, he glanced around. He didn't know what he expected to find. It was entirely possible that Cat and Ginette had gone off with someone else. They both loved Biloxi. For all he knew, they could be having a high old time in one of the casinos. Danny was right. This was New Orleans. Erratic and impulsive behavior was not only expected, but encouraged, and Sean knew better than to jump to any conclusions.

But that spot of blood on the car door… He didn't want to be married to Cat, but he sure as hell didn't want anything to happen to her.

He had no right entering Sarah's house without her permission, but she was miles away, refusing to take his calls, and time was crucial. In missing-person cases, minutes—let alone hours—could make all the difference, and he needed to know if Cat had been there.

Slowly, he walked from room to room until the only place

he hadn't searched was the bedroom. His skin prickled as he opened the door and looked inside.

He'd shared this room and that bed with Sarah for over two years. He knew the space like the back of his hand. Every corner, every crevice. He had no reason to suddenly feel so unnerved. No reason to feel the need to draw his gun before pulling back the closet door.

Something moved inside, and Sean jumped back, then laughed nervously when he realized he'd spotted himself in the mirror.

No one was there.

The house was empty, and he could find no sign that Cat had ever been there. Yet Sean knew something was wrong. Something kept tugging at him.

Then it came to him. The room had recently been cleaned. The air smelled faintly of lemon oil and ammonia. And now, as he glanced around, he realized the space was spotless. Sarah was neat, but she wasn't anal about it. She stacked clothes on the dresser, draped her robe over the back of a chair. Had books lying around everywhere.

Nothing was out of place.

Even the bed was painstakingly made up with fresh linens, but the comforter was missing.

Something else was missing, too. He just couldn't put his finger on what it was.

He walked over to the mirror. Spotless.

Glanced down at the dresser. Spotless.

As he moved toward the bed, something crunched beneath his shoe. Kneeling, he pulled on a pair of latex gloves, then picked up a glittering piece of glass and held it up to the light.

Traces of what looked like blood clung to the creases of the cut crystal.

24

Sarah was having a second cup of coffee the next morning when she looked out and saw a squad car pull into the drive. She watched as Lukas Clay got out and strode up the walkway. A moment later, the doorbell rang.

"This is a surprise," she said when she opened the door. "I'd planned to call you later to set up a time when I could come in and look at those files."

"That may have to wait." He shifted nervously and cleared his throat. "I have something I need to tell you. I'm afraid it's bad news."

"Maybe you'd better come in then." Sarah stepped back so he could enter, and then closed the door behind him. "What is it?"

"I'm sorry to be the one to have to tell you this, but…your father is dead."

Her heart skipped a beat. "When?"

"Early this morning. The nurse went in to give him a shot and she found him."

"He must have died in his sleep then." Sarah supposed that was the best way to go. And he'd told her on Sunday that he was ready. That he didn't want to linger. So this was for the best.

But Lukas was staring down at her strangely. "Your father didn't die in his sleep, Sarah. He was murdered."

She felt her face drain of color. "Murdered? My God. Are you sure? I mean…of course, you're sure. You wouldn't be here otherwise. It's just…I can't believe it."

"Maybe we should go in and sit down," Lukas said gently. He took her elbow and guided her into the living room. She dropped to the sofa, her legs suddenly too shaky to support her. Lukas sat down beside her.

"I don't understand." She turned and searched his face. "Why would someone murder him? He was terminal. Everyone knew he didn't have much time left. Is it possible someone was trying to spare him?"

"It wasn't a mercy killing, if that's what you mean."

"How do you know?"

He still had that strange look in his eyes. "There's no easy way to say this. Your father's throat was cut."

Sarah felt as if she'd been body-slammed against the floor. Everything inside her went still, and for a moment, she completely lost her breath.

She must have heard wrong, Sarah thought in a daze. Because the idea of someone stealing into her father's room while he lay weak and helpless…putting a knife to his throat…

"Oh, God." She pressed a hand to her mouth as a wave of nausea rolled over her.

"I know this is a shock," he said kindly. "But I have to ask you some questions. Just routine. We can talk on the way to the hospital if you like."

She nodded. "Would you mind giving me a minute?"

Rising, she hurried from the room before he could answer. Closing the bathroom door, she bent over the sink and splashed cold water on her face. Then she leaned against the counter and stared at her pale face in the mirror. Her father was dead. Murdered. His throat slashed.

Someone had robbed him of his final hours in the same gruesome manner that Rachel's life had been snuffed. The act was not just senseless, it seemed truly evil to Sarah.

Unless...

She squeezed her eyes closed.

What if her recent suspicions about her father were true? What if he really had abused Rachel? Did that mean he got what he deserved?

That judgment wasn't hers to make, Sarah thought weakly. Nor had it been the killer's.

Esme... I have to call Esme.

No, that could wait. She didn't want to break the news over the phone, and right now, she had to go to the hospital. There were arrangements to be made. Questions to be answered.

If he'd hurt Rachel all those years...

Don't think about that now. Just get through the next few hours.

But if he *had* hurt Rachel...

Something glimmered in Sarah's eyes that she hardly recognized, and she quickly turned away from her reflection. Drying her hands and face, she went back out to join Lukas. He helped her on with her coat, and they walked out to his car together. Sarah's movements were zombielike, and she knew reality hadn't set in yet. That would come later, when she was alone with too much time to think. Too much time to ponder the odds of her father and sister dying in the same horrendous fashion.

"Do you know of anyone who would want your father dead?" Lukas asked.

He was wearing the dark glasses again. Sarah couldn't see his eyes when he glanced at her. She couldn't tell at all what he was thinking.

Shivering, she wrapped her arms around her middle and shook her head.

"Do you know if he'd ever been threatened, maybe by someone he sent up?"

"No, but I didn't come home much after my mother died. My father and I didn't keep in touch."

"So what brought you back now?" Lukas asked.

Sarah stared out the window. "I heard he was dying. I wanted to make peace before it was too late."

"That's not the only reason, is it?"

She turned with a frown.

"You said you wanted to make sense of your sister's murder. You wanted to put all the pieces together." Slowly he turned to face her. "Maybe you already have."

Something in his voice sent a shiver up Sarah's spine. "I don't know what you mean."

"When was the last time you saw your father?"

"Sunday afternoon. I'm not sure of the time."

"Did any of the pieces fall together during the course of that visit?"

Sarah was starting to get seriously worried. "I still don't know what you're getting at," she said, although she had a bad feeling that she did.

"Someone reported hearing loud voices coming from your father's room. They said it sounded like an argument."

"My father was easily upset. Especially when he talked about my mother and sister."

Lukas was staring at her again. Sarah could feel the intensity of his eyes through the dark lenses. "I have one more question," he said. "If I don't ask it, you can bet that the county sheriff will."

"What is it?"

"Are you the primary heir of James DeLaune's estate?"

And just like that, reality came crashing in on Sarah. A cold, terrifying reality. "You can't think I did this! What would be my motive? Even if my father left everything to me, and I very much doubt that he did, he only had a short while to live. Why would I need to kill him?"

"I don't know, Sarah. Why would anyone kill a dying man?"

She thought about that question all the way to the hospital and all during the long hours that followed. As her father's apparent heir, she would naturally be the logical suspect. But as she'd pointed out to Lukas, if she'd wanted the money, all she had to do was wait for her father to die. Why take the chance on losing everything?

Unless money wasn't the motive at all.

And for Sarah, it wouldn't be. The accusations her father had leveled at her about Rachel's murder were far more damning. If anyone had overheard his allegations, they might well conclude that Sarah had a very powerful reason for bringing about her father's premature demise.

And the possibility that someone *had* overheard those accusations scared Sarah to death.

She wanted more than anything to go back to New Orleans and forget that any of this had ever happened. She thought about what Curtis had said on Sunday, how one moment could change history, one decision could change the course of a person's whole life.

And she thought about her father's last words to her. He'd accused her of killing her sister, threatened to cut her off without a cent. And then someone had killed him.

First Rachel, and now her father. Could she be next? Sarah wondered.

She wished she could grieve, but all she felt at the moment was fear.

And she didn't know which was more terrifying. That she could be a target...or that she wasn't.

When Sarah finally got home that afternoon, Esme was waiting for her in the kitchen. She'd brought over a chicken casserole, but Sarah couldn't eat a bite. She picked at the food while Esme talked about funeral arrangements.

"I don't want to wait," Sarah said. "I know that sounds cold, but I just want to get it over with as soon as possible."

Esme stared with mute disapproval.

Sarah glanced up. "What?"

"You can't put him in the ground so fast, people don't have time to pay their proper respects. Mr. James was an important man in this county."

"It's my decision," Sarah said. "And I don't want to prolong it. That only makes things harder."

Esme shook her head in exasperation. "Talking to you is like talking to a tree stump, child. You get it in your head something's got to be a certain way, then that's the way it'll be. No sense arguing about it."

"I'm glad you see things my way," Sarah teased.

Esme folded her arms, letting Sarah know that she wasn't

about to cave on everything. "Who you want to preach the service?"

"I don't know. I don't think we should have a church service. You know how Dad felt about that. I think a graveside service would be better. Something simple."

Esme clearly didn't agree. She gave Sarah an offended look. "Is anyone going to be allowed to pray at this service?"

Sarah couldn't help smiling. "Of course."

"Even with a graveside service, somebody got to say a few words," Esme insisted. "Else we'll all be standing around gawking at the casket."

"What about Tim Mason?"

The suggestion clearly took Esme aback. "What you know about Tim Mason?"

"Nothing, really. But he's a preacher, isn't he?"

"Yeah, he's a preacher all right."

"Then maybe I'll ask him. I met him the other day and I kind of liked him."

"You would," Esme muttered.

"What's that supposed to mean?"

"He's not what I'd call traditional. His notions on moral behavior leave a lot to be desired, you ask me."

Sarah shrugged. "Okay. Then we'll ask someone else. We can get anybody you want. I don't care."

Esme placed the dishes in the sink with a loud clatter and turned, her eyes blazing. "Well, you should care. This is your daddy's funeral we're talking about, not some stranger's. Mr. James was a hard man in a lot of ways, but he was always good to me." Esme's lip quivered and she dabbed at her eyes. "Gave me my little house free and clear, helped me send Curtis to school. It ain't right. First Rachel, now Mr. James. Lord, God, what is this world coming to when something like this could happen twice to one family?"

Sarah got up and put her arms around Esme. "I'm sorry," she said. "I didn't mean to upset you. We'll do whatever you want for the service. Let's just leave it for now. We can figure things out later. Come and sit down," she said. "Let me get you some coffee."

"You know I can't drink coffee. Keeps me up at night."

"How about a little whiskey?"

"Never touch it and neither should you. Eat your liver and your soul."

"Don't worry," Sarah said. "I rarely drink the hard stuff." Didn't mix too well with her pills, but she didn't tell Esme that.

"Esme, why don't you like Tim Mason?"

"I never said I didn't like him."

Just everything but. "I saw that look on your face when I mentioned his name. What did he do?"

Esme looked annoyed. "Lord, child, I forget how you like to worry a body to death when you get something in your head like that. Why you interested in Tim Mason all of a sudden?"

"I told you, I met him the other day. He was in Dad's hospital room when I got there on Sunday."

Esme's eyes deepened in agitation. "Tim Mason was in Mr. James's room?"

"Yes. Why?"

She glanced away. "Mr. James never had much use for preachers."

"I know that, but I get the feeling there's something you're not telling me," Sarah said. "You seem to have such a strong opinion of him."

"I already told you my reasons. I don't cotton to his views

on religion. And I don't have much use for his sermons, neither."

"Did Mama go to his church?"

"Now why you want to know that?"

"Because he said I looked like her. He even knew I went
away to school. I can't think of any other reason he'd know
that, unless Mama talked about me."

"All that was a long time ago. I'm an old woman. Half the
time, I can't even remember where I left my glasses."

"There's nothing wrong with your memory. It's a lot better than mine," Sarah said. "Can I ask you something else?"

"I ain't figured out a way yet to stop you," Esme grumbled.

"Dad didn't like Mama going to church, did he? He said
something the other day about her spending all her time there,
instead of being home where she belonged."

"Is that the question?"

"I'm leading up to it," Sarah said. "He implied that Mama
had done something he couldn't forgive. Whatever it was, he
said he couldn't get past it with her mistake staring him in
the face every day."

"I told you the medicine made him talk crazy. You can't
pay no mind to what he said."

"He seemed perfectly lucid when he told me he couldn't
stand the sight of me."

Esme's dark eyes glinted with sudden tears. "He told you
that?"

"It's nothing I didn't already know. What I don't know is
why. Why did he feel that way about me? I have my own suspicions about it, but I want to hear it from you."

Esme stared at her for the longest time. "You ask too much
of me, Sarah June. Just let it go, child. I always say, no good can

come from digging up the past. You need to let them ghosts be, so you can finally start living your life."

After Esme went home, Sarah poured herself a glass of wine and carried it with her as she drifted through the silent house. The ghosts Esme had warned her about were everywhere tonight.

Her father, her mother, her sister…all gone from this world. Sarah was the only one left. The black sheep of the family. She supposed there might be some irony in that, but at the moment, she wasn't in the mood to appreciate the odd paradoxes of her life.

She was exhausted and frightened, and contemplating what the next few days held felt a little like hovering on a tightwire strung across a fire pit. The funeral, an official investigation, yet more questions by the police.

She thought about calling Sean to let him know what had happened. If anyone could walk her through what she could expect from the police, it would be him. He'd called and left several messages on her voice mail, but she hadn't called him back. She hadn't even listened to what he had to say. And now it seemed unfair to drag him into this mess, when she'd told him countless times to stay out of her life.

Restless and edgy, she wandered over to the window to stare out at the street. Twilight had fallen. The pecan trees in the front lawn were black against a deep purple sky, and it had started to mist. Sarah could see the drizzle coming down in the glow of the streetlight in front of the house. The weather was gloomy and cold; the gathering darkness was already wearing on her nerves.

She stood there sipping her wine, her mind so cluttered that a movement in the shadows across the street didn't register at first. It was just a stray dog or the wind. She barely even noticed.

And then she saw him.

Derrick Fears had been standing among the trees where she couldn't see him. Now he stepped into the glow of the street-light as if to make sure she noticed him.

He wore a hood pulled up over his head, and his shoulders were hunched against the cold. Sarah could see very little of his face, but she knew he was staring at the house.

A light was on in the room behind her. He would be able to see her at the window.

Quickly, she stepped back, shielding herself with the drapes. She imagined him out there, laughing. Taunting her the same way he had at the farmhouse.

When she looked back, he was gone.

25

Heavy clouds covered the sky and lightning shimmered on the horizon as Sean pulled to the curb in front of Sarah's house and got out. He cast a wary eye around the neighborhood.

He and Danny had spent hours on a door-to-door canvass, but all they'd managed to turn up was an elderly witness who thought she might have glimpsed a strange car parked down the street from Sarah's house a few nights ago. But she couldn't say with any certainty that it had been there on Saturday night, when Cat and Ginette were also in the neighborhood. The only reason she'd noticed it in the first place was because the body style reminded her of the car her late husband had owned, but she couldn't swear to the color. It *might* have been dark green. Or brown. Or black.

The only concrete clue Sean had been able to uncover so far was the bloodstained sliver of glass in Sarah's bedroom. And that was hardly evidence, unless the blood type matched either of the missing women. A big, big leap, he admitted. Otherwise, it meant nothing. The tiny piece of glass he'd found in Sarah's bedroom could have been from something she broke months ago, or even years. Hell, it could be from something he'd dropped.

There was absolutely no proof of any kind that a crime had been committed in Sarah's house. No reason to believe she was connected in any way to Cat's disappearance.

But the fact that the two women had now been missing three days had Sean seriously worried, as did the possibility of a strange car in the neighborhood. A strange car that may or may not have been dark green. That may or may not have been the same car spotted near Holly Jessup's Shreveport home before she went missing. Before her body had later been discovered in New Orleans, just blocks from where Sean stood now.

He couldn't remember the last time he'd slept. Besides canvassing Sarah's neighborhood, he'd spent countless hours on the phone and in his car trying to retrace Cat's steps from the time she and Ginette had left the house. But no one had seen or heard from either of the women since Saturday night. It was as if they'd disappeared off the face of the earth.

But Sean knew from experience that nothing vanished without a trace. Something always got left behind. A spot of blood on a car door. A shard of glass on a bedroom floor.

As much as he didn't want to believe it, he couldn't shake the notion that something had happened in Sarah's house. He'd known her for over two years. She'd gotten under his skin in a way no woman ever had before or since. She was dark and secretive, and yeah, there were things about her past, about her sister's murder that troubled him. A part of him that still wondered what had really happened in that farmhouse.

But this was different. This was not fourteen years ago, when she was a kid. This was here and now.

The mere fact that he felt compelled to search her home in the first place was crossing a line that should forever change the way Sean looked at her. But he wasn't so sure that it would. He wasn't so sure that anything he found would ever change the way he felt about Sarah.

He reached back into the car for his bag, then closed and locked his car. The night was warm and he had on a light-weight jacket that covered his holster.

At least he didn't have to worry about being discovered, he thought as he headed up the street. He'd left several messages on Sarah's voicemail, and when she hadn't returned his calls, he'd tried her father's house in Adamant. A woman, the housekeeper he presumed, had told him that Sarah was out and wasn't expected back until late. So she was there and she was safe. And for now, he had her house to himself. Plenty of time to do what he needed to do.

A dog barked as he left the sidewalk and strode up the porch steps. Glancing over his shoulder, he inserted the key into the lock and stepped quickly inside.

Pausing just inside the door, he aimed his flashlight beam around the room. The house was silent and still, and as he made his way down the hallway, he felt that same tug of uneasiness he'd experience the day before.

Sean didn't believe in the supernatural, but he did believe in his instincts. Something was wrong in Sarah's house. *Something* had happened here. It was as if he could feel the echo of some violent act still quivering on the air.

Entering the bedroom, he angled the light over the walls and floor, into the closet. It was just as he'd left it the day before. Spotless.

Snapping on latex gloves, he pulled the drapes at the window and hung a sheet over the French doors so that he could turn on the overhead light. Kneeling over the spot on the floor where he'd found the piece of glass, he removed a tripod and video camera, then a spray bottle of luminol from his bag.

A victim's body could be dumped and the crime scene scrubbed clean to the naked eye, but without industrial-strength cleaning chemicals, there was always some DNA that remained. Tiny particles of blood could run down into the crevices between floorboards, seep into the baseboards, cling to the carpet and walls.

When the chemicals in luminol reacted to traces of blood, it produced a blue-green luminescence that could reveal spatter patterns, shapes, sometimes even shoe imprints in carpet. Household chemicals like bleach could produce the same results, but the glow was quicker to fade than with blood.

Sean sprayed a section of the floor, then turned off the light. A few seconds later, an eerie glow hung in the darkness over the area he'd coated.

Sean's blood went cold as he knelt to examine the pattern of the luminescence on the floor.

One glowing footprint appeared and then another. And they were shaped like the bruises he'd seen on the torso in the morgue.

He waited for the effect to fade, but instead the glow intensified and lingered.

He turned on the overhead light and the luminescence disappeared. Like nothing was there.

Grabbing the luminol, he sprayed another section of the floor and some of the walls. This time, when he turned off the light, the effect was astonishing.

Sean stood in the center of the room and slowly turned. The cloven footprints were everywhere. Trailing across the floor and glowing down from the walls.

"Sarah," he whispered. "What the hell is going on?"

★ ★ ★

Earlier, Esme had offered to spend the night, but Sarah knew how much she loved being in her own home at night. Sarah was the same way. She would have given anything to be in her own bed at that moment, safely tucked away from this madness.

Her father's house unnerved her. She'd never felt comfortable there, even as a child. Ghosts hovered in every room and dark secrets seemed to cling to every rafter. But the mysteries of Sarah's past were the least of her fears now.

Seeing Derrick Fears earlier had left her shaken, but it would be useless to call the police. He hadn't done anything wrong. He hadn't even trespassed on her father's property. Instead he'd been very careful to stay in the street.

But what if he came back while she slept? He'd gotten inside once. What if he tried to get in again?

Sarah made the dreaded rounds through the house. The kitchen, pantry and mudroom. Through the dining room, across the foyer, into the living room and on through to her father's study. Every window closed and locked, every door bolted and secure.

She lingered in her father's study. He'd once kept a gun in one of the desk drawers, and she even knew where he'd hidden the key. That was one of the advantages of being invisible. No one noticed you. People forgot that you were around.

Lifting the cigar humidor on his desk, Sarah found the key still taped to the underside. She peeled it loose and unlocked the bottom drawer. The gun was still there. A .38 Special that was a familiar weight in her hand. She'd held this gun before. More than once as a child. And now as an adult, she knew how to use it. Sean had seen to that.

Holding it at her side, she walked over to the mantel and

studied the pictures of Rachel. Smiling and beautiful. But maybe not so happy. Maybe not so innocent.

Suddenly, the room was oppressive, the lingering scent of cigar smoke a sickening reminder of a dark obsession.

Sarah carried the gun with her as she checked the upstairs. Her parents' room, Rachel's room, all the closets and bathrooms. By the time she reached her own bedroom, she'd managed to convince herself the house was secure. There was no way Derrick Fears could get inside. And if he did, she had the gun.

She swallowed a Xanax and went to bed. But for the longest time, she didn't sleep. She lay wide-awake, staring at the ceiling, listening for any sign of an intruder.

Finally her muscles loosened and exhaustion claimed her. Until a noise somewhere in the house brought her upright in bed.

Old houses settled, she tried to tell herself. Floorboards groaned, ancient pipes rattled. It was nothing.

But her heart was already pounding as she swung her legs off the bed and sat listening to the night. The house seemed almost too silent now.

Taking the gun from the nightstand, she moved to her bedroom door and slipped into the hallway, the pulsing drumbeat of her heart a frantic echo in her ears. At the top of the stairs, she stopped and peered over the railing.

The hair on her neck lifted a split second before a floorboard creaked behind her.

She whirled and stared deep into the shadowy hallway. Nothing moved, but she had the strongest sensation of another presence watching her from the darkness.

Her hand spidered across the wall, searching for the light switch. She was almost afraid the power had been cut, and the burst of brilliance startled her. For a moment, she didn't breathe as her hand tightened on the gun.

No one was there. She was alone in the hallway.

Quickly she went down the stairs and checked the front door. Locked tight. She moved cautiously through the dining room and kitchen to the back door. Locked tight. Everything was just as secure as she'd left it when she went up to bed.

So why the icy chill up her spine? Why the uncanny feeling that she wasn't alone in the house?

It was nothing, Sarah told herself. Floorboards groaned. It wasn't a footstep. Tree limbs scraped across a window. No one was trying to get in.

Understandable that she was jumpy, though. Her father was lying in the morgue with his throat cut. The identity of her sister's killer had been buried with her fourteen years ago. Who in their right mind wouldn't be jumpy?

Sarah went back upstairs and put the gun on the nightstand. She lay huddled under the covers, knowing that in spite of the Xanax, there would be no real rest for her that night.

She drifted for more than an hour, half asleep, half awake when her eyes opened suddenly and she lay staring into the dark. A new sound had awakened her, a rhythmic thumping that she couldn't place.

Her veins iced as she lay there listening to the dark.

Thump…thump…thump…

It was nothing. Old beams settling. Walls shifting. Sarah went through her earlier litany of reasonable explanations.

Thump…thump…thump…

Dust filtered down from the ceiling onto her face. She sat up in bed, her gaze lifted.

The attic. Someone was up there walking around. The one place she hadn't thought to check.

Thump…thump…thump…

The floorboards groaned beneath a heavy weight.

And then all went still.

Sarah's heart pounded a panicked staccato inside her chest. Someone was there. She could feel him. But the house was absolutely silent.

Which was why she was able to hear his breathing. Deep and unnatural. A feral gasping that lifted the hairs on her arms and the back of her neck.

Run! Get out of the house!

But Sarah couldn't seem to make her muscles work. Terror had paralyzed her, just the way it happened in a nightmare.

Besides, as long as she didn't move, he didn't seem to move.

She tested her theory by forcing her legs over the side of the bed.

Something scratched against the ceiling. The sound grew louder, frenzied as if claws were ripping right through the attic floorboards.

Sarah glanced around frantically. She'd never been allowed to have a telephone in her room, and now she realized that she'd left her cell phone downstairs in her purse.

She grabbed the gun and flew across the room to the door. The attic opening was just down the hall, and she tried to gauge the distance to the stairway. She had to get out of the house before whoever—*whatever*—was up there, decided to come down.

She opened the door to the hallway and paused to listen. She heard nothing. The scratching had stopped. The footsteps were silent.

Sarah's heart pounded and her chest tightened as she steeled herself for a dash to the stairs.

★ ★ ★

A little while later she stood shivering in the hallway as she watched a police officer disappear up the attic stairs. She could hear him moving around the space, but when he suddenly appeared in the doorway, Sarah jumped.

"Did you see anything?"

"There's nobody up here now, but I want to try something. Go back inside your room for a minute."

"Why?"

"You'll see," he said.

Sarah wasn't too keen on the suggestion, but she did as he asked.

"Can you hear me?" The officer's voice startled her. It sounded alarmingly close.

"Yes. You're clear as a bell."

"I'll be right down."

Sarah went back out to the hallway. When he appeared a few minutes later, he was brushing cobwebs from his sleeve.

"Sound carries through the heating vent," he said. "Whatever you heard was probably magnified. Might not have been as loud as you thought."

Sarah could feel that cold, dark panic swooping down on her again. "I heard breathing," she said. "And what sounded like someone scratching on the wood."

"Looks like you've got a bad squirrel problem up there," he said, still swiping at the cobwebs.

"That wasn't a squirrel I heard."

"Well, whatever it was is gone now. I don't know how anyone could get in from outside. The only access to the window is from the roof."

"Someone was spotted on the roof the other night," Sarah said. "That must be how he's getting in."

His brow lifted slightly. "You sound like you may know who it is."

Sarah shivered. "It's just a guess. I saw Derrick Fears out on the street earlier. He seemed to be watching the house."

"Well, that doesn't surprise me none," the officer said grimly. "We've had a few complaints about him since he got back to town. I locked the window, and there's a latch on the outside of the attic door. I fastened that, too, but it's pretty flimsy. If somebody wanted in bad enough, he wouldn't let that stop him. But it might slow him down, make him think twice." He glanced around. "I'll give the house a good going over, then have a look around outside. Probably won't be able to see anything until daylight."

Sarah waited downstairs while he searched the house, then walked him to the door.

"I don't think you'll have any more trouble tonight. If somebody was up there, he's long gone now. But I'll drive by every so often just to keep an eye on things."

"Thanks." Sarah closed the door behind him and turned the dead bolt. She could see his flashlight arcing through the darkness as he circled the house. Then he got into the squad car and drove away.

She lingered for a moment at the bottom of the stairs. Every light was blazing on the second floor, but no way was she going back up there tonight. She knew she wouldn't get a wink of sleep anyway. Putting the gun on the coffee table, she grabbed a blanket and curled up on the sofa to wait for daybreak.

26

When Esme came in at seven the next morning, Sarah hid the gun in her robe and went upstairs to shower. Numb with exhaustion, she slowly undressed, barely glancing in the mirror as she washed her face and brushed her teeth.

But as she stood under the hot water, everything came rushing back. The intruder in the attic. Her father's brutal murder.

Sarah couldn't help wondering if her family was being picked off one by one, and if she was now in the killer's sights.

She stayed in the shower for a long time, and when she finally came downstairs, she found Lukas Clay in the kitchen with Esme. He turned when Sarah came into the room, and his gaze seemed to linger as he nodded. His uniform was pressed and he looked freshly shaven.

"I heard about the call last night," he said. "I thought it might be a good idea to have another look around now that it's daylight."

"I appreciate the follow-up," Sarah said.

Esme stood at the sink, lips pursed, eyes bright with speculation. She folded her arms and glared at Sarah. "What call would that be?"

"I'll tell you about it later," Sarah said.

"You'll tell me about it right now, Sarah June, what in the world is going on? Why you being so secretive?"

"I thought I heard someone in the attic last night," Sarah said. "I panicked and called the police, but they didn't find anything. It may have been squirrels."

"Why didn't you call me?" Esme demanded. "I could have been here faster than the police."

A seventy-year-old woman coming to my rescue.

Sarah could picture it now, Esme in her housecoat and slippers, bearing down on a prowler with the pellet gun she used to scare off stray dogs. As tired as she was, Sarah couldn't help smiling at that image.

"I'll show you where the attic entrance is," Sarah said to Lukas. She could feel Esme's eyes on her as they walked out of the kitchen, and she knew this would not be the last she heard of it.

She paused in the foyer, glancing over her shoulder to make sure Esme couldn't overhear them. "I saw Derrick Fears standing outside the house earlier in the evening. I told the officer about him last night."

"What time did you see him?"

"It was early, just after twilight. I was in the living room looking out the window, but I didn't see him at first. Then he walked over to stand under the streetlight, as if he wanted to make sure I knew he was there." Sarah shivered, even though she'd dressed warmly in jeans and a wool sweater. She hadn't yet had a cup of coffee or anything to eat, but her stomach was suddenly churning. "He had on a hood," she said. "I didn't get a good look at his face, but I'm almost certain it was Fears."

Sunlight streamed in through the glass panels in the door and caught Lukas in the face. He moved away from the glare. "How long did he stay after you noticed him?"

"I don't know. Only a few minutes. But he must have been there for a while. I doubt it was a coincidence that he showed up just as I was at the window."

"If you see him around here again, call it in. If he keeps bothering you, we'll let his parole officer know about it. That might give him some incentive to move on."

"Do you think Derrick is the one who was in the attic last night? The officer said the window was unlocked, and the only way in is from the roof. That would explain why Esme saw someone up there the other night."

"I'll look around," Lukas said. "How do I get to the attic from inside?"

"Up the stairs and to your right, at the end of the hallway."

Sarah was still in the foyer a few minutes later waiting for him to come back when the doorbell rang. She answered, expecting to find one of the neighbors with a covered casserole in hand, the symbol of Southern condolences, but instead it was Sean, bleary-eyed and unshaven.

Sarah was so surprised to see him that she blurted out the first thing that came to mind. "You look like shit."

"I feel like shit. Can I come in?"

She stepped back, and as he entered, he gave her a quick appraisal. "You don't look so hot yourself. Long night?"

"You might say that."

He stood in the entry, restless and wary, as he glanced around. "So this is the place, huh? This is where you grew up."

"This is it." Sarah raked her fingers through her hair. "You really didn't have to drive up here, you know."

He turned at that. "I think I did, since you wouldn't return any of my phone calls. Did you even listen to any of the messages?"

"I thought it was best if we didn't see or talk to each other for a while."

"Did you?" His gaze lifted to a point behind her, and she turned to see Lukas walking down the stairs. Sarah wasn't even looking at Sean, but she could sense the sudden tension in his body, like a coiled cobra confronted by a mongoose.

When Lukas got to the bottom of the stairs, Sarah made the introductions and the two men shook hands.

"I'll have a look around outside before I leave," Lukas said. "See if I can find any footprints Terry might have missed in the dark." His eyes were only on Sarah now. "Don't forget what I said about getting new locks."

"I won't."

He went out the front door, and Sarah turned back to Sean, who was scowling down at her. "What was that all about?"

"I had a prowler last night. Someone got into the attic from the roof."

"You okay?"

"I'm fine."

But Sarah saw that his attention was caught again by something behind her. This time it was Esme. She'd come into the dining room and appeared to be unabashedly eavesdropping. When she saw Sarah's scowl, she pretended to dust the table with her apron.

"Let's go for a walk," Sean muttered.

They went out the front door, but Sarah led him around the house to the back path. They walked past Esme's cottage down through the pear orchard. The sun was bright and warm, and the breeze rustled through the dead leaves sounding like a rain shower.

In the distance, Sarah could hear the bells in the trees over the old Duncan graves. The sound made her shiver.

Sean's head cocked as he listened. "Is that a wind chime?"

"No, it's bells."

"It's kind of an eerie sound," he said. "Don't think I'd want to hear that in the dark."

He fell silent, and Sarah found herself studying him out of the corner of her eye. He wore a thin leather jacket over a gray T-shirt and jeans. Even haggard and weary, he was still one of the most attractive men she'd ever known.

"So how did you find out?" she finally asked.

He looked startled. "Find out...what?"

Sarah frowned. "You heard about my father, right? Isn't that why you're here?"

"Your father? No. What happened?"

"He's dead. I assumed that's why you came."

"I'm sorry," he said. "I know the two of you weren't close, but that kind of thing is never easy."

She drew a long breath. "Especially under these circumstances."

"What do you mean?"

"He didn't just die, Sean. He was murdered."

He stared down at her for the longest moment. "You mean as in someone pulled the plug?"

"I wish. No, it's...oh, God, it's so much worse than that. So horrible I can hardly bear to think about it, much less talk about it." She paused to take another breath. "Someone came into his room and cut his throat."

Sean was clearly shocked. "When did it happen?"

"Early yesterday morning. The nurse found him when she went in to give him a morphine shot."

"Do the police have any suspects?"

Sarah's hand trembled as she tucked a strand of hair behind one ear. "I think I'm their suspect."

Something flickered in his gaze. "Why would they think you killed him?"

Sarah waved a hand toward the house. "He was a wealthy man by some standards and I'm the only family he has left. I guess that makes me the logical suspect."

"But he was dying. He only had a few months left, you said."

"Yes, I know."

"So you could have just waited it out. Unless he threatened to cut you out of his will. But then you've never seemed to care about his money."

"But the police here don't know me like you do," Sarah said softly.

He looked out over the pear trees. A breeze ruffled his hair, and the light skimming down through the limbs highlighted a road map of tiny lines Sarah had never noticed before. His job was taking a toll. Aging him before his time.

"Sometimes I wonder if I really do know you," he said. "You keep so much of yourself hidden. All those secrets. I don't have a clue what goes through your head."

The edge in his voice alarmed Sarah. "Sean, if you didn't know about my father, why are you here?"

"I need to talk to you about Cat."

She didn't realize who he meant at first. "Cat? You mean Catherine?"

"I need to know if you've seen or talked to her recently."

Sarah was completely taken aback. But the way Sean looked

at her made the alarm buzz even louder in her brain. Something was wrong. He wouldn't have made the trip from New Orleans just to ask if she'd talked to his wife.

"Did you see her last Saturday night after I left your house?"

"No. I left to come here right after we talked."

"You drove straight through?"

"Pretty much. I had to pull over and wait out a rainstorm. Why? What's happened?"

He scrubbed a hand across his face. "She's missing."

"Missing? For how long?"

"Since Saturday night. No one has seen or heard from her. It's like she vanished into thin air."

Sarah frowned. "I don't understand. Why would you think I've seen her? I barely even know what she looks like."

"I thought she might have come to your house. Danny said she'd somehow gotten the notion that you and I were living together again. She implied that she intended to have it out with you."

Sarah could feel a headache pulsing at her temples. "Why would she think that you and I are living together?"

He didn't look at her. "I moved out."

Sarah stared at him in astonishment. "Why didn't you mention it? All the times we talked, you never said a word."

"I wanted to tell you, but I had the impression it wasn't something you cared to hear."

"Your leaving her...I hope it didn't have anything to do with me."

"Of course it had something to do with you, Sarah. What did you think? This isn't the time to get into that. All I want to do right now is find Cat."

"Of course." Sarah was still floored by the whole conversation. "Are you sure she didn't just go off for a few days to be alone?"

"She's not alone. Or at least she wasn't. She went out with a friend on Saturday night. Neither of them has been seen since."

"Is it possible they've gone off somewhere together?"

"The friend's car was found right off North Rampart. Less than a block from your house."

"And you think she was there to see me?"

"I don't know what to think, at this point. A small amount of blood was found on the car door. It didn't belong to her or the friend."

"Then who did it belong to?"

His silence registered like a slap in the face. Sarah's throat went dry. "You think it's my blood?" she asked incredulously. "You think I had something to do with her disappearance?" She caught his arm, and when his gaze swung back to her, she recoiled. "Oh, my God. That is what you think."

His eyes had gone cool and emotionless. Not the eyes of a former lover or even a worried husband. Sean was a cop now. "I'm just trying to piece together what happened. I thought it likely that she'd gone to see you, so I had a look around the house."

"*My* house?"

"I wanted to see if I could find anything that would indicate she'd been there." He had the grace to look slightly defensive. "I used my key to get in."

"You mean *my* key. The one you never gave back. Did you find anything?"

"A shard of glass that had some blood on it."

"That could have been there for ages," she said.

"Yeah, that's what I thought, too." He paused. "Do you know what luminol is?"

"Of course I know what it is. I lived with a cop for two years, remember?"

"Sarah, I sprayed it in your bedroom and the whole place lit up."

Her heart began to beat way too fast. She pressed a hand to her chest as if she could somehow slow the rhythm. "What are you talking about?"

"I found bloody footprints all over your bedroom."

Sarah could feel the slow creep of horror through her veins. "That's not possible. Unless the footprints have been there for years, too."

"I don't think so. The footprints were cloven. Just like we found on the first victim."

"Oh, God."

"Exactly," Sean said. "You reacted the other night when I told you the second victim's name. You recognized it. I saw it on your face. Holly Jessup. That name means something to you, doesn't it?"

"I read about her disappearance in the paper. I told you that."

"That's what you said."

"Sean, what's going on? Why are you looking at me like that?"

He shook his head, glanced away. "I don't know what the hell is going on. But somehow, everything that's happened is connected to you. You're the key to all this."

"To *what?*"

"The first victim's name was Amber Gleason. Her last name used to be Hays. Does that name ring a bell?"

Sarah shook her head. "I don't think so."

"Are you sure about that? Because we found a connection between the two victims. Amber Hays and Holly Jessup used

to live right here in Adamant. They went to high school with
your sister."

Holly Jessup.

Sean was holding on to her arms now. Sarah knew that if
she wanted to run, he would stop her. But it didn't matter.
She had no place to go.

His haunted eyes searched her face, as if looking for something to believe in. "Everything comes back to you, Sarah.
Tell me how that blood got in your bedroom. Tell me why the
only connection we can find between the two dead women
is you. Tell me how you knew about those footprints before
we found them on the first victim."

"I can't," she whispered.

Sean watched Sarah walk back through the trees toward the
house. He was torn by the desire to follow her back and the
need to maintain a professional distance. But whatever perspective he'd managed to hang on to had pretty much been
shot the moment he saw her.

He thought about the years they were together, all that baggage she'd carried around. The missing blocks of time, the
hazy memories. Both easily explained by the pills.

But now, he had to wonder if it was something more. Something that even Michael Garrett had missed.

Two women were dead, two were missing, and her father's
throat had been slashed. By her own design or otherwise,
Sarah was the catalyst for a nightmare scenario that reached
from a tiny town in Arkansas all the way down to New Orleans. She was in big trouble, and Sean didn't know how to
help her. He didn't even know whether or not to believe her.

The wind picked up, and he could hear the bells tolling in
the distance. He followed the sound through the orchard and

all the way across a field to the old farmhouse that was the site
of Rachel DeLaune's murder. He'd been there once before,
although he'd never mentioned the trip to Sarah. He'd stood
in the front room, in the exact spot where her sister's life had
ended, as he'd tried to put together what had happened. It was
there in the house that Sean had begun to wonder if he really
wanted to take his investigation any further. If the truth he
uncovered might force him to make a terrible choice.

He climbed the porch steps now, the bells still clanging in
the distance. The hinges creaked as he pushed open the door,
and the floorboards sagged against his weight as he stepped
through.

The house was cold and dim. The grimy windows filtered
the weak sunlight, and Sean wished he'd brought a flashlight.
He could barely make out the graffiti on the walls. Four-let-
ter words and phone numbers scrawled alongside the fading
satanic symbols.

He walked to the center of the room and knelt, his fingertips brushed across the dark stain on the floor. A chill swept
through him, and the hair at the back of his neck lifted. He
had the sudden feeling that he was no longer alone.

Slowly, he stood. Across the room, a door off a narrow
staircase stood open and he walked over to peer up into the
shadows.

"Someone there?"

He drew his gun and started up the wooden steps. At the
top, another door opened directly into a bedroom. An old
wardrobe stood against one wall, the mirrored door cracked
and blackened with age. Clothes and books and what looked
to be clumps of human hair were scattered across the sagging
floorboards, and the stench of rotting flesh stopped Sean in
his tracks.

A dead rat, he thought. He knew the smell of a human corpse and that wasn't it.

Crossing the room, he opened the wardrobe. Nothing inside. Not even the carcass of a rodent.

He reached out to close the door, then froze. For a split second, he could have sworn he saw someone standing behind him in the mirror.

No one was there. Nothing but dead space.

Something scurried across the floors in the shadows. A rodent—very much alive, he thought.

He turned back to the mirror, and now he saw what he had somehow missed before. A message written backward on the wall behind him.

I am you.

27

The body was released by the end of the week, and the funeral was held graveside at two o'clock on Thursday afternoon. The weather was beautiful, cloudless and warm, one of those late-winter days that seemed as if spring was right around the corner.

Sarah had gone to the mall the day before and bought a black dress with a matching jacket, and the weather was so mild, she hadn't even thrown a coat over it. But it was chilly in the shade of the awning and she found herself shivering when the wind blew.

Tim Mason delivered the eulogy after all, but Sarah heard very little of the service. She was in her own little dream world, until he spoke the line "…survived by his daughter, Sarah," and then she glanced up, her gaze meeting his for a split second before she looked away.

Her eyes strayed to the row of headstones nearby. Her mother, her sister and now her father. Everyone gone, but her.

Curtis stood in the sunshine, away from the crowd, and as Sarah watched, he knelt beside Rachel's grave, hand on his chin, seemingly as deep in thought as she'd been a moment ago.

When he looked up, Sarah was struck for a moment by the sadness in his eyes, by the air of confidence and purpose that always seemed to be at war with whatever it was from his past that still drove him. Shaped him. She thought again about what he'd said when he drove her home from the hospital that day. One small thing done differently and we become someone else.

When was that moment for her? When had she become someone else?

She shivered as she stared at her father's coffin, wondering what his last moment of life had been like. Wondering whose face he'd seen as he struggled for his last breath. And she thought of *his* words to her.

You did it. It was you.

Had he gone to his grave still believing her a killer? Had her mother?

Sarah looked up at the sky, cloudless and blue, and yet it seemed to her that twilight was already closing in. The sunlight spangling down through the trees had lost its warmth. The shadows had started to lengthen.

She looked at the faces all around her, wondering if one of them was the killer.

Or was the real killer the face that stared back at her from the mirror?

Sean, she thought. *Please help me figure this all out.*

But he had his own worries at the moment, not to mention his doubts about her. He'd gone back to New Orleans and she hadn't seen him since.

As the minister's words droned on, Sarah's gaze returned to her father's casket, and she felt the wrench of a long-forgotten memory, hazy now with the passing of time.

She couldn't have been more than four at the time. She was in her bed, lying wide-awake listening to a strange noise coming from Rachel's room next door...

Sarah got out of bed and opened her door. The noise was louder in the hallway. She padded on bare feet toward Rachel's room and stood right outside the door.

The noise distressed her. She didn't know what it was. She wanted to go wake up Mama, but she knew better. Her father would be mad, and he scared her when he got angry.

After a few moments, the sound stopped and she heard her father's voice speaking softly. So softly, Sarah couldn't tell what he was saying.

She wanted to turn and run back to her room before he caught her. He wouldn't like it if he found her in the hallway. She wasn't supposed to leave her room at night.

Mustn't come out. Mustn't tell.

The warning whispered through Sarah's mind.

The door opened and she could see inside Rachel's room. Her sister was lying on her side, not moving...not crying. Just lying there.

Her father came out of the room then and he saw Sarah in the hallway. Before he could say anything to her, she turned and raced back to her room. She jumped into bed and pulled the covers over her head.

As if that would protect her.

She heard his footsteps in the hallway. Pausing outside her door...

A moment later, he was at her bedside. He jerked away the covers and grabbed her arms, yanking her up off the bed.

"You little brat. You've been nothing but trouble since the day you were born," he said in a cold, angry voice. A voice that made Sarah whimper.

"*I'm sorry, Daddy.*"

"*Don't call me that. It makes me sick to hear you call me that. I'm not your father. You hear me? You're nothing to me but a god-damn mistake.*"

Sarah tried to cower away, but he wouldn't let her go.

"*What did I tell you about coming out of your room at night? Huh?*"

"*You said not to,*" *she whispered.*

"*You do it again and see how long it takes me to get rid of you. I should have sent you away a long time ago. Should have shipped you off to a place where girls like you belong.*"

Sarah knew what he meant. He'd told her before. He'd send her to a place for bad girls. A place where they locked you in a dark room and didn't ever let you come out. Sarah didn't want to go there. She was afraid of the dark. And she didn't want to leave Mama and Rachel.

"*I don't like the dark,*" *she whispered.*

"*Then you mustn't tell,*" *he said, his fingers digging into her arms.*

Sarah walked to the far side of the cemetery and found a bench where she could sit and be alone. She pulled her jacket around her to ward off the afternoon chill as she watched a pair of cardinals flit through the branches of a magnolia tree. The memory had left her shaken and heartsick.

A shadow fell across her and she turned in surprise.

"You look like a woman who is about at the end of her rope," Curtis said as he sat down beside her.

"What gave it away?"

"Your obvious preference for the company of the dead to that of the living, for one thing."

"The dead can't hurt you," Sarah said.

"That's true."

She stared at her shoes. They were a little too high and

a little too tight. She hadn't noticed until now that her feet were killing her. She reached down and pulled off her shoes.

"You do realize it's the dead of winter," Curtis said. "I would warn you about catching your death, but that would seem like a really bad pun at the moment."

"Yeah, it kind of would," Sarah agreed. "Not to mention that a doctor should know better. Even I know that colds are caused from germs, not the weather, and I'm the slow one, remember?"

"You were never the slow one." Something in his voice made Sarah glance up. The shade from the magnolia tree had deepened his eyes to jade as he looked out over the graves. "You were smart as a whip. Much brighter than anyone else I knew. You didn't just see things, you observed them. You didn't just watch people, you studied them. I think that's why those portraits you used to sketch were so horrifying. You had a way of seeing things in people, hidden things that were not always flattering. And then you magnified those traits so that the likenesses became grotesque caricatures."

"I never drew you that way," she said.

"Thank God." He glanced at his watch. "I hate to cut this short but I promised Gran I'd give her a hand this afternoon."

"We hired a bunch of people for that. Esme shouldn't have to lift a finger."

"You really think she's going to turn that kitchen over to strangers?"

Sarah winced. "Good point."

"Do you need a ride?"

"No, thanks. I'd like to just sit here for a while. I'm not in the mood to face all those people. Half of them think I killed my father for his money. The other half..." She shuddered.

"God only knows what they think. I hate all that whispering behind hands. Those long, speculative looks."

"Since when do you give a damn about what anyone thinks?"

"I care what the cops think," she said. "I'm not crazy about certain people thinking I'm a murderer."

"Certain people like your father?"

The question was softly spoken, but it sent a hard chill up Sarah's spine. She turned to Curtis, but she didn't say anything, just watched him in silence.

"I overheard your conversation at the hospital the other day," he said. "I didn't mean to eavesdrop, but the old man made no effort to keep his voice down."

"No wonder the police are so interested in me."

"I didn't tell them anything. And I don't think anyone else heard the specifics, just that there were raised voices coming from the room."

"Why didn't you tell the police what you heard?"

"Because I don't think you had anything to do with his death. And even if I thought you did…" He trailed off on a shrug. "He got what he deserved."

"I know what he did to her," Sarah said softly. "I remembered something earlier at the service. I saw him coming out of Rachel's room one night. He threatened to send me away if I told anyone what I'd seen."

A strong breeze swept through the trees, blowing dead leaves across the graves. The cardinals were on the ground now, pecking through the dirt.

"It continued, didn't it?" she said. "It never stopped until she died."

Curtis closed his eyes. "She never admitted it to me, but I suspected. Especially after she got pregnant."

Sarah's stomach churned. "Oh, God."

"She didn't want to admit that, either, but she couldn't hide it from me. I tried to get her to run away with me. I told her I didn't care who the baby belonged to. I'd raise it as my own. I almost had her convinced. Or at least, I tell myself I did. And then she was killed."

"Did my father know about the pregnancy?"

"I don't know."

"Curtis, do you think he could have had something to do with her death?"

"I've wondered about that, but I don't think so. He was crazy about her. Obsessed with her. But I don't think he would have taken her life. If I'd thought that, I would have killed him myself a long time ago."

Sarah shivered. "I've always wondered why he never loved me. Now I'm glad he didn't."

"You know why he couldn't love you, don't you?"

"You knew?" she said softly.

"I guessed," he said. "You looked so different from Rachel. She was so fair, you've got all that dark hair. And then one day, I saw—"

"You saw what?"

He shook his head. "I saw you and I figured it out."

"It's funny," Sarah said. "All my life I've never really known who I am. And now for the first time, I think I might actually like to find out."

Curtis smiled. "Maybe church would be a good place to start."

Sarah glanced up at him. "Are you trying to tell me something?"

"I think you already know."

★ ★ ★

Everyone had left by the time Sarah got up and walked back across the cemetery, pausing briefly to pluck two roses from the fresh mound to place one each on her mother's and sister's graves. Then she turned and followed the flagstone pathway to the gate.

Twilight was still more than two hours away, but the trees along the sidewalk blocked the sun. Sarah was cold and tired and she hadn't gone more than two blocks before her new shoes had rubbed blisters on her feet. She yanked them off again and carried them by the heels as she plodded along on the cold pavement.

A car pulled to the curb beside her, and she turned in relief, thinking it was Curtis. But her smile died when she saw the squad car, and a moment later, Lukas Clay got out.

He propped an arm on the top of his car as his gaze dropped to her shoes. "Everything okay?"

"Everything's fine. I'm just walking home from the cemetery." She gestured aimlessly with the shoes.

"Want a ride?"

She hesitated. "I guess that all depends."

"On what?"

"Did you just happen along or were you specifically looking for me?"

He frowned. "Does it matter?"

"It does if the ride includes a trip to the police station."

"I'm not here to arrest you, if that's what you're worried about. I'm just offering you a ride home. You look pretty miserable out here. But if you'd rather walk…"

"No, that's okay." She hobbled over to the car and climbed in. "Are you sure this isn't considered a conflict of interest? I am still technically a suspect, aren't I?"

"I don't think giving you a ride home is crossing any boundaries."

They were silent, until he turned down Sarah's street, and then she saw all the cars still lined up at the curb. "Stop," she said in alarm.

He shot her a puzzled look.

"I'm not going in there." She couldn't go inside her father's house and mingle with the people mourning his death. Not after what she'd just remembered.

"Where do you want to go, then?"

"I don't know. Anywhere but here. Just drop me off in town. I'll find someplace to hang out until everyone leaves."

"That could be a while."

She shrugged. "I don't care."

He scratched his chin. "All right, look. I've got an errand or two to run. You can ride along with me if you want."

She turned. "You don't mind?"

"No. But I'm headed out to the country. I won't be back for a while."

"That's fine by me."

They drove south on a two-lane highway that led them deep into the countryside. They were miles from town. Miles from anywhere, Sarah thought as Lukas turned onto a gravel road lined with hedges and shaded by pine trees.

The road dead-ended into a private lane, and as they drove through, the tires thumped on a metal cattle guard.

A few minutes later, they pulled up to a white clapboard house raised off the ground on stilts. The house had two chimneys and a large screened-in porch to keep the bugs out on warm summer evenings.

Sarah noticed new shingles on the roof and a fresh coat of paint on the gutters.

"Is this your house?" she asked as they got out of the car.

"Yeah, but I don't live here. I have a place in town. I only come out here every couple of weekends or so to do a little work."

"It's nice," Sarah said, gazing around. "Isolated, though." She rubbed her arms against a sudden chill. The day was getting colder.

"Come on in," he said. "I'll show you around. But watch your step. I've got several projects going at once, and you never know when you'll trip over a loose board or a stray hammer."

Cane rockers were lined up on the porch. In the summer, you'd be able to sit there and watch the lightning bugs, Sarah thought.

Lukas opened the door and she stepped inside. "Uh, you weren't kidding about the projects, were you?"

He'd stripped away part of the wallpaper, refinished part of the woodwork, and repaired part of the floor. Nothing, however, was finished.

"I'm getting the sense that you get bored easily," Sarah said.

"You know what they say about idle hands…" He seemed completely different out here, Sarah thought. More relaxed.

"Have a seat," he said. "I'll see if I can find us something to drink."

The room smelled of sawdust and varnish, tugging loose yet another memory for Sarah, but this one more recent. She suddenly had an image of all those *udjats* on the walls staring down at her.

She saw nothing like that in here, though. Just the opposite, in fact. A crucifix hung on one wall and a print of *The Last Supper* on another.

When Lukas came back from the kitchen with the drinks, Sarah was studying a photograph on the mantel.

He held up two chilled beers. "Glass or bottle?"

"Bottle is fine." She turned back to the mantel as he twisted off the caps. "Is this your mother?"

"Yeah."

"She's beautiful."

"Was. She died when I was eight. I don't know why, but my memories of her are kind of hazy. It's like I just stopped thinking about her one day." He handed one of the bottles to Sarah. "I guess it was easier that way."

Sarah returned the photograph to the mantel and picked up a small, wooden bird. "Did you carve this?"

"Yeah," he said. "It used to be a hobby of mine, but I haven't done any woodworking in years. I used to paint a little, too, but my mother was the true artist."

"I don't know about that," Sarah said. "This is beautiful."

A horn sounded outside and she turned to the window. "Are you expecting company?"

"A delivery," he said. "They don't like to drop things off way out here unless someone signs for them."

Sarah went outside with him and watched from the porch as he and the driver unloaded pallets of lumber. When he joined her a little while later, she was sitting in one of the cane rockers.

"Kind of cold out here," he said. "You should have waited inside."

"I like it out here. It's really beautiful. When you live in a city, you sometimes forget what a real sunset looks like. With a view like that, I could get used to all this peace and quiet."

"Yeah," Lukas said as he turned and scanned the horizon. "I've always welcomed the isolation."

28

Michael Garrett greeted Sean at the top of the stairs, and the two men walked back to his office together. Garrett was dressed in black slacks and a gray cardigan sweater over a crisp white shirt. Casual attire for him, Sean suspected.

He motioned Sean to a chair, then sat down at his desk, the gloom of early evening filtering softly through the window behind him.

"Thanks for agreeing to see me so late," Sean said. "I couldn't get away until now. The mountain of misery on my desk just keeps piling higher. I guess I don't have anything on you, though, do I?"

He was answered by one of those implacable smiles. "I'm glad you called. I hadn't heard about Sarah's father. Distressing news, to say the least." He shifted slightly in his chair. "Tell me about this new message you've found."

"It was scrawled across an upstairs wall in the old farmhouse where Sarah's sister was killed fourteen years ago."

"Was it the same message?"

"'I am you.' There's no way that can be a coincidence."

"No, I agree," Garrett said grimly. "The murders here in New Orleans would seem to be directly related to Rachel DeLaune's death fourteen years ago. It's entirely possible the same killer is killing again."

"But why?" Sean said. "Why *now?*"

For a moment, Garrett seemed lost in his own musings. "I've been thinking about everything we talked about when you were here last. Something about those tattoos has been troubling me."

"What is it?"

Garrett turned to his computer. "I want to show you something."

Sean got up and walked over to lean against the corner of the desk as he stared down at the Rorschach-like images Garrett had pulled up on the screen.

"The first two images are the inkblot tattoos from the victims. I lifted them from the crime scene photographs so that I could more closely compare them to the actual Rorschach inkblot. I've been looking for similarities, discrepancies, even the slightest enhancement that we may have failed to notice the first time."

"And did you find something?"

"I believe so." Garrett used his finger to point out various features in the images. "Clearly, there's a distinction in the mind of the tattoo artist between the light and dark faces. I thought he was telling us something important by the way he juxtaposes the faces in each image. Light, dark. Dark, light."

"The left side represents the mirror image, you said."

"That's what I thought at first. Two halves of one whole. But after further study, I realized I was wrong. Each face is slightly different and represents a separate entity. Each entity, with its own distinct drive and history, each with its own family of origin."

Sean's gaze was riveted on the screen as he leaned forward, trying to make sense of Garrett's summary. His arm brushed against the mouse, and one of the images skidded across the page. "Sorry," he muttered. "We didn't lose that one, did we?"

Garrett didn't answer. He seemed transfixed by something he saw on the screen. Sean could almost hear his mind clicking.

"What?"

"We didn't lose the image," Garrett said. "It's layered over the first image. Do you see what happened?"

Sean glanced at the monitor, puzzled.

Silently, Michael lifted a finger and traced the outline of a new face within the two merged inkblots.

"A fifth face?"

"An integration of the other faces. One body, one mind, four personalities." Michael sat back, his gaze still on the screen. "We're talking about a multiple," he said quietly.

A shiver of unease slid up Sean's spine. "A multiple? As in…"

"As in DID…dissociative identity disorder. What we used to call a split personality…one person, four separate identities."

Sean frowned at the soft note of excitement in the therapist's voice. "I've seen it in movies," he said. "But that kind of thing doesn't happen in real life, does it?"

"Oh, yes it does. It's rare. Very rare. A therapist could go his entire career without seeing a true case of DID, but…"

"But what?"

"As it happens, I'm seeing one…right now."

"Well, that's interesting," Sean said. "Especially the timing."

"I'd say *too* interesting…and too neat, as well." The excitement in Garrett's voice had turned to concern.

And now Sean was getting worried. "What are you getting at?"

"This patient came with a referral, but when I checked with my colleague, he wasn't familiar with the case, possibly because the person who came to see me was an alter-personality with his own name, his own history. I kept seeing him because he presented such an interesting case. But now I'm wondering if he sought me out for a specific reason."

"It was a setup," Sean said, feeling himself in familiar territory now. He knew nothing about psychoanalysis, but he could usually spot a con a mile off. "And it leads straight back to Sarah. This guy knew she was a patient of yours. That's why he sought you out."

"I'm beginning to think so," Garrett said. "But what would a deception like that gain him? Unless I somehow figure into his plan for her."

"His plan?"

"This isn't a random thing. It's like you said, everything is connected to Sarah. Why, we don't know. But for whatever reason, she's become very important to Jude."

At Garrett's words, uneasiness settled over Sean, bringing with it a sense of urgency. "Does he have a last name?"

"Cole."

Sean took out his notebook and jotted it down. "How long have you been seeing him?"

"Only for a few sessions."

Sean glanced up. "He came before the killings started, then. Does that make sense to you?"

Garrett had grown silent again. "It would if one of the alters somehow feels threatened by Sarah. Jude claims he's the protector."

"The protector of what?" Sean asked impatiently.

"DID usually develops out of an abusive situation, one that almost always starts in childhood. A person with DID can have many kinds of personalities of different ages, sexes, even nationalities. But certain *types* of personalities are almost always present. The protector, for instance, is the one that surfaces during the abuse and is crucial to the child or host's survival. The persecutor holds the child's rage. He's the keeper of the secrets and silence that surround the past abuse, and he can become quite volatile if he feels too much information is being revealed. Typically, the host has no knowledge of these other personalities, but they're often aware of him and each other. They interact and collaborate in their own world, which is why the host will often complain of hearing voices in his head."

"How would a whacko like this exist in real life and not reveal himself?" Sean said.

"People with this disorder can function very well, and they often lead creative and productive lives. But that's not to say they don't have problems. Nightmares, flashbacks, memory loss. These symptoms can create a chaotic existence, and DID sufferers tend to self-medicate."

"You mean like Sarah," Sean said slowly.

"Sarah has certainly experienced many of these symptoms, but she doesn't have DID. And the disorder in the individual we're talking about is so extreme that he may not be able to function well even under the slightest stress. In fact, I'd say he's beginning to lose control. Impulsivity is a characteristic of a disintegrating personality. I should have realized this earlier, when you described the crime scenes…the first one organized to the point of overkill, as you put it, the second one falling apart. And now he is, too."

Sean wanted to feel relieved that Sarah was in the clear, but at that moment all he could think about was how alone she was in that big house. "We have to find this guy," he said. "Does he have another appointment scheduled?"

Garrett nodded. "Yes, but not until next week. I can give you his information, but I don't think that'll be of much help. You're not going to find any record of a Jude Cole."

"Give it to me anyway," Sean said. "I'll put out a BOLO. Would you recognize a picture of him?"

"Yes, if it was taken while in protector mode. The disorder can be so extreme, physical appearances can actually change. In fact, the way he mutilates his victims' faces is probably a direct result of his own distorted self-image."

"The first thing we have to do is get you to a police artist," Sean said. "We need to know what this guy looks like. Without a face, we're searching for nothing but a ghost."

By the time Esme went home that night, Sarah was exhausted. She wandered through the house, wineglass in one hand, the .38 Special in the other, and the Xanax she'd taken after Lukas dropped her off mellowing out the rough edges.

Earlier in the week, she'd had all the locks changed and a metal grid fastened over the window in the attic. No one could get in now without going to a great deal of trouble.

But now, Sarah was preoccupied with an even darker history. She couldn't walk past Rachel's room without shuddering violently. She couldn't think about what had been done to her sister without feeling sick to her stomach.

Why had no one stopped him? Not Esme, not her mother, not even Curtis. And not Sarah.

Now that the funeral was over, she couldn't wait to get out of here. She had no idea what was happening with the investigation, but she couldn't be expected to stay in town indefinitely. She had a life, such as it was, to get back to. Any place was better than here.

But going back to New Orleans presented yet another worry. Sean had found bloodstains in her bedroom, two women from her past had been murdered and her ex-lover's wife was missing. Everything was connected to her, Sean had said. She was the key.

She dropped her gaze to the drawings she'd made of the inkblot tattoos. Two faces. One light, one dark. One good, one evil. A mirror image. Two sides of the same person.

A dark self.

Sarah's deepest fear.

There was a reason why she couldn't remember what had happened the night her sister was murdered. A reason why she'd been found covered in Rachel's blood. The answer had eluded her all these years, but the possibility, that terrible fear, had never stopped tormenting her.

Sarah stared at the images for so long the inkblots began to blur. She lifted the sketches from the desk to help her focus, and the light shining down through the paper made it transparent. The lines from the bottom drawing bled through to the top, creating the impression of a single image. A single face.

Sarah caught her breath as she angled the light up so that it shone directly through the paper. The hair on the back of her neck lifted when she realized what she was looking at.

The inkblots were made to go together. The message from the killer could only be interpreted when the images were viewed together, one on top of the other.

The blood in Sarah's veins was suddenly ice-cold. Her hands trembled as she stared down into the face of the killer.

And she knew that face. She'd drawn it before.

Ashe Cain.

The sketch she'd done of him must still be somewhere in the house. And it would be proof, at least for her, that he really existed. Proof that he—not Sarah—had killed her sister and her father, those two poor women in New Orleans. He was responsible for the cloven footprints. Not Sarah. Not the devil.

Ashe Cain.

He was back. Those messages at the crime scenes, the face in the inkblots had all been left for *her*.

I am you.

We're the same, Sarah. Our souls our mirror images.

"Fucking psycho," she muttered as she pawed frantically through the desk drawers looking for her old drawing books. She tore through the closet, the dresser, underneath the bed. And then she remembered that she and Esme had gone through her things before she'd left for boarding school. She hadn't been able to take all the books with her—she'd had dozens—so she and Esme had boxed some of them up and Esme had put them up in the attic.

The attic.

Sarah sat down heavily at the desk and took a drink of wine as she contemplated going up there to look for the drawing books. Maybe it would be better to wait until morning. Esme could go up there with her then and show her where they were stored.

But Sarah didn't want to wait until morning. She wanted to see that drawing tonight. It might well be the key to her vaulted memories. It could be the key to everything.

She took another drink of wine for courage and fingered the gun on the desk.

It wouldn't take long. Rush up there, find the box, rush right back. Three, four minutes tops.

Taking another sip of wine, she picked up the gun as she got up from the desk, then hurried down the hall. Up the stairs and through the attic door, heart pounding all the way. She flipped the switch, and the shadows cast by the harsh light from the bare bulb caused her to jump and clutch the gun frantically in front of her.

Quickly, she scanned the space. It was a typical attic, stuffed to the rafters with furniture, boxes and discarded toys. She even saw one of her old bicycles leaning against the wall and an assortment of sports equipment, long since abandoned.

The grid over the window was firmly in place. *Good*.

Sarah slid the gun into the waistband of her jeans and began searching through the boxes. They were all labeled and she had no trouble locating the ones marked with her name. Taking quick peeks under the lids until she found the one she wanted, she hefted the carton into her arms, turned off the light and hurried back to her room.

Once inside, she dropped the box on the floor and sneezed as a dust cloud exploded.

Then she stood frozen, gripped by nervous anticipation and an eerie dread. The cobwebs clinging to her hair and the spider that crawled from underneath the lid did nothing to alleviate her jitters.

With a shudder, she flicked the spider away and opened the box. There were dozens and dozens of books filled with her sketches and very few of them flattering. As Curtis had said, she'd once had a penchant for giving her classmates—especially those who had tormented her—macabre and distorted features, but the faces were always recognizable. That was what made them so creepy. With the aid of her trusty pencil, Sarah could transform even beauty queens into something hideous and grotesque. It seemed a little sick now, but at one time it had been her way of getting revenge.

"Better than murder," she muttered.

She thumbed through all the books, until she found the drawing she'd been looking for. As she stared down at his face, she half expected the page to erupt in flames. But Ashe Cain wasn't a demon. He didn't possess supernatural powers, just a sick and twisted mind.

The sketch had been meant as a Christmas gift, but Sarah had never gotten the chance to give it to him once she'd finished it. And now, here it was. His face staring up at her. That pale, terrifying visage that had crept through her nightmares for years.

She'd drawn him exactly as she saw him. No need to embellish features that had already been made eerie and surreal by the Goth makeup.

Sarah had never seen him without that makeup. She had no idea what he looked like underneath. But the set of his jaw, the shape of his face…that couldn't be changed by makeup.

She studied that face for the longest time.

Think, Sarah, think.

Did she recognize those eyes, the nose, the line of his jaw?

Warily, she lifted her gaze to the mirror, then let out a breath. Whoever Ashe Cain was, he was not her alter, although she reluctantly admitted that the drawing alone didn't prove much. He could still be a product of her imagination.

She took another sip of wine to wash the dust from her throat as she flipped through the journal. She saw a lot of familiar faces within those pages. Her mother, father and sister. Esme and Curtis.

Sifting through all those old memories was making her a bit light-headed, Sarah thought. Or maybe it was the dust. She got up to splash cold water on her face, but a wave of dizziness washed over her and she staggered back against the bed.

She sat down on the edge, placing her hands on either side to try and make the room stop spinning.

Any idiot knew enough not to mix pills and booze, she thought. She'd been asking for trouble for a long time now. But a little wine had never been a problem for her. Maybe tonight, though, she'd had more than a *little* wine.

She'd be all right. Just needed to lie down for a moment. Just needed to close her eyes.

Sarah opened her eyes. She had no idea how long she'd been out. Judging by the sour taste in her mouth, it might have been hours. But she could see the moon out her window. The soft glow spilled into her room, creating strange silhouettes. She lay still for a moment as she tried to orient herself, but her head felt full of cobwebs.

Wait a minute, she thought as she glanced around. Why was it dark in her room? She hadn't turned the light off before she lay down, had she?

And what was that strange scent? It smelled like...damp earth.

Her hands felt dry and crusty, and she lifted them in front of her, saw something dark all the way up to her elbows.

God, what was that?

Sarah swung her legs over the side of the bed and sat with her hands in front of her. She smelled like soil, as if she'd been out digging in the flower beds in the middle of the night. In the middle of winter.

Her brain still half-frozen, she stumbled to the bathroom and turned on the light. She was covered in dirt. It was all over her hands and arms, caked beneath her nails, matted on the knees of her jeans.

What the hell had she been trying to dig up?

Suddenly frantic to get it off, she turned on the water and started scrubbing. Then it hit her again about that light. She must have turned it off when she left the room because obviously she'd gone outside at some point.

Grabbing a towel, she went back into the bedroom and turned on the light to have a look around. She didn't notice it at first. She wasn't looking for anything like that.

And then everything inside her went completely still.

The little yellow bird from her grandmother was back in its glass case.

The little yellow bird she'd tucked in her sister's dead fingers fourteen years ago.

Someone had been in her room while she slept. Someone had left that bird for her to find.

And then her gaze dropped to her hands. Traces of dirt were still stuck beneath her nails.

What the hell had she been trying to dig up?

Her heart beat so hard she could scarcely breathe as hysteria bubbled in her throat. In full panic, she scooped her purse off the floor, the gun from her desk and fled.

29

Sarah hit the remote and the garage door crawled up inch by agonizing inch. She barely waited for the door to clear before reversing out of the garage, all the way to the end of the drive and into the street. Then she turned the car and floored the accelerator as the headlights cut a swath through the darkness.

Calm down. Get a grip before you wrap yourself around a light pole.

Breathe in…breathe out. In…out.

The bird she'd placed in her sister's casket fourteen years ago was back in its glass case in her old bedroom.

Sarah shuddered.

Not possible.

It was a different bird. Had to be. She should have looked for the tiny crack in the wing. All she'd thought, though, when she saw it, was to get the hell out of there.

Someone had come into her room while she slept and put

that bird on the nightstand to mess with her head. That was the only possible explanation.

But…she'd awakened with all that dirt on her. All over her arms, under her nails, on her jeans. As if she'd been on her knees digging…

No. No!

She didn't want her mind to go there, but the images were already flashing through her head. And the smell. God, the smell of the graveyard was all over her. Not just the dirt, but the funereal-home scent of hothouse roses. The smell was in her nose, on her clothes…

In…out. In…out.

She practiced the exercise all the way to the cemetery, after she'd parked, as she took the flashlight out of the glove box.

In…out. In…out.

As she slipped through the gate and the metal clanged shut behind her. As she crept through the cemetery, avoiding head-stones and graves.

In…out. In…out.

The DeLaune family plot was on the other side of a small hillock. As she crested the knoll, she could see the fresh mound of her father's grave piled high with flowers. Her mother's grave was nearest to Sarah, Rachel's was on the far side.

In…out. In…out.

She kept breathing as she walked past her mother's grave. Her father's grave. Stood at the foot of her sister's grave.

Staring at the disturbed ground.

A scream welled in Sarah's throat as she angled the flash-light beam onto the grave. A hand was sticking out of the loose dirt…

Sarah's heart slammed against her chest as she backed away

from the grave. She tripped over something and went down with a hard thud.

Oh, God.

The notion that Rachel's body had been desecrated sickened and horrified her. Who would do such a thing? And why?

To get your bird back.

Don't even go there. Don't. *Don't.*

She angled the beam over the ground and saw that she'd tripped over a shovel. She kicked it out of the way, then eased back up to the edge of the grave and shone the light over the dirt. Over the hand.

She saw now that the body was lying faceup, covered by only a thin layer of dirt. Decomposition had already distorted the features, but Sarah knew who it was, more from instinct than recognition.

It was Catherine. Sean's Catherine.

In the distance, a siren sounded. It didn't register at first, but then as the sound grew louder, Sarah started to panic. What if the police were on their way here? If they saw the dirt still on her hands and clothes, the shovel lying nearby, they could easily conclude that she'd been trying to bury Catherine's body. First her father...and now her ex-lover's wife.

Someone is setting you up, Sarah.

As terrifying as that notion was, it was far preferable to the alternative. That she had done this. That she had killed all these people.

No. Don't even think it.

She ran back through the cemetery, tripping twice over headstones, righting herself, trying not to think beyond the next few seconds.

Get out of here before the police come. Get in the car and drive. Just drive.

Fishing her keys out of her pocket, she tore through the gate and across the small parking area to her car. Hands trembling, she pressed the remote, then fumbled with the door handle trying to get in.

Key in ignition. Reverse. Get the hell out of here.

Just as she made the first corner, she glanced in her rearview and saw the lights flashing on the squad car as it made the corner and headed toward the cemetery.

Sarah left a message with Michael Garrett's service and he called her back immediately.

"Sarah? I've been trying to reach you for hours. I'm on my way to Adamant right now." His voice sounded so close, so steady and reassuring that he might have been sitting in the car beside her.

"You're on your way here? Why?"

"I'll tell you in a moment. Are you all right? You sound out of breath, and stressed."

Her shaky laugh held a hint of hysteria. "Really? Maybe that's because I just found a body in my dead sister's grave. And, oh yeah, the porcelain bird I put in her coffin fourteen years ago is now sitting on the nightstand beside my bed."

A long pause. "Where are you?"

"Driving around in my car. I can't go home because I think somebody's called the cops on me. I'm already a suspect in my father's murder, so what do you think they'll do when they find that body on Rachel's grave—" Sarah stopped short. It suddenly occurred to her that Michael didn't seem all that surprised by anything she'd just told him. Even the most experienced therapist would surely have some reaction to the events she'd just described.

Her pulse quickened in alarm. "Michael, what's going on? Why are you coming to see me?"

"I talked to Sean earlier tonight."

She swiped a strand of hair from her face with a shaking hand. "He told you he thinks I had something to do with these murders, didn't he? That's why you're on your way here. You think I'm in some sort of crisis."

"We both think you're connected to everything that's happened, but not in the way you mean. If what we suspect is true, you could be in a great deal of danger."

Her heart started to hammer, her every muscle tensed and quivering. "Who's doing this to me?"

"We don't know yet. All I can tell you at the moment is that you need to get to a safe place and stay there. I'll explain everything as soon as I see you. Have you talked to Sean?"

His calm, measured tone wasn't helping. Sarah could feel panic working its way up her throat. "You mean tonight? No."

"He's been trying to reach you, too. You weren't answering your phone."

"I didn't hear it ring," Sarah said. "I was really out of it earlier." So out of it that she hadn't heard someone come into her room and leave that bird.

Whoever it was must have turned off her phone, she realized. Just as he'd turned off the light in her room.

Everything that had happened tonight had been carefully orchestrated, and suddenly Sarah's mind shot back to that glass of wine on her desk. It had been sitting there when she went up to the attic….

The killer could come and go from her house as he pleased. Not just here, but her home in New Orleans, as well. Barring the attic window and changing the locks wouldn't keep him out. Nothing would.

An icy fear coiled around Sarah's spine. "It all goes back to Rachel's murder, doesn't it? Her killer is after me now."

"We think so. That's why you need to get to a safe place to hide until we can help you."

She checked for headlights in the rearview mirror. The road behind her was clear. For now. "There's only one way to stop this," she said on a tremulous breath. "You have to help me remember what happened the night Rachel died."

"I'll do anything I can to help you," he said. "You know that."

"Will you hypnotize me?"

"Hypnosis may not give you all the answers," he warned. "We've discussed this before. There could be a physical reason for your memory loss, in which case—"

"Memory regression hypnosis wouldn't work," she cut in. "I know all that. But it's worth a try, isn't it? What other choice do I have? He's eluded the police all these years. What if they can't catch him now? How long am I supposed to hide?"

Michael hesitated. "Try to stay calm and focused. We'll work this out together. Just tell me how to find you."

"I'm going someplace where no one will think to look for me," she said. "The directions won't mean much until you get here. Call me as soon as you drive into town and I'll lead you straight to me."

"Stay out of sight until I get there. Don't call anyone. Don't let anyone know where you are. Sarah, this is very important. *Don't trust anyone.* Even someone you've know all your life. Do you understand?"

"Just get here as fast as you can," she said.

The first thing Sean noticed when he pulled up to the house in Adamant was the open garage door. It was the middle of the night and Sarah's car was missing.

He grabbed his Maglite from the glove box and walked down the driveway to the garage, aiming the light inside and over the lawn. As he neared the house, he saw that the side door was flung wide, as if someone had left in a big hurry.

Instinctively, he drew his weapon as he moved toward the entrance, his light sweeping aside the shadows as he stepped inside. Even though the door had been open, the house was still warm. Sarah must have just left.

Quickly, Sean walked from the kitchen straight through the dining room to the foyer, where he paused at the bottom of the stairs. The lower level was completely dark, but he could see a light shining from one of the rooms on the second floor.

He cocked his head, listening. He heard nothing.

The house was silent. And yet he had the uncanny feeling that he wasn't alone. Someone was up there.

A warning whispered along his nerve endings as he moved stealthily up the stairs, his footsteps silenced by the thick runner.

At the top, he tucked the flashlight into his jacket and gripped the Glock with both hands as he eased down the hallway. A floorboard creaked underfoot and he froze.

A split second later, the light in the room went out.

"Sarah?"

No answer.

No sound at all except for the sudden throb of his own heartbeat in his ears.

Keeping his shoulder to the wall, he edged down the hallway, peering into the darkness for even the slightest movement. When he heard a window slide up, he lunged for the room, then paused at the door for a quick reconnoiter. A dark form was just slipping over the sill.

"Police officer! Stop!"

The intruder disappeared into the darkness. For a moment, Sean thought the guy had jumped, but then he realized there was a tree just outside the room. He hurried over to the window and aimed his flashlight toward the ground.

The dark clothing blended so well with the darkness that it took Sean a moment to spot him. Then he stared in disbelief. The man descended the branches so quickly his arms and legs seemed to be working in supernatural tandem.

Sean put away the flashlight and holstered the Glock, then climbed out the window behind him. But he wasn't as agile as his quarry. He fumbled for handholds and footholds and was only halfway down when he heard the soft thud of feet hitting the ground—then the pounding of footsteps.

Dead twigs scraped Sean's face and hands as he went down. He misjudged the distance as he jumped from the lower branches, and his right ankle twisted. He crashed to the ground, but he was up an instant later, whipping out the flashlight again to sweep the beam through the darkness. He saw a lone figure sprinting along the same path he and Sarah had walked down the other day, and Sean took off after the man.

Before they reached the cottage, the man veered off the path and headed for the orchard. Sean raced after him through the trees, but he was in unfamiliar territory and his target quickly outpaced him. By the time Sean emerged into the adjoining field, he'd lost him.

Breathing heavily, his ankle throbbing, he searched the darkness. After a moment, a sound came to him. Muffled, distant, and yet dissonantly familiar.

Bells...

And suddenly he knew exactly where the chase was leading him.

Ignoring the pain, Sean ran to the end of the field, down

the gravel drive, stopping only when he got to the edge of the overgrown yard.

The Duncan farmhouse stood silhouetted against the faint glow of moonlight. He'd only seen it in daylight, and hadn't thought it much to look at then. Just an old, dilapidated house where a tragedy had once happened. Where a young girl's life had been snuffed in a manner so brutal, the locals had never been able to forget it, and her sister had never been able to move past it.

Now, fourteen years later, Rachel DeLaune's killer had returned to the scene.

And Sean was on his own. He hadn't alerted the local authorities of his arrival, and a request for backup now would take a lengthy explanation and more time than he had to lose.

He drew his weapon and moved without the benefit of his flashlight through the tall weeds. Climbing the steps to the porch, he paused just outside the door to listen. Then he kicked the door open and flattened himself against the wall, pulse thundering.

The hinges creaked in protest. He waited a moment, then entered the house, gun lowered until he was through the door.

He stood motionless, his gaze scanning the darkness. For the longest time, he heard nothing. No footfalls. No loud breathing. Nothing but the incessant tolling of the bells.

The old house was cold and drafty, but sweat poured down the side of Sean's face. His hands were clammy, and he wiped first one then the other on his jeans so as not to lose his grip on the pistol.

He heard a very faint rustling above him. A rat possibly. Or maybe something else.

Sean moved across the sagging floor and opened the door to the narrow stairwell. It was pitch-black inside.

Shit.

He'd be a sitting duck once he entered.

But up the steps he went, easing the door open at the top, edging around the corner, using his flashlight now to slash through the darkness.

The room was empty except for the wardrobe, and he didn't think a grown man could fit inside. But as he turned, he noticed that the mirrored door sagged open.

Sean lifted his gun and quickly moved across the room. Standing to the side, he used his foot to fling the door open, then flashed the light inside.

A panicked rat scrambled over the edge. In the split second Sean had let his guard down, he realized his mistake. As the wardrobe door swung closed, he caught a glimpse of someone behind him in the mirror. And this time it was real. As silent as a damn ghost, the killer had followed him up the stairs.

All this went through Sean's mind in the second it took him to whirl. But even that was too much time. Taser darts caught him in the shoulder, and fifty thousand volts of electricity pulsed through his system. He felt as if someone had taken a hammer to his spine. His whole body tensed and cramped and went completely rigid. Shoulders hunched to his ears, arms frozen at his sides, he fell with a hard crash to the floor.

A voice said from the darkness, "Don't kill him yet. We need her gun first."

Footsteps moved toward him.

A face peered down at him.

Sean felt a flicker of recognition the instant before a gun handle crashed against his skull.

Sarah hoped that she could remember the way. It had still been daylight when Lukas Clay had brought her out here earlier, and now darkness and panic made everything look different.

The isolation of the country road seemed strange and surreal, like she'd wandered off into a dreamworld. Panic still tightened her chest, but now that she'd formulated a plan, now that she knew Michael was on his way, she felt somewhat calmer.

She came to the dead end and slowed to a crawl as she crossed the cattle guard. Another ten minutes and her headlights picked out the clearing just ahead.

The house was dark and the driveway was empty. That was good. Just what she'd been counting on. She pulled to a stop, leaving the motor running and the headlights on as she grabbed the flashlight and got out.

Earlier, Lukas and the driver had unloaded the lumber into an old barn. Sarah walked toward it now, checking the firmness of the ground to make sure the car wouldn't get stuck. Then she pulled around back and parked. Anyone coming up the road wouldn't see the car, but she'd be able to spot their headlights. She might even be able to get away before they stopped her.

Stuffing the flashlight in her bag along with the gun and her cell phone, she got back out and crossed the darkened yard. She pulled back the screen door and stepped onto the porch, hoping to find a spare key under a floor mat or flower pot.

No such luck.

She trudged around the house. The back porch had been demolished and the door was several feet off the ground. Sarah dragged over a sawhorse, and balancing herself on the beam, checked the door. Making sure the safety was on, she used the handle of the gun to smash out one of the glass panes in the door. Then she reached inside and released the lock.

Drawing all the blinds in the living room, she turned off her flashlight and curled up on the couch to wait for Michael's call.

Michael pulled into the driveway and cut the headlights. He'd called twice for directions and a third time from the gravel road to make sure he'd made the right turn. Sarah had offered to drive down to the end of the lane and wait for him, but he'd assured her that he'd eventually make his way to her.

And now here he was.

She came out to meet him and, even in the dark, he could see that she was exhausted.

She aimed the beam of her flashlight toward an old barn. "Pull around behind if you don't mind. You'll see my car back there."

After he'd parked and rejoined her, he said, "Where are we?"

"In the middle of nowhere."

"Yes, I can see that. I mean, whose house is this?"

"Would it make you feel better if I lied and said it belonged to a friend of mine?"

"In other words, we're trespassing." Not the greatest of conditions for the kind of deep relaxation he would need to induce in order to put her under.

"It's safe, though. No one knows we're here, and we'll be gone in a few hours. I'm anxious to get started," she said as they climbed the porch steps. "I took a Xanax earlier. It shouldn't be that hard to put me under."

"It's not always that easy," Michael said, following her inside. "You're dealing with a great deal of stress, and hypnosis requires concentration and deep relaxation. And you need to remember that it may not give you the answers you're looking for."

"Meaning, I won't be able to remember or I may not like what I remember?" They settled in the living room.

"Either or both. As I've told you before, tapping into the subconscious can produce unexpected consequences. Ideally, I would take several sessions to prepare you."

"Well, we don't have several sessions, we have right now, right here," Sarah said. She sat back and folded her arms. "Let me ask you something. Do you believe I killed my sister, my father, all those other people?"

He answered honestly. "No, I don't believe that. I've never had the sense that you're a danger to yourself or to anyone else."

"But someone is trying to make it seem as if I am. That's why everything is connected to me. The more I think about it, the more convinced I am that Rachel's murder is the key. Whatever happened that night, whatever I saw, has set all this in motion. And if I don't remember, I'll remain a suspect. You're the only one who can help me."

"Have you ever been hypnotized?"

"No. One of my therapists tried once, but it didn't take. I wouldn't go under, but I think it was because I didn't want to remember then. Now I do. Now I'm ready."

Michael studied her for a moment. He could see what she'd been through the past few days. The strain was etched clearly on her face, but she also seemed determined and more resolved than he'd ever seen her.

"I want you to sit back and get as comfortable as you can while I go over a few things with you. Essentially, hypnosis is deep relaxation and focused concentration that will allow a greater awareness of your subconscious thoughts and memories. It doesn't weaken your control, and you can do anything in hypnosis that you can do out of it, only you're less distracted.

Nothing can harm you physically. You'll be safe and you can stop the session at any time. You're in control, Sarah."

As Michael spoke, he could see her muscles starting to relax.

"Do you have any questions?"

"No."

"We'll start out with a few relaxation exercises. After that, we'll see if you want to continue."

"Okay."

After a few minutes of loosening up her muscles, he said, "Now it's time to concentrate. See that shimmer of light on the wall. Focus on the light and relax."

After a few minutes, he used a pinprick to test the depth of her trance. She was under.

"Sarah, you are very relaxed now, very safe, and I want you to go to a place that makes you feel happy and secure."

She smiled dreamily.

"You're going to travel to some other places, too, places you probably haven't been to in a long, long time. It's nothing to worry about. No reason to be frightened. The memories you uncover in those places can't hurt you. The images you see are only photographs of events long past. They can't harm you. You're perfectly safe. Do you understand?"

"Yes."

"Do you want to continue?"

"Yes."

"Take a deep breath. You're sinking deeper into your relaxation, but you're still in control. Always in control. Trust your subconscious mind to tell you what you need to know."

She frowned as if she didn't quite understand what he meant.

"I want you to think of yourself in front of a movie screen. It's directly in front of you, but it's blank. You're relaxed, still safe, still very much in control. Whatever you recall will appear on the screen as if you're watching a movie. It can't hurt you, but you can stop it anytime you want. Do you want to continue?"

She nodded.

He prepared her by taking her back to various points in her life. She remained relaxed and responsive. Always in control.

"Sarah, tell me what you see on the screen now?"

"Blood," she whispered. "I see blood."

Lukas was fairly certain he was on a wild-goose chase. He'd been getting the same message on his voice mail for days. "Have you checked that old storm cellar yet?"

The voice was disguised, but he was pretty sure he knew who it was.

He might have continued to ignore those messages, but when he'd picked up the phone earlier, that same voice had said, "How long do you think someone can stay alive down there?"

As he turned onto the gravel lane, he tried to remember exactly where that cellar was. Fears had said it was by an old burned-out house. Lukas had a vague recollection of playing out there as a kid. The best he could remember, it was straight back from the cattle guard.

He pulled to the side of the road and got out, using his flashlight to guide him through the trees.

It had been years since he'd been out in those woods, but some instinct seemed to kick in and he found the place without much trouble. All that was left of the old house were the outer walls and part of the roof. The fire had completely gutted it.

The storm cellar was about a hundred feet from the house, a domed concrete structure with an old wooden door that opened to steps leading down into the ground. As Lukas unfastened the bolt, he heard something inside that made the hair on his neck lift.

He threw open the door and the smell knocked him back a few steps. Hand to his nose and mouth, he aimed the beam into the opening. "Hello?" he called. "Anyone down there?"

He listened for a moment, then decided he'd imagined the earlier sound. Or maybe it was just a rat. Or worse, a den of rattlers hibernating for the winter.

Nothing was down there. It was a waste of time coming out here.

He turned and reached for the door.

And then he heard it.

A tiny whimper. Unmistakably human.

Slowly, he descended the concrete steps. It was cold and damp inside, and the smell was almost unbearable. Brushing cobwebs from his face, he angled the light around the cramped space. Wooden benches lined two walls and an old cot had been shoved up against the far wall where someone could sleep out the storm.

Someone was on that cot.

Lukas's heart flailed against his rib cage as he moved across the room and shone the flashlight over the body. She was dead. Had been for days.

He stared down at the decaying face, framed by a cap of short dark hair. He could still make out her features, and recognition niggled at him. He'd seen her somewhere before.

An image flashed through his head as footsteps sounded on the concrete steps. He whirled, lost his balance and tumbled backward onto the corpse. Something wet oozed onto his hand and he snatched it away, the flashlight still clutched in his fingers.

"You down here, you little bastard? I'll skin you alive when I catch you."

"Lukas, hide! Don't let him find you!"

The door slammed closed and the bolt slid home.

"Let's see how you long you last down there this time before you shit your pants."

Lukas curled himself into a ball on the floor, trembling with terror.

Because he knew now who had been leaving him those messages.

"You're still relaxed, Sarah, still in control, still feeling good. You're warm and comfortable. Perfectly safe. Do you understand?"

"Yes."

"What do you see on the screen now?"

"More blood."

"Where did all the blood come from?"

"It's on me."

"Are you hurt?"

"No."

"Where are you?"

"The old Duncan farmhouse."

"What are you doing there?"

"Ashe said for me to meet him there. He has something to show me."

"Is he there with you now?"

"I don't see anyone. Just the blood. It's all over my hands. In my hair…"

"How did the blood get on you?"

"I slid down. It's all over the floor."

"What are you doing now, Sarah?"

"Crawling."

"Crawling where?"

"I see her...she's on the floor... Oh, God..."

"You're safe, Sarah. No one's going to hurt you. Just relax."

She paused and caught her breath. "It's Rachel. I think she's..." Her breath shortened and her chest started heaving. "No. Please no."

"Do you want to stop, Sarah?"

"No. No!" She paused again. "There's so much blood...so much blood...I have to go...have to get help."

"Do you leave, Sarah?"

"No...she doesn't want me to."

"Who doesn't want you to?"

"Rachel. She's clutching my hand. She won't let me go." A terrified whisper. "I won't leave you. I swear I won't leave you!"

"Are you still there with Rachel?"

"Yes...but...her hand feels cold. So cold..." Her voice trembled with tears. "She's trying to tell me something..." Sarah gasped and drew back, her eyelids fluttering wildly.

"Someone's there," she whispered in a strange voice.

"Who's with you, Sarah?"

"I don't know. Can't see..."

"Whoever he is, he can't hurt you. You're safe and you can stop anytime you want to. You're still in control."

"He's there! I can hear him breathing."

"Where is he, Sarah?"

"He's behind you! He's right there behind you!"

Michael heard a floorboard creak behind him and he whirled.

★ ★ ★

When Sarah opened her eyes, she felt completely relaxed, as if she'd just awakened from a deep, restful sleep. Then she became aware of the unfamiliar surroundings and she sat up.

"Michael?"

No answer.

She went into the kitchen, then came back into the living room and called up the stairs. Parting the blinds at the window, she peered out into the front yard. But she couldn't tell if his car was still there or not.

Surely, he wouldn't have left without telling her. Maybe he'd just stepped out for some air.

Opening the front door, she went out on the porch. Someone was coming across the yard toward her. Her breath quickened until she realized who it was. He was hardly more than a silhouette, but she recognized the set of his shoulders, the way he walked.

He opened the screen door and stepped up on the porch.

"You must be wondering what I'm doing here," Sarah said. Then she saw his face, the look in his eyes.

The blood on his clothes.

Her heart twisted inside her chest. "Lukas?"

"Lukas isn't here, Sarah. He's gone away for a while."

"Then who are you?" she whispered.

He smiled. "I'm Jude Cole."

30

Sarah turned and lunged for the door. She slammed it closed and turned the dead bolt an instant before he put a shoulder to the wood. Screaming in frustration, he banged on the door, then kicked it.

In shock, Sarah backed away, not knowing what to do. Then she thought of her purse. The gun! Where was it? Where had she left it?

She searched frantically, but couldn't find it. Lukas must have already taken it.

Lukas...but not Lukas. He'd called himself Jude Cole.

Two faces, Sarah thought. One light, one dark. One good, one evil. The clues had all been there. Everything they'd needed to know. Not identical twins as she'd first thought. Multiple identities in one body.

Lukas Clay. Jude Cole...*Ashe Cain*.

A face suddenly loomed in a side window, and Sarah saw

him grin. He was taunting her now. He'd taken her gun, her cell phone. He knew he had her trapped.

"What do you want from me?" she screamed.

The face disappeared.

Fear was an icy chill down her back. She heard a window slide up somewhere in the house, and a moment later, the thud of his footsteps. He was already inside.

"Sarah…" It was a soft, terrifying singsong. "Sarah…"

She was already at the front door, turning the dead bolt. Rushing across the porch, she flung open the screen door and ran down the steps. Across the yard. Toward the barn. To her car.

At the last moment, she realized her keys were in her purse. And she had no idea where that was.

Groaning in frustration, Sarah slid to a stop, then dashed inside the barn.

The moon was up and a soft light filtered in through a high window over the hayloft. But everything below was in deep shadow.

Sarah glanced around in desperation. He had to have tools out here. A hammer, a pitchfork, *anything* she could use as a weapon.

But the search was taking too long. Any second the door would open and he would step inside.

Move! Get out of sight.

And then she saw it at the back of the barn. A car. An old green sedan.

The vehicle that had been seen in Holly Jessup's neighborhood before she disappeared. The car that was now hidden inside Lukas Clay's barn.

He'd killed Holly. He'd killed them all.

And now he'd come back for her.

Sarah's heart raced, her breath came in shallow gasps as she lifted the handle and opened the door. Sliding behind the wheel, she checked the ignition for keys. Searched over the visor, under the floor mats. Nothing.

Glancing in the back, she saw her purse lying in the seat. As if it had been placed there for her to find, Sarah thought.

She had to check it anyway. If the gun was still inside…

The barn door opened and he stepped inside. He saw her at once and strode toward the car, eyes forward, head down, arms swinging purposefully at his sides.

Sarah slid out from under the wheel and dove over the backseat. Onto Michael.

He lay facedown on the floor, silent and still.

Dead.

Oh, God.

She grabbed her purse, tumbled out of the car and ran, sobbing, toward the side door.

Something slammed into the back of her skull, and pain exploded behind her eyes.

Sarah stopped, stumbled, then fell face forward onto the floor.

Wrists and ankles bound tightly with cord, Sean lay on his side on the cold wood floor and tried to focus on the shimmer of moonlight through the grimy window. His vision was blurred, his memory hazy. He had no idea how long he'd been unconscious. He only dimly remembered the chase through the orchard that had ended at the farmhouse, the agonizing jolt of the Taser and then a face staring down at him.

Lukas Clay's face.

The bastard. It had been him all along. Or one of his personalities. What had Michael Garrett called them? Alters. The protector and the persecutor.

Which one had bashed him on the head and left him for dead?

No, that wasn't right. He hadn't been left for dead. For whatever reason, he'd been spared for the time being.

He struggled against the bindings, but that only made his head throb. He could feel the sticky wetness of blood on the side of his face, but he couldn't tell how badly he was hurt. Head wounds were tricky. Even superficial wounds could bleed for hours. But then sometimes they didn't bleed at all, and you could feel fine for days, only to drop dead getting up out of bed one morning. But Sean didn't think he needed to worry about that. Unless he found a way out of his current situation, he might not have days or even hours.

He heard the sound of a car engine, and he listened for a moment, trying to judge the distance, wondering if it was out on the road somewhere. But as the noise grew louder, he realized the vehicle was coming up to the house. He scooted himself inch by agonizing inch across the floor and pushed himself up against the wall until he could see out the window.

An old green sedan bumped along the driveway and pulled to a stop at the edge of the yard. The driver turned off the headlights, then got out and came around to open the back door. The moon was up, and Sean could see who it was.

Every muscle in his body tensed as he watched Lukas Clay lean into the back of the car and pull something out onto the ground. When Clay shifted his position, Sean saw that the lump lying in the weeds was a body, motionless and silent.

Clay grabbed the body beneath the arms and dragged it across the cold ground, up the porch steps and into the house.

A moment later, Sean heard a thud against the plank flooring below.

Clay went back out to the car and opened the trunk. He hoisted a second body over his shoulder, and when he turned, Sean could see a woman's limp arms and the sway of long, dark hair as he carried her across the yard to the porch.

Sean's heart thudded. It was Sarah. Had to be Sarah.

Was she dead?

No. *No.* Garrett had said that Jude Cole had some plan for her. She couldn't be dead yet. Sean could still get her out of here.

Desperation pumped through his veins as he tugged at the bindings around his wrists. The harder he struggled, the deeper the cord bit into his flesh, but he ignored the pain. Ignored the blood that had started to trickle down the side of his face again.

He was breathing so heavily, he almost missed the sound of footsteps. At first he thought someone was coming up the stairs, but then he realized the footsteps were on the porch, just below the window.

Pushing himself back up, he glanced outside as Clay made a third trip to the car. When he closed the trunk lid, he stood for a moment, a shovel in one hand, a hammer in the other as his gaze lifted to the upstairs window.

Sean jerked away and slid down to the floor, his gaze darting about the darkened space for a weapon or a way out.

His gaze lit on the wardrobe across the room, where moonlight glinted on the broken mirror.

Sarah smelled sulphur. The scent was faint, yet it seemed to be all around her.

She could hear the bells, too. Tolling over the graves. Tolling for the deceased and the doomed.

Was she already gone? All she could see was darkness. All she could feel was cold.

"You need to wake up, Sarah."

I can't.

"Can you hear me?"

She opened her eyes. Tried to lift her head, but the effort made the room spin. She squeezed her eyes closed and remained perfectly still until the dizziness subsided.

"Sarah?"

Who's there? She tried to ask, but no sound came out of her mouth. She licked her dry lips and tried again. "Who..."

"It's Michael. Can you hear me?"

Michael. He sounded so far away. His voice was muffled and strained.

Maybe he was dead. Maybe she was, too.

"We have to get you out of here before he comes back in."

And then Sarah remembered everything. It came back in a terrifying rush that left her trembling. Lukas Clay was Ashe Cain, and someone he called Jude Cole. And one or all of his identities had something terrible in store for her.

Sarah's chin rested on her chest and it took all her strength to lift her head. The room started a slow rotation, and she instinctively tried to steady herself with her hands. Then she realized she was sitting upright in a wooden chair, her arms restrained by a cord that encircled her chest and the back of the chair, her ankles fastened to the legs. She couldn't move.

She'd been placed in a circle of candles that had just been lit—she could still smell the sulphur from the matches. It was the scent she remembered from fourteen years ago.

There had been candles that night, too. She could see in her mind the way the flames flickered when the door opened. And then Rachel's terrified warning. *He's right behind you!*

Sarah had turned and stared into the palest of faces, the darkest of eyes. And then her gaze had dropped to the knife, still dripping with her sister's blood.

"Sarah?"

The voice startled her back to the present. "Michael? Where are you?"

"Over here."

The candlelight threw huge shadows over the walls and ceiling. It took Sarah a moment to find him.

And then nausea swept over her like a giant wave. What she saw...couldn't be real. None of this could be real.

Michael was sitting on the floor, his back to the wall, his arms spread out and pinned in place by nails through his palms. He had been positioned so that moonlight flooding in through the window on the opposite wall highlighted the macabre tableau.

"Oh, my God," she breathed.

Michael's head lolled against the wall. His face was bloody and bruised, but his eyes were open and he was conscious.

"Michael..."

"Just listen to me, Sarah." His voice was labored, so low she had to strain to hear him even in the silent house. "You have to understand what's going on here. It's the only way you'll be able to save yourself when he comes back. The man who brought us here calls himself Jude Cole. He's also Ashe Cain."

"His real name is Lukas Clay," she whispered.

"We're dealing with multiple identities. Right now the dominant personality is Jude Cole, and his only purpose is to protect Lukas Clay. All of this...everything he's done...is a carefully laid plan to protect Lukas...from you."

"Why?" she said desperately. "Why now, after all these years?"

"Because you came back and started asking questions. The moment you began digging in the past…you became a threat to Lukas. Ashe Cain murdered your sister, but Lukas is the one who would be punished. Jude can't let that happen."

"Why didn't he just kill me?" Sarah asked helplessly. "Why did he have to murder all those other people?"

"Because killing you outright won't stop the questions. He needs a scapegoat. The past can't be put to rest unless the killer is revealed. Everything he did was to that end. The tattoos. The satanic symbols. Even the victims were carefully chosen because of their connection to you. He's making it look as if you've lost control…snapped because of what you did to your sister."

"How do we stop him?"

"Jude is the protector. He's devious, but he's not a murderer. To kill, he has to trigger Ashe Cain's wrath. But Ashe is connected to you, too, Sarah. For whatever reason, he was obsessed with you. He became what you needed in order to get close to you. That fixation…is how you stop him…"

His voice trailed off just as Sarah saw the candle flames flicker. Jude Cole came into the room, a set of wooden poles gripped in each hand. Foot plates and straps had been connected to the shafts, and carved hooves had been attached to the bottoms. As he walked the poles across the floor, the wooden hooves made a loud thump-thump-thump that sent a shiver down Sarah's spine.

Homemade stilts. That was how he'd been able to make the cloven prints in the ground outside the farmhouse without leaving impressions of his shoes the night he'd killed Rachel.

He set the stilts aside and stood over Sarah as he removed a gun from his jacket and caressed the barrel. When he spoke, the voice that came from his mouth was not that of Lukas Clay. It sounded young and terrifyingly sinister.

"You're going to kill him," he said.

Sarah tried to shift away from him, but she couldn't move. Her breath came shallow and fast as a scream clawed its way up her throat.

"I'm going to unfasten you," he said. "I'm going to put the gun in your hand and you're going to kill him."

"You're insane," she whispered. "I won't kill anyone."

"You'll shoot him and then turn the gun on yourself. What choice do you have? You've killed all those people. Even your own sister."

His matter-of-fact tone was chilling. "No one will believe that," she said.

He cocked his head, smiling. "Everyone will believe it. They already think you killed your father. It's just like he said…" He nodded in Michael's direction. "You've snapped."

Sarah drew a shaky breath and lifted her head. "You've done all this for nothing, because I don't even remember what happened the night my sister died."

"He's helping you remember." Another nod toward Michael. "And now he has to die, too."

"To protect Lukas. That's why you killed those people."

"I didn't kill anyone."

"Then who did?"

Another smile. "You already know the answer to that."

She closed her eyes. "Why did he kill my sister?"

"You wouldn't understand."

She drew another breath. "Make me understand. Let me at least have that."

"Lukas's father thought he was so smart and clever, but he couldn't find the killer even though he stared him in the face every single day. That case stripped him of his pride. Took away the one thing he valued the most."

"But why Rachel?"

"Because she was the perfect victim. She was the thing *your* father valued the most. He did it for you."

Oh, dear God.

Sarah swallowed another scream. "You were both at the crime scene in New Orleans, weren't you? You and Ashe. You both tattooed that poor woman."

"He wasn't very good, so I didn't ask him to do it again. I'm glad I don't have to let him out anymore. He was always a lot more trouble than he was worth."

"He's not like you, is he? You have many talents, don't you, Jude?" This from Michael.

He turned with a cagey smile. "You can't trick me with flattery, Dr. Garrett."

Sarah watched him in the candlelight. He was devious, clever and sly…all the things that Michael had described. But he was also immature. He made mistakes.

"There's a big problem with your plan," Sarah said. "I'm not going to kill Michael, and I'm sure as hell not turning the gun on myself. So you'll either have to do it yourself or let Ashe come out one last time to do your dirty work for you."

"She's right," Michael said weakly. "You protect. You can't kill. That's not who you are. That's not why you were born. Only Ashe can kill."

"No," Jude said angrily. "I know what you're doing, but it won't work." He knelt and loosened the rope around Sarah's body enough to free her right hand. He moved around behind her so that he could hold her in place while he tried to force the gun into her hand. Sarah clenched her fist tightly. She had no idea she had so much strength.

"Stop it!" He sounded like a petulant teenager now.

"You have to let Ashe out," Michael said. "Let him come out to do what he was meant to do."

Suddenly, Jude stood and, still clutching the gun, put his hands to his ears. "I said *no!*"

"Ashe wants to come out, doesn't he?" Sarah said. "Let me talk to him."

"Shut up!"

Sarah had no idea if he was talking to her or one of the voices inside his head. He spun away and started to pace.

"Ashe?"

He stopped and was silent for a moment. Then his expression altered dramatically. The killer had been let out to play.

The pacing resumed, but now his movements were those of a predatory animal.

"Ashe?"

He wouldn't look at Sarah. He continued to ignore her when she said his name a third time. Instead, he strode over to Michael and put the gun to his head.

"Ashe, listen to me," Sarah said desperately. "Do you recognize my voice? Do you know who I am?"

His finger was on the trigger.

"Do you remember what you once told me? You said we're the same. Our souls are like mirror images."

He turned at that, and his gaze met Sarah's in the candle-light. She saw something in his eyes, a look she remembered from the past, and for a moment, she thought she had him.

Somewhere in the house, a door opened and closed very softly. Ashe turned toward the sound, and a moment later, he disappeared up the narrow stairwell.

Sarah had no idea who else was in the house. She didn't take time to think about it. The cord around the chair was still loose, and she worked frantically to free herself before he came back. *Arms first, ankles next, then find a weapon.*

Hurry. *Hurry!*

Sean's only weapon was the element of surprise.

He crouched against the wall, listening for the telltale footfalls on the wooden stairs so that he could time his attack. He'd only have one chance. A bullet would most likely take him down before he could regroup for a second assault.

But the man in the stairwell knew exactly where to step. He came up silently, just as he had earlier. Sean didn't hear a sound until Clay was right outside the door.

Sean swung the drawer he'd pulled from the wardrobe as hard as he could. The wood was flimsy and rotting, but the blow caught Clay in the chest and he stumbled back. Before he could regain his balance, Sean lunged, and the two men tumbled down the stairs, landing with a hard thud at the bottom.

Sean's head cracked against the floor, and the impact left him dazed.

"Sean!" Sarah screamed his name as she saw Ashe reach for the gun. Sean slammed the man's arm against the floor and the weapon went flying into the shadows.

Sarah's hands were free, and she quickly loosened the rope around her ankles. She dove for the shadows, but she couldn't find the gun, and Ashe's hands had closed around Sean's throat, squeezing tighter and tighter...

Her gaze lit on the stilts. She grabbed one and swung it as hard as she could against Ashe's head. He turned, eyes blazing, and lunged for her.

Sarah had no idea which persona he was now. All she knew was that she had to somehow stop him. She hit him again, this time with the end of the pole. The cloven hoof pressed deeply into his face before he jerked the stilt from her hand, and then he lowered his head and rammed into her with an enraged roar. They went flying back against the wall, and the impact knocked the breath from her. Sarah fell like a rag doll to the floor.

And that's when she spotted the gun.

He saw it, too, and scooped up the weapon before she could reach it. Sean was behind him and, sensing he was cornered, Ashe pressed himself against the wall, his gaze darting fiercely from Sarah to Sean.

As the anger drained out of him, he dropped to his knees, still clinging to the weapon. Not Ashe, not Jude, but finally Lukas Clay.

Horror glinted in his eyes, along with a terrible realization.

He lifted the gun to his mouth and fired.

Sarah sat huddled in a blanket on the farmhouse steps. She'd been sitting there for a long time, but the scene before her still seemed surreal. A line of squad cars and emergency vehicles formed a long train out to the road. The twirling lights mesmerized her for a moment until she forced her gaze away.

Michael had been loaded into one of the EMT vans and was already on his way to the nearest hospital. Sean was standing behind her on the porch, talking to one of the detectives from the county sheriff's office. Inside the house, crime scene officers from the state police were combing the rooms for evidence.

It was finally over, and yet Sarah felt more stunned than relieved. Too much had happened over the past few days. She would need time to process it. But for the moment, she tried not to think at all as she pulled the blanket more tightly around her.

Even in such a remote location, the curious had already started to gather. Following the sirens and flashing lights, they'd parked out on the road and walked across the field to the edge of the overgrown yard, which was as close as they were allowed to get.

One man stood away from the others. Derrick Fears caught Sarah's eyes and, even from a distance, she felt the impact of his stare. Then, with a slight shrug, he turned and disappeared into the darkness.

Sean sat down beside her. "You really should go to the hospital. Head wounds can be serious."

"Look who's talking."

He reached up and wiped a hand across the dried blood on his face. "Helluva night we've had." His gaze searched hers for a moment, then he turned to stare out over the field. "They found Cat's body in the cemetery, just where you said it would be."

Sarah swallowed. "What about her friend?"

"The state police received an anonymous tip about an old storm cellar in the woods behind Clay's property. They found the body inside. They also found what looked like a little kid's drawings on the wall, and old scratch marks on the door.

Sarah shuddered at the image his words evoked. "I'm so sorry," she whispered. "I don't even know what to say."

"You have nothing to be sorry about. None of this is your fault. If anyone's to blame for Cat's death, it's me. I never should have dragged her into this. I never should have married her to try and get over you." He turned then, his gaze burning into hers. "Sarah—"

She closed her eyes.

"I should have had more faith in you," he said softly.

"How could you, when I didn't have much faith in myself?"

"I told myself the reason I left was because I didn't want to have to make a choice. I didn't want to have to live with what I might find out about you. But the truth is…it was never about you. It was me. You called me an emotional coward once, remember? You were right. It wasn't your past that scared me off. It was how I felt about you. And now it's too late, isn't it?"

"I don't know how I feel about anything right now," she said with numb detachment. "I don't even know who I am anymore. What I've learned about myself, about my family, is going to change me. In ways I can't even imagine."

He took her hand and held it for a moment—a touch so gentle it brought tears to Sarah's eyes. "If you ever need me…"

"I know, Sean."

Sometime later, she walked alone across the field and through the orchard. A breeze stirred the bells over the graves, and Sarah shivered as her gaze lifted to her childhood home. The house was bathed in the cold, gray light of dawn. The charm was lost in all the shadows, the beauty hidden by a dark history she'd tried very hard to forget.

But a light shone from the kitchen window, where Esme waited for her inside. She turned when Sarah came through the door, and a moment later, bony arms wrapped her in a tight cocoon, rocking her back and forth the way she had when Sarah was little.

"I know, child," she soothed. "I know."

★ ★ ★ ★ ★